ARKLIGHT

TASK FORCE CRUSADER

J.M. MYRICK

All Scripture quotes are taken from the Holy Bible in New Living Translation (NLV).

The story contained herein is fictional in nature, although locations, characters, and historical depictions in the story are intended to closely follow actual events. The names of fictional characters, places, incidents, and events are the products of the author's imagination and have been used in this work of fiction. The resemblance of any fictional character to actual persons, living or dead, is purely coincidental. The heroic historical figures John Bell, Eugene Fluckey, Ian Fleming, and Simone Segouin (aka Nicole Minet), as well as the infamous Adolf Hitler, Heinrick Himmler, Dietrich von Choltitz, and Hildebrandt Gurlitt, are real figures; however, the author has fabricated fictional events in order to bind them to this story. The author's intention was to provide a narrative of historical fiction that closely followed the timeline of actual events in the history of World War II and beyond.

As a veteran, the author humbly thanks U.S. Navy Ensign John Bell, U.S. Navy Commander and Congressional Medal of Honor Recipient Eugene Fluckey, and British Commander Ian Fleming for their service to their countries, and the world, during World War II. The greatest generation.

Cover artwork design by www.ebooklaunch.com

ACKNOWLEDGEMENTS

Through God, all things are possible. Three years ago, had anyone told me writing was part of my journey, I'd have laughed. Yet here I am, writing the third novel of a trilogy. Enjoy your journey; each is unique and filled with wonderful surprises.

DEDICATION

For my Dad - a man of true character. He forged me into who I am, and for that, I'll be forever grateful. We lost you way too soon, but heaven gained a saint.

TABLE OF CONTENTS

TABLE OF CONTENTS

PROLOGUE

"But you are obsessed with whether the godless will be judged.
Don't worry; judgment and justice will be upheld."
Job 36:17

0100-Zulu Time 20August1944 (Paris, France)

Near the bank of the Seine River, British Commander Ian Fleming lay prone on a raiding craft, aiming his trusted, Welrod 9mm pistol. He trained the extended, suppressed barrel on a lone German sentry. Lieutenant John Bell and Petty Officer "Richie" Walter Steadman struggled to steady the raiding craft in the turbulent waters. Ian's shooting platform stabilized, and he squeezed the trigger, firing a single shot. The soldier's head snapped back, collapsing him to the ground just as the shoreline emerged through the dense fog. Tonight, they would undertake their most daring mission of the war; the liberation of Paris was already underway, but the Alsos mission team had intelligence of a different matter to obtain.

Fighting the upriver current, they closed in on the famous Tuileries Garden in Paris. Located alongside the monumental and historic park sat Hotel Le Meurice—the German headquarters for the occupation. Ian, Bell, and Richie had spent weeks developing a bond with *Francs-Tireurs et Partisan,* better known as the French resistance's FTP unit. The partisan group was made up of anyone old enough to fight. With the Allies closing in, FTP attacks on German occupational forces were in full swing.

The Alsos Team needed to act fast on the intelligence they had received. Through a contact, Ian had learned that Doctor Hildebrand Gurlitt was meeting at the hotel with the German Governor General, Dietrich von Choltitz. The Alsos Team had to locate Gurlitt, because he knew where to find the *Portrait of a Young Man* painting. The Knights Templar journal that Ian carried pointed to something hidden within the artwork. They hoped it contained another piece of Arma Christi – one of the holy weapons of Christ.

After meeting with Otto Hahn in Geneva, they had spent months looking for an opportunity to catch up to Gurlitt. The Battle of Paris provided the confusion and diversion, while the recently motivated, free French forces helped bolster the necessary manpower for the operation. The Alsos Team had reason to believe that Hans Frank was in possession of the stolen *Portrait of a Young Man*. He was safe in Poland at present, impossible to get to without the details a man like Gurlitt could provide. A degenerate art dealer by trade, Gurlitt was expendable by Nazi standards. So far, the Jewish art curator had found favor within the Reich, but tonight the team hoped to squeeze him for answers.

Bell pointed toward the shore, seeing three human silhouettes. Richie signaled them, and they flashed a red light. As the team drifted close enough to see the trio, Bell realized one of the resistance soldiers was much shorter than the other two. The raiding craft bumped the edge of their rendezvous location. Bell looked closer, seeing long hair and lipstick.

"Who's the broad?" he asked.

Ian looked back, wishing Bell could keep his internal thoughts – internal.

"And you wonder why you can't get a date," Ian said.

"She's wearing a skirt to a firefight. What do you want me to say?"

Richie smiled and shook his head.

"Lieutenant, she's also carrying some German's submachine gun - and by the look on her face, she understands us."

The female resistance soldier stared hard at Bell, who realized his criticism was not well-received by her or her two burly counterparts. The stillness was broken by the witty British spy.

"Please excuse us madam. I'm Ian, that's Richie, and the man you obviously dislike, that's John Bell. He's a bit obtuse, but he means well."

Bell's face flushed with embarrassment as he managed a two-fingered wave, gesturing his lack of tact.

"I'm Nicole – Nicole Minet. This is Claude and Richard. Antwon told us to meet you here. We are to show you the underground entrance into the hotel."

"Very good then," Ian said, offering a hand to the female.

Barely an adult, the petite brunette stepped aboard the raft, gripping her MP40 in one hand, holding Ian's hand with the other. Missing no opportunity to impress, Ian offered her his seat, electing to sit on the gunwale. The two men she brought jumped aboard, pushing the raft back into the Seine. Claude passed a paddle to his counterpart and the men rowed toward the Garden.

Bell sat behind the lovely French female; the vivacious scent of her perfume delighted his senses. He tapped her on the shoulder.

"I'm sorry if I offended you. I'm just not used to seeing girls – I mean, ladies… fighting wars. A gal like you shouldn't have to see this."

"You don't think I can fight? We shall see about that, American."

"Look lady, I'm just trying to apologize."

"How about you help row?" she said, digging an oar into the water. "Or are you too manly for that?"

Bell sighed, rolling his eyes. Ian looked back, smiling at his friend.

"She does have a point," Ian said, fighting back a laugh. "The oar is right beside you."

†††††

The rubber raiding craft drifted to a stop next to an oversized sewer inlet. Ian tied up the boat while his team disembarked, along with their French counterparts.

"This is the way to the hotel," Nicole said. "Stay close."

She entered first, careful to avoid the puddles. The team soon found their way into the bowels of Paris. Ian kept checking his watch as they trudged along, doing his best to forget the smell.

"Nicole, when will the resistance start their attack? It's overdue by my count."

"Don't you worry, Englishman. It will happen soon enough."

After a few more minutes, the group arrived to a choke point, just under the hotel entrance. Nicole pulled out a pack of cigarettes, offering a smoke to each of her men. They both wiggled one out of the package. Ian decided to join them.

"You think now's a good time for a smoke break?" Bell asked.

"Have patience, manly man," she said as Ian leaned in to light her cigarette, "we need to wait for the diversion."

Richie peered around the corner, looking up at the grate from below. He could see the lights on the side of the hotel and heard several German voices talking from above.

"Skipper, we aren't going anywhere with all those Germans up there."

Bell huffed and found a makeshift seat on an exposed pipe. Nicole looked at his slumped-over demeanor and laughed.

"John Bell, you act like this war is inconvenient for you? Like I am some silly little girl? We are risking our lives, for whatever this – mission is about."

Bell placed a hand across his face. The burden of the visions and dreams he had recently seen plagued him: Richie getting shot in a field he couldn't seem to identify; Ian, as an older man, reaching out for his help. He watched his friends in agony over and over, while awake and in his dreams. The pain of losing them transfixed his body. He stared at the damp concrete spillway, unable to focus on anything else.

"What's wrong with him?" Nicole asked.

"He's been having a rough time lately," Richie said. "This war has taken its toll on us all."

"Is he going to be able to fight?"

"That's one thing you don't have to worry about with the Skipper. He'll be fine."

The two Frenchmen inhaled the rest of their smokes while Ian used his time to better understand this French woman's desire to plunge herself headfirst into harm's way.

"So, Nicole, how did you become involved with all of this?"

She fanned away the smoke from her cigarette, making sure to blow it toward Richie, who had refused to partake.

"I started off stealing a bike from some German, and then I used it to deliver messages for the resistance. After that, I started to go out on sabotage missions. I've become rather good at it. Now, I'm going to help liberate my country from these Boches."

Ian was floored at her outright contempt of danger, and the way she held on to the MP40 told him she knew how to use it. He smiled at the young lady, making sure he looked at her from the ground up. She noticed his subtle pass, smiling back at him as she finished her smoke.

"Well, Richie. It looks like we're certainly in good hands," he said.

Bell stood up, taking a few deep breaths to clear his mind. He had internalized the visions, keeping them from his teammates, not wanting to cause them any alarm. The anxiety it caused him intensified his plight, especially under stress. He walked back over to Nicole. He stared past her, concentrating on what he wanted to say.

"Look, Miss, I haven't slept too much here lately. I'm hoping you can forget about… earlier."

"It's been a long, wretched war. Forget about it."

Bell took another head-clearing breath and smiled at the young woman's wisdom. At only 19 years old, she carried herself like a hardened, veteran soldier. He smiled, realizing that her wearing a skirt into battle might be the coolest thing he'd seen during the entire war.

Machine gun fire erupted from above. The FTP attack on the headquarters was underway. Numerous, thundering explosions resonated from a block away. Bell walked toward the grate's ladder, but Nicole grabbed him by his shirt.

"Wait. We go when I say."

Bell looked at her face and saw that she was waiting for something in particular. He took a step back as she motioned for her counterparts to move forward.

"Claude, tu vas vérifier. Richard, vous-couvrez," Nicole said.

"What are we waiting for?" Richie asked.

"You'll see."

The ground rattled as a German tank clattered over the grate. It seemed as though the march of a hundred boots followed behind in the armor's wake. Chalky bits of debris fell from the ceiling.

"Security garrison. Now that they are gone, we should have a clear path inside," she said, motioning for her men to open the grate.

Claude climbed the ladder to assess if the route was clear. He motioned for the team and exited the sewer. Richie crested the top of the ladder, seeing a fireball of explosions on the adjacent block. The sound of small arms fire echoed through the streets of Paris. It appeared that every German soldier available was addressing the attack. The entrance to the hotel was only a few feet away. Nicole took the lead, gathering the rest of the team in the shadows outside the door.

"You three, follow me," she said, looking at Ian. "We will go around back. It's the closest entrance to General Choltitz's residence. If Gurlitt is still here, that's where he'll be."

"Claude, Richard – bonne chance, mes amis."

The Alsos mission team followed Nicole to a corner, where she stopped after seeing several soldiers posted at the door.

"What's the plan for this?" Ian asked.

Nicole looked at her watch and smiled.

"We watch them leave... any minute."

Ian had only a second to digest her statement. The clatter of automatic gunfire echoed from inside the hotel. Claude and Richard's diversion went straight to plan. Every German, except for two sentries, charged inside. Nicole turned to Ian and winked.

"Hold my gun," she insisted. "I'll distract them. You take them out."

"But wait," Ian said, as she sauntered off across the courtyard.

Ian stood there, in a state of dumbstruck confusion, holding her weapon, watching her approach the sentries. Bell, and then Richie, patted him on the back as they passed by, stalking ever closer to the German guards. Nicole used a few cars to mask her approach, but soon allowed the enemy soldiers to see her walking toward them. The men looked at each other, amazed to see a beautiful woman smile at them with chaos rumbling all around. They both approached her, rifles at the ready, until one soldier decided she was close enough.

"Halt!"

The well-trained resistance fighter knew she had them right where she wanted them. She grabbed the bottom of her shirt, and then lifted her blouse up, showing the Germans her exposed waistline.

"But, I'm unarmed," she said, her bold lipstick accentuating her smile.

The glimmer in her eyes enticed both of the soldiers. She didn't mind if they looked. Her shirt cleared her brassiere. The guards were mesmerized by her figure, never seeing the two American Raiders approach. With stealth-like precision, Bell and Richie plunged their combat knives into the German's backs; they were no strangers to getting their hands dirty. Both of the guards collapsed to the ground, their fate sealed. Nicole dropped her blouse and approached the fray. The Nazi soldiers' muffled yells were covered by the Americans' hands.

"Serves you right, Boches!" she said, spitting on one of them.

Bell ended his target's struggle, still in utter disbelief that Nicole had no fear. The woman had an extraordinary ability to overcome any situation. Her confidence was second to none. He felt ridiculous for how he had greeted her, and he now saw the great potential in her actions. Ian arrived at the entrance, covering the others. He still held Nicole's prized weapon.

"You didn't scratch it did you?" she asked.

"Of course not, darling."

"Let's get inside and find this Gurlitt you seek. My men won't be able to hold out much longer."

Nicole took the lead, finding the stairwell to the top floor. The four of them ran up the stairs until they reached the upper landing. She pushed the door open, on the prowl for the enemy. She could see the entrance to General Choltitz's quarters down the hall. Sporadic machinegun fire echoed down below.

They waited for the right moment. Ian peeked over her head and could see the group of soldiers in between them and the general.

"Now how do you propose we deal with this?" he asked. "Undressing in front of them, while it's certainly my favorite tactic, might be a bad idea."

"True," she turned toward Ian holding a grenade at eye level, "but this should do the trick."

She pulled the pin and released the spoon, which flipped to the floor. She looked back, winking at Bell.

"Timing is everything," she said with a smirk.

She opened the door, the grenade primed, fuse already burning. Her underhand throw propelled it toward the gathering German force. To Ian's surprise, she had already grabbed another grenade from his belt and before the first grenade exploded, the second was in the air, ready to clear anything left standing.

BOOM.

The stairwell shook from the concussion. Plaster popped off the walls and ceiling.

A second, *BOOM*.

Nicole was through the door in an instant, finding downed German soldiers all over the floor. A few staggered to their feet down the hall. Dust, smoke, and debris hung heavy in the air. Nicole squeezed the trigger of her prized MP40, firing at anything still moving. Ian followed along, unable to match her speed. Bell and Richie covered the rear.

"This is what you get!" she yelled, continuing to cut down every soldier catching her attention.

Ian and Richie backed her up, clearing the floor of the opposition. Bell turned, seeing the door to General Choltitz's suite blown open by the blast. Through the smog of haze, he saw two stunned soldiers inside. He finished them before they could recover their senses. The close quarters battle ended in a mad minute. Bell soon found himself in the office, his team flanking his position.

The room was adorned in rich wood paneling; an ornate desk sat in the center of the room, and a stone fireplace occupied the interior wall. Bell gazed out the window, seeing the flash of small-arms fire and explosive-fueled fireballs erupt in the streets below. The four Allies stood in the middle of the room. A set of hands emerged from behind the desk. The face of General Dietrich von Choltitz emerged. He stood surrendering—hands extended, palms out. In the face of certain death, he had little choice. Bell approached the general, feeling around his waist, checking him for weapons.

"He's unarmed," he said to his colleagues, before jabbing the barrel of his submachine gun in Choltitz's side. "Where's Gurlitt, asshole?"

Ian stepped up; he knew Bell would play their trump cards immediately, and they could not risk letting Gurlitt escape. They needed to get Choltitz to talk.

"Dear General," Ian said, "what my friend here is trying to say, is: please have a seat. We need to chat."

Nicole walked up to the general, her attention moving top to bottom.

"France will no longer stand by while you Boche have your way."

The general sat down in his chair. He was in no position to argue her point. Silence gripped the room, until Ian grabbed Choltitz by the jaw. He pulled their captive toward him, looking him in the eye.

"Well, old boy, it looks as though you're in a pickle. The Allies are advancing, Paris will be liberated within the week, and I bet Hitler wants you to burn everything as you retreat."

"How did you know that?" Choltitz asked with nervous beads of sweat building on his forehead, his eyes darted across all four of his captors faces. "He's mad!"

"Frankly, I agree. We all know Hitler's crazy. But, you have to ask yourself one question: do you want to hang with him, or do you want to get out of this war with some of your honor still intact?"

"I assume you have an offer to make?" Choltitz asked.

"That's the spirit. It's simple really. You give us Gurlitt, and we leave here tonight, without killing you. We can also make you a few assurances," Ian said, looking toward Nicole.

Nicole stepped between Ian and the general.

"What do you mean, leave? He's coming with us, right?"

"Just relax," Ian said. "Let's see where this… negotiation goes, darling."

She huffed, turned, and walked toward the door, pulling out a pack of cigarettes. She stood next to Richie, who covered the team from counterattack.

"I don't know about this, Ian," Bell said, pacing the floor opposite the general.

Choltitz looked at Ian, his eyes narrowed. Ian had made his point. This was personal and the general realized it.

"Gurlitt left Paris – only hours ago," Choltitz said. "Since the resistance started their attacks yesterday, he left while he could. Maybe there's something else we could arrange?"

Ian closed his eyes and rubbed the bridge of his nose at the news. Nicole walked back over to Ian, handing him her already burning cigarette, lighting another for herself. Disappointment rarely revealed itself during Ian's negotiations, but this was their only chance. *Portrait of a Young Man* needed to be found. Bell walked up to Ian, and Richie retreated from the door to the hall, closing in to confer.

"Ian, this sounds like it's all for nothing. If we can't get a line on that painting, we need to scram," Bell said.

"He's right," Richie said, looking at his friends. "We need to get out while we can."

The German Küblewagen, complete with an iron cross on the hood, entered at the rear of the hotel amid the chaos encircling the building. Nazi officers Colonel Claude Weber and Lieutenant Alfred Kieffer had decoded an intercept they received. One word caught their attention, focusing their efforts. A mention of the Alsos Team was deciphered after several other keywords pointed them toward Paris.

They had spent time interrogating Doctor Otto Hahn, after he had arrived back in Berlin. Under the heel of the Gestapo, he reluctantly divulged enough, eventually directing the SS officers toward the Alsos Team's interest in Gurlitt.

As they approached, they saw two dead German sentries laying at the backdoor entrance to General Choltitz's residence. Weber cracked an insidious grin, knowing the Allies would have no chance to grab Gurlitt, who was already on a plane, bound for the fatherland. The two officers knew they were taking a chance wading into the fray, but if they could capture the Alsos Team and secure the Knights Templar journal, the Reich would gain the advantage once more. The path to the ultimate weapon, which had been lost in Bizerte, was now within reach.

"We need to go check on the general," Kieffer said.

"You go up and take the center stairwell," Weber said, his face atwitch. "I'll go around the side and come down the hallway so we can cover each other."

Weber drew his Luger and ran around to the side entrance, anxious to meet his enemy. Obtaining the journal and returning it to the Führer would go a long way toward restoring his status. After the failure in Bizerte, and again in Geneva, he needed to catch a break. His pace quickened, running to reach the top floor in time.

Ian pressed his pistol into the forehead of Choltitz, finger on the trigger.

"General, you have about five seconds. Give me one reason not to kill you."

Choltitz smiled and relaxed, thinking he did have something else to offer.

"Gurlitt might be gone, but your friend here mentioned a painting. I know where he has hidden, or sold, much of his art collection. Maybe… I could help you with that?"

Ian pulled back the Welrod, realizing the mission might not be all for naught. Sweat from his hand dripped from the grip of the pistol. Failure wasn't an option, and the pressure upon him showed. The bitter clash of war continued to erupt in the city below.

"Where's the Raphael painting, *Portrait of a Young Man*?"

"Is that all you desire? It's firmly in the collection of Hans Frank, deep inside Poland. It's far out of your reach…"

Choltitz smiled, not knowing why these men were so interested in stolen art. A war raged all around them, yet this took precedence. A meeting entered his thoughts in the moment—that one awkward night in Berlin.

Bell looked through the door, gripping his M3 submachine gun. He overheard that Frank had the painting. Krakow, Poland would be their next target of opportunity. Hans Frank's estate.

"Ian, that pretty much confirms it," Bell said. "Let's get the hell out of here."

Shots rang out from the stairwell, grazing Bell's left arm. He turned, firing back. Nicole saw another uniformed SS officer move across the hall in the opposite direction. She leveled off a burst of fire in his path. Richie turned to back Bell up, but stopped short, feeling compelled to ask Choltitz a question. After Bizerte, any information regarding Gurlitt could be useful down the road.

"How much art does Gurlitt have hidden away?"

Nearby, Ian pressed the Welrod against Choltitz's cheek, wiping the emergent smile of hopeful rescue off his face.

"He has everything—from pieces of the *Ghent Altarpiece*, to hundreds of smaller works. It is an incredible collection."

Richie thought of the *Adam Panel* of the *Ghent*, still buried in Tunisia. Hans Frank would be their next target as they pursued the stolen artwork; they might get another shot at Gurlitt, but for now they had to evade capture.

"Ian, let's go!" Bell yelled, laying down an automatic string of hot lead. "There's nothing left for us here."

Nicole stepped back from the doorway and Richie took her place to keep the German officer pinned down. She walked over to Choltitz, pointing her MP40 submachine gun at his heart.

"Don't do what Hitler wants," she pleaded. "Don't burn Paris. If you just surrender peaceably, the FTP will protect your family. We know where you keep them. Otherwise, I'll kill you right here, right now."

The general could see the fire in her eyes. He broke contact with her gaze for a moment, surveying the two American commandos laying down a barrage of gunfire into the doorway ahead.

"I'm a practical man. I have feelings for this city. Even though we are enemies, I am no enemy of Paris."

Nicole winked at the general and then turned to fight her way out of the hotel. Ian removed his pistol.

"We're letting you live. Let the city live, and when the time comes, surrender with honor, General."

Choltitz sat back in his chair with an expression of relief consuming his face. Despite the firefight only feet away, he knew that the German advantage was forfeit. This was an opportunity to walk away from a crazed leader. The Reich was lost, and with it, a futile attempt toward a final solution he had never understood.

Ian pressed against the wall, ready to exit. Bell's arm was bleeding, but he didn't even realize he was hit. His M3 clattered in the direction of the stairwell. Richie's bursts of directed fire shredded the walls of the hallway.

"What's the play, Skipper?" Richie asked.

Bell changed his magazine.

"Follow my lead. Cover our asses!"

Bell entered the long hallway, his M3 bursting rounds through the door of the stairwell. Richie instinctively followed the group into the hall, directing his fire in the opposite corridor, toward the other Nazi.

Nicole tilted her MP40 barrel up and ran past Bell.

"There's another way! Follow me!"

The Alsos Team out-flanked the two German officers, finding another stairwell. They ran down the stairs until they reached the bottom floor. Nicole pried the bullet-riddled door open and saw two German soldiers. She fired a burst from her weapon, dropping both men. She stepped into the hallway, her gaze meeting Claude and Richard's lifeless bodies. By the looks of it, they had fought hard.

"C'est la vie… mes amis," she said, turning for the exit. She could take no time to mourn the loss of her men.

She led the Alsos Team out of the German headquarters, and they made their way back into the sewer tunnel. Their lungs burned as they slowed their pace, nearly back to the Seine River. Bell felt the sting of his wound when he used the ladder, dropping into the sewer. They weren't happy about missing Gurlitt, but Choltitz's knowledge of Hans Frank was enough. It was something to go on. Even if *Portrait of a Young Man* did in fact hold a piece of Arma Christi, they still needed to figure out a way to get into the heavily occupied German stronghold—in Krakow, Poland.

Ian pulled out the Knights Templar journal, making a few memos in the back of the book. He noted that Hans Frank held the painting, that Gurlitt might be the key to unlocking some of the secrets, and also that Frank would be their next target. Once Paris was liberated, they would have another base of operations to work from. The journal held many cryptic secrets; every clue would help direct their path moving forward. They wanted nothing more than to get to the truth, and most importantly, they needed to secure the ultimate weapon. The Nazis could never be allowed to use it.

✝✝✝✝✝

The shooting stopped abruptly. Weber quick-peeked the corner, peering down the hallway toward General Choltitz's residential office. He exposed himself, confident the assault force had abandoned the floor. His Luger was clutched in his hand. He held it forward of his body, edging ever closer to the office's doorway. The squeak of hinges from the other stairwell alarmed him, until Kieffer appeared to his front. The two Nazi SS officers split the doorway into Choltitz's office.

Weber spun into the middle of the passageway, seeing the general light a cigarette from behind his desk. A look of pleasant surprise erupted on Weber's face, his right eye twitching from stress. He lowered his weapon, entering the office.

"Herr General, how did you survive?"

Choltitz took in a long draw from his unfiltered smoke, watching the two men he knew, now at his door.

"Colonel Weber. Lieutenant Kieffer. Did you get Gurlitt on the plane back to Linz?"

"Yes, Herr General," Weber said.

"Sit. I need to tell you something. This war is almost over for me."

Weber walked across the room, confused by the German leader's remarks.

"But sir, we can still win this. The Führer has foreseen it."

Kieffer stood behind the colonel, keeping an eye out for any movement in the hall. He listened intently, already sensing what the general seemed poised to say. Everyone knew, but no one had the guts to admit it. The general sat back in his chair and breathed out a large cloud of smoke.

"Hitler has lost his mind. I know he showed us a grand vision for world peace—strength through force and power. It made sense, so many years ago. But now, we have the entire world closing in around us – and the atrocities we've committed… are not right. His foolish ambitions are not going to work. We'll all be lucky if they don't hang us when this is all over with. I'm done with this madness."

Colonel Weber sank in a chair on the side of the desk; he sat deflated, the nervous twitch still apparent on his face. Choltitz took another pull of his cigarette.

"Do you know why we're here?"

Weber shook his head, puzzled by the general's question.

"We're here because Hitler wants to destroy the ideal of God. He thought if religion could be wiped out, the ideologies of faith would die. True peace could be obtained if religion was no more. We're here, because of Doctor Hildebrand Gurlitt, the late Doctor Heinrick Clarke, your boss

Heinrich Himmler, and Adolf Hitler. All of this – it's not for the purpose we were led to believe. The entire war effort is in pursuit of a single weapon… a weapon that Hitler said would secure true peace. I see it now as something that will only bring about complete destruction."

Weber sat forward, both interested and confused. He had never gotten the whole truth from anyone so close to the seat of power. The singular goal somehow had meaning to him. The SS doctrine, Himmler's Order of the Black Sun, it all made better sense now. Choltitz extinguished one smoke, immediately lighting another.

"I was a part of a meeting, only a few weeks ago," Choltitz continued. "Gurlitt, Himmler, and the Führer himself, were discussing the loss of some journal. I believe it was carried by Doctor Clarke and lost after he was killed in Casablanca. It didn't concern me at the time, but after my encounter tonight, I remembered something interesting."

"General, Kieffer and I are both familiar with this journal. After Bizerte, we have been running into many strange occurrences regarding it. This Alsos Team for instance."

The general inhaled the smoke.

"The ones who attacked me?" he asked.

"Yes, Herr General."

Choltitz leaned forward and said, "You see, Gurlitt had followed up on some information regarding the journal. He told Hitler that he had made a remarkable discovery. I didn't catch everything, but Gurlitt said that he found an object hidden inside the *Just Judges* panel of the *Ghent Altarpiece*. He was skeptical at the time. However, he whispered whatever it was to Hitler directly, and the Führer was elated at the news. Gurlitt mentioned afterwards that the painting was marked with the sign of some saint. He kept mentioning something about Arimathea."

Weber and Kieffer both knew the Knights Templar journal contained many secrets. They exchanged a glance. Kieffer believed the information they had collected in Bizerte was powerful, but to wage an entire war effort for a single weapon… it must be something of more immense power than he had imagined.

Kieffer digested the general's statement, seeing something completely different than his cohort. To control the weapon meant to control the world. To bring about world peace – that was what Hitler wanted. It was what the Reich intended. Kieffer saw Choltitz as weak, unwilling to follow the Führer. The general deserved to die, but there were more important things to do. Kieffer had to find out what Gurlitt knew. The young lieutenant saw what he could be to the Reich. They had to get to Himmler with what they knew. Maybe he would allow them into the inner circle.

If Kieffer could find the ultimate weapon, destroy the ideal of God, and bring peace on Earth, he could become a visionary, himself, and start anew the future of mankind. He could lead the new world of tomorrow. The power he could wield over the world would be limitless perfection. Without a God for the dullards to cling to, everyone would be free to embrace the new world order. Kieffer now understood Hitler's vision. It was beautiful. He would do anything to see it through.

"Kieffer," Weber shouted, bringing the young SS officer out of his lustful trance.

"Yes, Colonel?"

"We must gather our things. We need to leave Paris at once!"

"Is the general coming with us?"

Choltitz turned to look out his window over the Seine River, thankful to still be alive. He gazed over Paris, seeing several small fires, listening to the intermittent crackle of firearms in the distance.

"No. I'll cover the main army's retreat. Paris has fallen, gentlemen. Now, I must do the right thing and turn her over with dignity."

CHAPTER 1: SQUADRON

"Commit everything you do to the Lord. Trust Him, and He will help you."
Psalms 37:5

1300-Zulu Time 19May2020 (1800-EST Arklight HQ)

Spear Team's newest addition, Lieutenant Anne Carter, entered the room with her Integrated Suppressed Rifle (ISR) at the high-ready. She stepped just inside the door, scanning her sector for threats. Captain John Steadman, known as "Steady" among the Teams, crossed behind her, collapsing the space as he moved with well-practiced precision. Now the youngest of the group, Anne knew she had much to prove—especially in this world of elite men. Her compact frame didn't fool anyone on Spear Team, all of whom had already seen her prove herself formidable in single hand-to-hand combat. Commander Billy "Chappy" Chapman entered third, bumping Anne in order to gain some clearance from the doorway. Lieutenant Colonel Mitsuru "Wisp" Tanaka was fourth in the room, picking up the center and sweeping back toward John.

"Clear," he said, closing down the middle of the room while Chappy collapsed the other half, moving away from him.

Anne stepped toward the far corner. The sweat built on her forehead from the stress of a hundred entries. Salt from the perspiration burned her eyes. The grime from expended cordite soiled her face. She continued to collapse her sector, until the threat emerged.

She pulled the trigger in a controlled burst, firing into the intended target.

"Cease-fire! Cease-fire!" Major "Rico" Mims yelled from the observation platform above.

"Dammit, Anne. You've got to get this down," Chappy growled.

"Shit. It looked like a gun," she said, inspecting the mannequin-like target dummy.

Chappy sighed and walked out of the shoot house door, grumbling to himself. John stepped up to Anne, unbuckling his chinstrap.

"Don't let them get to you. We make our mistakes in training – so they don't happen out there."

Wisp looked over John's shoulder into the target she had shot.

"Anne, you don't have to be so trigger happy. Use more precise aim and spend a few less rounds. No more than three to five on each target inside a structure. Remember, we have to keep in mind that innocents could be close by."

Anne nodded her head and tilted her helmet back. Major Allen "Zip" Doha stood above the three of them, a large smile on his face.

"Steady, I got it." he said.

John looked up, squinting from the lighting.

"You got what?"

"She's finally earned a call sign."

"I'm all ears," John said, turning to see Anne's reaction.

"Trig!" Zip called down. "You know, she's good at math and stuff – plus, she's a touch *trigger* happy. Get it?"

Anne huffed. John knew it wouldn't stick, only because nothing had to date. Wisp started laughing and patted her on the back.

"Well, Trig, you ready to call it a day?"

"Hell no. Reset the floor," she said. "Let's run it again. I want to get it right."

Wisp had a surprised look on his face.

"If on-the-trigger-Anne wants more, I'm in."

"If I mess up, we mess up. I get it."

John smiled at her determination and looked up at Rico.

"You heard her. Reset."

☩☩☩☩☩

Zip entered Spear Team's ready room, stopping in front of the honor board. He placed his hand over the collage. All the losses Arklight had suffered. Dagger Team, Arrow Team, Doc, and Sam were all displayed as a vivid reminder. Even the best laid plans fail. The pictures of friends, colleagues, and the courageous still haunted the remaining six operators of Arklight. Admiral Nathan Grant, their commanding officer, and Command Master Chief James "Boomer" Lincoln had spun up two training teams, but they wouldn't be ready for months.

Anne had been practicing nonstop for Arklight's upcoming mission. John and company needed her expertise for what would follow. She had proven herself a true asset to the team and to the mission; after Nashville, John requested she be added to Spear Team, especially given the heavy losses they had suffered during their encounter with Magnus. She specialized in mathematical theory and physics, giving the team an edge in deciphering Professor Amaldi's notes.

The professor first discovered the advanced binary code from the *Adam Panel* of the *Ghent Altarpiece* in Bizerte, Tunisia, just prior to Spear Team's arrival. Anne and Rico were able to create a special decryption system to translate the code. Once completed, the system revealed that the binary contained the plans, experimental theories, and mathematical formulas for the European Union's Large Hadron Particle Collider, located in Geneva, Switzerland. The exact plans, followed in absolute precision, were now reality.

The *Ghent* had been created in the 15th century, leaving Arklight completely puzzled as to how an advanced binary code found its way onto the painting in the first place.

"Zip, how's Gator doing?" Wisp asked.

"You know they had to amputate his right hand. It just never would heal properly."

Chappy tapped the team's honor board and jogged over to Zip, grabbing his shoulder on the way into his equipment cage.

"I talked to him yesterday," Chappy said. "He's in good spirits, but the recovery, after so long – it's getting to him. That damn sewer was full of some nasty stuff."

"You're right about that," Zip said, rubbing his thigh. "I had a pretty nasty infection, myself."

Rico entered, with Anne following. He touched the board as he walked by. She stopped to take in the losses. She missed Joker, especially. He was with her during Basic SEAL training (BUD/S) and became a good friend. Anne turned her attention to the medals hanging on the board. She remembered something Zip had mentioned earlier in the day.

"Zip, when you told me about what happened to Doc and Sam—it sounded like you were blaming yourself for what happened in Bizerte," she said.

"Out of the blue, like usual," Zip said, shaking his head. "It's not blame, Anne. It's about the thousands of kids, half our age, who died far too young during that war. It's probably hard for you to understand. You weren't there. But, if you could have met them, seen their faces, you'd know."

"Amen to that, brother," Rico said, tapping Zip's fist with his own.

John entered the locker area, stopped, and looked over his team.

"Get cleaned up and get to the lab. We've got a few things to cover with the admiral. We'll be wheels-up after. Prep your kits."

Chappy smirked while he stripped off his plate carrier.

"Hey Trig, you ready for this?"

Anne broke her gaze from the honor board and turned toward her assistant team leader. Her eyes narrowed. There was no way in hell that call-sign would stick.

"I've been waiting for this my whole life."

Chappy pulled off his sweaty combat shirt and wiped the grit from his forehead. The scar from where Magnus' bullet caved in his helmet still marred his face.

"Be careful what you wish for. We barely made it out alive last time we went after Arma Christi."

"Don't forget, I'm the one that rescued you old farts," she said.

Wisp looked at Chappy, anxious to spur a reaction.

"What now, Chap?" he asked, fighting back a smile.

Chappy stood back from his shelving. He nodded and smiled at the confidence Anne exuded.

"Get out of here before you see an old man naked!" he said, blasting water at her from his squeeze bottle.

"Aye-Aye, Commander." She jumped into the adjacent changing room. The door shut, and Chappy continued to change. The others entered their cages, prepping their gear.

"John – you sure she's ready for this?"

"She's as ready as we can make her."

Rico walked over, pulling off his helmet.

"Boss, she's still missing a step here and there. I'm not so sure."

John smiled at Rico, knowing he felt threatened by her brains. The decision was already made.

"Look, she's got it where it counts. You guys need to trust her. She'll come through when it matters."

"I believe in her," Zip said, walking to John's cage. "All you two need is a little faith."

Chappy sighed and looked at Wisp.

"What's your take, Mr. Personality?"

"I think she'll fill in well," Wisp said. "Besides, we have bigger fish to fry. We're out of time and I don't see anyone else we can rely on."

Zip smiled and tapped Rico on the arm on his way past.

"Outvoted!" Zip said, "Three to two, she's ready."

Chappy turned around and grabbed his shower bag.

"I, for one," he said looking at John, "don't agree."

"I feel you," John said, "but I think she can handle it, and frankly, we don't have a choice. We need her. Plus, it's my call to make, brother."

Chappy nodded and walked toward the shower. There was a time not so long ago this debate would have lingered. His thoughts fell away to something else: Emaline. He longed to see her again, but knew that would never happen. She had been dead for over a hundred years, and trying to reconcile that fact still baffled his mind. Still, her words danced in his head, urging patience and tolerance and causing him to smile in spite of both himself and his reservations about Anne.

"Whatever call you make. I'm with you, Steady."

†††††

Admiral Nathan Grant stood in his office overlooking the underground hangar of Arklight's headquarters. Buried deep below Mayport Naval Air Station, the base didn't exist on any map. He looked across the concrete deck, observing the five C-17 Globemasters parked below. The massive, hydraulic airplane lift was pushed all the way up to the external hangar above. It remained one of the only ways in and out of their base of operations. Crews scurried about on the deck of the bedrock-walled hangar, preparing Spear Team's plane for their first real mission since the worst night of Nathan's life.

Gazing across the activity, he took a moment to appreciate that the bulky support pillars still impressed him, and the hydraulics of the lift were a true feat of engineering. He saw Spear Team exit their ready room, walking in a group to the lab on the main floor. He watched as the six members moved in unison. It was evident to him that their training had paid off over the past few months. After the losses they suffered on the last mission, every bit of positive thought was needed to carry the plan forward. The burden of losing good men, and in such brutal fashion, still haunted him – every hour of every day. The phone rang, startling Nathan from his thoughts.

He picked up the receiver.

"Admiral," his secretary said, "General Rod Johnson is on the secure line."

"Patch him through," he said, his mood lightening.

"Rod! How are things going?"

"Pretty well. I should ask you the same, though."

Nathan fell back into a brief silence. "I'm a little nervous about launching this mission."

"That's why I called. Archie and I wanted to let you know we're thinking about you and Spear Team. You have our full support and our prayers, Nathan."

"I appreciate that. It's good to hear from you."

"Well let me change that by reminding you that you're still on the line for a golf rematch, and I have a man on the inside who says it doesn't look good for you."

"It was that terrible rental club, you blowhard. But I've got my lucky 9-iron back now, my friend, and you don't stand a chance."

"We'll see about that," Rod laughed. "I'm looking forward to it. Godspeed."

Nathan hung up the receiver, ending the call. Despite the banter and the well wishes, he felt alone and abandoned, on an island of grief. Arklight had been operationally crippled since Magnus' attack, but he knew they had to move forward. The Secretary of Defense (SecDef), Archie MacManus, had cleaned up the catastrophic mess they had left behind. Had it not been for his efforts, Arklight would have been exposed to the world, jeopardizing everything they sought to accomplish. The incident was explained away as another terrorist attack, foiled by the efforts of the intelligence community. No civilians were harmed, which kept the heat to a minimum. However, no one would ever know the sacrifices his men had made on that fateful night. Nine genius-level, elite soldiers perished at the hand of Magnus O'Keefe, and those losses could never be replaced.

Nathan squeezed his fist in anger and looked upwards.

"Am I to forgive someone so evil?" he asked, alone in his office.

He closed his eyes. All he wanted was a vision, like the many he had seen before. Something to guide him, something to establish even the slightest path of purpose. He saw nothing.

"All in good time," he said to himself. "Patience, Nathan, patience."

††††††

John and the team stood in the lab, surrounded by the many artifacts they had retrieved. The *Adam Panel* of the *Ghent Altarpiece* sat on the floor, propped against the wall. The Titulus Crucis, known as the Title of the Cross, sat on the center table in the sterile room. The *Storm on the Sea of Galilee* sat next to the *Adam Panel,* and the 30 pieces of silver it contained sat in a plastic box Chappy carried toward the center table. The box separated the 29 pieces of pure silver from one other piece; that particular silver coin was folded over another coin made from pure gold. The Titulus Crucis and the 30 pieces of silver represented two pieces of Arma Christi. Spear Team's previous missions saw the pieces recovered.

Many discoveries were made during both previous missions. One painting led them to the other, and that same mission now pointed them toward another piece of the *tunc clavem*, or, as they knew it, the Time Key. They had learned that the Time Key functioned to unlock the Ark of the Covenant, which was believed to contain the ultimate weapon. They possessed the coin John carried in his pocket – the very one Confederate General John Bell Hood had minted, just prior to the Battle of Nashville in 1864. A single bronze coin, folded over gold, from King Solomon's mine. John held it in his hand, admiring the archaic minting of the general's namesake upon it. He thought back to when Navy Ensign John Bell, Hood's great-great grandson, gave it to him in 1943, standing just outside of Bizerte. The family keepsake, given away to a stranger from the future. John Bell didn't know what he possessed at the time.

The single bronze coin stood apart from the 30 of silver. The two folded coins, one bronze and one silver, were originally extracted from the mines of King Solomon. Of course, 30 coins, including the one of folded silver, were paid to the infamous disciple, Judas Iscariot. They were cursed symbols of the betrayal of Jesus Christ. The coins carried the shame of all mankind, highlighted by the act of Judas, himself. The 29 pure silver coins were believed to somehow work in conjunction with the Titulus Crucis. Nothing had transpired to date, but John remained hopeful that something would eventually trigger a reaction. Chappy sat the plastic box on the center of the table as all six members of the team gathered around.

The door to the lab opened, and in stepped the admiral, ready to move their long-anticipated mobilization plan forward.

"John, thanks for getting your team down here. We need to make sure we all understand what the objective is. Chief, you patched in?"

Anne heard the garbled transmission and turned to the coms panel inside the room. Her knowledge of Arklight's communications systems was unparalleled.

"Hang on, sir. Let me," she said, typing away.

A moment later, the chief's image appeared on the main screen. The red lighting and lit screens behind him told everyone he was secured in his briefing room, known to the Teams as *the Ark*.

"Admiral - sorry for the signal interference. We're about 5 hours flight time from Okinawa. The satellite is giving us a little feedback."

"Chief, we have you locked in for now," Anne said as she struck a few keys.

"Thanks, Anne."

"What do you have for us, Chief?" Nathan asked.

"My source on the ground said that Magnus might already be in Okinawa. He hasn't made a move toward our target yet, but he's close enough to make me nervous."

"Received, Chief. Do we know if he has any assets in the area?" John asked.

"Best we can tell is, yes. There are any number of contract groups he could be in bed with, and let's not forget the organized crime elements. He could reach out to groups like the Yakuza – or worse."

John nodded and looked around the room, not surprised by the chief's intel. It had taken a longtime to reacquire Magnus. He knew that the reemergence had significant meaning. The chief looked into the screen.

"Sir, we're looking at a pretty sticky situation, if you ask me. Getting into Shuri Castle will be hard enough, but running into Magnus. That'll seriously complicate our objective."

"I'm aware of that," Nathan said, "but we don't have a choice. The best intel we have says the *Portrait of a Young Man* painting is still hidden below the castle. The journal indicates it contains the Spear of Destiny. That's what we're after, and it's what Magnus is after. It's the final piece of the Time Key."

John looked over the pieces they had possession of, and he knew the two folded, mixed-metal coins would somehow work with the Spear of Destiny, or as some called it, the *Lance of Longinus*. Together they would create the Time Key, which would open the Ark of the Covenant. Of course, Arklight still had no idea where the Ark was hidden, or what purpose the ultimate weapon served. They had learned many things to this point, but finding the Spear that had stabbed Jesus Christ would hold more answers. If it required them to face down Magnus, that would be something the whole room would sign up for.

Magnus had killed their brothers, and now they had a chance to find him. A chance to settle the score.

"Chief, just find out where Magnus is," John said. "We'll do the rest."

"That's what I'm talking about," Chappy said, elbowing Zip. "That bastard needs to pay."

Nathan didn't want to lose focus.

"Chief, have we been able to locate Magnus' father, Maximillion O'Keefe?"

"Not since he fell off the grid just prior to Nashville. He's gone totally dark, but we did dig up one anomaly."

"What's that?" Wisp asked.

"Our friends at Langley just located an old account that was routed through proxy a couple of years ago. It looked shady. The account showed multiple payments totaling over 5 million dollars, made to an excavation firm in Canada."

John looked at Chappy.

"Coincidence?"

Chappy rubbed the bridge of his nose, knowing coincidences don't exist in this line of work.

"Where in Canada?" he asked, looking at the screen.

"The best we can tell is that they were somewhere in Nova Scotia. PNK Excavating is the firm. It's just outside anything I'd consider normal for his expenses."

Chappy typed the information into the computer. A simple search revealed several excavation and archeological dig sites. There was everything from ancient first nation projects to buried pirate treasure digs ongoing. Chappy looked over the group with concern.

"John, we need to get out there. Maybe they found something we didn't know about."

The team stared at the data while Zip pulled up satellite imagery of the known sites. John watched as he zoomed in, which jarred a memory from the journal. He grabbed the Knights Templar journal off the counter and flipped it open, finding the page.

"Zip, stop there."

"What is it?" Chappy asked.

"Look here on page 124." He pointed to a sketched shape.

"Dude, you're freaking kidding me." Zip blurted out.

The shape of a particular island on the imagery was an exact match to a sketch in the journal. John saw another cryptic Latin phrase written below the sketch.

"Wisp, what's this say?"

The tall linguist looked over the phrase.

"It says, '*The doorway to loyalty and betrayal, honor and desecration, eternal life and death, resurrection and damnation.*' Whatever that means."

Chappy had a sick feeling in his gut and John stepped back, trying to process what the phrase pointed toward. Without any context, they all knew it wouldn't make any sense.

John looked at the main computer screen. Birch Island, Nova Scotia sat front and center.

"You got anything else to drop on us, Chief?" asked the admiral.

"Looks like I've given you enough for now. With your permission, Admiral, I'd like to keep digging until we launch the mission."

Nathan nodded.

"Sounds good. Spear Team will be headed your way soon."

"Roger that. Get some sleep on the way, Spear Team. Boomer out."

The group stood around the newly discovered information, and John grabbed the Titulus Crucis.

"Admiral," John said, "whatever Maximillion is up to in Nova Scotia, we need to figure that out. Soon."

"I totally agree. I'll head up there, myself, once you and the team get on mission in Oki. I'll check this lead."

"Sir, you shouldn't go it alone, given what we know," Anne said.

"I need to meet with the SecDef and General Johnson, anyway. Given the nature of the find, I'm sure they'll be interested. I'm betting they decide to come along."

"John, look at this," Chappy said, continuing to zoom in on the map.

"There's a rather large excavation site on the Eastern edge of the island," Rico said, pointing. "Just above that triangle-shaped swamp."

They looked at numerous trailers and drilling equipment lined up along a cleared section of land. Maybe they had fallen further behind in their pursuit of the Arma Christi. Whatever Maximillion and Magnus were up to, they had to get to the bottom of it. John believed the situation was beginning to spin out of control. He continued to hold the Titulus Crucis in his hands. Something hit him.

"Admiral, we've travelled back in time twice now," John said. "I can only guess that God is somehow using us, but I haven't been able to see why. Not yet anyway."

Nathan rubbed his face, almost accustomed to the constant frustration the near endless pursuit caused him.

"Me either. I do know that all of this is leading somewhere, but I have to ask – what's the cost?"

The team all stood silent. Rico looked at the admiral with a solemn respect.

"Sir, we set in motion all of these things from our first interaction with Richie—I mean Walter—and John Bell. We set them on a path that led to right where we stand. If you think about it, it led us into Nashville. That's where we discovered this mission. Besides, there's nothing like an 8th inning comeback," Rico said, smiling.

"He's right, sir," Zip said. "We're as much at the center of this as the Alsos Team. Richie, Ian, and John Bell followed the journal's secrets for years, but only because of us."

The admiral still got flustered hearing the name Richie. Navy Raider Walter Richard "Richie" Steadman was John's elderly grandfather. A veteran of WWII, hero to the country, and a still-operational CIA asset, known by his codename to a select few people. Nathan knew him first as Pappy, but later, he revealed himself as Walter. The almost 100-year-old man still withheld information about the Knights Templar journal, even under direct questioning. His deep-set relationships with the SecDef and General Johnson prevented Nathan from physically choking the information from him. Nathan knew Walter would only pass along what intel he saw fit; this strained their relationship. Nathan tried not to take it out on John, who still blamed himself for the losses they had suffered.

"Richie, or Walter, or whatever he goes by these days, failed to give us information that could have saved the lives of many men," he said. "I don't believe he has our best interests in mind."

John sensed the admiral's distaste for his grandfather. He looked at Zip and walked around the table. He still clutched the Titulus Crucis in his hand and wanted to redirect.

"I think all the men are trying to say is that this starts and ends with us. You can't deny we've seen some incredible things, and everything currently points to Okinawa and *Portrait of a Young Man*. It has to contain the Spear. Once we secure it, maybe we can find out what this is all about."

John sat the Titulus Crucis on the table, inches away from the coins. No sooner than he took another step, the ancient piece of petrified wood moved. He stopped. Everyone in the room focused on what was happening. The Titulus Crucis slid across the table toward the container of coins. The 29 coins rolled and flipped over each other, planting themselves against the horizontal edge of the container. The wood reacted like it was magnetized to the coins, flipping on its side, pressing itself to the plastic container.

Nathan felt chill bumps all over his body and could only look on in awe. All of the Arklight operators, including John, stared on in amazement.

Rico said, "What the hell's going on, John?"

"I wish I knew…"

The coins and wood let go of their hold on one another. Everyone began to breathe once again. The admiral felt a sharp pain in his eyes, forcing them shut. He was struck with what he longed for; a vision jumped into his head. He saw John standing next to a wall, staring ahead. The disappointment and sorrow was apparent on his soot covered face. The intensity of the vision made the admiral look away in visible discomfort. Another shock registered: Nathan saw a marker on the rock.

"Touch the stone, John," he said.

"Stone?" John asked.

Nathan shook his head, disoriented.

"You okay?" John asked, extending his hand, grabbing the admiral to hold him upright.

The instant John touched Nathan; he became overwhelmed with a vision of his own. There he stood in a craggy corridor, his grandfather standing beside him. He handed Walter something. He clutched the table, then staggered and shuddered.

"Take it!" he yelled.

The rest of the team watched the two men snap back into themselves. The vision disappeared as quickly as it came on. John and Nathan stared at each other, eyes as wide as saucers.

"What the hell was that?" Chappy asked.

"I saw my granddad, as a young man – like in Bizerte."

The admiral stepped forward, rubbing his face.

"This mission is a go," Nathan said, knowing he now had something to do. "John, whatever it takes. Understand?"

"Yessir."

"Just do what you do, and don't lose track of why we're here. I've got something I need to handle. I'll take care of the Birch Island lead."

The admiral turned, possessed with a thought, and left the lab.

Something told John that Nathan had seen more than he shared, but John had done the same. The blinding vision nearly caused him to forget about what they had just discovered.

"How could a piece of wood and metal have that sort of reaction to one another?" John asked, breaking the dead silence in the room.

Chappy looked around and then straight at John.

"Are you going to tell us what that was about?"

"I need a minute, Chap."

Anne was awestruck at what she had just witnessed.

"Is this a common thing around here?"

"You ain't seen nothing yet," Chappy said.

Rico picked up the Titulus Crucis and examined it, as if it would jump out of his hand at any moment.

"It's never reacted like that before," he said. "It's even been in the same container as the coins. I-I don't... there's no scientific explanation for it that I can think of."

Anne grabbed the wooden piece from Rico's hands.

"The only explanation would be that the molecular make-up of the wood can take on the same properties, becoming fero-magnetic. Potentially, the wood could become magnetic to the coins."

"Maybe, but how would it become magnetic all of a sudden?" Rico asked.

Anne didn't have an answer. Rico stepped back rubbing his chin.

"Let's just agree, it's freaking weird," Wisp said.

John looked around the room and laughed.

"Some of you still don't see what's happening here," John said. "This is a quest of sorts. We're all being asked to digest something we don't understand – to have faith in something we can't see. But each of you, except Anne here, have felt the power guiding everything. This is our crusade to find the truth. The Arma Christi, the Templar journal, and whatever this ultimate weapon is supposed to be. Don't be naïve. Open your minds. We're fighting as much of a spiritual war as a physical one."

Anne stood silent, reflecting upon what she had gotten herself into. She had been atheistic her entire life, believing in what science had taught her. Questions began to flood her mind. *What are we doing chasing after pieces of folk-lore and legend? We're surrounded by advanced technology and we possess great scientific knowledge, yet all of these men — these intelligent people — seemed focused on something paranormal. Why?*

She had to start looking at things objectively so she could steer John and the team toward the real truth: it's all explainable. Magnus needed to be their focus.

How could such gifted men, elite warriors, be fooled into thinking spirits and heaven exist? Whatever the case, she realized that no matter what, she would need to be prepared. The mission would lead them further into the mysterious world of the Knights Templar.

††††††

The team stood outside the lab in the hangar bay. John walked up to Anne and tapped her on the shoulder.

"Can I have a word?"

"Sure, sir."

He turned and started walking toward the team's C-17, which was being loaded with their operational gear. Anne followed, walking up beside him.

"I need you to do something for me," John said. "I need you to keep an open mind about this mission. You're going to see things that will change how you feel. Don't be afraid to question them."

"Honestly? I've already seen some things that concern me. Not with the mission, but with the team."

"Like what?"

"With the exception of Wisp, you all seem to believe this mission has some greater, divine, inspired purpose."

John was floored by her candor, and it caught him somewhat off guard.

"I see," he mused. "I tell you what. Give us this one mission, keep an open mind, and I promise you'll have a different perspective afterwards. Well, provided we aren't all killed in the process."

Anne thought about it for a moment, sure that she would be the one to straighten them out.

"I'll keep an open mind. But you need to do the same. What happened in the lab – that's explainable. I just need some time with it to find the answers."

"Okay, Anne. You've got a deal," John said. "Now, I need you to do something for me. Remember that laser-etched overlay we made of the *Adam Panel*? I need you to create something for me, no questions asked. It's not an easy task, but I need it before we brief in Oki."

"Sounds like a challenge—I'm in. What's the thing?"

CHAPTER 2: FORCE

"Evil people desire evil; their neighbors get no mercy from them."
Proverbs 21:10

1400-Zulu Time 23May2020 (2300-JST Naha, Okinawa)

Magnus choked out the lone security guard, under the slow flicker of light in an alley tightly wedged between two buildings. His hand traced along the ripples of the man's windpipe, squeezing cartilage along the way. The vibrations of each of his labored attempts to breathe were strangled into stillness. The thin, middle-aged guard was locked in a death-grip by the Welshman; tears rolled down his face. He gasped, his face locked, begging for mercy. One quick jerk crushed his throat. His eyes flared with terror at the realization that his life was forfeit.

The body was dragged behind a small dumpster and left in the shadows. Magnus wiped the man's saliva off his hand, onto the sleeve of his jacket. Now a fugitive, and knowing he was on every no-fly list in the world, Magnus had shaved his head to help mask his appearance.

All of his black market arms dealing had gained him valuable allies. The nefarious elite continued to aid in disguising his movements around the world, and the endless bankroll provided by his father gave him more than adequate funding to continue his campaign to retrieve the Arma Christi.

His last experience taught him there was an entire division of the U.S. government dedicated to the continuation of the Knights Templar pledge to protect the so-called Weapons of Christ. He had come face-to-face with his enemy and knew they possessed many of the pieces he needed for the ultimate weapon. By their movements, he deduced they were well-trained and also well-funded, with equipment and logistics. The FBI covered up what happened in Tennessee, and the media ate up the lie that Magnus was an IRA terrorist. They had created a false narrative, alleging that he was tied to Mohammad, Al-Shabaab, and even the Taliban. His picture was posted everywhere—the 'Maniac of Mosul' they called him, from his disgraced Special Air Service days.

Ever since he and his mercenaries were overrun that night below Oliver Tower, he had been working on a comprehensive plan to destroy his newfound enemy. Whoever they were, they stood in the way of him attaining the ultimate weapon – his opportunity to achieve true power, control, and wealth. He had amassed his own personal army of mercenaries, paying top dollar for their loyalty, and above all, their discretion. The little incursion tonight would pave the way toward his own ultimate victory.

Magnus pressed the send button on his radio.

"The guard's down, mate. How's it look?"

Ronnie, Magnus' ever-loyal American mercenary, pulled the scoped rifle into his shoulder. Night-vision enabled him to see inside the residence. The .308 Light Tactical Sniper rifle felt at home in his hands.

"I got no movement above," he said, peering through the scope. "Your target's all alone."

"Copy. Moving."

Magnus grabbed the metal storm drain in the alley. He looked up to the second-floor balcony of the multi-level structure. Once he ensured no one was watching, he scaled the drain, climbing onto the roof above. On his feet, an easy jump to the balcony found him within striking distance of his unsuspecting target.

"Still clear... only some foot traffic to the south," Ronnie said.

Magnus adjusted his earpiece, crouching in front of the sliding patio door. He glanced through the glass. There she was, sleeping mere feet away. They had been tracking her movements for days and finally had everything in place, ready to go active. The door was an older design, and Magnus checked to see if she had left it unlocked.

"Damn," he whispered. "Ronnie, I've got to break in. Watch my back."

"You're all clear."

Magnus lifted the entire door panel while studying the rudimentary locking mechanism on the latch. Once he elevated the door, the base was off of the tracks. He tugged toward himself, and the door slid free, making only the slightest sound. His target, Ayana Matsui, never moved while his presence loomed over her, re-positioning the door. Once his hands were free, he entered the sleeping quarters and scanned the room for any threats.

Ayana slept, and Magnus crept through her apartment, looking for the two items he needed. Quietly, he entered the hallway and within a few steps was standing in her modest kitchen. He reached into his pocket, retrieving a small flashlight. He turned it on, using a red lens to find her keys and her ID badge – items of the most importance if they were to gain access into Shuri Castle. He saw them both sitting on the countertop, right where he figured she would lay them. He reached out with his left hand grabbing the keys, careful to not make any noise. He then grabbed her ID badge and closely inspected the Shuri Castle logo.

The Welshman felt confident in his plan, but still needed to secure one more piece. He turned, extinguishing the light. The still-sleeping silhouette of Ayana lay in her bed, oblivious to the vile presence in her home. Only a thin sheet, cotton pajamas, and air separated her from the terror now hovering above. Magnus stood at her bedside, facing the point of no return. He reached under his woolen jacket, feeling the suppressed pistol against his side.

He bypassed the cold steel for a syringe filled with a GHB derivative, designed to render an adult unconscious for hours. He grabbed the knock-out drug, pulling the cap off with his teeth. With one quick move, he placed his hand over the young curator's mouth, inserted the needle in her arm, and put his knee across her chest. Her eyes opened wide with shock, and her right arm grabbed Magnus' hand, which was holding the now-empty syringe. Horrified, she could only take in the man's face staring back at her. Magnus enjoyed every moment of terror before she lost consciousness. It took a few seconds for the struggle to end. He released her, watching her small frame fall limp on the bed.

Ronnie watched the intensity of the fray. The sheer enjoyment on Magnus' face concerned him. He struggled to understand why this was so important, and more importantly, why Magnus seemed to enjoy the misery he brought upon others. *What a sadistic asshole,* he thought.

"You're still clear," he said, shaking the chills off. "Bring her out the front door. The van will meet you there."

Magnus looked out the window, toward Ronnie's perch two blocks over, and gave a thumbs up. He grabbed the balcony door, lifting it back in place. It was important to not alert anyone of their presence. Ayana was supposed be off of work for another two days; she had no close friends, as her work was the passion of her life. No one would come by to check on her disappearance, and by tomorrow, it would be too late to do anything to disrupt the plan.

Magnus reached into the small of his back, pulling out a large bag he had folded in place to fit. He rolled it out on the bed and folded the Japanese woman inside. She weighed about 100 pounds from what he could tell, which was light compared to things he was forced to carry in his military days. The large duffle bag was stuffed with the human cargo and he sat on the bed, reaching through the two padded handles. He grabbed hold and stood; Ayana tightly packed into his makeshift kidnapping rig.

The night concealed his exit from the front door. He walked down the stairs and onto the street, to the waiting van. The door slid open and he turned, sitting on the metal cargo deck. A pair of familiar hands grabbed hold of the cargo, pulling it across the floor.

"I'm in. Drive." Magnus said, adjusting his jacket. "Don't forget to pick up Ronnie around the block."

The white paneled van pulled into an enclosed warehouse in the middle of Naha, Okinawa. Shipping containers littered the docks surrounding the warehouse, providing additional camouflage for the true clandestine nature of the building's occupants. As the vehicle cleared the entrance, two of Magnus' goons inspected the area to the rear of the van and then heaved their respective chains to close the large, roll-up door, which secured them inside. The van glided to a stop, and the side door popped open, with Magnus and Ronnie stepping out onto the concrete floor. Ronnie motioned to a couple of men waiting for orders.

"Take her out of the bag and put her in the cage. If she tries anything, you know what to do."

"And don't rough her up, yet," Magnus said. "I need her uninjured for tomorrow."

The two men grabbed the bag containing Ayana and walked it to the small detention cage in the middle of the warehouse. Magnus smiled, happy to secure his easy entrance into Shuri Castle. Ronnie walked to a table laden with documents, plans, and an old underground map they believed to be a tunnel network, located under the castle.

"Well, now that we have the girl, what's next, boss?"

"You and I still have one more thing to accomplish tonight," Magnus replied. "Let me make a quick call, and we'll get on with it."

Ronnie sat his sniper rifle on the table.

"I'll take a load off," he said, plopping in the first chair he could find. "Take your time."

Magnus nodded and walked across the warehouse floor. He looked to his left, seeing the majority of his hired help asleep on cots. A few others secured gear, and two men kept watch. To his right, he admired the three up-armored SUVs, the array of firepower stacked on the floor, and the numerous packages that would get delivered to their staging areas tomorrow morning. Confidence was high. He was sure the plan would catch his enemies off-guard and ill-prepared.

He pulled the satellite phone from the cargo pocket of his pants, extended the antenna, and pressed the speed dial. After a few seconds of connecting, the line rang and a familiar voice answered.

"Well, boy, did you secure the manager?"

"I did, Father," he said, ticked that Maximillion still called him that. "It was a piece of cake."

"Good. Is everything else in place?"

"Yes. We're about to enter phase two."

"We can't afford any more issues. This plan of yours better work. They'll know very soon that we have the package."

Magnus smiled at the thought.

"Did you locate it?"

"Yes," Maximillion said, "the journal was right. It led us straight to it. The information your grandfather secured from Gurlitt turned out to be what we needed to contextualize the search."

Magnus rubbed his shaved head, feeling rough stubble under the weight of his hand. Peace through strength. Maybe his grandfather was right all along.

"The information? You mean from 1964?"

"Yes, indeed," Maximillion replied. "What he and Weber uncovered that night led us here. Of course, it took forever to find the other part, but we're very close to having the ultimate weapon in our hands. Remember: it's useless without the Time Key. Don't fail me, boy."

"My plan won't fail, Father," Magnus said, choking back his anger. "It'll take a little time, but they won't ever see us coming."

"They better not. Your grandfather didn't want to allow you this honor, but I insisted. You'll be rich beyond your wildest dreams. We will rule over true peace in this world – together. Father and son."

Magnus closed his eyes imagining the power, the wealth, and the world under the weight of his boot heel.

"Aye, Father. I'll let you know when we're clear. If all goes well, I should be leaving within 36 hours."

"Don't screw this up."

The line went dead and he flipped the antenna down, deactivating his device. He stood motionless on the floor, thinking that the foolish stories his grandfather used to tell might actually carry some truth. The Knights Templar journal had been in his family's possession his entire life, until he gave it to Mohammad, that day in Dallas. He knew that his grandfather, Alfred Kieffer, had been a Nazi SS officer during WWII. He changed his name to O'Keefe after the war, in order to hide from the authorities. The Kieffer name was his heritage, but greed continued to be Magnus' drive. The Fourth Reich ruling the world through the power of the ultimate weapon would please his elders. But, for Magnus, only supreme rule would afford him everything he wanted. Unending, unlimited, unyielding power.

He snapped out of his daydream of grandeur. He thought about his last trip to America and the soldiers he encountered; John's face was permanently burned into his memory. How they appeared in that dank basement, overwhelming his superior numbers, still angered him to the point of rage. Nonetheless, losing *The Storm on the Sea of Galilee* to those American soldiers had now turned into an opportunity for the Welshman.

Another second of quiet lingered, ending as he turned and walked toward Ronnie.

"You ready, mate?"

"As long as you're paying me, I'm ready anytime."

†††††

The van slowed at the 90-degree corner of Aka-Marusou Dori, the street at the base of the castle wall. The side door opened as the van stopped. Magnus looked straight ahead, seeing a 10-foot-high concrete wall. He faced due north and knew it was the first step into Shuri Castle. Ronnie exited the van, looking in both directions, seeing nothing move either way. Magnus threw the grappling hook up the wall, setting it. With two quick tugs up the rope, he grabbed the rough edge along the top. Both he and Ronnie were over the barrier in seconds, inside the heavy brush just off the edge. The van rumbled off to stage for their pick up. The two men listened for any sign they had been compromised.

Magnus turned to face another 15-foot concrete wall, observing that a steep climb was possible through the scrub brush. He took the lead, maneuvering his way to the top, finding the intersecting edge of the thick, concrete obstacle. He pulled himself over and motioned for Ronnie to follow. They had to stay undetected tonight in order to recon the civilian security force working inside the castle. Tomorrow night, they would need to know every position.

"We've got to find some high ground," Magnus said.

"The two-story on the south of the courtyard looks pretty good," Ronnie said.

"Okay, mate."

The two men were dressed for the occasion: gray fatigues, some light weapons, and a backpack filled with tech was all they needed for the sneak and peek. Magnus crouched, hidden from sight, checking the few vehicles in the parking lot. They were all unoccupied. He scanned the area, looking for the on-site security cameras. He could see one, but the angle was too great for it to catch their movement.

He readied the grappling hook for another 15-footer. This final climb would get them into the upper area of Shuri Castle, and from there, they

ARKLIGHT: Task Force Crusader

could get to work. The rubberized hook clicked against the hard rock wall. Magnus checked the rope, and he was up in a matter of moments. Ronnie followed along, and the men found themselves in a courtyard behind the southernmost building on the grounds.

The castle had been constructed utilizing ancient building techniques, unlike many of the other castles in Japan. The Ryukyuan limestone walls were still original in some spots, but the repaired areas were easy to identify. The clay-tiled roof was foremost on Magnus' mind, since walking on it could prove difficult. Ronnie tapped Magnus on the shoulder and pointed to the map.

"We need to walk on the center line of the roof. Just move slow, then we can drop down on the other side. The security camera relay is supposed to be there."

"You better be right. Otherwise, it might get lively in here."

"It's no problem; I've been on these types of roofs before, and they're stronger than they look."

Magnus had taken one step toward the access ladder leading up to the roof when Ronnie grabbed his arm. The Welshman almost pulled away, until he saw why he was stopped. Two security guards stood just feet from their location. The lighting along the main pathways illuminated the open areas, but only a few streaks pierced the bushes on the perimeter. They waited, and the guards soon wandered off in separate directions.

"Clear," Magnus whispered, now scaling the access ladder to the roof.

Ronnie followed. The men had a solid view of the grounds, with the exception of the main courtyard in front of the main hall's throne room. The clouds in the sky masked the men as they moved like cats across the roof. Magnus lay prone along the edge, checking the area below.

"This is it."

"Sure is," Ronnie said as he low-crawled to Magnus. "There's the relay hub. Between the air-conditioning units."

Magnus looked across the courtyard of the castle grounds. He saw that it was in a controlled access area – a perfect funnel to trap his prey. A gate at the end of the corridor was closed; it represented the only way in or out. He grabbed the grappling hook from his pack and crawled to the roof's peak. He seated the rope's anchor across the center of the roofline and dropped the rope into the space below.

"Get on with it," Magnus said, motioning for his man to move.

"I'm goin'."

The mercenary grabbed the rope and lowered himself into the controlled area. Magnus pulled out his binoculars, surveying the location from above. Ronnie slid to the ground, making his way into the darkened outdoor corridor. Once on the ground, he saw two security guards through the window, sitting half-asleep at the monitoring station. Several of the air-conditioning units were on, covering any sound he might make. The control box for the security cameras was easy to access, and he made quick work of infiltrating the closed-circuit system.

Ronnie located the primary lines for the network and separated them. He reached into his backpack and retrieved what he needed: a purpose-built housing with self-tapping gator clips for the main lines. The battery would power the monitoring system for more than enough time, and the relays were already in place outside the castle walls. The clips were attached to the camera feeds. He powered up the unit and stuck it inside the relay panel box. He closed the door and pressed the mic on his radio.

"Bug in place," Ronnie said. "You copy?"

Another voice came across the radio earbud.

"Standby. Checking the feed."

Ronnie watched the two guards talking inside. The monitoring station had several active screens with motion-tracking enabled. He noticed all of the screens flicker for a brief moment before returning to normal. None of the guards paid it any attention.

"We got the signal," the radio crackled. "It's good to go."

"Copy that," Ronnie said, giving a thumbs up to Magnus above.

He was relieved the guards didn't notice the tap to their screens, but he remembered his training and how complacent most security tended to be when standing a post. They now had the ability to monitor all of the cameras in the facility, which was the main objective for the operation.

Magnus focused through his binoculars, watching several guards walk about inside the castle. He shifted his gaze to the main hall, recording every position of cover and concealment available. He gambled everything on his enemies coming for *Portrait of a Young Man* within the next 24-48 hours. If he was right, he could gain the advantage, cripple his enemies, and recover what his father needed. Of course, what his father needed only served as a means to an end, and that was what Magnus wanted.

Ronnie reached the roof and pulled up the rope before crawling higher, to Magnus' position.

"Did you copy the radio traffic on the bug?"

"Yeah," Magnus said, "we're damn-well ready this time."

"What about the tunnel entrances?"

"We'll set those up on the way in. There'll be enough explosives to collapse the entire tunnel system."

"Those bastards won't escape this time," Ronnie smiled. "You've thought of everything."

Magnus pulled the binoculars away from his eyes and leaned over toward Ronnie.

"I hope they die in miserable fashion. One way or another, they'll lead us back to where they have the Arma Christi stashed. I've made sure of that."

"We'll kill 'em all," Ronnie mused.

"If they somehow survive, they'll have the Japanese Police all over them. So, it's a win-win for us, mate," Magnus said, a slight smirk emerging on his face.

"What else you got?"

"That's it, for tonight. Let's call the van and get back to the warehouse."

"Roger that."

†††††

Magnus and Ronnie sat their gear down on a table inside the warehouse. Their preparation was complete, and it was time for them to get some rest. From what Magnus had determined, his newfound enemies operated at night, using special stealth-tech. They were well-trained and well-equipped; a secret branch of the United States military, with a specific mission, running in full opposition to his own endeavors.

In the aftermath of Nashville, Magnus had escaped the police perimeter using underground tunnels to get to the Cumberland River. Once there, he and Ronnie were able to exfiltrate the area. During their ride out, Ronnie noticed something unusual sitting at the airport, in front of the Tennessee Air National Guard hangar—he had never seen one, much less four, C-17 Globemasters sitting on the tarmac at the facility. Magnus surmised those aircraft were most used by the teams they had encountered. If that same group was to get to Okinawa, they would arrive by air to Kadena, Air Force Base. That was about two miles from the warehouse, which sat between the castle and the base.

Ronnie extracted the live round from the chamber of the LTS rifle platform.

"Magnus, we're going to be moving around a lot. You sure our escape and evade plan's solid?"

"I've used the same service for years. They called today, and the plane is fueled up and bloody well ready to go. I've paid a handsome sum to maintain our secrecy."

"Just double checking, man. The JP's will be all over the place once we make our move."

"I've got it covered, mate." Magnus walked off and dug out the satellite phone vibrating in his pocket. The phone buzzed again.

"That didn't take long," Maximillion said.

"I told you, I've got everything covered."

"You better. We just extracted it. It's utterly remarkable. Once I get it crated, I'll be headed back to prepare the device," Maximillion said, noticeable excitement lining his voice.

"It actually exists?"

"Not only does it exist, it's more impressive than I even could have imagined. It survived in a damp grave for almost 622 years. We can now finish what the Führer, himself, started in WWII. Your grandfather was right – the ultimate weapon does exist, and in our hands, we will take back what's ours. Peace will happen, and science will pave the way."

Magnus had long-known his family's ambitions, only sharing them internally for his own well-being; however, he couldn't help but feel a new sense of purpose after hearing his father's upbeat voice upon recovering what he had been on a quest for his entire life. Once Magnus assembled all of the pieces to the weapon, he could relieve himself of the burdens his father had placed on him. He smiled, wondering how great it would be to answer to no one. Killing those in his way mattered now, more than ever.

"Yes indeed, Father. I'm glad you found it. I won't let you down. The future will be ours. I assure you."

"See you when it's done, boy," Maximillion replied, a new level of satisfaction ringing in his voice.

The line went dead. Magnus took a deep breath, knowing Maximillion's quest heralded the beginning of the new world order. The Large Hadron Particle Collider had been operational for many years, refining the exact frequencies necessary to bend reality, itself. The science of the device had proven to be remarkable, opening portals and creating the energy fields needed to activate the Time Key. His father's tireless research on the project had spanned decades. After identifying the God particle and creating the necessary energy outputs, his project stood complete. The date of the collision was already scheduled. The time drew near.

Magnus believed that his father served no further purpose after seeing the science of the project through to completion. He grew tired of his demands, sick of his patronizing tone. The plan to unleash the ultimate weapon all rested upon the acquisition of the Arma Christi. Magnus *would* find the pieces needed to construct the Time Key.

By his own tally, his enemies possessed most, if not all, of the pieces. He needed to secure them to unlock the weapon. With the intelligence his grandfather had provided him, he knew the American soldiers would come. He prepared for them to appear in the castle, and he knew they would bring *Portrait of a Young Man* straight to him. *Why search for it when it was coming gift-wrapped?* He didn't know where they would appear, but when they did, he'd be ready.

He walked over to the table. Ronnie had stripped off his gear, ready to get some sleep.

"Everything good to go?" Ronnie asked.

"Better than ever," Magnus said.

"Hopefully that lady we kidnapped will stay out of it, until at least lunchtime. I'm beat."

"She's going to have an eventful day. Of course, I'll likely have to teach her some manners."

Ronnie shook his head, knowing some of Magnus' techniques.

"I'll keep her quiet."

Magnus walked toward a cot and looked back.

"You do that then. I'll get you some extra cash for your trouble."

Ronnie watched Magnus lay down and looked over at one of the guards. A question entered his mind.

"Hey, I've been meaning to ask. Why is this so important to you?"

Magnus sat up on the cot and untied his boots. This was the first time Ronnie had asked any real questions.

"I think I pay you enough to not ask questions."

"You know I don't give a rat's ass. I'm just curious."

"Take your curiosity and piss off, Ron," Magnus said, stretching out. "All you need to know is that this is important, and you're getting paid quite well for it. Now how about you let me get some sleep?"

Ronnie sighed and looked toward the lady in the cage.

"Make sure you wake me up when she starts to stir," Magnus added, rolling over.

One of the guards nodded and continued to pace the warehouse— an effort to stay awake.

A nervousness struck Ronnie. This felt like more than a job. He knew what he was doing, he searched for something to cling to, but Magnus had ill intentions – for everything he touched. The paid in full loyalty sat awkwardly on his heart. He turned over on his side, rationalizing the means to an end. Ronnie didn't believe in anything, or anyone; money was real. Besides, he hated people anyway. After four tours overseas, his heart had grown cold. Regular people, or *sheeple* as he liked to call them, had no clue to what real hardship was. They didn't understand what he had been through. All in the name of freedom – freedom to take stuff. Money was freedom. Money talked, and he wanted lots of it.

Ronnie took a deep breath, ready for an extended vacation. Only a few more obstacles stood between him and his dream. Millions of dollars would soon be his.

CHAPTER 3: CONTINGENCY

"But the Lord's plans stand firm forever; his intentions can never be shaken."
Psalms 33:11

0530-Zulu Time 24May2020 (1430-JST Kadena, AFB)

The roar of jet engines thundered across the tarmac. John stepped off the rear cargo door of the C-17, enjoying a warm, fresh breeze dancing across his face. He turned and looked up the ramp, watching the other five members of Spear Team gathering their gear.

"Captain Steadman!" The bass of a welcomed, familiar voice rattled his ears, even above the noise of aircraft taking to the sky. "Hope you got some rest."

John glanced over, unable to suppress his smile.

"Chief," he said with a note of fond respect, "good to see you."

"How was your flight?"

"Long… It's been awhile since I've been to Oki. How's our target looking?"

The chief curled his well-manicured mustache and adjusted the ball cap on his head.

"Well, I wish I could say this is going to be easy, but I'd be lying, Captain."

"If it were easy," John said, "we wouldn't be here."

"And some of us know you'll do whatever it takes to get us home, you old pirate," Chappy said as he jumped off the plane wearing his standard flip-flops and shorts.

The chief smiled, pulling an unlit cigar out of his mouth.

"Pirate?" he smiled. "Looks like the resident yeti has gotten all sentimental on us."

"Remember: you're talking to an oci-ffer," Chappy belched, as he walked past.

John and Chappy walked to the waiting transport while the chief stayed behind to greet Rico, who was now emerging from the cargo bay of the aircraft.

"What's the word, Chief?"

"Same ole' shit, different day my friend. How about you?"

"Just living the dream. You know, jet-lagged and sea-bagged."

The chief twisted his cigar and slapped his friend on the back before lighting the sweet stogie.

"Got any good news for us?" Zip asked as he approached.

"Yeah, you guys get to try and land your asses on a dime at 100 miles per hour. But, other than that, everything is just freakin' peachy."

"You know how we like to make an entrance," Zip said, smiling on his way past.

Wisp walked by next—his typical, stoic demeanor markedly unconcerned.

"As long as I can get a cheeseburger," he said, "I don't care what we do."

Zip poked at Chief.

"He's been craving a burger since Guam."

A familiar female voice sounded from the cargo bay.

"Does he always complain this much before missions?" Anne asked.

The chief turned back around, seeing his young protégé and smiling like a prideful father. She carried six nylon satchels for her teammates.

"Anne! Glad to see things haven't changed with Spear Team. Looks like you get to carry all the bags."

Zip looked toward the transport, and then back.

"I'm just glad I'm not the low man anymore," he said, smiling ear to ear. "Throw the bags in the truck, Lieutenant. I ain't got all day!"

Chief grabbed Zip by the shoulder, turning with him to walk toward the transport.

"I'm glad she's getting the same treatment, just like everyone else."

"She's a tough one… just don't tell her I said so," Zip laughed.

Once aboard their transport, the team was driven across the tarmac. The staging area was located in a procured hangar on the northwest side of the airfield. Air traffic in the area was heavy, with military flights of all types departing and arriving. The smell of salt air blowing in from the East China Sea was all but consumed by the abundance of jet wash fumes.

Anne stood in the bed of the transport truck, looking over the cab as they crossed the taxiway. It felt good to be operational, at last. Her wish had come true; however, she was struggling to fight back the fear, nerves, and doubt of her first Arklight mission. She took a deep breath, knowing the very best had prepared her – for whatever may come.

The truck squealed to a stop in front of the hangar. The CIC and the Ark sat inside with dozens of umbilical cables connecting them on the floor, throughout. Chief jumped out of the passenger side, looking up at John.

"Sir, we have a ton to cover before we launch."

John took a quick glance over the area, seeing numerous, stacked gear boxes sitting on the deck.

"Roger that," he replied. "Let's go ahead and get this thing briefed."

He looked back at Chappy.

"Hey brother, get everyone in the Ark. We brief in 15."

"Roger that."

John turned back to the front, seeing the chief already headed toward the back of the hangar for his pre-briefing ritual. He felt a hand grab his arm.

"Sir," Anne said, "here's the drone you wanted me to build. What's it for?"

"Remember, no questions," John said, admiring the craftsmanship. "And thanks... So, what am I looking at?"

Anne was holding a tiny, square, robotic device.

"It's a one-time use, laser-encoding drone. I know you wanted me to make a copy of the binary code on the *Adam Panel*, but I had another idea along the way. I just started building it, and it's pretty neat. Easy to operate as well."

"How's it work?" John asked.

"It's basically a robotic memory printer with a laser-etching device attached. Rico helped me make it out of an old recon drone and some other parts. I programmed it with a complete copy of the binary code, so it's capable of reproducing it on another flat surface. The drone can simulate the codex using geo-synced markers and other surface-detection software."

"Whatever you just said sounds complicated."

Anne shook her head and held the device at eye level.

"You just set it down and hit the button. It does the rest. I figured it was smaller to carry around, and maintains better security for the code. You've got a copy ready to go anytime you need it."

"That could prove useful, and you're right about the size being an advantage – thanks for going the extra mile. Just another reason I wanted you on our team."

"That means a lot, Captain."

"You're with us now. Just call me John, or Steady. Okay?"

"Yes, Cap… I mean, John."

Anne exchanged a brief smile, turned, and walked toward the CIC to see who Chief had brought along to help out. John held the device in his hand, amazed at what something so small contained.

How do you work? I can't even begin to get my head around it.

John smiled, knowing this had real purpose, even if Anne didn't realize it. He walked out the back door, stuffing the mini-drone into his cargo-pocket.

"Captain," said the chief.

"Can you just call me John? We're far past formalities, my friend."

"I guess I owe you that. What's on your mind?"

The chief had already taken a few puffs of his cigar prior to John's arrival. The thick smoke caught John's senses.

"Got an extra?" John asked. "It could be my last."

"Don't say that crap," said the chief. "This'll work out. It has to."

"Don't be so touchy, Boomer. I'm just trying to beg a Cuban off of you, brother. Though it sounds like something is on *your* mind."

Chief dug out an extra cigar and passed it to John. He rummaged through another pocket for his lighter.

"I spent some time with Gator – you know, before we left. I think I screwed up."

"What do you mean?" John asked, as he lit the sweet, savory stogie.

"I – I told him about the mission."

"How much did you tell him?"

"All of it."

John puffed on the cigar, thinking about the agony and self-blame he carried along, himself. Killing all those near-defenseless Confederates still bothered him. Magnus showing up had to be part of what he, himself, had brought upon Arklight. A wave of emotion hit him in the moment. He froze in thought, consumed by the loss of so many.

"Did you hear me, John? I said, I told Gator everything. You got anything to say about that?"

Tears welled in John's eyes, and he lingered for a moment. All the suffering that was experienced in that one night. Nine good men, gone in an instant. *For what?* John thought, *if I would have found another way.* If only he could go back.

"John? You okay?" asked the chief.

"I'm just sorry, Boomer. Sorry for Gator. Sorry for what happened."

"It's not your fault. Things just happen, man."

"But do they?"

"No buts about it," he replied. "There was nothing anyone could have done to prevent Magnus' reaction. He's a damn evil bastard. We just need to go get him, and let's end this."

John wiped the sorrow from his cheeks, embarrassed his emotions got the best of him.

"You're right, Boomer."

The chief placed his hand on John's shoulder, grown from the experiences of the past. He was helping heal Gator with the knowledge that his sacrifice was for something far greater than any of them would ever understand. He rescued Gator from the abyss, and at least now, he could go into everyday with understanding. Action serves purpose.

"John, I'll tell you something I've learned from all of this. Funny – me telling *you* something I've learned. This—all of this—is meant to teach us something through the process. The good, the bad – hell, even the ugly. It's all meant for something. You said it to me once: this is leading us to something extraordinary."

John stood like a stone, puffing on the cigar, reminding himself of that evening he encouraged the chief in Nashville. *It's funny how the world works*, he thought.

"I've been feeling sorry for myself," John said. "Looking back on something that's gone. I suppose, I've lost sight of a few things. Lost my way."

"It's nothing you wouldn't do for me."

The sun still shown bright in the sky, but time was in short supply. They needed to get on with the briefing. Boomer looked at John.

"Let's enjoy these, put yesterday behind us, and move on into tonight, tomorrow, and beyond."

"Sounds like a plan."

††††††

"Where the hell have you two been?" Chappy asked.

"Sorry. We got caught up for a minute," John said, shutting the door to the Ark.

"I was ready to brief this thing without you," Chappy replied.

John looked at Chappy, extended his middle finger, and scratched his nose. Chappy smirked and walked around the console.

"Ty, secure the Ark."

"Roger that. Wait one… Ark secure, Chief," his voice crackled over the intercom from CIC.

"Gentlemen and lady, sorry for the delay. Captain Steadman and I had a few details to discuss."

The chief made a few key strokes on the keyboard and a three-dimensional map of Shuri Castle appeared. He raised the image to eye-level for Spear Team to view.

"Ty, go ahead and get the admiral on a secure channel and bring up the intel briefing on O'Keefe."

"Copy that, Chief."

Monitors in the Ark highlighted images of Magnus, phone records, spreadsheets, black marketeers of the Yakuza, and several researched photos of the Knights Templar journal. John could see the information growing and expanding. He looked around the room.

"Before we get too far into this," John said, "I need to say something." Everyone's gaze trained on him, unsure and expectant. He breathed and began, "I'm responsible for what happened in Nashville."

Wisp asked, "What do you mean?"

Concern crept into the teams' expressions as they continued to look at John.

"I made a bad call," John said. "I feel like, those Confederates didn't have to die. They didn't stand a chance against us, and we... no, I – ordered their deaths. That decision, the one I made, brought Magnus upon our friends."

"That's a load of crap, John," Chappy said. "There's no way any of that could have been avoided. It's not your fault, man."

"Look," Zip added, "you *know* how tricky it is to deploy less-lethal on the battlefield. It would've gotten us killed."

"Steady, if anyone's to blame," Rico said, "it's me. I'm the one who let my emotions drive me. I've got to live with that, but... blame you? Put it behind you, man. We're still here. That's what matters."

"I wish I'd been there," Anne said, her eyes welled.

Chappy stroked his beard and dropped his head.

"John, we need your head in the game. Nobody here, not me, not the admiral, or the chief – not even Gator, blames you for any of this. So, no pity parties today, boss. Let's get back in the game, find Magnus, and kick his sorry ass."

"Yeah, I'm out of regrets," Wisp said. "Plus, I never make mistakes."

John breathed a heavy sigh, smiled, and nodded his head. It took a load off his chest, knowing his team still believed in him. Tonight would be another chance to set them back on course; an opportunity, a moment of real freedom, and with any luck, answers awaited.

"I'll let it go. I will... I just had to get that off my chest. I'm ready."

"First and foremost," Chief said, getting back into the brief, "Magnus O'Keefe. Ty, bring up the CIA asset."

The map of the castle disappeared and the screen below displayed an image of a Japanese man.

"Meet CIA asset Touma Nakamura of the Yakuza Yamabishi clan. He's been vetted through both the CIA and the NSA. He's been providing information on Magnus' movements. Evidently, he's an unsatisfied customer."

The screen changed to photos of Magnus, a group of men, and cars in a parking lot.

"According to the source, Magnus met with several Yakuza heads, three days ago, on the mainland of Japan. It appeared he was brokering another arms deal."

John looked at the man to Magnus' left.

"That guy beside Magnus – that's the other guy from the basement."

"Sure is," Rico confirmed, "have you been able to ID him?"

"You guys think this is amateur hour?" the chief replied.

A biographical analysis of Ronald S. Nelson came up beside the pictures.

"It says that he's a former special forces operator. Four tours overseas," John noted. "What's a guy like this doing with Magnus?"

"Frankly, that I don't know, though the facts suggest it's for the money. Ronald here has been working mercenary jobs for about 6 years."

"So where's Magnus now?" Wisp asked.

"As of yesterday, the asset reported he was still on the mainland, but satellite couldn't confirm. We haven't had a visual in two days. However, according to our CIA folks, the asset has been very reliable in the past."

"I don't like it, John," Chappy said. "Magnus could be anywhere."

The chief looked at John.

"That's a possibility," he said. "Also, there's been no chatter reported by NSA. For all we know, the asset is working with Magnus."

"Chief, Zip said, "zoom in on Magnus' lapel."

A few keystrokes and Zip's blood grew cold at the visual. The pin on Magnus' lapel was the Black Sun symbol. A gifted symbology expert, Zip shook his head as the information crashed down, confirming his fear.

"This is really bad."

"What?" Anne asked.

John looked at the image. He recalled what he knew of the history of the symbol; the Black Sun appearing here and now made some sense to him, but Zip's concern was at a much higher level.

"That symbol is a Nazi occult symbol. It was a Nazi SS secret marking found on the floor of Wewelsburg Castle in Germany at the close of World War II… Zip, it looks like you may have more to say."

Zip stepped up to the table, and all attention locked on him.

"There's a story – a conspiracy theory, if you will – among some really talented professors I know. Seeing the Black Sun, right here, right now, gives the theory merit."

Chappy was ready to hear it.

"Well?" he asked. "You going to share or keep us waiting?"

Zip knew this would be hard to believe, but seeing the symbol meant something.

"Okay, I'm just going to tell you," he said, taking a deep breath. "John's right in that the Black Sun is a Nazi occult symbol, but there's a legend behind the symbol. It's said that those who wear the Black Sun are the most loyal believers of Hitler's cause. I'm talking about an enemy that has a vivid singular purpose. They believe they are chosen to save the world and bring about peace on Earth."

"I've read about a secret sect of the SS," John added, "called the Merovingian group – bearers of the Black Sun. Some called them 'The Order of the Black Sun.'"

"That's all true," Zip continued. "The story on the Merovingian's dates back hundreds of years, recording as they took up the mantle of opposition to the Knights Templar. They were once, in fact, allies – the Teutonic Merovingian Knights and the Templar Knights; however, their purpose changed. All of a sudden, they wanted to wipe out religion and the thought of God, changing the ideology of the world. They believed if all religion were gone, true enlightenment would fall upon mankind. A peace would follow, and their Führer would lead humankind toward genetic perfection."

"That's one strong and messed up theory, Zip," Rico said. "So, they're convicted in their cause. That doesn't change anything."

"It might yet," Zip replied. "The emergence of the Black Sun in Japan… the Axis powers, meeting once more, right now. That's got to mean something."

"It means we need to get to the bottom of this," John said.

"There's one more thing, Steady. The main part of the theory is what bothers me."

"Spit it out," Anne said.

Zip swallowed and wet his lips.

"The Order of the Black Sun was believed to have not only staged Hitler's death in 1945, but to have protected him in South America, after the war. It's said that they continued to work toward their vision of a new world order and the abolishment of religions all over the world."

"That's crazy," Wisp said, "what do you reference this information on? Wild conspiracy theories, or actual facts?"

Zip knew it was thin, but needed to complete the story.

"Think about everything we've been through. Think about Magnus, his conviction to find the Arma Christi, the Knights Templar journal, and how all of this has come together. We're facing a formidable enemy, who believes in their purpose. I'm not saying this is a strong theory, but it's the only thing that makes sense."

"So, if this is correct—and that's a big if," the chief said, "Hitler was primarily behind the pursuit of the ultimate weapon. And this weapon is something that can destroy the belief in God?"

Anne wanted to speak out, but all of the information being discussed left her without words. *Does science stand against religion? What does the Nazi occult have to do what's happening today? What have I gotten myself into?* Chills quivered down her spine as she classified the information away as lore and legend.

"It kinda makes sense if you think about it," Chappy said.

"With no religious guidance on Earth," Rico said, "there would be no argument against immorality, scientific experimentation, you name it. Everything is on the table."

"That's what General Hood basically said in Nashville," John said. "In the hands of evil, the ultimate weapon will destroy all things. In the hands of the righteous, the ultimate weapon would be the light of the world."

"I want to make sure we're all clear," Chappy said, "whatever happens, we can't let whoever these people are get their hands on the weapon."

"No doubt," Rico said, "this is some weird kinda stuff."

The team shared quiet looks across the room in the revelation of Zip's theory. A powerful and driven enemy opposed Arklight. The appearance of the Black Sun on Magnus' jacket, here in Japan, gave everyone an uneasy feeling. Time was running out; the mission had to go on.

"Well, now that everyone is sufficiently freaked out," the chief said, "here's the infiltration plan. Let me be clear: this is an unsanctioned black-ops operation. Compromise equals a Japanese cell, a trial for espionage, and likely the death penalty."

"Okay," Chappy said, "so don't get caught. Copy that."

"Satellite imagery shows a small guard force working at night in the castle," Anne said.

"Only 8 guards on duty tonight. Two in the control room, two at the front gate, and four singles on foot patrol. They tend to congregate around the main buildings. They have radios, duress buttons to the police, and are armed," Zip added.

Chief pointed toward the western courtyard of the castle's grounds.

"Here's your landing zone. You'll jump from 35,000 feet. It's tight, but you've been practicing on smaller. Winds should be calm. No moon tonight, so watch your intervals."

John scanned across the table, tracing the glide path with his finger.

"Tonight, we'll use the new reactive camo parachutes, helmets, and the gear we've been training with. We should be invisible on approach."

"Roger that. What about the roving guards?" Chappy asked.

"Intel reports they rarely leave the shops in and around the main castle," said Anne.

"We'll use the less-lethal TX-9 tranq-guns on the guards. It should keep them out for 8-12 hours, depending on body composition," John said.

Zip looked over the 3D map of the castle.

"High-ground, or you want me with you?"

"Stay with us," John said, "but bring a tactical option."

"Explosives?" Rico asked.

"The tunnel network should be open, but there are two weak spots we identified," the chief said, pointing at two places toward the east end of the complex.

"Rico, bring the usual," John said. "Make sure you build some options, in case we need to breach our way out."

Rico nodded and started thinking about the charges he would construct.

John looked across the center table toward the chief.

"Well, Boomer, what's exfil looking like?"

"I got contingencies upon contingencies. Primary exfil will be by Stealth-hawk helicopter. Rally point will be the main courtyard in front of the castle. Secondary exfil is by spy-rig."

Wisp grimaced. The endless torque on the line, the spinning, and the wind made for a special kind of motion sickness.

"Are you serious? I really hate that idea. All the spinning makes me vomit."

"Take a barf bag," Chappy said, nudging Anne, motioning his head at Wisp. "Looks like we know who's going on line last."

Anne smiled and shook her head. The earlier conversation about the occult had left her mind as she focused on the mission at hand. This was what she had been training for, and her time was now.

"Tertiary exfil, we have a moving van that will be staged into place by a couple CIA operatives. Once you land inside, they'll stage a breakdown outside the North gate."

"Sounds good," John said.

"Of course, if things get crazy, we can just steal a car," Rico said.

"Spear Team, the only way out is to get back here on U.S. soil. As soon as you exfil, both our birds will be spun up, ready to depart the country under fighter-escort to international waters."

"Our mission's clear," John said. "We get in and disable the security contingent quietly. We have to find the painting in the tunnels and get out before anyone knows we were there. We launch at 1230 Zulu. Final checks by 1100."

Everyone stepped back from the table. Chief pulled out a fresh cigar.

"Ty, is the admiral linked in?"

"Yes, Chief."

"Patch him through."

The large monitor on the wall flickered to life. Admiral Nathan Grant was at his desk within the Arklight headquarters. His formal suit and tie ensemble told them all he had somewhere to be.

"John," Nathan said, "I'm getting ready to depart for Nova Scotia. Are things ready to go on your end?"

"Yes, Admiral. I think we're as ready as we can be."

"I wish I could say the same. I'm stopping in DC to pick up the SecDef and General Johnson. I'm told Walter might bless us with his presence."

"I hope you can find some common ground, sir," John said, detecting the source of the admiral's frustration.

"Me too, John. I'm trying to manage my expectations with a glass of bourbon. Hopefully we can get to the bottom of this and put a swift end to whatever the O'Keefe's are up to."

"We'll do our best, Admiral," Chappy said.

Nathan looked down for a moment before staring back at the camera.

"Chief," he said, "send me the video of the briefing. You'll have to get me up to speed on the Black Sun info. Very interesting stuff, Zip."

Zip nodded at the camera.

"I wish it was something a little brighter."

"Whatever the case, we'll get through this, one way or another. Failure isn't an option."

John looked at the faces around the room.

"Is there anything else, sir?"

"I guess not," Nathan said, with the choking stab of concern lumped in his throat. "Good hunting. Stay safe. Insertion approved."

"Roger that, sir," said the chief as the monitor went blank.

Silence fell over the room. John took a moment to look over his team.

"You heard him. Get some rest. Final gear checks at 1100 Zulu. You know what to do."

CHAPTER 4: REICH

"In those days people will seek death but will not find it. They will long to die, but death will flee from them."
Revelation 9:6

2200-Zulu Time 23April1945 (2300-CET Tailfingen, Germany)

A concussive explosion shredded the German tiger tank in the middle of the street. Vehicles burned in the roadways. Rubble littered the landscape. German soldiers continued to walk down the sidewalks with their hands in the air. Nazi Germany's Third Reich was all but finished in their war against the world. Operation Big was already a success, but the Alsos Team had to locate Professor Otto Hahn. The man had sacrificed himself, helping to thwart the Nazi advance.

Richie, Bell, and Ian followed behind the main Allied assault into the city. Their focus was on capturing the university, all the while locating and freeing Otto Hahn. German resistance was sporadic within the city center. Only the hardened SS troops who remained fought the advance. The Alsos Team knew there would be entrenched pockets of resistance both in and around the school. A carefully laid plan was developed to get the Alsos Team into the university; however, it would still require great skill and cunning to sneak behind the enemy lines. As small-arms fire crackled all around, Ian approached the commanding officer of the rifle company they were coordinating with.

"Captain, you ready?" Ian yelled over the gunfire.

"Yeah! I got first platoon distracting them on the left flank! Just watch out for the tanks moving in from the east!"

Machine-gun fire hammered down the street and erratic explosions shook the ground below their feet. Ian turned around, jamming his helmet down low on his head.

"Looks like it's time, gents."

Bell stood up, just high enough to see over the Sherman tank that was providing them cover in the street.

"How far to the sewer entrance?" Bell asked.

"By my estimate," Ian said, "it's around the next corner."

"Try not to get shot this time," Bell said, looking at Richie.

Richie smiled in return. A thunderous explosion from the Sherman's barrel rattled his teeth. Physically, he had fully recovered from their experience in Krakow, Poland, but emotionally he was still on the mend. Kieffer almost ended his life that day. *What doesn't kill us, makes us stronger.*

"It's not like I could help it, Skipper," he said, working to talk over the fresh ringing in his ears.

Bell winked at his friend and peeked around the edge of the tank.

"Let's get moving."

The three Alsos Team members flanked to the right of the main assault. The plan was to enter the sewer system and use it to gain access behind the enemy lines, around the university. Richie carried a backpack full of explosives, to distract the Nazis if needed. Bell clung to the hope that they could locate Otto Hahn and his team. Ian had already arranged for them to be transferred to Farm Hall in England afterwards, where they could continue their research and aid the Manhattan Project.

Ian held his M3 submachine gun, pointing it toward the sky. He stopped at the corner of a blown-apart house, looking ahead. Richie continued running past Ian, finding concealment behind some luggage, abandoned in the street. Bell stopped beside Ian, peering around the building's façade.

"Where's the grate?" Bell asked.

"It should be right here," Ian said, "according to the map."

Bell looked around, anxious to get off the street.

"There it is—under the wagon. Middle of the street."

A rickety, old, horse-drawn wagon sat blocking the grate. How it had survived the military onslaught was anyone's guess.

"Richie. Over here." Bell said.

Richie looked behind him, seeing Ian and Bell lift the grate from the cobblestone pavement. They tucked in, crawling under the wagon. Ian was soon out of sight, dropping into the sewer. Richie ran to them, bumping into Bell, who dropped below. After a few seconds, all three of the Alsos men stood in the smelly, damp sewer, ready to head toward the university's main building. The vibrations from the explosions above kept the entire network resonating with a low, bass-like thud. Dirt, debris, and concrete dust fell from above, signaling every impact.

"Looks like we got ourselves into another tight spot, gents," Ian said.

"No kidding. This place stinks!" Bell said, holding his lapel over his nose.

"Well, Skipper," Richie said, "hopefully it won't take long to get to the other side."

"Let's hope not," Bell replied.

"At any rate, let's get on with it," Ian replied.

✝✝✝✝✝

Gunfire echoed in the distance. Light streaked into the sewer below. Bell stood on the ladder to the small courtyard above, which sat behind the university's main building. It was far enough beyond the German lines to avoid the direct fighting. With the Allied advance at their doorstep, the Alsos Team knew the Nazi SS would throw their full force into the defense. Nothing stirred above them. Bell pushed up on the grate, sliding it across the concrete and into the grass. His head poked up, scanning the courtyard for enemy soldiers.

"All clear," Bell said.

He climbed out of the sewer and took a few deep breaths of fresh air. His head craned over his own shoulder, smelling the soaked in odor on his jacket.

"Nasty," Richie whispered.

Ian was up next, surveying the small courtyard. A pleased look emerged on his face, recognizing where they were.

"Excellent work, old chap, you've put us right where we need to be."

"I'm still good for a few things," Bell smiled.

He reached down into the sewer, grabbing Richie's hand; his wound may have healed, but the effects continued to zap some of his strength. The memory of Richie getting shot in Poland still tortured Bell, but seeing his friend on his feet again gave him hope. Richie was last into the courtyard. The overcast sky provided a shadow-free environment.

"Where to now?" Richie asked as he pointed his M3 toward the main building.

"This way," Ian said. "Otto got word to me that he and his men would be in the lower laboratory."

Richie approached the massive, wooden double-door leading into the building. Another explosion rocked the far corner of the property, and he looked back with concern.

"No worries, Richie," Ian said. "That infantry captain knows the plan."

He shook it off, pulling the door open. Bell covered the entrance, and the trio entered the crumbling structure, still unbeknownst to the Nazi occupation forces. Richie held cover down the hallway in one direction while Bell took the other. Ian stepped between them, pulling out his map of the floorplan.

"Looks like we need to go your way, Bell. Second hallway on the right. Third door downstairs – on the left."

"Gotcha," he said, stepping off toward the objective.

"I got rear guard," Richie said.

Ian spun toward Bell, and the two men aimed their weapons down the hallway. They needed to move fast. The Allies were gaining ground all over the complex. The Nazis would rather kill assets like Otto Hahn than let them fall into the Allies' custody. The small team maneuvered with precision down the hallway, encountering their first set of guards inside the scientific wing.

Without hesitation or communication, Ian and Bell fired a burst into each of the black-uniformed SS soldiers. The men fell into a heap, collapsing upon the once mirror-like floor of the building.

"Come on!" Ian shouted, running toward the room marked on the map.

Bell charged along behind him, knowing the Germans would be in a full state of panic. The gunfire inside the building would bring more Nazis into the fight. Ian made it to the door, hearing commotion inside. Bell arrived behind him, grabbing his shoulder for their well-rehearsed entry plan. Once Richie arrived on the other side of the closed door, Ian nodded, signaling they were ready.

Richie faced the door, thrusting his foot into the knob side. The door struck open with a bang. Ian and Bell leapt through the breach, looking for threats. Controlled bursts of submachine gun fire rattled the space. Richie stepped through third, picking up the center of the room. Time slowed down. Their focus sharpened.

A wide-eyed SS soldier looked at Richie. He held his Luger to the head of Otto Hahn. The distraction of the entry provided a second to work amid the chaos. Richie locked his arms forward, pressing his weapon into position, acquiring his sights, and pulled the trigger, releasing three rounds in quick succession. The SS soldier had no time to react. The well-placed group dropped the man where he stood, and Richie charged forward, placing one more shot into the man's skull.

Hahn sat in his chair with a gory spatter across his face. Shock consumed him. He opened his eyes, seeing Ian's familiar face and watching him fire a deafening burst into another Nazi soldier. Otto remembered Ian and the other two men from Geneva. They made good on their promise to get him out after all. The ringing in his ears deafened him. He stared at Ian, trying to read his lips.

"Otto! Professor? You okay?"

Hahn nodded, dazed by the violence and killing he had witnessed. He looked down at the soldier, who, moments ago, was about to take his life. He looked back to Ian.

"You came for me?"

"I wish you would have come with us back in Geneva," Ian replied. "We could have avoided – all of this quite unpleasant killing."

Hahn stood to his feet, flexing his jaw as he looked around the room. One of his colleagues lay executed on the floor. A terrible memory of the sacrifices made. He shook his head at the sight.

"I'm glad to know my messages reached you. We have so much to discuss. The things I must tell you."

"Let's get you and your people out of here first," Bell interjected.

"He's got a point, Professor."

Richie looked into the hallway, seeing several SS soldiers running for the back of the building, away from the Alsos Team.

"Ian, it might be safer to wait here. The Nazis look like their retreating."

"Jolly good."

Bell took off his backpack and pulled out a SCR-536 Walkie-Talkie, extending the antenna.

"Epsilon-One calling the 132nd Recon, over."

Static crackled and a voice answered.

"132nd to Epsilon. You inside?"

"Affirmative 132nd. We're holding in place. Continue assault, over."

"132nd, copy. Sit tight. We're coming for you. Out."

Ian overheard the good news. Richie continued to watch the hallway, closing the door for a lesser profile. He and Bell pushed a desk in front of the other entry-point, barricading it shut. Ian got the other scientists in order, having them sit on the floor. The room had high windows, and the walls of the building were thick. With adequate protection from small arms fire, loads of fighting outside to occupy the Germans, and the SS in full retreat, Ian turned his attention towards his talk with Hahn.

Hahn found a chair, and Ian sat across from him. The cunning British spy reached into his breast pocket and pulled out the leather-bound Knights Templar journal. Known as the *Sermita in Armis*, or 'Path to the Weapons,' the journal had guided the Alsos mission team throughout Europe. While the official Alsos mission revolved around capturing German scientists and technology, this team focused on Hitler's obsession with Arma Christi, *the Weapons of Christ.*

The Nazi regime had stolen priceless works of art from all over Europe. Thanks to Arklight, the *Ghent Altarpiece's Adam Panel* was well hidden in the desert outside of Bizerte, Tunisia. Bell had shared much of their story with Ian, but still withheld Spear Team's involvement. After Krakow, the Alsos Team held only the Arklight secret from one another. The conspiracy they had stumbled upon was bigger than any country. There was too much at stake, but promises had been made. Hitler had to be stopped, and so the three men made a pact with each other. Their mission would stay true to the Knights Templar journal; they would tell no one of its existence. Even still, each of them continued to skate around the specifics of their Arklight interactions.

†††††

"Kieffer, hurry up," Weber said as he scrambled around the front of the Mercedes.

The young SS Lieutenant carried two overstuffed bags to the trunk and flipped them into the back of the vehicle. Weber jumped into the driver's seat. Two shadowy figures sat behind him. Kieffer jogged to the passenger side of the car and jumped in. The Allies were fast-approaching the eastern edge of the city. The fate of the Reich rested upon a well-orchestrated plan, cunning deception, and sleight of hand.

"Let's go," Kieffer said.

Weber mashed on the accelerator and the long, black Mercedes rumbled away from the villa. His chest swelled with Nazi pride, knowing that he was hand-picked for the most important mission of the war effort. He glanced into the rearview mirror, amazed to be in the presence of his idols. Both men had shaved their heads, even trimming away their mustaches. It was an amazing transformation... but those eyes. The fire still burned in the powerful stare of his Führer.

Heinrich Himmler looked calm; every calculation made months in advance. Weber knew Himmler to be an excellent strategist and planner, but what he had prepared now was pure genius.

"Heir Führer, I have everything in place. Just like you asked," Himmler said, sounding like a child begging the affections of his father.

Hitler sat with his gloved hand covering his face, detesting the fact his Reich had fallen. His overriding desire to save the world, by ridding it of those he believed to be undesirable, was now a fading notion.

"You've been with me from the beginning, Heinrich. I've always loved you the most. You deserved my trust. My attention. The others – they were too concerned about their own power. That is why we failed. Why my vision failed to be."

"But sir, we didn't fail. This is just a new beginning. It's just like Putsch in '23. We just need to regroup. Play the long game."

Weber watched Hitler turn from the window. His expression changed, to that of curiosity. Himmler had struck a nerve. A memory that fueled him throughout the war.

"You've never let me down, Heinrich. Tell me this plan of yours."

Himmler smiled with devilish intent.

"I've called in The Order of the Black Sun, Heir Führer. Your best body-double has been placed inside the bunker, under the Chancellery. Eva wanted me to give you this."

Himmler handed Hitler a folded note with the outline of her lips copied perfectly in red lipstick, pressed on the paper. It was folded around a picture. He unfolded the paper, seeing his long-time mistress and newlywed bride. She wore flowers on her dress and lie in a field just outside the Berghof. He remembered that day well, holding up the note.

'My dear Adolf,

The time has come to say goodbye. Heinrich told me of the plan, and I will do my part for both you and the Reich. Bring peace to this world at war, cleanse the Earth, and start the new world order. I believe in you as I always have.

Love, Eva.'

Colonel Weber couldn't believe the emotion welling in his leader's eyes. He had never seen his Führer cry – much less show weakness.

"Colonel! Look out!"

Weber yanked the wheel back onto the roadway, and Kieffer looked at him with concern.

"Heir Colonel, we need to get them to their destination. Do I need to drive?"

"No, Kieffer, I was just checking behind us."

†††††

Bell waved through the window at friendly forces moving in front of the science building. The rumble of Sherman tanks, the hustle of American soldiers, and the sound of P-51s overhead put his heart at ease. Richie found a chair in the room, grouping with Ian and Professor Hahn.

"Professor, tell me what happened after Geneva," Ian said.

Hahn sat forward in his chair. His handkerchief was spotted with German blood that he had wiped from his own face. The scientist sighed and cleared his head.

"I was transferred back to Berlin, where I continued to work on my nuclear fission research. The Gestapo was still watching me, very closely.

After the July 20th assassination attempt failed to kill Hitler, I was rounded up – with many others. It… it was a terrible ordeal. The Gestapo and the SS slaughtered anyone they thought had a hand in the plot. I remember being blindfolded, beaten, and dragged away."

"That sounds awful," Ian mourned.

"It was a nightmare, which only got worse. The two men you knocked out in Geneva showed up… I tried to hold out, but they threatened my family. They held a gun to my wife's head. I… I had to tell them everything."

"Is that how they found out we were in Krakow?" Bell asked.

"Yes," Hahn said, his stare telling the story. "I can see you all made it out, and for that, I am thankful."

"Richie here took a bullet from that bastard Kieffer, but he's still with us," Bell said.

Hahn looked at Richie with concern.

"I'm very sorry that they broke me."

Richie pressed on the wound spot, feeling that it was still tender.

"It's okay, Professor. If they did that to me, I would have told them anything to keep someone I love alive."

Hahn smiled, wiping his face once again.

"After they finished interrogating me, I was placed under strict guard and ordered to complete my work. My colleagues and I stalled all we could, hoping the Allies would get to us before we finished."

"Finished what exactly?" Ian asked.

"You remember Amaldi's research?" Hahn sighed.

"Yes, of course" Richie said. "He broke the code on the *Adam Panel* of the *Ghent Altarpiece*."

Bell had heard the conversation as it developed and walked closer.

"Tell me this all doesn't go back to Bizerte?" he asked.

Hahn looked back at Bell, who stood between him and Richie.

"I'm afraid so. It also goes back to a splinter group of the Knights Templar – from long ago. Have you ever heard of the Merovingian Teutonic Order?"

"What the hell's that? A drink?" Bell asked.

Hahn smiled.

"The Teutonic Order joined the Knights Templar during the great crusades, hundreds of years ago. But, after the Battle of Grunwald, the Order fell into decline. I had to do some research, but I found something interesting. You see, their doctrine was to bring peace by force. By creating a master race, while eliminating others. Sound familiar?"

"Sounds like the plan of the Third Reich," Ian said.

"During my internment here, I saw many things that frightened the life out of me. One of which was Heinrich Himmler."

"As in... the leader of the SS?" Bell asked.

"Yes. His fascination for the occult developed into something very dangerous. We tried to stop it, but they took it."

"Took what?" Ian asked.

"Using Amaldi's code, what we had learned in Bizerte, and notes given to us by Hans Frank, we developed a pocket atomic bomb."

"A functional atomic bomb? How big is it?" Richie asked.

"Small enough to fit into a car's trunk. Theoretically, with a yield of 5 kilotons."

Bell turned and walked away with his hands on his head.

"Where is it?" Ian asked.

"Himmler took it yesterday. He rejoiced at the design. Said that the Order would rise again."

"Wait a second, Professor," Bell said. "You said Hans Frank brought you some notes? The Butcher himself?"

"Yes. He was accompanied by another fellow. I think his name was Gurlitt... Hildebrand Gurlitt, I believe."

Richie, Bell, and Ian all looked at each other, remembering their missed opportunity to nab Gurlitt in Krakow. They wanted Frank at the time, but they all realized now that Gurlitt was a much larger player than they had understood.

"Tell us about Gurlitt," Ian said, adjusting his position.

"He arrived one day, carrying an artifact of some significance. It was an ornamental chalice of some sort. It was of great importance to Hitler. I overheard Gurlitt mention something about a 'final solution.' He spoke of a weapon of great magnitude—that the artifact was the key. Gurlitt said it was the key to controlling unlimited power."

Richie's blood turned to ice, knowing this was a bad mixture. Nazis, a pocket nuke, and the key to Amaldi's discovery. Gurlitt knew much more than they gave him credit for. The Allies were closing in on the Nazi Reich, but this new information added yet another wrinkle to the story.

††††††

The black Mercedes rumbled southward and into the countryside. Weber smiled, knowing they were almost to the waiting aircraft. All of them would soon board a plane bound for Casa Winter, located on the Canary Islands of Spain. From there, they would take the finest, most advanced U-boat in the Nazi fleet, bound for Argentina. Himmler had prepared the perfect exit strategy, secured a powerful weapon, and had mobilized The Order of the Black Sun. Under his guidance, the Black Sun had grown from their Germanic origins within the Teutonic Order. This most secret society of the Reich accepted only the most dedicated and loyal members of the SS.

"Heir Führer, the Reich will not just survive," Himmler said. "We will take our revenge. We will complete what we set out to do. Eva will sacrifice herself and your body-double in the bunker. I have left strict orders for my SS to poison them both. It will be painless. After your double passes, they will make it look like a suicide."

Anger swelled on Hitler's face. Reduced to such trickery. It felt below him, but his survival in the face of overwhelming defeat took precedence over pride.

"I've taken the same great lengths," Himmler continued. "I have a man who will pose as me. He will draw the Allies away from us, and when the time is right, he, too, will end his life. They will think us both dead."

"Heinrich, your level of planning has never ceased to amaze me. How do you propose we take our revenge?"

Weber glanced into the rearview while Kieffer stared ahead, listening most intently.

"With absolute patience, Heir Führer. We play the longest game, use our resources in secrecy, and infiltrate the governments of our enemies. We disappear and play the spy game. It will take decades, but with the right people in place, inside all governments of the world, we will rise. We will raise the new world order. We will have peace, by destroying our enemies. Your vision of a master race – world dominance – will be my greatest gift to you."

Hitler's gaze narrowed. He took in a deep breath. Weber checked the road, glancing at his idol, who looked at Himmler.

"So begins the Fourth Reich," Hitler declared. "Their God was right about one thing: the door is open for peace. Our preparations will open the path for all to follow. Like our truth-bringer Abaddon told Sir Heinrich so long ago, 'I was the one to come.' Our physical reign may have been short, but the next coming will bring about an everlasting peace, through the technology we will develop."

Himmler smiled. The teachings of The Order of the Black Sun had stuck with his leader. In time, he would exert his vision for peace throughout the world, creating a new world order. A world not bound by religion, but by that of scientific superiority and genetic excellence. His Führer saw the vision. Himmler was prepared to spend the rest of his days making it reality.

The vehicle came to a stop in the grassy field. The twin engines of a civilian plane sputtered to life. Kieffer exited the car and opened the door, extending his arm forward.

"Heil Hitler!"

His leader stopped in front of him. The intensity of his eyes burned a hole in the young SS officer.

"Kieffer is it?"

"Yes, Heir Führer!"

Hitler held his arm up, making the symbolic gesture of Nazism in return.

"This will be the last time I'm ever in the fatherland. No more salutes – no more use of my name. For I will be dead, only to rise again."

Hitler turned to Himmler.

"We must keep a very low profile. We go by our new names from this point forward, yes?"

"Yes, Heir – my leader," Himmler replied.

Kieffer dropped his salute and realized none of them would be back to Germany. The base in Argentina would be their place of exile. It would provide them everything they needed to begin infiltrating every government on Earth. Hitler *was* the Nazi party and Himmler saw that – saving him, he thereby saved the future. Everything else could be rebuilt.

Kieffer looked at his new identity. The craftsmanship of the documents was flawless. Colonel Weber toted the bags and a metal trunk from the car to the flight crew. He watched them load it aboard the plane. Hitler and Himmler climbed the stairs to the passenger section.

"Alfred O'Keefe, from Wales," Weber said, looking over Kieffer's shoulder.

"Did they get the device loaded?" Kieffer asked, still looking at his new identity.

"We are all set."

"So, what identity did they give you?"

Weber pulled out his documents, flipping open the cover.

"Johnson – Joshua Johnson. Apparently, I'm a U.S. citizen already. A businessman. Most excellent."

The two men relished their new identities and would soon enough infiltrate the countries they had been assigned. The plane was loaded with Himmler's most trusted SS officers, who would see Hitler to his new home in South America.

Hitler and Himmler would soon begin their worldwide domination at such a slow pace; no one would realize it until it was too late. Timing was everything, and finding the Knights Templar journal was the key to the Reich's survival.

CHAPTER 5: BREACH

"If one person falls, the other can reach out and help. But someone who falls alone is in real trouble."
Ecclesiastes 4:10

1300-Zulu Time 24May2020 (2200-JST East China Sea)

"Who's freaking bright idea was this?" Zip asked, struggling to stand under the weight of his kit.

"Yeah, thanks," Chappy said, staring at John. "Who else would come up with an insertion this crazy?"

"Stow it you two," John said, adjusting his loadout. "Make sure your bottle pressures are good."

The team stood inside their pressurized travel box, which was inside the cargo hold of the C-17. Everyone wore specially insulated suits over their entire tactical kit. These suits' radar-absorbing material would create near invisibility, similar to their reactive camouflage utilities. The parachutes they would use on tonight's High-Altitude High-Opening (HAHO) jump into Naha, Okinawa were reactive as well. They each had their full combat systems, helmets, plate carriers, weapons, and even a few specialty pieces of equipment to carry. On top of that, a full parachute rig, oxygen bottles, a jump mask, a supplemental power kit, and an additional jump helmet, equipped with the latest multi-dimensional waypoint guidance system.

Rico carried the most weight – 150 pounds to be exact. His stout frame could handle it with relative ease, while Zip's thinner frame struggled under the 135 pounds weighing him down. The drone of the C-17 engines slowed as the aircraft reached its 35,000-foot deployment ceiling.

"Five minutes to insertion. Your glidepath: 22 miles to target. You'll need to deploy at 27,000 feet minimum," said the pilot over the intercom.

"That's not too far," Wisp surmised, plugging the glide path calculations into his wrist-mounted command module.

"Nah. We've made 34 miles from 27,000 before in Roswell," Rico added. "Should be a piece of cake."

"Anne, make sure you drop your HUD this time. Remember, that's the first thing you do after stabilizing your chute," Chappy said, grinning with obvious enjoyment.

She remembered their first training jump a few months ago. It was a harrowing learning experience. Both at night, and from extreme altitude, she deployed her chute just like she had trained to do, but forgot to flip down her thermal enhanced night-vision heads-up display. Without using the guidance system, she couldn't see the other members of the team. The camouflage made them invisible to the naked eye. Had Chappy not been looking for her, she would have run into his canopy. Anne gulped in some air, gave a thumbs up, and nodded her head.

"I'll use my HUD when you learn to start lifting the toilet seat," she replied with a nervous smile on her face.

The entire group enjoyed a brief laugh to her response. John looked around, checking over his team, proud of their journey thus far. He couldn't help what happened on the last mission, but tonight he had taken better measures to protect life—at least where the opportunity presented itself. The events of this night would get them closer to solving the Knights Templar mystery and might even provide some answers into what the O'Keefes' were planning.

John stood at the door, mask in place, ready to enter the cargo bay.

"Spear actual to Command."

"Command, Spear actual; reading five-by-five. How's Spear six holding up?" the chief asked, his voice crackling over the radio.

John saw Anne react. She was embarrassed, but glad to be cared for. She was like a daughter to the chief after all they had been through. She extended her middle finger.

"Command," John radioed, "Spear six is ready and able. We're good to go."

"Command copies. Your first waypoint check-in with be at 25,000 feet. Your glide path vector to target will be at 96 degrees from jump-point."

"Spear actual, copy – out."

Anne shuffled out of the pressure door. She carried over twice her own body weight under the load of equipment. Her legs and back burned, and she was already welcoming the subarctic freefall to come, just to relieve the strain. The rest of the team exited the travel box, making their way to the aft cargo door. A yellow light buzzed in the cargo bay, and the pilot's voice blared over the intercom.

"Two minutes," John said. "Door opening – standby…"

Bone-chilling air rushed into the cargo bay. The ear popping release of pressure would have been bad enough on its own, but the cold was stabbing at their senses, as well. Anne's small slice of exposed neck stung with pain. She reached for the area, only to feel a tug on her collar. Wisp winked through his illuminated glass faceplate as he tucked away the exposed skin. Anne gave him a thumbs up, turning her focus into the rectangular void of frozen gloom to her front.

A buzzer alarmed.

The green light flashed.

Anne didn't have time to react from the middle of the jump group. All the strain on her bones felt the release. Wind punched her body as she passed through the slipstream. She was in flight, falling faster as she approached the opening altitude. The six team members drifted apart as they approached terminal velocity. Anne took slow, deep breaths, keeping her nerves at bay. She watched her altimeter hit 30,000 feet.

John arched his back at the hard deck, flaring his hands. He yanked the deployment strap, and the snap of his parachute flung his feet downward. The visor of his helmet rotated, like a digital compass on a gimble. His descent slowed and he articulated their location for heading. He released his chute handles and flipped down his HUD system, triggering the thermal highlighter.

"Spear actual… deployed at 27,000," he said, looking for a count. "I have 4 – no, 5 chutes in sight. We have good deployment. On glidepath to target."

"Command to Spear actual, copy on descent. Tracking via satellite, looks nominal."

"Spear actual, Command. Guidance engaged, following track. We have a short LZ."

"Command copies."

With the wind at their backs, Spear Team approached Shuri Castle, circling in from above at a steep angle.

"Son of a… Steady! Two guards in the LZ," Zip said.

"Zip, Wisp, execute the contingency takedown," John said, focusing on his alternate plan.

"Roger that," Zip relayed, switching on the auto-guidance for his parachute platform. He reached for his weak-side-holstered tranquilizer pistol, drew it, and transitioned it over to his strong hand. The guidance would keep him on the proper glide path to target, and he was a sniper who never missed a mark.

The TX-9 tranq system integrated a small, yet powerful, hypodermic, electrically charged taser injector that would temporarily paralyze the target; a nanobot-computer system then delivered the exact proper dose of sedative. The state-of-the-art, less-lethal pistol had worked flawlessly in training, where each of the Arklight operators had "volunteered" to be tested by the device, after John had insisted on it.

Wisp flared his chute away from the group, tracking west of Shuri Castle.

"Spear three to Four. I've got the guy to the south on the walkway," Wisp asserted, knowing he had preference.

"Spear actual, everyone else – flare west. Follow Spear three's line to target. Watch your intervals."

A series of clicks emitted from the radio.

"Command to Spear actual. Confirming two heat signatures within the LZ. We register seven more signatures on the property."

"Actual copy," John said, reorganizing his plan on the fly. "Spear actual to Spear two," he said, wanting to communicate his thought to his assistant team leader, "execute ground game with Spear five and six on the south end. I'll take three and four north."

"Spear two, copy," Chappy said while he watched Zip and Wisp commit on their targets. He marveled at their trained precision.

Zip guided in from the south; his target turned and looked straight at him. The USMC sniper saw the stocky Japanese security guard twist his head, trying to make out the strange anomaly in the sky above. A slow, steady squeeze of the trigger at 40 yards and Zip hit his mark. The security guard tried to reach for the dart in his chest, but his body locked into position, charged with 50,000 volts of electricity. He folded to the ground, jerking and twitching from the shock.

Wisp glided in next, calculating the other guard's pace; timing was everything for him as a martial arts expert—he always preferred to get close. The security guard felt a presence, and, hearing the flap of the parachute, he turned to his right. He was met with an invisible force on his chest and flew backwards, slamming onto the hard pavement. Wisp hit the quick release on his parachute and drew his TX-9, firing a tranq injector into the guard. The man's body locked in place for a moment before he fell limp under the effect of the sedative.

"On your right," John said, missing Wisp by a couple of feet.

The soft snap of parachute material echoed inside the stone walls of the courtyard. Spear Team had landed along the western side of the Shuri Castle complex; elsewhere, they had seven more guards to go. The security guard's relief team wouldn't start arriving for several more hours.

"Spear actual, Command. We're on the ground. Start the clock."

"Command copy."

The slightest clink of metal on metal, nylon rubbing against nylon, and a few rips of Velcro could be heard. John looked back, seeing his team stow their jump gear into one large cargo bag. The chief had come up with this old school extraction method, and it had John shaking his head in disbelief. Chappy, Rico, and Anne collected all of the bulky gear, stuffing it into the large bag Chappy had parachuted in with. Wisp and Zip took their positions, looking into the castle grounds, covering the team.

"You good, Chap?"

"Almost," Chappy said as he laid out a three-foot blimp-shaped balloon. "This crazy-ass contraption gonna work?"

"It better, or there'll be no hiding the fact we were here," Anne said.

She zipped all of the gear inside the bag and buckled the safety straps. Chappy pulled out a pressurized helium bottle and twisted the valve, filling a specialized balloon. He nodded his approval as the balloon activated the reactive camouflage material it was made from and transferred the charge down the attached line to the cargo bag. He flipped down his enhanced night-vision goggles, watching as the tethered balloon lifted into the night sky.

"Set."

"Spear actual to Command," John said, "Evac-1 is flying. We are transmitting."

"Command to Actual. We're tracking. Specter is cleared inbound. 15 minutes to extract."

"Copy." John turned to his team and pointed toward the castle grounds. "Let's move out. Secure the courtyard, before Specter arrives."

"Roger that," Chappy said, motioning to Anne and Rico.

The three of them headed to the south wall of the complex, and John checked his wrist-mounted command module. Chappy's team would take the two office guards and the south gate guard. John's team, meanwhile, would handle the two north gate guards and the two other roving guards on the eastern side of the complex. They needed to establish control and maintain stealth; only then could Arklight locate the secret entrance of the castle's below-ground hold.

†††††

Chappy checked his command module.

"Anne, cover left. Rico, take point. Spear two for Actual – we're at the jump-off point."

"You're clear. Execute," John said, checking his module for the overhead view.

Rico heard the order and started checking down the right corner of the building. His Integrated Suppressed Rifle had a newly-fitted TX-9 delivery system mounted under the barrel. The ISR was the newest generation of the .300 Blackout series. A short-barreled rifle with a computer-assisted heads up display gave Arklight a distinct edge in the field. The limited-range system was excellent for Close Quarters Battle, complementing the reactive camouflage systems used by Spear Team.

In the shadows, Rico was invisible to the naked eye, but the bright security lights caused noticeable refraction off his uniform and equipment.

"Stay right to the next corner," Anne said, "We should be good up to the next point."

She looked up, seeing the security camera overlooking the courtyard. It was mounted in front of the security office. She stepped behind Rico, following his exact line through the light-streaked corridor. Chappy checked to the rear of the team, ensuring they were maintaining stealth.

"There it is," Rico said, settling into a darkened recess just outside of the office.

Chappy flipped down his night-vision, scanning the area for threats. One camera had a fix on the door. A floodlight illuminating the area was an easy target. He aimed his ISR, steadying the shot. A single whisper emitted from the muzzle, and the specialized subsonic fragmentation round struck the light's bell housing. The crack of broken safety glass barely made a sound.

The entrance to the security office dimmed.

"Let's move up. Less-lethal. I'll get the door. You two take out the guards," Chappy said, wanting to see Anne get her first operational shot off as a member of Spear Team.

†††††

"One guard, 2 o'clock in the courtyard. He's lit up like Christmas," Zip said, adjusting his position against the craggy stone wall.

John looked over Zip's shoulder.

"That's one of the roving guards. Spear actual to Command, any visual on rover two?"

"Command to Spear actual. We have rover two on the move to the east. He's behind the main castle. Out of range at present."

"Actual copy."

John looked back over his shoulder. Wisp's white-hot silhouette lit up his goggles.

"Let's move to the North gate. Hold on this guy until we give the go ahead."

Zip nodded and John peeled away to his left. The North gate was the one entrance left open during the night. Through intelligence and surveillance, Arklight had been able to determine that no deliveries were scheduled tonight; they planned to close the gate after neutralizing the guards. John walked behind Wisp, who stopped just before rounding another corner. Bright flood lights shone down around the stone wall. Wisp saw the angle contrast along the ground.

He peered around the corner, trying to catch a glimpse of the North guard shack. Both guards sat inside, oblivious to their surroundings. The men were playing cards and conversing over a steamy, hot drink. He smiled to himself, overhearing the men speaking Japanese; they were lamenting about how slow the night was going.

John tapped Wisp, who withdrew.

"What's it looking like?"

"Both guards are sitting in the shack – playing cards. They're as complacent, as we expected. We should be able to take them quickly, Steady."

John looked over his command module, seeing all of his assets in place. They had to get this right – if only to avoid all of the angst they experienced last time.

"Spear actual, Spear two. You set?"

Static crackled over the radio with two clicks, signaling they were ready.

"Spear actual to Spear four, set?"

Two more clicks were heard. They had 5 guards in their sights and the other two were isolated on the other side of the complex. Eight minutes left before the extraction bird flew over.

"Spear actual to all: execute, execute, execute."

†††††

Rico and Anne closed on the knob-side of the security office door. Anne stepped around Rico, taking point on the entry. Her smaller size had proven advantageous in training; in most instances, she could stand in front of anyone on their team, and they all could still see over her, which sharpened their tactics and sped things up when it came to close quarters battle.

Chappy observed that the security door opened inwards, and he placed his hand on the knob. He looked toward Anne, waiting for her to nod she was ready. He could see she was over-thinking the problem.

"Anne, you've done this a thousand times. Just take your sector. Trust your training."

She took in a deep breath and cleared her mind. She nodded, Chappy turned the knob, and the large steel door was pushed open. Neither guard reacted. They didn't hear the door at all. Anne stepped through, feeling Rico was behind her. The two operators used their stealth of movement, working down the wall of the office toward the two guards, who remained unaware of their presence. Chappy came in the office last, his attention on the guards sitting at the security desk.

One problem they didn't foresee was the industrial glass between them and the guards. The TX-9 rounds needed an unobstructed path to their intended targets. Rico and Anne had taken a knee and were sliding on the ground toward the men. The guards sat back in their chairs, watching the monitors. The distraction of a television show they watched had their full attention. Chappy couldn't help but notice it was a show he, too, enjoyed.

"At least they're into zombies," he muttered. He settled in along the entryway, knowing this part of the operation was about to get unconventional.

"I've got cover on them," he said over the radio.

Anne struggled to manipulate her ISR while pulling out her TX-9 pistol. The rifle-mounted version was too much for her small frame to shoulder effectively. She clicked her mic twice, sliding her way ever closer to the guard. Once in position, she came up on a knee, taking aim on one of the unsuspecting men. Rico closed in until the metal of his rifle struck the hard-concrete floor with an unmistakable *click*.

Anne watched her target turn toward the sound. A choking tension came over her when the man stared at Rico. Knowing he was about to alert his partner, she fired the TX-9, striking him in the neck. He fell to the floor, paralyzed by the electric charge. The other guard jumped up, ready to help his co-worker. Anne took aim, firing another TX-9 round, striking him in the chest.

Chappy watched the first guard go down, and saw Rico pull himself to his feet. Anne fired on the second guard, but something wasn't right. The man was still standing.

"Anne, get on that guy!"

She scrambled to her feet, just as the guard turned in her direction. The guard's eyes grew wide at what appeared to be an aberration closing in to take his soul. Rico stepped forward, but Anne was already on the guard, drawing him away from the security desk. The sedative was working in his system, but he could still sound the alarm. She placed the man into a lateral vascular neck restraint, choking the oxygen from his already foggy brain. Rico placed his gloved hand over the man's mouth, securing his arms while Anne clamped down. The guard fell limp, and Anne dropped him to the floor as gently as she could. Rico assisted her, taking most of the weight.

By the time Chappy arrived in the security room, both guards were out, despite the near compromise.

"What the hell was that all about?" Chappy asked.

"My bad," Rico said, deactivating his camouflage. "Anne, good pick up."

"No problem."

"Whatever the case, that was close," Chappy said, still reluctant to complement her actions.

"Rico, you take that bank of cameras. I'll take this one," Anne said, pulling off her rucksack.

Chappy moved back to the door in case someone showed up while the other two placed the security system into a loop. Rico wired a small USB transmitter into the security computer.

"Spear five to Command, we have their system in loop. You should have access."

"Command copies, we're in and... we have control."

††††

John listened to the traffic, knowing they were clear to move.

"Zip, take out rover one."

A few seconds ticked by. John thought he heard the faintest noise in the distance.

"Spear four to actual. Rover one down."

John clicked his mic twice as Wisp moved into the light of the guard shack to the north. They advanced in tandem around the harsh, bright lighting of the area. The two guards never changed their demeanor and instead continued to look at their card hands. Once across, John decided to employ technology instead of risking compromise. The guards had too much light around them. There was no good way to enter the shack without taking a chance that they would alert the other guards, or worse yet, trip the silent alarm.

"Wisp, deploy a couple of our little friends."

"Roger that?"

"Times running short. Specter's close."

"Yeah, I know," Wisp said, as he pulled two bug-sized drones from a case.

John raised his forearm, moving his command console into a flattened position. He pushed the command access screen, choosing TX-9 drone deployment. He geo-synced the guard's positions, assigned a drone to each man, and placed the tiny, flying robots into two program zones displayed on his wrist monitor. The single-use drones utilized advanced AI to attack their targets. The TX-9 versions delivered the same paralyzing system as the pistols. You didn't need to aim, but you still needed to be precise.

John saw both drones prompted on his screen, ready to be activated. He nodded at Wisp, who held them out in his gloved hand. John hit execute. Both drones were gone in a flash, disappearing from sight.

A *thud* resonated against the wall of the guard shack.

"Ahhh…"

Another *crash* vibrated against another wall. Wisp fought to keep the visual he had in his head at bay. The thought of two grown men being attacked by miniscule bugs, rendering them both unconscious, somehow seemed funny in the moment.

"Let's go check it," John said, elbowing him.

They closed on the entrance to the shack. The door was already open. Both men lay unconscious on the floor.

"Get the gate," John said. "I'll collect the drones."

Wisp stood up, stretched his back, and walked across the pavement to the large barred security gate. The gate covered the entire entrance and would deter anyone from entering the castle.

John entered the guard shack and collected the small one-inch drones from the neck of each man. He placed them into his dump pouch, then moved the guards into a position where they wouldn't be seen. He turned off the lights and closed the door to the guard shack. Wisp closed and locked the gate.

"Spear actual to Command. North gate secure. Moving on rover two."

"Command, copy. Rover two is on the move toward you. Three minutes until Specter's on station."

"Actual, copy. Chap, you moving on the South guard?"

John heard two clicks as he fell in behind Wisp. They had to move toward the east, in order to intercept the other roving guard. Zip appeared, moving to their right, falling into a loose wedge formation across the grounds.

†††††

"Dammit, she's on the phone." Chappy said, seeing the South gate's guard sitting in a small shack. She was very animated, talking at near warp speed on her cell phone.

"Spear two, Command. We've got a chatty-Kathy here. Can you give us a hand?"

"Command, Spear two, standby."

Anne closed on the female guard while Rico took another angle to cover. Chappy watched her pull the phone away from her ear and throw it on the small table inside.

"Looks like she got hung up on," Anne said.

"I got her," Rico said. "She's stepping out of the shack."

He leveled off his TX-9 and fired a dart into the young woman. She fell to the ground, like a tree chopped at its base. Anne closed in, meeting Rico where she fell. They grabbed her, dragging her into the guard shack. The gate was already shut. They turned out the lights in the small building.

"Spear two, Actual. We are all clear. You've got two minutes to locate rover two."

"Copy that. We're looking."

†††††

John's thighs burned under the stress as they glided in a fast walk, trying to maintain stealth. There was no sign of rover two. His command module said the guy was right around the corner. The courtyard on the east side of the castle was a maze of short walls and plant life. Some segments were still under construction, littering the ground with debris.

"Command to Spear actual. 30 seconds until extract."

John felt the first bit of perspiration run into his right eye.

"Where is this guy?" he asked.

Zip and Wisp scanned the area, but they could see nothing.

Suddenly, the guard rounded the corner, running into John's chest.

"15 seconds to extract."

John grabbed the smaller man with one arm around the neck and his gloved hand over the man's mouth. Wisp closed in, helping to secure the man. Zip took aim with his TX-9.

"Crap, he's biting me."

The Japanese guard bit into John's glove, catching skin while mule-kicking him in the shin. A nasty headbutt caught John in the mouth, and the smaller man spun out of his grasp. Wisp grabbed the stocky man, but he twisted his arm out of the hold. The guard bladed himself, his arms centered, he was ready to fight. As much as Zip wanted to see Wisp and John tangle with the guy, he squeezed the trigger on the TX-9, dropping the man where he stood.

"Spear four to Command. Rover two is down."

"Command copy."

The transmission came through as the roar of a C-130 approached the castle. The large cargo plane had a mounted V on the front and centered itself on the balloon's line from the ground. Known to most as the Fulton surface-to-air recovery system, or STARS, it had not been used since 1996. Chief had Special Operations Command pull it out of mothballs to solve a problem. Arklight needed to extract all of the used gear in order to maintain deniability. John turned in time to see the aircraft thunder overhead, grabbing the balloon line and snatching the large bag off the ground. The plane would circle back to Kadena.

"Spear actual to Command. Looks like a successful extraction. We're moving on the objective. Castle secure."

"Command to Actual, we have no threats on satellite or ISR. Nothing moving in the compound except friendlies. Command out."

"Actual copy," John said, kneading his bitten hand. "Chappy, meet us at the main castle entrance."

"Roger that."

†††††

Magnus sat back and lit a cigarette. The glow of the computer monitor highlighted his athletic frame. One of Magnus' hired guns sat at the keyboard following the blurs as they streaked across the screens, distorting the focus. Smoke wafted in the air. Ronnie walked in, noticing the strange apparitions on camera.

"These guys are good," Ronnie said. "You can hardly see them."

"I bet someone is watching over them as well," Magnus replied.

"A tasked satellite?" Ronnie asked.

"Two of the bloody things, most likely."

Ronnie looked toward Magnus, who pulled the cigarette from his lips, exhaling smoke.

"That was pure genius to get in there and hijack the cameras last night," Ronnie said. "What's the play?"

"You let me worry about that. You just take care of business on your side of the house."

"I can do that. Is the extraction plan still solid?"

"It's all set. Just don't leave anyone alive," Magnus said, his eyes narrowing.

"Roger that."

"Is our guest awake yet?" Magnus asked.

"She is, and she's behaving."

"Good, I'll have a word with her."

Ronnie nodded, turned, and walked toward the cage. Ayana sat back against the bars; fearful she wouldn't see another day. He leered though the cage door, pulling the key to the lock out of his pocket.

"Ayana, I know you're scared," Magnus said, his demeanor light. "We aren't going to hurt you. I simply need some information."

"You should let me go. Then, I'll tell you whatever you want."

"It ain't that simple, lady," Ronnie said, opening the cage. "Come on. Time's short."

She knew she could walk out or they would drag her out. She looked at Ronnie's hand like it was diseased. He grabbed her by the back of the neck and guided her forward, toward Magnus.

The Welshman exhaled in delight. He could smell her fear as Ronnie pushed her ever closer.

"Ayana Matsui," Magnus said, "the youngest curator ever hired at Shurijo Castle. They say that the castle holds many secrets. More than any other castle in Japan."

"Who are you and how do you know me?"

"Who I am is unimportant," Magnus said, his face closing in on hers. "Let's just say that I need your help. If I don't get it," he brandished his knife, "more extreme measures will be taken."

Chills ran down the young woman's back. Ronnie's grip across the nape of her neck tightened. She sensed a wicked nature in Magnus, believing he would follow through on the threat. There was only one choice. Ayana fought back the tears, finding the words.

"What do you want?"

CHAPTER 6: ENTRENCHED

"The wicked plot against the godly; they snarl at them in defiance."
Psalms 37:12

1400-Zulu Time 24May2020 (2300-JST Shuri Castle, Okinawa)

John entered into the castle's main hall door. Brilliant reds, golds, and blues patterned the walls. Zip took in the sights, entering second and clearing to the right of the grandiose chamber. A few more steps found the duo walking across the main throne room. Shadowed under indirect LED lighting, the craftsmanship was awesome to behold. Hand-carved, ornamental woodwork stood all around. Dragons and fire graced the walls in patterned gold-flecking. Wisp and Rico entered the room moments later, taking up the center positions between John and Zip.

"Whoa. This place is impressive," Rico said.

"This is the Throne of Seiden," Zip said, taking in the symbolism. "See the calligraphy hanging above the throne? It's from the Chûzan Empire – dating back to the 14th century. Very cool."

"This land has been ruled by Chûzan for generation after generation," Wisp said, reading the symbols aloud, translating for the team.

Chappy stepped into the room, followed by Anne. The space was easy to secure, with diminished light streaking against the outer walls.

"Spear actual, Command. We're at the rally point. What's the perimeter looking like?"

"Looking good, Actual," the chief's voice grumbled over the radio. "Poseidon is monitoring from international waters. Satellite is clear."

"Copy that, Chief. We'll be going dark soon."

"Understood, Actual. Godspeed. We'll see you on the other side."

"Roger that. Spear Team, spread out. Take a look around."

John scanned the room, knowing the journey would be littered with perils. With Magnus in country, there were some real concerns this time around. He closed his eyes, and information flashed through his mind. As if on a movie screen, masses of information played out behind his eyelids, visualized in his brain. Of all they had learned, there was no way to know what information would be relevant this time around.

"No innocence in war," John uttered.

"You say something, Steady?" Chappy asked, scanning the darkened surroundings to ensure he and John had split far enough from the rest of the team.

"Nothing," John said, "It's just something that keeps popping in my head."

"What's that?"

"'No innocence in war.' I keep having to remind myself this is a just war, and there's no morality in it—that part's up to God. *We* understand what this is about. Not sure about everyone else."

"Look bro, I think they know what's at stake. They'll come around. It's just a matter of time. Besides, Anne hasn't seen it for herself, yet."

John gazed across the room, watching the others inspect all the ancient artifacts. Anne's face had a kind expression when she was at ease, which wasn't often. It was easy to see the intensity smoldering within her.

"Chap – we're lucky to have her. She'll come around."

"Either way, I know you'll do what's right, in the right time."

John smiled at his long-time friend and teammate. He twisted his wrist to view the command module.

"Okay, Rico, you got the water charge?" John asked.

"In my pack. Where do you need it placed?"

"According to the schematics, and bear with me – the 1992 reconstruction seems to have covered the lower bunker from the shelling in 1945; that was after the initial reconstruction in 1947, so, according to our best estimates, and using the information in the Knights Templar journal—there," John said pointing. "That should be a hidden entrance from this room into the tunnels."

Rico pulled up the drawings, scanning the room for structural supports. He looked up, counting the trusses supporting the ceiling.

"Steady? I know they rebuilt this place, but if you look at the ceiling, you'll see the supports are different on that side of the room."

"Okay, yeah – I see it," John said.

"Okay, see where they extended the support on the east wall?"

"Yes."

"There's a slight downward slope to the floor, below that section."

Rico walked over to the that area of the room. Zip, Wisp, and Chappy shined their lights up on the ceiling. They couldn't make anything out of what Rico described. Of course, Rico was the engineer.

"So, what the hell are you talking about, Rico?" Chappy asked.

Anne's brow furrowed. Even though she wasn't an engineer, she understood load dynamics.

"This is a symmetrical room," she said. "The west wall has a different support structure than the east wall. The extended trusses and the floor pattern on the east suggest a door may have once existed there, confirming the info in the journal."

"Thanks, Anne," Rico acknowledged. "Chappy's a little dense sometimes."

"Forgive me for asking, jack-wagon," Chappy said, throwing his arms up in the air.

"Look man, I don't question your computer genius, so just shut up and let me do what I do," Rico said, lowering himself to the floor in front of the east wall. He felt the sloped ground.

Zip elbowed Wisp.

"He's doing that thing now," he said, watching Rico work.

"What's that mean?" Wisp asked.

"Just wait for it," Zip smirked. "He's in the zone."

John watched over Anne's shoulder as she crunched some calculations. He wasn't sure what she was doing, but surmised it to be an equation of sorts. She raised her head, forcing John to reel in his curiosity.

"Rico," she said, "check for a buckle, or maybe a seam, on the floor – two feet to your left."

John watched Rico slide to his left. He blew dust about, clearing the seams, feeling along with his fingers.

"Damn. You're good, Anne. I think I got it. Yeah – it's running along the wall. There's a faint breeze."

"What're you talking about?" Chappy asked.

"Come here, I'll show you."

Chappy dropped to a knee and lowered himself to Rico's position. Frozen in place, Rico had a giant smile on his face.

"Show me what, dude?" Chappy asked.

Rico pushed himself away from the crack, motioning for Chappy to get where he was.

"Put you face where mine was, Chap. You'll feel it."

Chappy moved over and saw a small crack in the concrete floor. Then it hit him: a constant rush of air cooled the sweat on his face. He came up to his knees.

"So, what's a drafty old castle floor got to do with anything?"

Anne walked over to the spot, pointing to the ground.

"That draft is from the hidden World War II tunnel system, located under the castle. This spot on the floor is the main staircase access that was covered up after the war. When they reconstructed the castle in 1992, they cemented over the stone, using it to cover the stairs."

Rico stood up in agreement. John thought it a good time to share some history.

"During World War II, the 32nd Japanese Army operated out of Shuri Castle. The Allies knew this and shelled this place for three days during the Battle of Okinawa. However, what they didn't know was that the Japanese had dug tunnels below the castle. They held out during the shelling, forcing the 1st Marine Division into a fight. Ultimately, it didn't work out for the Japanese, and eventually, they were forced to retreat. Heck, a few hours from now will mark the 72nd anniversary of when the *USS Mississippi* began the bombardment, as a matter of fact."

"That's neat and all, John, but the mission's to recover the painting. I'm assuming it's hidden somewhere down there, so what's the plan?"

John's intimate knowledge of history didn't thrill Chappy, but at least he got the gist of things.

"Rico, can you rig a charge for the floor without blowing this place apart?"

Anne walked to Rico and they both took a long look at her command module.

"That should do it," he said. "Yes; based on Anne's calculations, we can cut through with a shaped water charge. It's going to take us a few minutes, but other than a little overspray, we should be able to get through without damaging the rest of the room."

"Okay, do it then," John said.

†††††

"They're inside," Magnus sneered. "Time to go."

"Me and my crew are ready to move out," Ronnie said. "You're a smart bastard, Magnus. Everything is going just like you said it would."

"Don't cock it up, Ronnie. We'll have several phases to get through before we're home-free. You'll be sitting on the beach drinking Mai Tai's before you know it."

"Understood, boss."

Magnus looked in the back of the van where Ayana sat bound and gagged. Her eyes were tearing up. Her fear showed, and her uncertainty was evident. Two of Magnus' men sat on either side of her, their bulk crowding her space.

"Take the gag out," Magnus said.

She turned her head away as one of the men slipped the gag down under her chin and snatched the rag out of her mouth.

"Ayana, look at me," Magnus insisted, grabbing her chin and focusing on her face. She pulled away once again. He unfolded his knife, placing the cold, steel blade flat against her face and using it to turn her head his direction.

Ronnie felt a lump invade his throat, chafing his neck. He saw her as an innocent – caught up in something she had nothing to do with. She wasn't a threat.

"That's more like it," Magnus said, his blade under her chin. "Now, I know you've been asking yourself, why did I take you? Simple really – you're going to be our guide into Shuri Castle."

"Get a ticket," Ayana said, turning her head away. "It's open to the public. Now let me go."

"That's not the type of tour we need. There are secret entrances into the castle from town. I want you to show me those."

"You give me a map, I'll point them out. Then will you let me go?"

Ronnie could tell she was scared and recognized an opportunity to get what Magnus wanted, without continuing to bargain her own life.

"It's almost that simple," he volunteered, "but we're taking you with us to verify. Plus, we can't let you go – until we leave. That's only a few more hours at this point."

Ayana heard the reasonable sound of Ronnie's voice. She felt that he intended to keep his word, but the other man, the Welshman, scared her. His stare was cold, like a snake staring down prey before a kill.

"Okay. If that's all I need to do, I'll show you. You promise to let me go?"

"Like I told you before," Ronnie said, "no one will get hurt. We just need to get into the castle tonight. There are some bad people that have broken in. They're looking to steal an artifact."

Ayana sat back in shock. Her concern shifted.

"What people?"

Ronnie pulled his cellphone out of his pocket and tapped into the live feed. He flipped the device over and showed Ayana. She saw for herself.

"Why not just tell the authorities? Why not alert us at the castle? We could have done something to prevent this."

"It's not that simple. Your entire security team has been neutralized – most likely killed. This group would overwhelm anything you could throw at them. That's where we come in. We can stop them."

"Why kidnap me? What are they trying to take?"

"Let's just say this group operates above anything you could imagine. We had to do it this way, because they're tapped into every bit of technology there is. If they knew we were here, they could destroy us. This is why we had to take you like we did. We need to sneak into the castle to stop them."

"What are they taking? You could have told me this earlier."

Magnus saw that Ronnie seemed to have a positive effect on Ayana; she believed him. He knew if Ronnie was successful, things would get easier. Ronnie looked over to Magnus, who nodded his approval to share.

"During World War II, a famous painting was sold to the Japanese Empire called *Portrait of a Young Man*," he said. "Emperor Hirohito was here with that painting at one point. We believe that painting is still hidden beneath Shuri Castle in the tunnels."

Ayana's fear slipped away, and curiosity emerged on her face.

"I've heard the stories… however, we have searched every square inch of those tunnels. There's nothing down there."

Ronnie continued to build his rapport. He pulled out a tablet containing the digital copy of the Knights Templar journal.

"I'm sure you've checked, but have you checked the old tunnels?"

"What old tunnels?"

"These," he said, showing her the modern map of the current tunnel system she knew about and then using the digital Templar map to overlay the image, exposing hidden tunnels and compartments. Ayana leaned forward, no longer shaken, but interested.

"I've never seen this before. That explains some of the markers we detailed back when I was an intern."

"What markers?" Magnus asked, careful to manage his overbearing tone. He wanted to encourage her to share what she knew.

"There are several stones inserted into the rock of the tunnels. They've never really made sense to me, but if this map is correct, they're positioned adjacent to the secret passages."

"That's where we need to go," Ronnie said, cutting his eyes toward Magnus, "because this group we're after knows this information as well."

"We have never been able to excavate this area because of historical protections in place. This would be a huge discovery."

"We just want to protect it. We need to get in there, undetected, stop these thieves, and protect history."

"Untie me. I'll help you. I won't try to run away. This is too important."

Ronnie looked back at Magnus and nodded to one of the men sitting beside Ayana. They pulled her forward and cut the bonds off of her wrists and ankles.

"See? Things aren't as they appear, Ayana," Ronnie said. "Look at my phone again."

She sat forward, seeing her entire security team down. They had fallen victim to a precision attack at the castle. She saw blurs on the screen.

"What happened?"

"These are the people we're telling you about. They just entered the castle an hour ago and killed your entire security detail," he said, pointing to the screen. "Here's where they entered the main building."

She watched, now sure of Ronnie's story. Everything he told her made sense.

"Ayana, is there an entrance we can use to enter the castle tunnels from Naha?" Magnus asked.

"Yes; I'll take you there. But there's no way into the castle grounds from the tunnels."

"You let us worry about that," Magnus said, pleased with Ronnie's efforts to flip the situation. He confirmed the feeling with a firm grab of Ronnie's shoulder.

"Time for you to head towards your target, mate."

"Will do. We'll get in position and wait for your go."

"I'm expecting a call from our source. Once he lets us know the infrastructure is crippled, you can take out the command element."

"It's a lot of moving parts, but you've been spot on so far, so... see you at the rendezvous."

Ronnie exited the van and turned around.

"Mag, Can I have a quick word?"

Magnus stepped out of the vehicle as his team prepared to depart for the castle.

"What is it?"

"If she helps us, I mean... will you really let her go when this is over?"

"Sure, I'll set her free on the way to the rally point. She bought your story well enough."

"Okay. Good luck. Just think, you'll have what you need soon, and I'll be on that beach inside of two days."

"Like I said, Ronnie – stick to the plan."

"I got you."

The warehouse stirred with activity as both groups loaded into their vehicles. Two vans headed toward Shuri castle and two others headed toward Kadena Air Force Base. Magnus maintained a firm grasp on the operational particulars, and with Ayana, he would get his stealthy entrance into the castle. He needed to wait on Arklight to bring him his prize.

Ronnie knew his part of the operation was going to be risky. Attacking an active military base, evading security and the Japanese Police, *and* making a getaway seemed like a long-shot. The margin for error was non-existent, but he felt confident in the plan. They wouldn't know what hit them, and they wouldn't have time to discover who hit them. At least not before they were far out of the country. Magnus had unlimited resources at work, and money was no object. Ronnie laid back in his seat, knowing the payday would set him up for the rest of his life.

†††††

John rolled his jaw around. The concussion from the blast wasn't as bad as he thought it would be, and the water all but vaporized into thin air.

"Hell yeah! Homerun," Rico said, still trying to equalize the pressure in his ears.

"Did we set off any alarms?" John asked.

"Negative," Zip said, "it registered on two of my sensors. I think we're good."

Rico and Wisp pushed a fractured stone down the breach point. A broken set of stairs was noticed under the debris.

"We got a good entry point," Chappy said as he entered the stairway.

It descended downward to a deeper point, some 30 feet underground. Chappy came to a wall, and more stairs continued into the murk below.

"Kill the white light," John said. "Let's go under NVGs and save our batteries."

He flipped down his night-vision goggles and followed the next stairwell down another 20 feet, arriving on a rolling rock floor. The space was narrow, the air damp and cool. It was fresh air at least, which also meant there had to be an exit, or at least ventilation, somewhere ahead. Chappy felt the slightest breeze cross his face as he proceeded deeper into the craggy tunnel.

John followed along, glancing at the map on his wrist-mounted command module.

"Chappy," he said, "there should be a marker ahead on the right."

Anne saw several markings along the walls of the tunnel. Japanese writing seemed to be everywhere in the space. She touched a few symbols as she passed. Wisp saw her reach out for some of the more ornamental calligraphy.

"Those are from World War II," he said, reading a few along the way. "Final notes to their families."

Rico guarded the rear of their single-file stack.

"I've watched a couple of documentaries about the Battle of Okinawa," he said, "It was some of the bloodiest fighting in the entire war."

"No doubt," Zip added, "My grandfather fought here. Like right here on Oki. He was a wind-talker with the First Marine Division."

"You may have mentioned it, oh, a few hundred times," Anne smirked.

"He was a real hero. Being here, even today, is kinda surreal."

"Your granddad was a real-deal Navajo code-talker? Did he ever mention this place?" Wisp asked.

"No," Zip said. "He never talked about the war. None of them— him or the other elders—really ever discussed it. He said it was too painful."

"Yeah, my grandfather never talked about it either. Or at least that's what I was told," Wisp said.

"I didn't know he was in the war. You've never mentioned it," John commented.

"Yeah, he was ashamed. At least according to my grandmother. She said he was supposed to fight to the death, or commit seppuku. He chose to live with his shame, but died before I was born."

"Damn," Rico said. "That's pretty heavy."

"I've never really thought about it much," Wisp said. "But coming here, to this place, it just entered my mind."

"I totally get it, brother," Zip said.

Chappy found a discolored stone inset into the rock of the tunnel.

"John, what do you make of this?"

"That's got to be it," he said, looking at his map.

"Spear actual to Command," John radioed, "we're at the first marker."

Static emitted over the radio system.

"Looks like we're dark," Chappy said. "Rico, come take a look at this."

Rico worked his way around his teammates, arriving to the front. He looked over the smooth rock surface, finding a spot of interest to the left of the marker. He reached into his load-bearing vest and pulled out what looked like a scope. The wide end had several buttons affixed along the aperture and an eyepiece. He switched it on, flipped up his NODs, and placed the device up to his right eye.

"What's that?" John asked, focusing his night-vision to get a closer look.

"It's experimental tech from our friends over at DARPA. A trans-matter particle x-ray device – at least that's what I would describe it as. They call it T-PAX."

"That's only a theory," Anne said.

"Not anymore," Rico said with a smile on his face. "This section of rock was engineered to fit in the space here… it's really an ingenious design. Take a look." He handed the device over to John.

John grabbed the small, scope-like device and pulled it up to his eye. He saw a grainy image of spectrum blues and grays. A white image highlighted what he needed to see; a line was traced around the entire rock, and a hidden void existed behind it. He looked up to the ceiling of the tunnel. The white line continued to a light gray piece of rock.

"You've got to be kidding me. Amazing. You can actually see the mechanical wheels behind the rock. Chappy, hand me your extendable baton."

Chappy reached behind his holstered pistol and pulled out the baton, handing it over. A swing of John's arm opened the weapon, and he used it to push on a stone trigger in the ceiling. To the naked eye, it looked like any other part of the tunnel. The T-PAX showed everything behind the solid surfaces. John pushed the rock upward, and a clang released the rock wall at the marker. The entire piece opened, swinging inward.

"That's pretty cool," Zip said.

John handed the device back to Rico.

"That's some awesome tech right there," John said.

"Only the best for Spear Team, Steady."

†††††

"Stop the van," Ayana insisted.

"You heard her. Stop here," Magnus said.

"Okay, this is the main tunnel entrance location. It's in the basement of that house. The park owns the property, but we haven't used it in some time. This is where we enter the tunnels for our research projects, since all access has been cut off from the castle."

"Are there any guards posted?"

"No, but it has an alarm. The guard station monitors it from inside the castle. My keycard will override the alarm and will get us inside."

"Excellent," Magnus said, knowing the cameras had been dealt with.

"I can let you in and go contact the authorities," Ayana said, trying to find a way out of her current predicament.

"No. You're coming with us. The authorities could be compromised, as far as we know. You saw it in the video," Magnus said, almost fooling himself, "they killed your entire security team. These are some really bad people."

Ayana thought about what she had seen and what she knew. It was all plausible, at the very least. She didn't like Magnus, but he did have a point.

"Okay. Let's go, then. I'll need my keycard and my keys. Once I unlock the door, I'll have to disable the alarm."

"Shall we?" Magnus asked, sliding the van door open to exit.

He and Ayana walked to the front door. She inserted her key and pushed the heavy door open, and they stepped inside. Magnus watched her insert her keycard into a slot and enter a six-digit code. The light on the pad turned green and he scanned the interior of the home. Nothing about it appeared remarkable.

"The rest of you are clear to enter," he radioed.

Several armed men entered the front door. They all scanned the area with trained intensity, making certain no one was present.

"Where's the entrance?" Magnus asked.

"Downstairs," Ayana said, "Follow me."

She walked across the living room, cutting between a couple of the eight mercenaries who were here under Magnus' charge. She grabbed the knob on a door that led them all downstairs into the basement. Magnus followed her down, seeing that the house had been built over the entrance to a rather large cave. The mouth was over 12 feet high and 15 feet wide.

"How'd this get here?"

"The Japanese soldiers who occupied Shuri Castle during World War II dug several tunnels," Ayana said, "for everything from resupply to escape. There was an ancient tunnel system already in place from the original construction, back in the 14th century. We believe it was simply enlarged during the war. This particular entrance—or exit, I should say—is how the 32nd Japanese Army escaped under the bombardment of the U.S. Navy in 1945. At least that's the popular theory."

Magnus smiled, knowing that this access would give him an advantage and an invaluable drop on the soldiers already inside. Their satellites wouldn't detect any movement around the castle because their approach was from underground. He possessed a digital copy of the map system to aid their crafty entrance, and they had the curator, who seemed to be convinced of their story.

"Go ahead to the first turn," Magnus said. "I'll be there in a minute."

The mercenaries pulled down their night-vision goggles and proceeded into the tunnel. Magnus smiled at Ayana.

"You've done a great job, Ayana. I appreciate it."

Ayana's dark, cropped hair fell across her face as she looked down to hide her disbelief of his admission. She worked to regain her composure, looking up and smiling uneasily.

"You're free to go. Just don't say anything about this, to anyone."

"I won't say a thing. I promise."

She nodded and looked Magnus in the eye once more before turning to walk away. The stairs were close and she exhaled, allowing the tension to leave her chest.

A piercing pain stabbed at her back, taking her breath away. A hand grabbed her around the neck. Another white-hot jolt in her back. She tried to inhale. Shock coursed throughout her body – she gasped. The frozen pinch of death's embrace left her speechless. The last thing she saw were those glacial blue eyes, just as life faded away.

"This has to be the spot," Chappy insisted, looking at his map.

"Then where's the painting?" John asked, his claustrophobia beginning to test his patience. "The journal was clear. It says on page 112, *Two doors will reveal the Young Man. The Spear is stone, the stone is the path.*"

Anne looked around the cavernous space. The underground area was large. There were stalactites formed along the ceiling, and even a few mounds of stalagmites peppering the floor. Layers of bedrock ran like colored streaks along the walls.

"Can we go to white light for a few?" she asked. "Maybe it will show us something?"

"Sure," John said, still confused about why they had not located the painting. Everything pointed to this spot, but even with the T-PAX, they couldn't locate a hidden space.

The cavern illuminated as each team member shined brilliant white light against the walls of the underground room. The multitude of colors trapped in the lost cavern glowed for the first time in decades. Rico still searched to find a seam, or anything useful with the T-PAX.

"Steady, this is a solid space," Rico said. "There's only the way we came in, and the tunnel leading out, toward the city. I don't see anything else."

"The desperation they must have felt," Wisp said, following the Japanese writing on the walls.

"What's that?" Rico asked.

"This soldier wrote, *'We are under attack. If I am killed my name is,'*" Wisp said, inhaling sharply at the name.

"Name is?" Anne asked.

Wisp swallowed. His face turned sullen.

"*Tanaka,*" Wisp said, acknowledging his own namesake, "It goes on to say – *'Ghosts came here.'*"

"No way," Zip blurted.

"It could be any Tanaka, right?" Chappy asked.

"I guess," Wisp acknowledged. "That's strange."

"Wow, what's the probability of that?" Anne asked.

"She's got a point," Chappy said, shaking his head. "Finding that – now. It's a little unsettling at the least."

"I wasn't referring to the name," Wisp said, "check this out, on the wall. Is that an outline of a spear?"

John walked over, shining a light on the spot. He searched his mind, needing an answer. *No painting? How can it be?*

"The spear is stone, the stone is the path," John sighed relief, touching the outline of the spear-like pattern.

A blinding glare pierced his retinas, emitting from the stone. A rush of wind encircled his body, and everyone turned away, unable to move. That feeling overcame all of his senses. He looked up.

Chappy staggered backwards, feeling the push, like his feet were magnetically charged to the ground. Every member of the team froze in place. An electric, blue light descended from above, filling the entire space and standing their hair on end.

"Tell me this ain't happening already!" Chappy yelled.

"What the hell?" Anne asked, a twitch of fear nipping at her spine.

John smiled, feeling the presence around him; it confirmed there was purpose to their mission. The power descended upon him, charging his body with a feeling of peace he longed for. Every nerve tingled. A warmth grew in his heart, and all of his worries fell away.

"Look up, Anne," John said. "We will serve *Your* purpose!"

A brilliant flash of light sparked, blinding her. An embracing warmth encircled her senses, like nothing she had ever felt before. Chills erupted all over her body. A charge coursed through her, making her feel invincible.

Another flash sparked, and the cavern faded to black. Nothing remained.

CHAPTER 7: PRIDE

"Our ancestors trusted in you, and you rescued them."
Psalms 22:4

1400-Zulu Time 24May1945 (2300-JST Near Shuri Castle)

Bell, Richie, and Ian climbed up a steep, rocky slope, nearing the rendezvous point. The narrow trail was covered by a thick jungle canopy of foliage and palms of all descriptions. The air was so dense and humid, it felt as if you could cut it with a knife. The team had been on the move for nearly a month. Their travels lead them to the Pacific, still hoping to find the painting that had escaped them in Krakow, Poland. Now armed with information from Professor Otto Hahn, they needed to get to the bottom of a broader Nazi conspiracy. Raphael's painting *Portrait of a Young Man* had been stolen by the Reich and traded to Japan in payment of wartime support. The Alsos mission team believed that the painting contained a piece of Arma Christi known as the Lance of Longinus—or, The Spear of Destiny.

"Bell, old bean, do you even know where we are?"

"Dammit, Ian. Yes. I not only know where we are, but I also know where we need to go. Raiders do more than just swim," Bell said, giving his comrade a look. "The rally point with our escort is just at the top of this hill. Look for an old broken statue up ahead."

Unable to see the exchange, Richie sensed Bell was on edge by the sound of his voice. The war in Europe had ended, and after Tailfingen, they had to make sense of the Nazi plan. Richie pushed a damp palm leaf away from his face, seeing Bell traverse the rock-strewn hill ahead of him.

Ian tapped Richie on the shoulder.

"He hasn't been the same. Since Krakow. Not since you got shot."

"I think this war is finally getting to him," Richie replied. "Maybe after this mission, we can get a little R&R."

"That sounds quite excellent. I know a great little place in Thailand – Tapu Island, it's called. Remind me to call my contact there when we get out of this godforsaken jungle. I'll have her set us up for a stay. The scenery is exquisite. And I'm not talking about the beaches."

Richie couldn't help but smile at Ian's plan. If the man had three wishes, they would concern beautiful women, expensive booze, and zesty tobacco.

Bell reached the summit and squatted in the foliage. Their objective sat in the distance, with a heavy presence of Japanese soldiers both in and around the location. Shuri Castle rested atop the next hill, overlooking the village of Naha, Okinawa. Naha appeared to be deserted, but still untouched by the war effort. Operation Iceberg had started in April and battles had been raging across the island ever since. Shuri Castle was a fortified pocket of resistance and continued to pose problems for the Allies. According to intelligence, the 32nd Japanese Army was dug in at the heavily defended castle. In a few hours, the battleship *U.S.S. Mississippi* would begin directing fire at the castle in an effort to drive out all resistance. The First Marine Division sat poised to continue the ground assault in what had become some of the toughest fighting of the war.

The castle, with its curved terra cotta roof, red paint, and tall stone walls, exemplified the definition of Asian design. Bell watched through his binoculars as hundreds of Japanese soldiers moved about the fortress. There was no direct way in, and there was no one insane enough to try – at least until the Alsos Team arrived on the island.

"You two get up here," Bell said. "Tell me if this looks right to you."

Richie crested the hill and saw him crouched, looking through his binoculars. Ian wasn't far behind, checking the rear and holding his M3 submachine gun at the low-ready.

"Let me see, Skipper."

Bell handed Richie the binoculars, and he looked ahead, seeing the large force of troops guarding the castle. He pulled the binoculars away from his face and surveyed to his right. An ancient, broken, open-mouthed Sisha statue sat a few feet away. Ian stopped next to it, admiring the stone piece.

"Interesting," Ian said. "Looks like a cross between a lion and a dog."

"A guy from division said that the Japs believe they ward off evil spirits," Bell replied, looking back at their objective.

A twig snapped from behind the statue. Ian raised his weapon, flicking his half-burned cigarette to the ground. Richie and Bell both turned in the direction of the sound.

"Easy fellas," a deep, American voice grumbled. "I heard you guys talking and figured you weren't Japs. I was told to meet you here."

The Alsos Team saw a shadow emerge through the tropical leaves of the jungle. The familiar frog-skin camouflage pattern of his uniform took shape as he held his rifle out, barrel up, on approach. The thick, tall Marine entered the opening, towering over Ian. He was followed by a short, stocky fireplug of a man carrying a radio on his back.

"I'm Sergeant Decker, 1st Mar Div Recon. Everyone just calls me Big Jack."

"What's the code word?" Ian asked.

"Oh yeah, it's Thunder."

"Lightning," Ian said, dropping his rifle along his side.

"Who's that with you?" Bell asked.

"That's the best damn scout in the division," Jack said. "PFC – well, hell, I still can't pronounce his first name. That's Doha, but we just call him Red. He's a code-talker. He'll keep us in touch with division."

Doha was short compared to Ian, but standing next to Decker, he was like a stump. Broad and strong, his stature exuded confidence.

"Now that we've sloshed through this freaking nasty jungle," Red said, his English refined and articulate, "can one of you tell us why?"

"For an Indian, you speak well," Bell said.

"I grew up in Phoenix, asshole," Red said with an edge to his voice.

Red turned, facing Ian and wiping the sweat from his brow.

"You seem like an intelligent one," Red said. "Why'd you get me and my friend here dragged out of our racks to meet you behind enemy lines?"

Richie watched Jack turn away, losing interest. He also noted the frustration that had crept along Red's face.

"Look, guys. I'm sorry we had to get you involved," he interjected. "Let's start over. I'm Richie. That's Lieutenant Bell and Commander Fleming. We need your help."

Both the Marines snapped to attention.

"I'm sorry, sir" Red said. "No one told us you were officers."

"I've never seen officers come out here like this," Jack added by way of apology.

"At ease, gents," Ian said, reaching into his pocket for a cigarette. He fished out a pack and his Zippo lighter.

"Sir," Red said, as he handed Ian a small circular can, "I wouldn't do that if I were you. These Japs can smell a cigarette from a mile away. They'll snipe you before you take a second toke."

"What's this?" Ian asked, examining the tin.

"It's snuff, sir," Jack said, his posture relaxing. "A Marine's best friend if you ask me. All the nicotine, none of the dyin'."

"What do you suppose I do with it?" He opened the can, smelling the sweet tobacco.

Red looked at Decker and winked.

"You put a pinch between your cheek and gum. Make sure you spit and don't swallow."

"That sounds utterly barbaric," Ian said, handing the can back to Red. "I'll just wait until I can have a civilized smoke."

"Whatever floats your boat, sir."

Bell watched the Marines each take a pinch of snuff and place it in their mouths. Jack had stains of the stuff dripping down his chin. The marine didn't even bother to wipe away his favorite past time – it just blended in with the grit already on his face.

"We were told that your unit stumbled upon what you thought might be a cave leading into Shuri Castle," Bell said, "Is that true?"

Jack spit a stream of brown to the ground. Ian pursed his lips, offended by the smell.

"Dammit, Red. I told you not to file that report. Now look what you got us into."

Red stared at Jack for a moment before shifting his gaze back to Bell.

"Yeah. We found a cave yesterday. On the outskirts of Naha," Red said, pointing toward the village below. "Ran into some Jap regulars at the entrance. They were wearing the same unit insignia as the ones in the castle, best we could tell. Once we got close enough, we saw a couple of tunnels that looked like they might even be attached to the castle. I mean, after Iwo, they're known for tunneling through just about anything."

Ian looked at Richie and then toward Bell.

"Well then," he said, "do you think you could show us that cave?"

Red glanced toward Jack and they shared a smile.

"What's so important about this cave? I mean, they're going to start dropping ordinance on that entire area in a few hours. Division told us to clear out, and now you guys are telling us you want to sneak in?"

Richie stretched his neck and took a deep breath.

"Our orders are classified, but I can tell you this: we have to get into that castle and recover something important. Important enough to send two officers this far behind the lines. Not to mention sending you two up here to meet us. So, I'll tell you what – you guide us in, and I'm willing to bet we can make it worth your while."

Jack raised his brows, considering the notion; the spoils they could encounter in that castle could set them up nicely for after the war.

"Okay, say we do this. How in the hell do you think we move into that castle without alerting the Japs?"

"Look," Ian said, "me and these two Raiders have gotten into some seriously guarded places since this war started. You're just going to have to trust us."

"You're Raiders?" Red asked.

"We've been in this thing since Torch," Bell replied.

Red looked at his Marine buddy.

"These guys have a good rep, Jack. I say we give it a go."

Jack spit a dark stream onto a palm frond close to the ground and then looked back over the group.

"It's your funeral. It's not like I got a whole hell of a lot of options. We'll take you in the way we went yesterday. Just follow our lead."

Richie knew the Marines sensed an opportunity, but he also believed they would do the right thing if forced. Sergeant Decker and PFC Doha located the trailhead that would lead them to the cave entrance. Red took point, moving with a silence that would outshine a cat. Bell followed Richie; he looked back at Ian.

"I hope we make it out of here in time. Division was clear that the bombardment will commence at 1730 Zulu, no matter what. That doesn't leave us much time to find the painting and get out."

"You Yanks and your schedules. We'll be fine. No offense, but the Navy is usually late anyway."

"Whatever the case, you've still got to make good on your promise."

"What promise?"

"I heard you talking to Richie about Thailand again. If we get out of here alive, we're going."

"Yes, indeed," Ian smiled. "After all, you're my two best mates." They entered the tropical jungle of the war-torn region.

††††††

Inside, a lantern flickered against the jagged walls of the cave. Red sank to a knee at the edge of the wood line, holding his fist in the air. Everyone else knew to freeze in place. He peered to the right and left of the cave entrance, seeing nothing move. A moment later, two silhouettes appeared on the uneven wall inside. By their shape, they were Japanese army regulars. They approached the mouth, moving toward Red with their rifles slung over their shoulders.

The smell of rotten fish hung heavy in the air—trashed left-overs from dinner. Red watched the two khaki-clad Japanese soldiers as they exited the cave's entrance, walking into the lush green foliage. Both men carried standard Type-99 rifles with bayonets affixed. They settled into sentry positions on each side of the entrance.

Ian pulled out his tried and true, silenced Welrod 9mm pistol. He motioned to Bell on his right. Red caught the movement in his peripheral vision and tried to wave Ian off. Jack closed in on Red, taking a knee beside him.

Red's eyes slanted; his brow furrowed.

"Are they trying to get us killed?"

"If they screw this up, we're getting the hell outta here," Jack answered.

"These Japs are going to hear them and bring this whole damn place down on us."

He gripped his rifle, pulling it into his shoulder. Jack watched Bell pull his knife out as he approached the first sentry. The look in Bell's gaze was intense – focused on the task at hand and driven by belief. Jack reached over the top of Red's rifle, pushing it down.

"Wait. These fellas know what they're doing… look at 'em move."

Bell crouched behind the right sentry. Ian found a perfect firing angle on the left.

Red looked around for the other guy, Richie. Jack tapped him on the shoulder, pointing upward to a rocky overhang. There, Richie crouched over the sentry on the left, ready to pounce. Red relaxed his posture, sitting back on his heel, marveling at this group's stealthy precision.

Richie took one more silent scan of the area, ensuring there weren't any other hidden enemy positions. He looked down to Bell, giving a hand signal for all clear. Bell made eye contact with Ian across the entrance, making sure the shrewd Brit was set. He looked back to Richie, holding up his left-hand counting: three, two, one.

In quick succession, Richie dropped onto his enemy, using the force of his knee to drive the soldier to the ground. Red and Jack heard the air leave the man's lungs as he crumpled underneath Richie's weight. The other guard turned, his eyes wide with shock and his rifle pointed at the fray. Bell saw his opportunity and charged the armed sentry. The enemy soldier heard the steps as Bell approached, turning to react. The man's jaw dropped, frozen in his footsteps. The sensory overload from multiple attackers caught him off-guard. Bell parried the rifle with his left hand and skillfully directed his knife into the soldier's chest.

Ian began to close the distance between himself and the fighting, scanning for the other sentry. Bell appeared in front of Ian holding his knife, blood dripping from the tip. The two men shared a nod. Ian turned his attention back to Richie, who was still atop the other soldier, silencing his screams. Richie tightened his hand over the man's mouth, and his struggle ended as his body fell limp.

Red exited the dense thicket of trees with Jack following his lead. The two Marines closed in on the Alsos Team, joining their rally-point perimeter.

"That was some real commando stuff right there," Red said.

"Let's just say," Ian whispered, covering the open entrance to the cave, "we've been at this from the beginning."

Big Jack Decker stood firm and grabbed Ian by the shoulder.

"Look, guy, I see you've got some balls, but me and Red here, we've been fightin' in the Pacific since freakin' Tarawa – so don't patronize us. How about you tell us what this is all about, or we walk. I didn't sign up for this crap."

"Yeah… you guys have way too much skill to be cannon-fodder. What's this really about?" Red asked.

The two Marines stiffened their posture, refusing to budge on their demands. Bell sighed, flexed his jaw, and rubbed the bridge of his nose in frustration. Ian shook his head but continued covering the cave. Richie had built up some rapport, or so he thought.

"Truth is," he said, wiping the sweat from his face, "you aren't going to like what I tell you. Then you're going to think we're crazy. So, we appreciate you showing us how to get here. Be careful getting back through the lines."

The two Marines realized Richie meant what he said. They were free to go back to their division and continue the fight on their terms. Big Jack tapped Red on the arm.

"Sounds good to me. Let's get the hell outta here, Red."

Red didn't move. He stood firm, staring ahead in silence. It was as if they were playing poker after going all-in and Red sensed the bluff. The two warriors refused to break contact. Red saw something inexplicable, deep within Richie's gaze. A familiar intensity burned in his heart. Something told Red that he needed to see this through, or he would regret never knowing what lay at the end of this rabbit's hole.

"Red, let's go," Jack repeated.

"No. I'm staying."

"Have you lost your damn mind?"

"This is something I need to see through. It's my vision quest."

"You promised after Iwo – no more unnecessary risks," Jack said. "You remember that?" What we lost?"

"This is different." Red turned to face his friend. "Go if you want. I'm stay' in."

Decker pulled off his camouflaged, steel-pot helmet, raking his hand through his sweaty, high-and-tight, hair. His stare would have been enough to intimidate any other man, but Doha stood firm, much in the way of his Navajo ancestors—stalwart and coursing with a keen sense of purpose.

"We've been through hell already," Jack said. "You're really willing to die now?"

"You remember when we got pinned down that day on Iwo? All our guys getting cut down, right in front of us?" Red asked.

Jack's eyes welled from the memory of that terrible day. Every impact flooded his thoughts. Memories of that awful, black, volcanic sand jumping off the ground. Everything sank in that stuff, even the bullet-riddled bodies of his fallen brothers.

"Why you gotta bring that up? We lost everyone… all of them."

"You think I don't know that?" Red asked. "I bring it up because we were charging some objective on some map for a few *feet* of ground. This… this is different. My vision is clear. I have to stay because this really matters. I can't explain it, but it's important."

"I told you that day," Jack said, wiping his face, "no matter what – we were going to stick together. You saved my life that day, buddy."

"You don't have to stay. I understand if you want to go."

Bell walked over to the Marines.

"You two going to get on mission – or kiss each other goodbye?"

"Skipper, can you give them a minute?" Richie asked.

"This is no place to air this crap out," Bell said. "We're lucky the Japs haven't interrupted this little love spat."

Jack turned away from Red and reached out for Bell, grabbing him by the collar. He outweighed Bell by a hundred pounds.

"Officer, or not – you keep talk' in and I'll…"

"Whoa, Big Jack," Richie said. "He didn't mean anything by that; we're just exposed here, buddy. Look around."

Rock crushed under foot, echoing within the cave. A shadow appeared on the rough wall, then another, and another. Ian looked back at the rest of the team, pointing into the cave with enough vigor he caught Bell's attention.

"They're coming," Bell said, "spread out."

Bell grabbed Red by the arm and ran into the brush to the right of the entrance. Richie looked at Jack, then back to Ian as he slid toward cover.

"You stay' in or go' in, big guy? It's decision time," Richie said.

"Dammit," Jack conceded. "Okay."

Richie turned, ducking toward the left. Jack followed, locating a boulder to hide his large frame behind. Richie started searching for Ian, knowing he had the only modified pistol among the team. The voices echoed inside the cavern, carrying out into the jungle.

Ian dragged one of the dead sentries into the fern-sheltered wilderness. He posted at the edge, waiting for the Japanese patrol to exit. His Welrod was pointed toward three figures stopped at the threshold. It was the new guard. They would surely sound the alarm.

"Bloody hell," Ian said under his breath.

Two of the Japanese soldiers carried rifles, but one—an officer—carried a pistol on his right hip and a samurai sword on his left side. The officer looked over the area.

"Akai yoake," he said, "akai yoake."

Red grabbed Bell by the arm, and whispered into his ear.

"It's their challenge phrase of the day."

The Japanese officer peered into the surrounding area. Ian saw his expression change. He drew his head back, on guard.

Ian steadied his aim on the closest guard, firing off a single shot, striking him in the head. A warm spatter misted in the face of the officer, who looked away with the sting of gore in his eyes. The other guard turned to react. Red threw his bone-handled knife, striking the soldier in the upper back with lightning precision. The officer wiped off his face and turned in a panic, only to be met with the wide right fist of Big Jack. His head snapped back, rendering him unconscious. The officer folded to the ground like a rag doll dropped by a child. The team made quick work of the sentries while Jack disarmed the officer.

Richie closed in, stunned by the veracity of the punch.

"Damn, Jack. You made quick work of that guy."

"Gold gloves finals, 1940. I still got it."

Bell walked over and looked at the unconscious officer.

"What should we do with him?"

"Unfortunately, he's a liability," Ian said, as he pointed his pistol at the man's head.

"Wait," Red said, holding his hand out to Ian, "he might have some use."

"What are you thinking?" Bell asked.

"This guy has all the codes for the day. He's an officer – he knows the castle. I mean, capturing him could be a game changer."

"Yeah," Jack said, "but how many Japs have we captured, and how many of them talked?"

"He does have a point. They aren't known for sharing," Ian said.

"Bell, let's hold on to him," Richie said. "We can tie him up and gag him. If he doesn't cooperate, then maybe we go another route. All I'm saying is, it can't hurt to see if he has something to offer."

Bell placed his hands on his hips, considering the limited options: kill the guy, or tote a hundred and fifty extra pounds of deadweight a mile behind enemy lines, under a battalion of enemy troops. He knew a year ago he would have chosen differently.

"Okay, Richie. Who's gonna carry sushi-boy?"

"I'll take point," Ian said, turning his gaze toward the cave. "My knees aren't what they used to be."

Richie handcuffed the officer and stuffed his handkerchief into his mouth. Some tape was wrapped around his head, securing the gag into place. Red looked at Jack.

"They don't call you Big Jack for nothing, Sarge."

Decker dropped his head back, looking up into the dusky canopy of trees. He let out a deep sigh before grabbing the much smaller officer, draping him over his broad shoulder.

"You can carry him next, skinny," Jack said, looking at Richie. "Red, watch our six."

Ian infiltrated the cave, following it deep within before finding a corridor with ascending stairs carved out of the surrounding stone. He entered, followed by Bell, Richie, Jack, and then Red. The soft glow of oil lanterns flickered inside the long passage. The Alsos Team and the Marines began their upward trek, working their way toward the castle proper.

Ian snaked his way through another short stretch of tunnel, keeping an eye out for any sign of enemy presence. The staircase corridor had led them through a small labyrinth of underground tunnels, some natural and others manmade. Richie and Ian consulted the Knights Templar journal along the way, mapping the underground network within its pages. They spent time sketching and backtracking, trying to find the right path into castle. After a few wrong turns, Red took the lead, using his tracking knowledge to identify where the Japanese had marked the correct route on the walls.

He stopped at a small opening and motioned for Ian to come forward. They both surveyed the beyond, listening for any sign of movement ahead. Once Ian was sure they were alone, he turned on his flashlight, illuminating what appeared to be an underground storage room. He entered and stood among crates of items along the walls of the cavern. Ammunition, food stores, and barrels were stacked around the rock walls. Ian shined his light down a walkway between the crates, turning a corner to see another set of stairs leading up. They looked well-traveled – possibly the route into the castle.

Bell closed in on Ian, startling his thought.

"Where the hell are we?" Bell asked.

"I think we're in the lower level of the castle," Ian said. "Look at the stairs over there, the stores in here."

"I was starting to lose faith we'd find the right path."

"Let's get everyone up and check this room for the painting. There's stuff stacked everywhere."

Ian followed Bell to the opening leading out, and they gave the all clear. Richie entered the room as the others pulled the unconscious Japanese officer through the opening. He stood in the cavern, shining his light to the left, where he saw another footpath through the mountains of crates, stacked furniture, and wooden boxes.

The click of boot heels on rock resonated from the stairs entering the cavern, alarming the men. Ian pushed Richie to the left, in between several small crates and piled up items along the bedrock floor. Bell and Red helped Jack stuff their captive into a crag between the boxes and the exit before disappearing, themselves.

The soldiers closed in on the Alsos Team, and Ian pulled out his pistol, ready to do work. Two flickering orbs shined along the walkway. He watched the four soldiers. Two were carrying small crates, which they set down only feet away. The other two men carried oil lanterns, providing enough light for them all to find their way. Ian stood frozen, mere feet away from the enemy. The four men took their time placing their cargo atop another crate. The soldiers moved with no crispness; they all looked weary from the war.

Ian looked at the soldier's feet and realized they were standing less than a foot away from Bell, who dared not breathe. He watched his friend shrink into the smallest possible crack until – *creak*. The four enemy soldiers turned and saw Bell's arm.

Before they could react, a blinding flash of light shot into the cavern; electric blue light charged the room and a cyclone of air funneled across the floor. Richie remembered Bizerte. It couldn't be. *What were the odds?* His eyes were forced closed from the brilliance. Everyone—ally and enemy alike—shielded their eyes, blinded by the flash. A final spark shrouded the walls of the cave, bringing a vivid burst of pure energy that cascaded down the walls. Blue-tinted lightning arced overhead. The space faded to black. The lanterns held by the Japanese soldiers had been blown out.

Richie strained, opening his eyes first, staring into an array of faint green dots hovering in front of him. "John?"

A moment passed. Richie saw a flicker of movement in the pitch-black space.

One of the Japanese soldiers had something in his hand. He closed in on one of the green-eyed figures.

"Duck!" Richie yelled.

John jetted to his left, ducking to avoid whatever Richie saw.

"Ian!" Richie yelled.

Two shots exited the Welrod. Within a split-second, the entire cavern lit up. Six green lasers illuminated the entire chamber, followed by the metallic clank of automatic gunfire, which leveled the other three Japanese soldiers. Ian pointed his pistol at the ultra-modern soldiers, until he realized a strange familiarity. Bell rolled from his hiding spot, seeing a familiar face not far away.

"John? That you?"

"Bell?" John asked, surprised to hear his voice.

"Yeah, what just happened? Are you really here?"

Jack let loose the unconscious Japanese officer, and he pointed his rifle toward the alien, camouflaged men in the room – until he saw her. Anne stood several feet away. Her stature staggered him. He looked closer, struggling to see. It was then that her face caught the lumbering Marine off-guard.

Red stood in disbelief, staring ahead into a face he couldn't deny.

"Decker. Doha. These guys are with us," Bell said.

His words had little impact as the two Marines stood awe-struck by what they had just witnessed. Richie walked over to Big Jack, pushing his rifle to the ground.

"Jack, they're Americans. Our friends."

"What the…" Red said, as he continued to stare at Zip. His mind raced.

"Did you say *Doha?*" Zip asked.

CHAPTER 8: ARK

"...but God said to me, 'You must not build a Temple to honor my name, for you are a warrior and have shed much blood.'"
1 Chronicles 28:3

1400-Zulu Time 24May2020 (1800-AST Nova Scotia, Canada)

The specially modified Blackhawk helicopter cut through the dwindling light of the day as it traversed Mahone Bay. Flanked in their aircraft by two other stone-gray warbirds, Secretary of Defense Archibald MacManus, along with Deputy SecDef Roderick Johnson, and Admiral Nathan Grant, caught their first glimpse of Birch Island. The SecDef pulled his headset microphone closer to his lips.

"Gold Squadron, you're clear to execute."

"One-Alpha-Six, copy."

The two flanking Blackhawks broke formation, dropping down below the command helicopter. One chopper made its way to the construction zone east of the triangular swamp. The second helicopter approached a clearing due south. Archie had called in a few favors, pulling this operation off with Canadian approval. He had chosen the best flight from his best squadron of Development Group (DEVGRU), more widely known as SEAL Team Six.

"Nathan, you better be right about this. I had to grease the wheels with a lot of promises. I think I signed over my house to the Canadian Prime Minister."

"Sir," Nathan said smiling, "you saw the intel for yourself. I think it's pretty compelling. The O'Keefe's are up to something. Besides, if I'm wrong, maybe you won't have to pay for the renovations now."

Rod tapped Archie on the shoulder and said, "There's no telling what Maximillion knows."

Archie nodded in acknowledgement. He adjusted his headset, watching the action on the ground.

"Let's just hope this isn't another dry well."

The three leaders watched the two teams take down the area. Nathan looked through gyro-stabilized binoculars, zooming in on the two detained men. One of them wore a white shirt with PNK printed on the back.

"One-Alpha-Six, we got two detained. No sign of the HVT."

"Sierra-Delta actual, copy," Archie said into the mic as his head sank toward the deck of the chopper.

"Sir, Maximillion might not be here, but the info might pan out, yet. Look at the trailer by the excavation site," Nathan said.

Archie could see PNK printed on the placard.

"Maybe these two can tell us something."

Rod pulled his mic up to his mouth.

"Sierra-Delta two to One-Alpha-Six. Clear us an LZ."

"Roger that," a gritty voice said. "Popping green smoke."

†††††

A tall, muscular, brown-bearded operator approached the exterior door to the SecDef's helicopter. He grabbed the latch, sliding the door back toward the tail. His multi-cam uniform, plate-carrier vest, and helmet-mounted, quad-eyed, panoramic night-vision goggles were set in the upright position. Sparkling orange hues from the early stages of the sunset reflected off his eye protection as he stepped back. The engines of the Blackhawks had already powered down, but the rotors continued to bleed off energy.

"Sir," said the SEAL, "we've secured the area. Our birds will be circling for overwatch."

Archie stepped from the chopper to the dirt-layered ground, his dress shoes and slacks catching dust. He reached out for the squadron leader's hand.

"Good job, Commander. Let's hold this until we figure out what's what."

"Sounds good, sir. The two detainees are right over there."

"Understood."

Rod and Nathan exited the helicopter, both dressed in fatigues. They all followed the Commander across the gravel and dirt clearing, approaching a semi-trailer next to which were two young men on their knees, hands on their heads. Both men looked like contractors, outfitted in jeans and work boots. They had dirt and grease smeared over their clothing. The one with a short black beard dropped his hands, wanting to ask a question. One of the operators closed in to handle the man, but Archie held up his hand.

"What did we do? Who in the hell are you?"

"Son," Archie said, "do you think you're in a position to ask questions?"

The bearded man looked at his coworker and grit his teeth. Nathan stepped closer and made eye contact.

"What's your name?"

"I'm Cabot. This is George."

"Have these two been searched?"

The Commander nodded and motioned for his men to give Nathan some space.

"Cabot, I'm Nathan. George, you can put your hands down. We're here because we're chasing a fugitive of the United States government. We have reason to believe he has been here over the past few months."

George dusted his pants off as he stood to his feet. Cabot also stood, facing Nathan. Archie and Rod stepped back, happy to let Nathan ask the questions.

"This is a little much don't you think?" George asked.

"He's what we refer to as a high-value target, or HVT. If you two can answer a few questions, I think we can let you go on about your business."

"Look man, we just work here," Cabot said. "We were sent back today to take down some drilling equipment and get it loaded on the barge."

Nathan reached into his pocket and pulled out two pictures. He first showed a picture of Magnus O'Keefe.

"Ever see this guy around here?"

George shook his head, while Cabot studied it a little longer.

"No, he doesn't look familiar."

"What about this man?" Nathan asked, swapping pictures. "He may have funded this whole operation."

Cabot looked at the picture. George nodded.

"That's the guy in charge," Cabot said. "I remember him coming out several times. He had us do some drilling that was – different."

"What do you mean by different?"

"Like he had specific spots that had to be drilled to certain levels at certain times," George said, remembering how strange it was. "The guy was a real pain in the ass… like really particular."

Rod and Archie leaned into the conversation, hoping to glean more from this lead. Nathan reached into his right cargo pocket and pulled out the Knights Templar journal, opening it to page 124.

"And did you find anything?"

"Yeah, but after we hit the mark and sleeved the hole, he shut us down," Cabot recalled.

"What was at the mark?" Rod asked.

"I wish I knew," Cabot said, looking at his coworker and scratching his head.

"It's like another island across the bay," George added, "it's full of strange markings, symbols, and the tales of lost treasure – they go on forever."

Nathan turned and showed the men the drawing of the island. He pointed to a set of markings on the paper.

"What do you make of this?"

Cabot studied the drawings and looked toward the swamp, orienting himself. George was quick to respond.

"That's right where we sleeved the tunnel. These other points were what they guy referred to as, um…"

"Pitfalls," Cabot said, snapping his fingers, "he told Tim, our foreman, that we had to relieve pressure on those particular points for…"

"He called it *the tent*," George said.

"We even dubbed the work area as *The Tent*," Cabot said, looking at George. "We thought it was just another shot at treasure hunting. All and all, the guy paid us well enough not to ask too many questions, if you know what I mean."

Nathan closed the journal with one hand and rubbed his forehead with the other.

Cabot's eyes widened when he saw the cover of the journal.

"That's one of the symbols we saw – right there," Cabot said.

Nathan looked down at the cover of the ancient leather-bound book. In the center was a fighting lion below a crescent moon with a star on each side. He pointed to the lion.

"This exact symbol?"

"Yessir. I happened to see it on a marker stone, just before we sleeved the tunnel."

Rod huffed at the news. Archie sighed. Nathan needed to ask another question, but he was already sure of the answer. He lifted the photo of Maximillion once more.

"When was the last time this man was here?"

Cabot looked down, rubbing his beard.

"They kicked us off sight a few days ago, but my buddy, Andy, he drove the ferry they leased. When I saw him this morning, he mentioned that they pulled out late yesterday."

Archie took a deep breath and patted Nathan on the back.

"At least we're not far behind."

"Yeah, but we couldn't get a satellite tasked until today. They could be anywhere by now."

"True," Rod said, "but maybe we can get someone down that tunnel and see what they found."

His phone rang and he stepped away. Nathan turned back to the two workers.

"Do you know what's down there?"

George shook his head.

"No," Cabot said. "All I can tell you is it's 90 feet deep - exactly. The sleeve we inserted is about 150 feet long – and at a precise 40-degree angle. It's right over there, if you want to see it."

"I absolutely need to see it," Nathan said. They stepped off in that direction.

"Hold up," Rod said, rejoining Nathan, the men, and Archie.

"What is it?" Archie asked.

"You're not going to believe this," Rid said. "We just got hailed over the SOCOM emergency channel. A black-site chopper is requesting clearance to land.

"Walter," Nathan grumbled, placing his hands on his hips.

"The one and only."

"Tell them they have clearance. Make sure our overwatch birds are aware," Archie said. He watched Nathan grow tense and begin rubbing the back of his neck.

"He's going to tell us a bunch of bad news, sir. I can already feel it."

"Maybe. But, as you know, we ain't got to like it…"

"We just have to do it," Nathan said, finishing a cardinal thought among the SEAL teams.

"Commander," Rod said, motioning to the Gold Squadron leader, "secure these two gentlemen and make them comfortable until we find out what the hell is going on."

The tall, armored, SEAL nodded, "Roger that, General."

✝✝✝✝✝

Nathan stood in front of the 6-foot diameter tunnel sleeve, which lead toward a point 90 feet under the middle of the swamp. A white tent covered the entire work area around the pipe, shielding it from the rain. He had already snapped a handful of chem-lights, tossing them into the steep-angle of the pipe. Three of the SEAL operators prepared two ropes, rigging them to descend.

"Sir – sir!" a voice said.

Nathan snapped out of his daze.

"Yes?"

"Are you sure you want to be the one to go down?"

"It's my mess, sailor. I'll be the one to clean it up."

The young SEAL nodded his head, continuing to lay out the rigging. Nathan remembered the last time he met with Walter during an actual operation. Nine good men were lost, because he didn't – he couldn't – share what he knew. Even in the debrief, Walter didn't show his hand, citing that, *'somehow Nathan will be shown what to do.'*

Nathan threw another light-stick down the pipe and shook his head. Walter was right about one thing: Nathan shared a powerful vision with John, full of a sorrow he didn't understand. He saw the Earth as a wrecked, scarred hell. All hope seemed lost. He watched people fighting, desperate to survive, some in bondage – some worse. His eyes closed; he could hear the tormented screams, feel the desperation in the air. Everything burned.

"Nathan, you okay?" Rod asked.

He snapped out of the horrible dream.

"Yes. Is *he* here?"

"Turn around and see for yourself."

Nathan gathered his thoughts and turned to see Helen. She was dressed a little more casual than usual. Jeans, a pair of boots, and a polo shirt that didn't quite conceal the pistol on her hip.

"Helen," he said, shaking her hand, "good to see you."

He looked past her as Walter hobbled up, clutching his cane, followed by Archie.

"Walter, I wish I could say the same for you."

The old man, now in his nineties, huffed, stopping to look at Nathan.

"You still don't get it, do you?"

Helen stepped back, anxious to get out of the way.

"You're in for it today," she said, with a knowing smirk on her face.

"I don't get what?"

"What all of this is about. Why you can't see it?" Walter asked, his hands shaking as he propped himself over his cane. Nathan huffed and crossed his arms.

"How about you enlighten me. Enlighten all of us."

The old man shook his head and pursed his lips at Nathan's outburst.

"How about you two cool it," Archie said. "What brings you to us today, Walter?"

A brief silence fell over the group. The sun was setting over Nova Scotia. Helen placed a folding chair behind Walter. He never looked back, trusting she placed it right where it needed to be. The wisdom he possessed and what he was about to impart would take a lot out of him.

"Nathan, I know you're angry with me. I'm sorry you feel that way, but you have to listen to me. *He* has something to share."

The admiral sighed at the request and squatted lower, taking a knee in front of Walter. Rod reached over, grabbed a small crate and settled upon it. Archie joined Helen, propped against the wall of a metal shipping container.

"I need you all to know that I didn't know where to come. Not until I heard about this operation. Everything came together when I found out the three of you would be here. It was then…"

"What are you talking about, Walter?" Rod asked.

The old man loosened his collar. Helen walked over to him and placed her hand on his shoulder. Her stare told Nathan she believed him, whatever he was about to say.

"It's okay. Tell them."

Nathan watched, still aware of Helen's concern. She stared back at him with stern determination; she had never been this involved when Walter was talking, which was enough to topple him from his knee and backwards onto his rear end in the dirt, like a child being read a story.

"I'm going to tell you some history. At least the parts that matter, anyway. Have any of you heard of Prince Henry Sinclair?"

Nathan shook his head, but Walter already presumed the question was rhetorical.

"He was a Templar Knight," he continued, "*the* actual Templar Knight who was sworn to protect the Ark of the Covenant. During the last year of the Crusades, the Knights Templar recovered the Ark in some of the deadliest fighting of the period. It was taken from the Holy Land, under the protection of the Templar. This information was protected by them, and later the Freemasons, for hundreds of years, and represents why John Bell and I became involved, as Templar Masons."

"Why have you never shared this with us before?" Archie asked.

"It's part of the 33rd level Templar Mason oath – to never share our knowledge with outsiders."

"Then why now?" Nathan asked.

"According to the oath, if the Ark of the Covenant becomes compromised, we are to do whatever is necessary to protect it."

"The Ark of the Covenant? I don't understand." Nathan added up the collective of information in his head. "Maximillion? Are you saying what I think you're saying?"

Walter furrowed his winkled forehead and looked Nathan in the eye.

"If what I saw this morning holds true, then yes."

"Wait, the Ark was here?" Archie asked.

"I thought he found something, but I wasn't sure what. How would the Ark have gotten *here*, of all places?" Nathan asked.

Walter held his hand out, palm up.

"Nathan, hand me the journal."

Once the book found Walter's hand, he flipped it open, using it as a reference.

"In the early 1390's, the Knights Templar had been almost completely extinguished throughout Europe, with the exception of few loyal knights. A new order of Knights emerged in the chaos, sworn to protect the Arma Christi already liberated from the Muslims. These first Freemasons, as they would come to be known, realized the true nature of the Arma Christi and the power it contained."

Walter pulled off his Freemason ring and handed it to Nathan.

"At that point, Freemason teachings tell us that the Ark of the Covenant had been hidden beneath the Cathedral of our Lady of Chartres, in France, since the late 13th century."

"What does this have to do with it today?" Rod asked.

"Let him finish," Archie said, holding a hand up.

"The Templar became conflicted during that time, and a secretive civil war broke out. A splinter faction, called the Teutonic Knights of the Templar, believed the Arma Christi should be brought together and assembled into what became known as the ultimate weapon. They wanted to wipe out all resistance to the Templar, creating a new world order of peace and prosperity. They became obsessed, twisted by the teachings of their first grand master, Sir Heinrich. It was the Teutonic Knights who first tried to steal the Ark."

"What did the Templar do?" Nathan asked.

"The Templar Knights were able to stop the Teutonic Knights. The Templar believed that the Arma Christi possessed great power, but in the hands of men, it would be corruptible – vulnerable to evil."

"So, this… all of this, goes back to the journal – to Prince Sinclair. Doesn't it?"

"Yes. Prince Henry Sinclair was the Templar's most trusted and respected knight. Naturally, he was tasked with protecting, even hiding the Ark, and some pieces of Arma Christi. That caused him to do something in the mid 1390's that no one expected. He sailed across the Atlantic, discovering a new land and a new people."

"Wait a second. I thought Columbus was the first to sail across the Atlantic… in like 1492? You're saying this guy did it a hundred years before him?" Rod asked.

"Think about it: if the Templar knew a fraction of what we know right now, it would be the greatest knowledge of their time. Worthy of great secrecy – and great lengths to hide it from discovery."

"So, the Ark was brought over here 100 years before Columbus?" Nathan asked.

"No one, not even me, knew where the Ark was taken, until…" Walter scratched his head.

"Until – what?" Archie asked, still trying to digest the truth.

Walter handed the journal to Nathan, who still held the ring.

"Look on page 36, under the rectangular drawing."

Nathan saw the drawing. It had strange symbols drawn in three lines within the rectangle that was traced around them. Under the shape was a set of letters.

Nathan read them aloud, "*H-I-S-E-o-O*… What does it mean?"

"Henry I. Sinclair – Earl of Orkney."

"What do the rectangle and the symbols mean?"

"That's the genius of Sinclair and the Knights Templar journal – nothing makes sense until the pieces come together."

"So, what has to come together?" Archie asked.

"Everything," Walter said, turning to face the SecDef. "Sinclair used another island, here in Mahone Bay, as a base of operations. He strategically placed markers and symbols, and even hid a little treasure, just in case anyone found out about his trip overseas. Remember, he was hiding one of the most important, Godly relics ever known to mankind. He made it his mission."

"Yeah, I get that," Archie said, tugging at his jacket. Dusk was upon them. Daylight was in scant supply.

"Walter, I appreciate the story," Nathan said, standing to get a harness on, "but I have got to get down that hole. It isn't getting any brighter out here."

"Is there more?" Rod asked.

Walter sighed at the younger generation's haste.

"Prior to one of our Alsos missions, late in the war, we came across some intel about Heinrick Himmler, head of the Nazi SS. According to the source, another high-ranking Nazi by the name of Rudolf Hess—you remember, the guy who was captured in Scotland?—well, what we discovered from Hess was that Hitler sent him, with Himmler, to Halifax, Nova Scotia in 1933. They had found out about a rectangular stone that had been unearthed on another island, here in Mahone Bay, at a depth of 90 feet. That stone had strange symbols carved into its face, identical to the one drawn here in the journal."

"How did they know about the stone? What was their—?" Nathan began.

"This is why I need to tell you everything. Now let me finish."

The old man shifted his gaze upon Nathan, who had now stopped moving entirely. Walter's eyes squinted, and he stared ahead.

"Nathan, the Nazi SS had a secret faction. They called themselves The Order of the Black Sun. Some even referred them as the Teutonic Order of the Black—"

"Wait a second, are you insinuating they're linked to the Teutonic Knights? If so, this goes back a long way. The Templar and Teutonic Knights, and the journal... it was stolen by the Nazis prior to World War II."

Walter nodded his approval.

"So, in 1933, Himmler and Hess stole the 90-foot stone and burned down the building it was in at the time. That stone was hidden away by Himmler. We might hold the journal now, but the Nazis held it for many years. Unfortunately, Maximillion held it long enough to put the pieces together, well before us."

"What do the makings on the stone mean?" Rod asked.

"It took me a long time to figure that out," Walter said. "Until just this morning, actually."

"Well?" Nathan asked.

"The answer is there, in your hand."

He had forgotten he was holding Walter's ring. He held it up flat in his palm to inspect.

"It's just a ring," Nathan said. "I don't see anything special about it."

"You know who made that ring?" Walter asked.

"Who?"

"I'll get to that," Walter said, settling back in his chair.

"Now the games start – right?" Nathan growled.

"No, I just want you to understand, the ring is special. Prince Henry Sinclair eventually returned to the Orkney Islands of Scotland. But, in 1401 the Teutonic Knights caught up with him, and they tried to steal the journal. Although they killed Sinclair, his son escaped with the journal, and his father's ring."

"This is Sinclair's ring?" Nathan asked.

"It's been passed down from generation to generation—given to the Templar Mason who were tasked with protecting it from the Teutonic Knights, or, as we know them today, The Order of the Black Sun."

"I still don't see anything *special* about it."

"I never did either," Walter said. "I tested it, inspected it, and even prayed about it for years. Today, I guess He felt it was time to show me, and in turn, time for me to show you."

The sun had set and evening surrounded them. Some of the SEAL operators turned on the generator-driven lights at the dig site. Walter took the ring from Nathan, stood up, and sat the ring on the chair.

"Helen, can you find something flat? Maybe a clipboard with some paper?"

She turned, knowing she had one in their helicopter. Nathan stood up and looked toward the pipe leading beneath the swamp. Several of the operators had fashioned a pulley system to lower him into the tunnel. He was ready to see what was below. Helen jogged back to the group and handed the clipboard, loaded with plain white paper, to Walter.

"The sun always rises," he said, "through one window in my bedroom. It's been that way for as long as I can remember. It's one of those things you take for granted, a beautiful sunrise. Until you realize, of course, there may not be many more in your future."

"I can appreciate that, Walter – but what the hell are you saying?" Archie asked.

"I've kept this ring under lock and key for years. For some reason, last night, all I wanted to do was hold it. I wanted answers. I feel asleep with it in my hand. When I awoke, it was gone from my grasp. I started to panic, until I looked over on my nightstand – and there it was. No sooner did I breathe again when the sun broke the horizon, through that same window."

"Okay," Nathan said.

"Do you have a flashlight?" Walter asked, turning to him.

The admiral pulled out one of two mini-flashlights he carried on him at all times and handed it over.

"Helen, can you hold this on its side – right here."

The old CIA operative took the flashlight opposite the clipboard and twisted the ring to a precise angle from the paper. He turned on the light. With a prism-like effect, symbols appeared on the paper. Nathan closed in, realizing they matched the symbols of the rectangle in the journal. Walter flipped the ring over, finding the light once more. He twisted the ring in the light. Words formed where the symbols once shined.

"Read what it says, Nathan."

Nathan got very close to Walter, trying to focus on the phrase.

"It says, *The Armor, hidden and spread, hold the Key to the Temple. Our Covenant touched by Grail; the future is written on Birch – 1398 H.I.S. – E.o.O.*"

"What does it mean to you?"

"It means…" Nathan said, chills erupting on his arms, "it means I'm not going to like what I find at the bottom of this hole. Am I?"

†††††

Nathan held the rope looped at the small of his back. The friction heated the palm of the rappelling glove as it slid through his grasp. A harness was pulled tight around his waist. He turned his head over his shoulder, watching for any sign of the bottom, using a flashlight to guide his descent. Rod's movement above him was the only thing disturbing the light as the two men crept ever-deeper into the steel-lined tunnel.

"You okay, Nathan?" Rod asked.

"Yeah, just slow going. How about you?"

"Just following your lead. Looks like we're passing the halfway point. It's a little steeper that we thought, huh?"

"And slicker," Nathan said. "Watch your footing."

"Roger that. Oh, and so you know, I'm not a fan confined spaces."

"Then why come? I told you I'd be fine."

Rod looked over his shoulder at Nathan below. The borrowed hardhat sat high on Rod's head. Its fixed light made Nathan squint.

"Sorry, about that," Rod said. "I just didn't want you to go it alone."

"Seriously. You can get them to pull you up. I got this."

"And let you hold this over my head?" Rod huffed, laughing a little, "I'd rather get bamboo shoots under my toenails."

Nathan laughed and continued dropping a little faster in an effort to dissuade Rod's resolve. Now it was a game to Nathan; he wanted to see if a man he respected had any quit in him.

"I see you," Rod said. "Trying to see if I got my nerve still, are you? It's on."

Rod matched every glide on the rappel with Nathan's. They soon forgot about everything but the competition – something men of purpose often do to forget about the danger.

"Slow up! I see the bottom," Nathan said.

"That was easy enough. Reminded me of—"

"It's a chamber! Sorry, I didn't mean to cut you off."

Nathan's feet hit the floor, and he radioed to the top of the tunnel.

"Anyone copy?"

Rod found his footing at the bottom. The pipe had entered the chamber at the same steep angle. The walls were made of what appeared to be concrete, with timber supports staggered throughout the small room. A pair of drag marks stretched into the space ahead, ending at the edge of pipe. Something was pulled out.

Nathan saw two powerful flashlights that had already been set up. He turned them on and redirected them, rotating the light into the structure. One of the beams of light passed by a timber batten covered in symbols. He swung the beam back around and stopped. They looked very familiar to those on the 90-foot stone.

"Check this out, Rod."

"Man, for this to survive over 600 years under a swamp – that's some impressive engineering for the time."

"The mark right here – it's Henry Sinclair's crest," Nathan said.

Rod moved past Nathan, following the streaking to its origin in the small chamber.

"Whatever was here, they dragged it from this spot," Rod said, looking around the confined space.

"Do you really think the Ark of the Covenant was down here?" Rod asked.

Rod further inspected the scuff marks scraped into the ancient wooden floor.

"Based on what Walter had to say? Yes," Nathan said.

"I wish we could find something more concrete."

"Keep looking around," Rod said. "The sooner we find something, the sooner we get out of this damp tomb."

"True," Nathan said, thinking of a distraction. "You never finished what you were saying."

"Oh yeah, it was nothing. I just remembered a place, outside the orphanage I grew up in as a kid. It was basically an old sewer culvert – similar to the feel of that tunnel descent."

"I never knew that about you. How did you wind up there?"

"Long story," Rod said, "but when I was 14 years old, I woke up in a hospital. The nurse told me I was rescued at sea and brought in to them. Well... long story short, they said I had a head injury because I couldn't remember anything before the hospital. Eventually, I was turned over to the state and raised in an orphanage."

"I guess it's not something that comes up often in conversation." Nathan said.

"Nah. Lucky for me, at least I had my name sewn into my clothes. I never knew my parents, but at least they seemed to care about me – before they died."

"I'm sorry, Rod. I didn't know."

"It's okay. I've lived with that my whole life. It was a boating accident, according to everything I was ever able to locate. It is what it is. I guess the tunnel was bringing back a little more anxiety than I might have realized."

"I was pushing you," Nathan said, "I'm sorry."

"No. Seriously, it helped me get down here. It's not so bad. Plus, I've dealt with worse things. If it wasn't for tragedy, I would have never met my wife. She keeps me on the straight and narrow."

"She's a good woman. You're lucky for that, too."

"Yeah, she's always supported me," Rod said. "No matter what."

Nathan took his handheld flashlight and scoured every surface until he found something definitive. He stopped, staring at the discovery. It startled him at his core. Rod could see him locked in place.

"What is it?" Rod asked.

The request was followed by quiet. He moved toward Nathan.

"I've seen some remarkable things, especially since taking over Arklight. But, this… this is by far the most disturbing."

"What?"

Rod edged up, but no sooner stopped moving when he saw the reflection from above. Nathan's flashlight beam danced over the 2-foot by 3-foot pure gold piece. The plate was inserted into a small hole along the ceiling in the chamber. Several images had been hammered into the surface of the golden plate. Rod tried to make out what he saw, but Nathan had already deciphered what it meant.

"The lamb broke seven seals; the four horsemen appeared; the white rider was first; death will come; the earth will quake as the angels with seven trumpets appear," Nathan said.

Rod saw the depiction as it was read aloud. His veins began to pump ice, and chills covered his body.

"Why put references to the tribulation be down here? I mean, doesn't the Ark represent God's presence? Not his wrath," Rod said.

"Maybe it's a warning, but… I think it's something else entirely."

"What's that?"

"After Nashville, John found a phrase in the journal. It referred to a Temple," Nathan said. "It seemed to reference something physical, but not a place. John told me that he thought the Temple was the Ark. After all, it made some sense by that point. Now look at the top of the gold plate."

Nathan moved his flashlight and pointed to what was hammered ahead of the tribulation reference. A depiction of the Ark and the Time Key together, followed by a cylindrical object and a man.

"We already know the Time Key and the Ark function together – who is the man and what's he holding? I can't see that last part."

Rod turned his light onto the piece and started shaking his head.

"I've seen this before. It can't be."

"What's it say, Rod?"

"That's Joseph of Arimathea and the Holy Grail. But look at the ring encompassing all of the pieces – it encircles everything."

"Like a Large Hadron Collider?" Nathan asked. The silence between them was pointed. "We haven't had anything in the journal reference the Grail. This whole thing is unusual."

"Well, if this plate is as real as we think it is, somehow, the Ark, the Time Key, the Holy Grail, and the Hadron Collider all function together. Do you think they represent the ultimate weapon? That they will somehow bring about the Apocalypse?"

Nathan was concerned, albeit not surprised by, Rod's questions. This was the physical evidence he had been looking for, where everything else had been speculation. Rod reached toward the plate.

"What's this?"

Rod pulled the handle, hoping to release the plate from the ceiling. There was a squeal from above, accompanied by a *thud*. The space shook and rumbled. Air rushed past their faces.

"Rod!" Nathan said, scrambling back. "Get to the shaft!"

He scampered to his feet, tugging on the rappel rope secured to him. He yelled into the radio, holding it aloft as water poured into the chamber.

"Pull us up!" he shouted, grabbing Rod with his free hand. "Get us out, now!"

His belt tugged against his waist and he made eye contact with Rod, making sure they both escaped the flood. Within seconds, they were hoisted out of the water, into the pipe, and toward the exit. At least they both saw the plate. Nathan didn't want to have to share the scene he saw, but he knew now without a doubt – the Ark of the Covenant was in Maximillion's hands.

CHAPTER 9: FAMILY

"For the sake of my family and friends, I will say, 'May you have peace.'"
Exodus 15:6

1500-Zulu Time 24May1945 (0000-JST 25May1945 Shuri Castle)

"It seems we're in need of a proper introduction," Ian said, walking toward John.

John flipped up his night-vision goggles.

"Bloody hell! You're the same Yanks that saved my hide back in Bizerte." Ian said, a smile extending across his face.

"Everyone hold up a minute," John said, looking at Jack. He turned his head and pointed to the U.S. Flag on the side of his helmet.

"We're American soldiers here to help. It's okay, big guy."

Chappy elbowed Richie and nodded, like an old friend. They stood next to each other, waiting to see if Jack or Red would have some sort of aneurism.

"What're their names?"

"The big one's Jack," Richie said, "and the short one's Red."

"Fellas – pssst," Chappy said, snapping his fingers, "hey – look at me. Yeah, we're just guys like you. No big deal. Just take a couple of breaths before you pass out. We'll explain everything."

John took the opportunity to recover Rico and Wisp's attention.

"You two – set some sensors back the way we came in. That should be the way up to the castle. Rally on me when you get done."

"Steady," Wisp said, "are you going to tell us what just happened? I mean running into these guys, again – here?"

"I know. We've got a lot to discuss."

"No doubt."

"Anne?" John asked.

She stood, weapon at the ready, her head scanning side to side. She kept flexing her eyelids, still blinded.

"Anne, everything's okay. Stand down."

"What happened?" Anne asked. "I don't feel okay. I'm freaking out a little bit."

"Long story, stand easy. You're among friends."

Bell saw her lift the night-vision and drop her balaclava. He was mesmerized by her appearance. Yet another strong female soldier standing in front of him. He remembered to check himself, given past experiences.

"Ma'am, I'm Bell. Lieutenant John Bell."

"That's great, dude." She lowered herself to the crate to sit and gather her senses. "Who the hell are you, again? What just happened?"

Bell looked back at John, remembering the night they first met on that beach in Bizerte.

"It's 1945," he said. "Damn good to see you fellas. And you, ma'am."

Anne shook her head, now regaining her vision. She saw Bell's uniform, his equipment. She looked past him, seeing the others of the Alsos Team.

"Please tell me this is a freaking joke," Anne said.

"It's no joke," Bell replied. "We... I mean, Richie and I, ran into the rest of your team a couple of years ago in Bizerte. It changed everything."

Anne looked at John, remembering that night. He stared back at her.

"He's telling the truth," John acknowledged. "I told you, you need to keep an open mind."

"An open mind?" Anne asked. "This is a little more than that, John. This... this is ridiculous! I mean I thought I knew, but... this is far different than I imagined."

"I tell you what," John said. "Focus on dropping a sensor array. Get that up and running so we don't have any unwanted company. When you get back, I'll explain everything."

"Okay. This is beyond weird."

"Oh, and seriously, Anne, you're really in World War II, underneath an entire division of Japanese soldiers. It's the real deal. Don't get compromised – understand?" John asked.

Anne turned to find a high-point on the room for the sensor. John watched some of the others interact around the room. Zip shook Bell's hand, while Richie patted him on the back. Red and Jack stood back, still reeling in shock. Chappy approached the two Marines.

"Who the hell are you?" Jack asked.

Chappy laughed and couldn't believe what he was seeing. Two Marines, in full combat gear, amid World War II.

"You want the long version, or the short version?"

"It don't matter," Red said, "just tell us what the heck's goin' on."

Chappy nodded and held his hand out, stepping into an open area a few feet away.

"Sit down over here, fellas."

†††††

John watched Chappy guide the two Marines to one side of the cavern. He stepped down onto the floor, and made his way toward the middle of the stone-walled room to join Bell, Ian, Richie, and Zip.

"We never imagined we'd see you here," Bell said.

John looked past Bell and saw Richie's face.

"It's good to see all of you," John replied, shaking his young grandfather's hand. Presently a man more than twenty years his grandson's junior, Richie smiled, glad to see John once again.

"Pardon me," Ian said, "Bell, Richie – how do you know these gentlemen?"

Bell paused, knowing this would be tricky, despite all of the knowledge they had shared with one another. Richie and Bell had left their Arklight secret buried, even after Germany. It was time for the whole truth.

"Um, right. Ian," Bell said. "I need you to understand something. Everything concerning them is classified—a matter of National Security. But, they have had no direct bearing on the Alsos missions, since the start."

"Go on," Ian said. "I'm all ears."

"They appeared in Bizerte the morning we captured those scientists. They're why the Nazis folded. They're the reason the Allies got into the city that day. We helped them, and they helped us."

"I don't understand. Why didn't you say anything? I told you about my rescue, and what they did for me. You knew... and didn't..."

"Well, no, you didn't really," Bell countered. "You just said some strange Americans rescued you. I had my ideas, but you never said..."

"Hold on a minute," John said, holding his hand in the air. "Neither of you told each other about us?"

Both of the men stared at one another and then at John. Richie stepped closer to his grandson.

"I'll make this right," Richie said, patting John on the shoulder, "Ian, we wanted to tell you, but John here – he's my grandson. We made a promise to keep their involvement a secret. You know how Bell is with his word – it's his bond."

"Grandson? He's twice your age," Ian said.

John laughed and shook his head at the obvious.

"Ian, these guys travelled through time. They're from 2016," Bell said.

"Well, 2020 this time around, to be accurate," John said.

Ian's brow curled and his attention wandered around the room.

"That's bloody-well fine, but..."

"Ian, really?" John asked, looking at the Brit.

"I suppose I wasn't very forth-coming, myself," Ian said.

"What's that supposed to mean?" Bell asked.

"It means, I never told you that I was in Bizerte that exact same night, did I?"

Bell and Richie both focused on Ian. They remembered his vague story of escape, but hadn't pressed the point.

"Well?" Bell insisted.

"I don't remember much, but this one," Ian said, pointing to John, "and two others, saved me that night. They took a painting and some other items out of Bizerte. Let's just say, I'm acquainted."

"So, we were *all* there, the whole stinking time," Bell said. "That's just great."

Zip had spent the majority of the conversation watching the others interact. His speechlessness finally broke.

"Bell, Richie, and – well I don't know you, sir," Zip said, "but it's great to see you guys again."

A few embattled smiles broke through the confusing reunion.

"I'm Ian Fleming, and you are?"

"You're *the* Ian Fleming?" Zip asked.

"Zip, can it," John said.

"Certainly," Ian said, his lips pursed at the strange inflection, "Her Majesty's MI-6 at your service."

Zip looked at John, realizing he stood in front a future icon. A dangerous thing to discuss, or even let on about. Ian looked on with some intrigue.

"Allen Doha," Zip said, extending his hand. "Everyone just calls me Zip."

"What a coincidence, old bean," Ian said as they shook. "That Marine over there – his name is Doha, if I recall it correctly."

††††

Anne set up the array, watching the two groups talking below. She took her time, picking through a few items stacked around the cavern. Her own eyes soon discovered this was real. Everything in the crates appeared to be new, even though she couldn't read the Japanese writing. Her mind considered the possibilities, still unsure how they had arrived in the past. She did feel sure this was the exact same cavern, but one second ago, it was empty. The next second, it had a few lights and was full of ordinance, weapons, and even furniture.

She made her way forward, spotting Rico and Wisp below, on the other side. She climbed down to their level. Rico was setting up a sensor on the stairway that lead up.

"What's going on?" she asked.

"I know you're freaked out. It bothered me the first couple of times. It's one thing to 'know' about it – but feeling it? That changes things."

"So, this is what happened in Nashville? Bizerte?"

"Not exactly," Wisp said, checking his command module.

"Okay – can either of you just shoot me straight?" Anne asked.

Wisp and Rico looked at each other, smiled, and synced the camera sensor to their systems.

"Sending you the code for the camera, Anne. Let's move back a little ways, in case visitors arrive," Wisp said.

She stepped back and addressed her command module, entering the code and connecting her to the camera array. The newest system allowed for multiple operators to sign into each surveillance device deployed. Arklight had also equipped each system with a small auto-destruct trigger that actuated once all connects were lost. The team knew leaving any trace of technology behind would have major implications.

"Okay. You know a lot about Nashville," Rico said, "but you were never briefed on Bizerte."

"Well?" Anne asked.

"I know," Wisp said, holding his hand up, "but compartmentalized is classified. You know how the admiral is."

"Maybe I need to know at this point."

They looked at each other and Rico nodded.

†††††

"So, Jack, that make sense?" Chappy finished.

"Yeah, but it doesn't make this any less unbelievable."

"Who's your Japanese friend on the floor?"

"He's an officer we captured on the way in. That British guy, the commander, said to bring him along. Thought he might be useful."

"Nothing but dead weight so far," Red said.

"Right," Chappy smiled, feeling a connection with the Marines. "So, your name is Doha?"

"That's right. What's it to you?"

Chappy laughed and glanced around a large crate. He saw Zip talking to the others and motioned to catch his attention.

"Zip, get over here."

A few seconds later, Zip rounded the crate, finding himself standing face-to-face with his grandfather. The thought had dawned on him earlier, but there was so much happening, he wanted to be sure first.

"PFC Ahiga Doha and Sergeant Big Jack Decker," Zip said. "It's almost just as I imagined."

"What the hell are you talking about?" Jack asked, exchanging a glance with Red.

"Did you explain?" Zip asked Chappy in a daze.

"I did. But maybe ole' Red here doesn't see the resemblance."

Red reached out with his right hand, placing it on Zip's shoulder. It reminded Zip of his youth.

"You're related to me?" he asked. "But, how?"

"You're my grandfather."

"No way. Now you're just messing with us," Jack said, throwing a hand in the air.

Red saw the conviction in Zip's face. His own bloodline from the future—here, in this place. It staggered him, and he struggled to understand. Zip placed both of his hands on Red's shoulders. They stood, locked, analyzing each other's faces, taking in the mirror-like image.

"Looks like your prisoner is starting to stir," Chappy said.

Jack drew back the butt of his rifle, ready to deliver another knock-out blow to the head.

"Wait a second," Chappy said, pushing himself between Jack and the prisoner. He knelt down, getting a closer look.

"He might be useful, yet."

†††††

Anne, Rico, and Wisp entered the center area of the cavern with John and the Alsos Team. Anne had gotten enough information to feel a little more at ease and also now knew not to discuss anything about the future. It was rule number one for Spear Team. She walked up behind John and started sorting out who was who. Ian was easy because of the accent, but Richie was even easier as he stood next to John. She turned her head, adjusting her ISR rifle. She began to study Bell, who noticed her gaze.

"So," Bell said, mistaking her interest, "what's a pretty girl like you, doing in a place like this?"

"Really?"

"What?" Bell asked, bending his head back and lifting his hands as an innocent. "I just was trying – I ... never mind."

All Anne could imagine was the man being almost 100 years old, and dead, back in their time.

"I'm sorry," she shook her head. "Bell, is it?"

"Don't worry, he has that effect on everyone, darling. I'm Ian, Commander Ian Fleming, by the way."

"Darling?" Anne asked, mindful of the era.

She blushed, not totally unaffected by Ian's well-practiced charms. Bell turned red for a different reason, but he was no stranger to offending women, or just about anyone for that matter. Rico saw Bell and reached out for his hand.

"Bell – Richie. Man, it's damn good to see you guys again," Rico said.

Wisp connected with Ian and nodded his remembrance of Bizerte.

"Steady, what's the play?" Wisp asked.

John remembered they had a mission to complete, along with the unsettling fact that there was no painting here, in their time. There was no sign of the Spear of Destiny. He was now, however, standing close to John Bell. *What about the coin?* John reached into his front pocket for the Civil War coin Bell had given to him in 1943—the same coin General John Bell Hood had minted before the Battle of Nashville. His fingers slid ever-deeper into his pocket, and there it was. It was still there. He grabbed it between his index and middle finger, pulling it out.

"Bell, you remember this?" John asked, holding the coin up.

"My coin," Bell said. "You've still got it."

††††††

Having no interest in John's retelling of the coin story, Chappy leaned around the crate with a growing smirk on his face. He saw Wisp's tall frame in the walkway.

"Hey, Wisp, I need you to come translate for us."

"Okay," Wisp said, curious to see why.

A few moments later, they joined the other group, in the rear of the cavern. He made eye-contact with the two Marines before looking on the ground. The prisoner's demeanor showed little fear – just anger concerning his capture. Wisp began to speak in Japanese.

"You are our prisoner," Wisp declared. "We expect you to act with honor. Do you understand?"

The prisoner nodded and made a few mumbles in the gag.

"You will not be harmed if you cooperate with us. You will be released, after we leave."

The man's brow furrowed and he mumbled something indiscernible.

"I'll remove the gag, but if you try to call for help – you will regret it."

The man nodded and Wisp untied the gag, removing it from the prisoner's head. The Japanese officer knew his predicament was dire as the gag was pulled down. Wisp sat back on his boot and looked at the prisoner.

"What's your name?" Wisp asked.

"Hino."

"Do you speak English?" Wisp asked.

The officer shook his head.

"What's your full name, rank, and unit?"

"Fujio Hino. 1st Lieutenant – 32nd Japanese Army."

Wisp wasn't sure of who the man was, but he could see the fire in his eyes. He looked back at Chappy, speak freely in English.

"Where did you grab this guy?" Wisp asked, looking back at Red and Jack.

"At the entrance to this place," Jack said.

"I think we need to talk this over with John," Wisp said, looking at Chappy.

†††††

The entirety of Spear Team, the Alsos Team, the Marines, and even their captive gathered in the middle of the cavern. They were surrounded by crates, ammo boxes, and a variety of valuables hidden away from the destruction of war. Ian had fished out the Knights Templar journal, holding it in his hand. John clasped the folded coin given to him by Bell back in Bizerte.

ARKLIGHT: Task Force Crusader

"Steady, all sensors and cameras are in place," Rico said. "No contacts. We're clear."

"Thanks. Look, everyone – I know this is a highly unusual situation. My team came here with a plan, and all I can tell you is… we didn't expect this. We expected to be alone – still in our time."

Jack pulled off his steel helmet and scratched his head.

"What the hell's a sensor?"

"Don't worry about it, Jack," Chappy said. "It just tells us if the enemy is near."

"Huh?"

Bell looked at Richie and then Ian.

"We came here because of the journal," Bell said, "We've been all over Europe looking for one stinking painting, and it's supposed to be here."

"Page 112, Ian," John said, realizing the paradox. "Open it and tell me what you see."

Ian flipped open the journal and discovered it was a page he had chosen to make notes on. The very page he had drawn the tunnel system on—the one that got them into the cavern.

"It had nothing on it, before I drew this earlier." He turned the book to show John.

"I'll be," John mused. "That's the… never mind."

"Tell me why you picked that page," Ian urged, his gaze locked on John's face.

John and Chappy looked at each other. Rico could see that the map matched everything they had researched.

"Look at that. How weird," Rico said, marveling over the fact that Ian had just written some of the information that helped bring Arklight to Shuri Castle. Whatever the case, the bigger problem remained the painting. They knew now that neither group had possession of it. Spear Team needed to trust the Alsos Team and the Marines. It was no time to hold back.

"Look, Ian," John said, "I need you to write this – exactly as I say it. Write it on page 112 and, you can't ask me any other questions about it."

"It could be important, need-to-know information. Matter of fact – I believe we're in a need-to-know state presently."

John looked at Richie, who already knew.

"Ian, some things are too dangerous to know," Richie said.

"I suppose you have a point, but now isn't the time for that debate."

"Can we get to writing?" John asked, flipping open his notes from Spear Team's briefing.

"I'm ready whenever you are," Ian said, his pen in hand.

"Two doors will reveal the Young Man. The Spear is stone, the stone is the path. Got it?" John asked.

Richie, at least, heard it loud and clear.

"That's the painting," Richie said, "*Portrait of a Young Man*. That's the same one we're looking for. It has to be here."

"Small world," Zip said.

"More like a weird, bad dream," Wisp added.

A few seconds of silence settled among the group. Jack looked at Red.

"A freaking painting? All this – for a painting?" Jack asked.

"Can someone please explain to us what the hell is going on?" Red asked, looking at Zip.

"I wish we had that kind of time," John said, "but we don't. Just know as ridiculous as all of this sounds, the fate of the world hangs in the balance."

"We're used to that. This war has been going on for years already."

Zip smiled, knowing how battle-hardened his grandfather had come to be.

"Look, this is a lot to take in, I know," he said. "But, you have to realize something: this *has* to stay a secret. I won't be born for years to come, and you can't tell anyone, anything about it. It would ruin history. Does that make any sense?"

Red's eyes searched around the room in thought. He looked at Jack once more.

"He's got a point."

"Okay," Jack said, "we can keep our mouths shut – but what's in it for us?"

Zip's grandfather always talked about his war buddy Jack when he was growing up, but Zip had never gotten to meet him. There were so many stories, but nothing about this mission. They must have stayed true to their word.

"What do you want?" Zip asked.

Jack's forehead wrinkled in thought.

"I don't know."

"Maybe we can cross that bridge later?" Red asked.

"Let's just focus on staying alive for now," Zip said.

John and Richie stared at each other during the exchange. They both felt like Zip had a story to tell of his own.

"We need to put our cards on the table," John said, watching Zip deep in thought. "We used the journal in our time, along with some other intelligence, to find out that *Portrait of a Young Man* was hidden under this castle. But now I think some of the information we had was yours."

Bell and Ian looked at Richie. Anne found a crate to sit on next to Chappy. Her head was swimming.

"I'm lost," Anne said.

"Me too. Don't feel bad. This is a mess," Rico said.

Richie grabbed the journal from Ian and stood beside John.

"We've been through Sicily, Switzerland, France, Poland, and Germany tracking this one painting."

"Why?" Wisp asked.

"Because we believe that it holds a secret. Ever hear of a piece called the Lance of Longinus – the Spear of Destiny?"

"Yes, of course," Zip said. "It's the piece of Arma Christi we've been after. The spear used to stab Jesus Christ on the Cross. It's part of the *tunc clavem*."

John exhaled and tilted his head back. Zip just shared too much.

"What's a *tunc clavem*?" Ian asked.

"Before we go there," John said, "finish how you got here."

"Long story short," Richie said as he flipped through the journal, "we tracked the painting down to Hans Frank, but it was Hildebrand Gurlitt who told us the painting was in Okinawa. It was traded by the Nazis to the Emperor of Japan for war support."

John saw the picture forming.

"We saw a picture of the Emperor with the painting... here in the castle. So, that makes sense."

"Well, the last best information we got says it should be right here."

"Like right here in the castle – or right here in this cave?" Chappy asked.

"I'm hoping somewhere in this underground network, but it could be anywhere," Ian concluded.

John thought about the phrase he had given Ian. It was what led them into the cavern, but now it was just something he told Ian to write. It was enough to make his head pound.

"Back to my question. What's the *tunc clavem*?" Ian asked.

Maybe this, too, was part of the paradox. John looked at Rico, knowing he would disapprove of his tactics, but in this case, he felt led.

"Gentlemen, in our time we've discovered some things about the journal, about the Templar, the ultimate weapon, and maybe what this is all leading to."

Bell sat forward.

"Is this not too dangerous for us to know? You know, the future?" Bell asked.

"Maybe knowing will give us an edge?" Ian asked.

"Perhaps," Rico said, "or it could spin everything out of control – altering history and destroying the future."

"Only one thing has been in my head," John said, looking at Bell, "at least since we ran into you. Want to know what it is?"

"What?" Bell asked.

"'My future is in your hands,'" John said. "'Rescue me from those who hunt me down relentlessly.'"

"A Psalm of King David," Bell said, remembering a faith he had almost forgotten because of the war. He thought for a moment, realizing how far he had fallen since the beginning. The war had changed him, but seeing John again reminded him of who he should be. "Yeah, I'm tired of trying to figure all of this out. Maybe a little faith is in order."

"Maybe so," Rico said.

John looked at Rico, history on his mind. A simple nod to John signaled his decision. John looked around the room and everyone stared back at him. He arrived to Chappy and stopped.

"Don't look at me," Chappy said.

John paused, thinking about all they had experienced.

"We've discovered so much. The *tunc clavem*—or in English, the Time Key—is a compilation of different pieces of Arma Christi. These smaller weapons, the Titulus Crucis, the 30 pieces of silver paid to Judas Iscariot, and the Spear of Destiny, work together to form the Time Key."

"Okay, that's what we know," Bell said.

"The Time Key has to be assembled into one piece. The device will then be used to open what's referred to as the *Temple*," John continued.

"What's that?" Richie asked.

"That's the part we don't completely understand. According to an old Templar legend, the Time Key is what will open the Ark of the Covenant."

"Whoa," Bell said, "that's the ultimate weapon – isn't it?"

"I believe so."

"What's it supposed to do?" Ian asked.

John cut his eyes to Anne, sharing a look, knowing she would feel differently. She drew her head back and narrowed her gaze.

"You remember your mission to rescue Professor Amaldi in Sicily?" John asked.

"How did you?... wait – the future," Bell said. "Yes."

"The code he discovered – the one that the Nazis were trying to decipher? That code was more than plans for an atomic weapon; it was the blueprint to a large, circular particle collision device."

"Yes, Otto Hahn confirmed all of that for us, but what about the pocket nuke?" Ian asked.

"Pocket nuke?" Wisp replied.

John's stare widened at something he hadn't heard before.

"Ian – say that again."

"When we caught up to our friend Otto in Germany," Ian said, "he told us that Himmler and Gurlitt gave him enough information to build a 5-kiloton pocket nuclear weapon. I, for one, believed him. He's been an Ally since Geneva."

A sickness crept over John at the collision of information.

"Geneva?" John asked.

"Yeah," Richie said, "we ran into Hahn there. That's where he confirmed the code Amaldi found. He also mentioned Gurlitt."

"Well, then this next part gets even more disturbing – especially after what you just shared."

"Just spit it out," Bell said.

"The Large Hadron Particle Collider was built in Geneva many years ago in our time. The collider, the Ark, and the Time Key all function together somehow. My best guess is that they open a gateway or a portal of some kind."

"How so?" Bell asked.

John looked at Anne.

"Can you explain?"

"Sure," Anne said, pushing up to her feet. "The collider uses magnets to speed up subatomic material, moving them in opposite directions. It slowly uses its charge to increase the rate of movement to light speed, and beyond. Then, they use the magnets to precisely align the material where it slams together creating – well no one really knows. Some say it's dark matter, some say black holes, and others say pathways into other dimensions."

"I don't know what that all means, but it sounds very bad," Ian said.

"It's supposed to be advancing science, but in this light – it does sound bad," Anne said.

"John, don't beat around the bush. Just tell us what you think," Richie said.

"Kieffer. Alfred Kieffer—"

"The Nazi bastard who shot Richie?" Bell inquired. "What about him?"

"His son and grandson are the ones trying to get to the ultimate weapon in our time. All of this is connected," Rico said.

"So, he did escape," Bell said, elbowing Richie. "I bet what we heard was true."

Ian looked at Bell and then to Richie.

"John, finish telling us what this weapon really is," Ian said.

"Here's the short version – but this is just a guess. The Ark and the Time Key have to be brought to Geneva, or somewhere around the collider. They spin up the particles and collide them at the same time the key is inserted into the Ark, or the Temple. Here's the catch. In the hands of evil, the weapon will bring about a hell on earth. In the hands of the righteous, a better life."

"What's that supposed to mean?" Richie asked.

"I don't think anyone really knows," Zip said, "but it sounds bad – like in an everyone-will-die sort of way."

"We have to get to it first," Bell said.

"The problem is," Chappy interjected, "the Kieffers, or O'Keefes, or whatever they go by, have had possession of the journal since like the late 1960's. We just retrieved it four years ago, so they have one hell of a head start."

Anne shook her head and held up a hand, as if she were back in grade school.

"Am I to believe that all of you believe this – nonsense? It all sounds like some ridiculous quest. I assure you, there's an explanation. Old legends are simply things too technologically advanced for people of the time to understand."

"Don't mind her," Chappy said, rolling his eyes. "She's new."

Anne huffed and turned off to think. John watched her walk away and turned to the rest of the group.

"Now that we all know what's at stake, we need to work together."

Bell nodded in agreement

"What's the play?" Ian asked.

"I'll take part of my team to recon the area and leave two here for overwatch," John said. "You guys start looking for the *Portrait of a Young Man* in this cave. We should be able to keep the enemy off of you."

"Jolly good plan," Ian said. "It's better than what we had in mind at the onset, anyway."

CHAPTER 10: STALKER

"Physical discipline may well save them from death."
Proverbs 23:14

1500-Zulu Time 24May2020 (0000-JST 25May2020 Kadena, AFB)

The nondescript, white box van eased to a stop at the main gate. Security Police conducted their usual sweep for bombs and signaled for the front window to be rolled down. Bright lights shined into the driver's compartment. Ronnie handed the young Air Force SP his clipboard.

"Good morning, sir," said the SP.

"I guess you're right – it is morning now," Ronnie said. "Been a long night, Airman?"

The SP broke a slight smile and looked at the clipboard.

"Where you headed?"

"We have a delivery to the airfield. Hangar 9, I think," Ronnie said.

"Yeah, I see that. What's the cargo?"

"They didn't say. By the code on the invoice, looks like aviation parts."

"You got your ID card?"

"Right here," Ronnie said, handing him a forged civilian worker card.

The SP inspected the card and flipped it over, checking the watermarks.

"Well, Mr. Young, looks to be in order," said the SP, handing back the ID and the clipboard.

"Cool. Hey… you guys take it easy," Ronnie said as he rolled forward and accelerated away from the gate. After passing the backup SP group posted inside, Ronnie knocked on the pass-through door.

"All clear, Stevo."

A bald-headed, stocky man slid open the door, his German accent thick and gritty.

"I told you that ID was flawless."

"Good work. Now we just need to get through the gate to the airfield. Once inside, we'll find the bastards we need to take out. And hey, make sure your men understand that we have a few minutes before the base comes down on us. If they don't make exfil, they get left."

The man turned to address a small unit of armed men.

"You Brandenburger dogs understand? We're in and out – kill'em all."

†††††

"Admiral, slow down, sir, you're losing me," the chief said into the receiver as he paced inside the Ark.

"Maximillion beat us to it is what I'm trying to tell you," Nathan said, "We got to Birch Island and found where they excavated it. They have the Ark of the Covenant."

"Damn. What the hell are we supposed to do now?"

"I don't know, Chief. But, there's something else we discovered."

"What's that?"

"There's possibly another piece of the Time Key we over looked. We found a gold plate in the room where the Ark was stored. It had a picture of a man. A man I believe to be Joseph of Arimathea."

"Who's that?"

"The Bible links him directly to Christ. He asked to be responsible for taking Jesus to his burial site. The scriptures refer to him as the secret disciple."

"I'm still not following."

"Legend has it that Joseph used the Holy Grail to catch the blood of Christ. The real Grail has never been found because Joseph hid it away. He knew the blood of Christ was too powerful to fall into the wrong hands. Maybe he also knew about the Time Key – that the Grail was the final piece needed."

Chief stroked his mustache and shook his head in distress.

"Sir, do you think John has been right? You know… about all of this leading to the end?"

"I've been skeptical from the beginning, but after seeing what we just saw, I'm starting to believe it's real. This entire sequence of events – it's leading to something."

A pause held on the line with some faint static.

"Chief, we need to focus on getting the Spear of Destiny. We still have an advantage. We hold most of the Arma Christi, and they might not know we have it. Time is on our side. When Spear Team gets back, tell John about the Grail. I'll see what I can find in the journal."

"Roger that. I'll call you after."

†††††

As they lifted into the ink-black sky, the rumble of two F-15E jet fighters shook the hangar where Arklight had taken temporary residence. The Command and Information Center (CIC) and the Ark sat inside. Two C-17 Globemasters were parked on the tarmac, facing away from the hangar, with their cargo doors open. The chief exited the Ark, his mind struggling to fit the pieces together. He stepped up to the door of the CIC, seeing several uniformed personnel sitting at various computerized terminals.

"Tim, what's the sit-rep?"

A tall, skinny ensign looked across the luminescent corridor. Faint lights of blue, red, and green flickered in the mirror of his pupils.

"Still no changes at the target site, Chief."

"Any signs of movement around the castle?"

"Negative… Everything looks quiet."

The chief craned his head around to see his new communications officer hard at work. Anne was hard to replace, but Ensign Carol Sparks filled her shoes the best way she knew how – with constant, meticulous attention to detail.

"Carol, anything from Spear Team?"

She typed in some mission notes as she looked back at the chief. Her hair was in a bun, her voice confident.

"Nothing since they entered the throne structure. All trackers and coms are offline."

"Roger that. I'm stepping outside for a few. Call me if there are any changes."

"I will. We're in good shape," Carol said.

Chief exited the CIC and walked through the ajar hangar doors. Warm, fresh, salty night air filled his nose with each breath. *Just like Coronado*, he thought back to his younger days in the teams. He approached his team's C-17, stepping on the rear ramp and walking inside.

"Where are my cigars?"

He overheard the screech of tires sliding to a stop on the coated tarmac. The sound came from the other side of the second C-17. A door slammed, then another. The chief stood up and walked back to the ramp. A dozen men, armed to the teeth, ran toward the hangar. No uniforms, no markings of any kind.

"Magnus…"

The chief reached for his pistol, feeling nothing of comfort on his hip. It was inside the Ark. Two men approached, clearing the C-17 to his right. Something had to be done. He reacted and prepared by stringing some loose netting across the floor, ankle-high. Seeing men moving in his direction, he retreated further inside the aircraft's fuselage. Shots rang out from within the hangar. Muzzle flashes reflected past the slit in the gigantic doors like a strobe.

"Dammit," Chief said, his brow furrowed. "Work the problem, Boomer."

††††††

Ronnie followed behind his main assault force as they entered the hangar, firing at anything that moved. He stepped to the right of the entry point and saw some of his men closing on the CIC. The other five flanked to his left, collapsing their sectors of fire back toward the main force. A tall, thin sailor cut down the angle from the door. He fired several shots from his pistol, striking one of Ronnie's men. That didn't concern him as much as the hole in the wall – next to his own head.

"Push right!"

Ronnie saw his men firing at the sailor. Clouds of dark mist floated in the air as one of his men fell. He ran to the downed mercenary who was bleeding from an open head wound.

"He's done! Keep pushing!" Ronnie yelled.

The remaining mercs on the right worked to see inside the CIC, taking cover when small arms fire erupted in their direction. Ronnie looked to his left and motioned for the flanking force to close in on the resistance.

"Get in there!"

Another burst of fire plinked off of the metal of the hangar. Both of Ronnie's teams stalled. He pulled a grenade from his chest rig, snatched the pin, released the spoon, held it for a one-count, and threw it into the doorway of the steel box.

BOOM.

"Move!" he cried, rushing past his men. He led with his rifle, looking through the door of the structure. Equipment sparked and smoked, flickering with damage. Two bodies were down, including the one dead sailor they had shot. He scanned the room.

"Where are you?" he muttered, directing his men in to clear with a hand signal.

††††††

Boots left the soft surface of the tarmac and *clinked* onto the rear ramp of the chief's C-17. Light streaked into the long corridor of the cargo bay. Boxes lined the interior of the aircraft. The chief knelt behind a crate, halfway into the plane. He closed his eyes, sharpening his hearing as the two armed men approached. Time wasn't on his side, but he had to get to his kit and get in that hangar. The metallic *clicks* drew within feet of his position. One of them was breathing through his mouth. *First timer,* he thought, reaching for his CQC folder in his trouser pocket. He locked the tanto-blade of the combat knife into place.

"Watch out for that net," the lead man said, turning back to look at his companion.

The chief exploded from his hide, closing on the lead assaulter. He parried the man's weapon, plunging his knife deep in the jugular. The second man jumped back in shock, raising his weapon in defense. In perfect form, the chief locked his concentration upon the next threat, placing his right foot behind the already limp legs of the first man. Tightening his grip on the knife handle, he grabbed the upper arm of his dying adversary with his left hand, jerking the man around with one twist, throwing him into the second assaulter.

A round fired off as the two men collided, striking Chief in the upper left arm. He felt the round pass through the muscle, but gave it little thought. He charged at the off-balance gunman, knocking him into the bulkhead of the aircraft. His partner collapsed in a bloody heap at his feet. The second assaulter raised his head in time to see the chief's knife stabbing downward. The man used his left arm to block, but the momentum was too much to overcome. A piercing pain cut through the man's eye socket, followed by a forearm crushing down on his windpipe.

Sweat dripped off the chief's nose from the instantaneous stress. Gasps choked out of the man – his final, suffocated attempts at drawing breath. He looked toward the hangar doors as the second assaulter's body fell limp. Chief pulled the rifle away, picking over the dead man's gear for spare magazines. No one else had emerged from the hangar.

Through the hangar doors, he saw several more flashes of light surge, accompanied by cracks of thunderous gunfire. His hands found two grenades, and he stuffed them into his trouser pockets.

"I take my freaking pistol off for one minute," he grumbled. "Shit!"

†††††

"They're in the back, next to that other steel box!" Ronnie yelled over the sporadic discharges.

The men to his left were pinned down behind several clunky crates. His team wasn't much better off. The easy prey he had hoped for turned out to be well-armed. He waved his arm at one of his men on the left until he got his attention. Ronnie grabbed a second grenade and held it up, followed by three fingers. The man nodded as dust and debris showered down on him from the withering fire.

"On my mark!"

Ronnie stepped back from his cover and pulled the pin, eyes locked on the other team. His man across the hangar mimicked his movement, followed by two others. Ronnie pointed his finger in the direction of his throw so the others could see. He lobbed the baseball-sized grenade across the hangar. Three others released, curling into the air – all descending in the area of the Ark.

Four simultaneous concussive blasts rocked the area around the Arklight personnel. Screams and moans of pain replaced what had been sure-fire resistance. Ronnie gritted his teeth, feeling certain he had just taken away his opponents' will to fight.

"Move in!"

††††††

Blood dripped from the chief's elbow as he press-checked his newly acquired AR-15A3 rifle. He verified that the holographic sights were functional and stuffed three extra magazines into his back pockets. His own kit was inside the hangar, out of reach. Time was running out. He searched over himself, realizing he was soaked in gore. The throbbing burn in his arm was no match for the pain he would feel over losing his people.

He tilted the barrel of the rifle into the air and exited the C-17. A series of explosions sounded from inside the hangar. He dashed toward the fight. His grip on the rifle was as natural as any craftsman holding a tool of their trade. The famed SEAL still had fight in him, even though his body had aged past his prime.

A plan formed in the chief's head as he approached the large doors. The emergency call box was on the far side of the hangar, and based on the direction of the gunfire, he had a chance to get there. He stopped at the door, slicing the angle to his right. He knew the assaulters were moving toward the CIC and the Ark. The explosions gave their position away.

He caught some movement through a few crates and boxes on the floor. He looked deeper inside the structure, seeing more movement on the left. *I'm behind them.* He had surprise on his side. Once he confirmed the general location of the enemy, he craned his head through the doorway, looking for the call box. There it was against the opposite wall; he had to chance it. His sat-phone was in the Ark, but at least this line would go straight to base security.

Chief entered the hangar, splitting cover on the teams moving in on his people. He hoped they could hold out long enough for him to outthink their attackers. It was an excruciating tactical move, but he knew he might not survive, anyway – they were outnumbered. Fact was, they needed all the help they could get, and that took priority over charging into a firefight ill-prepared. With stealth-like precision, he weaved his way backward, monitoring for any signs that the enemy was aware of his presence.

He reached the phone and pulled up the receiver. Each ring felt like an eternity, especially once his mind had time to tune into the screams of pain across the hangar. Those grenades had taken an awful toll on Arklight's mission team. Tears of rage filled his eyes. A choking lump hung in his throat.

"How could this happen?" he uttered aloud, looking up.

The line picked up and a female's voice answered.

"Base security, Airman…"

"Listen up – this is Master Chief Lincoln, Hangar 9. We're under attack by a small force of about a dozen hostiles, heavily armed, with assault rifles and grenades. I need a quick reaction force immediately – or we're all dead."

"Sir?"

"You freaking heard me… get some meat-eaters headed this way. The base is under attack – Hangar 9."

"But…"

He left the receiver hanging from the box. He saw movement and closed in on several men to his left. The other group was too far ahead. The men he saw were obvious flank support. Someone, maybe all of them, had military training. He knew he needed to maintain surprise.

†††††

Ronnie exited what remained of the CIC. He cut the corner down with the barrel of his rifle, eyeing the forward corner of the Ark, to his right. Sparks snapped into the air from all of the damaged computer equipment. Hazy, white smoke rolled upwards. He heard someone in anguish.

"Hang in there," a voice said from behind the Ark.

Another sizzle of electronic disruption crackled as Ronnie motioned for his men to move forward. Three of them pressed past as he held up an exposed wiring harness with his offhand. He heard movement behind him to his left and looked over his shoulder. The men on his flank had cleared some offices on the other side of the expansive hangar. He squeezed the mic on his radio.

"Magnus, you copy?"

A few seconds later, static crackled over the air.

"Go ahead, mate."

"We're on target and I think we got 'em all. What's your status?"

"Excellent. On target ourselves. We're in position. Looks like they tranqed the security team. No contact yet."

"Okay, I'll call you when we get clear."

Ronnie turned to see his men pointing their weapons around the corner of the second large steel container. One of the men turned his head.

"I got six more down back here," the man said, "Do you know how many we're looking for?"

"Not sure. Any alive?"

"Two are still breathing, but just barely."

"Okay, coming," Ronnie said, squeezing his mic once more, "Stevo, keep checking the offices. Take out anything that moves."

"Gotcha."

Ronnie turned his attention forward and walked around the corner of the Ark. His men had their weapons trained on two other wounded, uniformed personnel. A female wearing a flight-suit had a tourniquet around her upper right arm. Dark crimson covered the sleeve and her face was marred with superficial scratches. A man lay next to her, blood oozing from his nose and ears. He had lost consciousness, still clutching onto a rifle. Four other victims lay scattered about the floor, some in pieces splattered against the metal wall of the hangar. The mercenary in front of Ronnie grabbed the rifle, throwing it far from reach.

"Hey," Ronnie said, nudging the unconscious man with his foot, "wake up, douche-bag."

The man stirred; his swollen-shut eyes rolled around in his head. The female coughed, her body heaving. She looked at Ronnie. Her nose and ears still bled.

"You're American… but why?"

"Why? Because – there's money in it, lady. Lots and lots of money."

He watched as tears streamed down the woman's cheeks. The sorrow held no place with him. Her team, the entire CIC staff, was no more. She looked to her left and saw that the damage to her arm. Ronnie knew she was critical. The man next to her, lay unconscious. Ronnie saw the tourniquet on her arm. It saved her life for now. He watched the man's chest rise and fall in a labored fashion. She tried shaking him with her good hand.

"Tim, wake up," she said.

Ronnie knelt down and looked at the leather badge on the man's uniform.

"Gunnery Sergeant Timothy Blackwell. Looks like he's not going to make it I'm afraid." Ronnie said, looking at her badge. "Ensign Carol… Thomas."

She turned with what energy she could stir and looked at Ronnie.

"What do you want with us? We're just a logistical research group."

"How many people are here?" Ronnie demanded.

She looked around, scared they had gotten everyone. But she didn't see the chief, or the aircrews. She hoped they had gotten away, or were bringing help.

††††††

A fire of emotion burned inside the chief's chest. His full attention locked on his first target, like a shark to prey. The man stood back, watching the other four clear the rooms along the back wall of the hangar. The chief gripped his knife, slinging the rifle across his back. He was feet away, ready to attack, when he heard a voice in the distance. Someone was still alive. It gave him some hope, but he knew they wouldn't last long.

In one rapid movement, he closed in on the man; cupping the merc's mouth to control the head, he jabbed his knife into the upper back.

163

Without hesitation, he retracted the blade and cut across the neck, severing the vocal cords. The chief's tight grip controlled the brief struggle until his enemy collapsed. He deposited the body on the floor and moved up, looking for the next opportunity to level the playing field.

Base alert sirens sounded in the distance. At least they took his call seriously. He realized he could use the pulse of audible sirens to his advantage. The chief rolled the rifle off his back, grasping it with expert intent. He led with the barrel toward the offices, catching two men exiting one door, while another two stood ready to enter the next office. They were all lined up in front of him.

He had to move fast. He shouldered his weapon, taking calculated aim below the body armor of the assaulters. He switched the safety to full-auto, gripped the rifle, and aimed for the pelvic bowls and the thighs of the men. *Cripple them quickly and follow up,* he thought. The rifle stock locked between his cheek and shoulder, his eye picked up the holographic sight, and he squeezed, holding the trigger down.

The clatter of rifle fire swept left to right, cutting through all four men. Small clouds of pink spray fogged the air under the lights of the hangar. The bolt of the rifle locked back. The chief pressed the magazine release, reloading the rifle with a fresh stack of rounds from his back pocket. He reacquired the screaming heap of armored men, who were bleeding and writhing in pain on the ground. He closed in on the group, placing a single shot in each of their heads.

On his way past, he grabbed an extra magazine off of one of his foes, noticing a throat mic around his neck. A red light flashed on the radio. Chief snatched off the throat mic and detached the ear bud from the dead man's ear. He stuck the bud up to his own, listening to the traffic.

"Stevo, that's a bit of overkill over there. You got 'em?"

The chief covered the mic with has hand and scrubbed it back and forth, hoping the resulting noise would pass for static.

"Yeah," he said.

"We've got to go."

The sirens continued, masking his movement. He heard police sirens closing in the distance. Security was on the way.

"Harris," Ronnie said, looking at the guy next to him, "you and Jones go check on Stevo and his team. Tell them we need to extract, now."

The two men nodded and moved toward the other side of the hangar. Carol coughed up spatter, continuing to stare at Ronnie with contempt. He looked back at her as she clung on to consciousness.

"Don't freaking look at me. You probably don't even know what this is all about anyway. You've been lied to, just like the government does to all of us. You're on the wrong side."

Her brow knotted at his statements. The pain she felt made her entire body ache.

"Wrong side?" she asked.

Ronnie stood up, took off his backpack, and pulled a length of four separate, yet attached foam pieces from the inner compartment. He pulled a clear strip off of one piece and stuck it to the metal wall of the hangar.

"Yeah, wrong side. Do you even know what you're doing here?"

She watched as he placed each length of foam on the wall, creating a perfect square. It was just feet beyond where she lay. A frigid chill caused her to shake uncontrollably. Ronnie looked back at her.

"That's shock setting in. Do you know why you're here?"

"We're here," she coughed, "to fight evil people – like you."

"Yeah, whatever... You're here because somebody told you to be here – you're getting freaking paid, just like me. That's why you're *really* here."

She coughed again, wiping her mouth off.

"What are you doing?"

Ronnie poked something into the foam, taking enough time to make sure it was set in place. He looked back at her as he stepped away from the foam device, reeling out what looked to be wires.

"I'm gonna go get my money, Carol. That's what I'm doing. The only difference between you and me? I'm not a slave to the system."

"Where are you going?" she asked as terror crept over her.

Ronnie stepped around the corner of the Ark. She realized what he was doing.

"Please, no!"

He initiated the shaped charge, blowing a square hole into the wall of the hangar. He walked back around the corner, looking down on

Carol's broken body, charred and tattered with bits of debris. Somehow, she was still breathing.

"Sorry, lady. Suffering's just part of life."

He stepped through the wall and into the night.

††††††

The chief flinched at the explosion, ducking out of instinct. He looked in the direction of the flash, just next to the Ark. His rifle was at the low-ready as he turned the corner. Two more men stood, guns trained at him. He couldn't engage them both and survive. He dove across the corridor as rounds blasted in his wake, some catching him in the leg. A white-hot stinging in his calf told him his mobility was compromised. He ignored the pain, reaching in his pocket for one of the grenades he had picked up.

Rounds splintered the wooden crates and cordite filled the air—the two men were whittling away his cover. They moved aggressively, pressing a tactical advantage, firing toward the corner. One weapon clicked empty, and the man moved, switching magazines.

"Cover!"

"Copy that. Cut it down!" the other yelled. "We got you, asshole."

The merc pulled his rifle stock tight into his shoulder and stared down the rail, his eye focused on the sight. The other followed, fixated straight ahead while his associate cleared the remaining angle.

"He's gone."

They walked up beside one another, confused to where their target went.

A cold chill shot up the chief's spine. The throbbing burn made him want to vomit as he circled behind the two mercs. He released the grenade, sliding it across the floor, striking one of the men in the foot. The mercenary turned and looked down, feeling the impact, confirming his fear.

BOOM.

The grenade blast shook the hangar. The chief recovered, staggering toward his kit, still locked in the travel box next to the Ark. He fell to the floor, the intensity of the pain trembling his body. Once he unlocked the

166

box, all he could think to grab was his medical kit. The trail of crimson smear that followed him would panic most soldiers, but for the chief, it was calming. The bleeds weren't critical, although they burned like hot-pokers imbedded in his skin. He cinched a tourniquet down on his upper-right thigh and jammed gauze into the wound, gritting his teeth with each press.

His hands were sticky with gore, not all his own. He fought to get another tourniquet on his upper arm. Pain vibrated throughout his body with each turn of the lever, cutting off the pulsating flow to his limbs. He strained with his better arm to uproot a dose of pain-killer once he had completed his temporary medical measures. He had to finish clearing the hangar, and he prayed someone was left alive. Sirens closed in; base security was almost on the scene. He reached into his kit and grasped his spare handgun before standing to his feet. He limped toward the Ark; hopeful his team had somehow survived the brutal attack.

Electric sparks flickered inside the CIC. Monitors were riddled with bullet holes, and wires arced from the destruction, glowing like severed arms, reaching skyward for help that wouldn't arrive. Bodies were scattered about, dashing the chief's hope. Nothing stirred. He stumbled his way through the CIC, rounding the corner toward the Ark. Even with shaky hands, his pistol led the advance. He heard voices entering the hangar behind him.

"Alpha team, clear right! Bravo team, take the left!"

It had to be the base's special reaction team. He continued to labor his way through the debris-covered corridor. He moved along the backside of the Ark. Boots on the ground, one moved – only slightly. On the opposite wall, he saw a square hole leading outside. He continued clearing, until he saw Carol. Her body was tattered and shredded; there were so many bleeds, he didn't even know where to start. He collapsed to his knees beside her, seeing she still held onto Tim Blackwell.

"Why?"

Carol strained to open one ruptured eye, squinting at him. Her face was bruised and battered.

"You made it," she coughed.

"Carol, hang in there."

"I… I have to tell you," she said, struggling to speak, "It's beautiful…"

"What?"

"Follow it through," she mumbled, "the darkness can never extinguish the light."

His chest burned with despair as she took her last labored breath. He looked past her, seeing his entire team slaughtered on the floor. He fought to breathe, choked by emotion. Tears flowed down his cheeks. His hand covered her open eyes, forcing her eyelids to shut. Footsteps closed in behind him as he collapsed on the floor, struggling to fight back the sorrow. He rolled on his back; his stare still locked on Carol. Beams of light closed in, until one shined down on his face.

"We got a survivor!"

†††††

Ronnie drove through the airfield gate, staring in the rearview mirror. He could see the commotion inside of the guard shack as he past. The timing of the operation worked out, and he had no spare baggage to contend with. None of the men he had used for the operation made it to the rendezvous point. He was the only one to make it out. He keyed up his radio.

"Magnus, you copy?"

"Go ahead," Magnus said.

"I'm free and clear. Their command and control element is done."

"Excellent work, mate. Did you plant the tracking devices on their planes?"

"I know we got one tagged. Resistance was stiffer than we anticipated. I'm the only one who got out."

"Did they get killed, or captured?"

"I'm not sure," Ronnie said. "I had to get out while I could."

"Get to the extraction point. Only a few hours now, Ronnie. You'll soon be rich beyond measure," Magnus said, laughing.

"Sounds good," Ronnie smiled. "See you there."

Magnus pulled his radio away and pointed to one of the men in his group.

"Set up the ambush spot there," Magnus said, turning to look at the high ground. "Put overwatch there and there."

Several other men blanketed the area, ready to address anyone who emerged from the main hall of Shuri Castle. Magnus stood ready, his trap set. He keyed back up his radio.

"Ronnie, I may be in a bit of a rush when I show up, so be ready."

"Copy that. Just radio me when you're inbound."

CHAPTER 11: BETRAYAL

"Then Satan entered into Judas Iscariot, who was one of the twelve disciples."
Luke 22:3

1600-Zulu Time 24May2020 (2000-AST Nova Scotia, Canada)

The Blackhawk's landing gear settled on the tarmac. Rod Johnson slid open the side door and stepped out of the chopper, beneath the whine of the turbines. Two other helicopters landed nearby, both stuffed with SEAL Gold Squadron operators. He watched the men disembark and head toward the C-130 that was tasked to take them back home.

Nathan walked up beside Rod. The two men watched as Walter's CIA helicopter circled in for a landing. The Halifax-Stanfield International Airport had cleared space for the U.S. military aircraft, but Nathan wanted to clear out before they overstayed their welcome. The sun was settled low on the western horizon. The Arklight Gulfstream could get them back to Mayport NAS before midnight.

"Well, Nathan, looks like we got lots to discuss on the ride back."

"Yeah, I just wonder what's on Walter's mind. He knows more."

"True. I think it's time for ole Walter to clue us in on *everything* he knows about that damn journal."

Nathan laughed, "I wouldn't hold your breath."

Rod smiled and patted Nathan on the shoulder before turning to walk away. Nathan stood still, watching Archie and Helen help Walter off his helicopter. The three of them approached him, stopping short. Walter propped on his cane. He looked over Nathan's shoulder, watching Rod shake hands with one of the Gold Squadron men. Both Helen and Archie flanked Walter, and the look on their faces was solemn.

Walter focused back on Nathan.

"Maximillion has the Ark," Walter said. "The time is upon us."

"What time are you referring to?" Archie asked.

Nathan and Walter exchanged glances – they both reflected in silence. A frigid breeze rippled across Nathan's face, shivering his spine. The visions of death, suffering, plague, and famine all hit him at once. A light burned through it all with nightmarish intensity. A singular, brilliant, clear sunbeam shone in the distance. Nathan's face grew pale, and his stomach soured. Walter placed his hand upon his shoulder. Instantly, peace settled in Nathan's heart. The light warmed him.

"You and John are the key," Walter said.

Helen grabbed Archie by the arm.

"Archie, how about we go ahead and board the plane?"

"Sounds good to me," Archie said, patting her hand. "I need a drink."

Helen laughed as they walked toward the Gulfstream. Walter squeezed Nathan's shoulder, looking toward the jet, his eyes distant. Everything was about to change.

✝✝✝✝✝

At Shuri Castle, Magnus looked over the live video monitors in the security office. A labored snore distracted his concentration on the camera feeds. He pulled out one of his pistols, aiming it at the noise, and discharged a single round into the head of the tranquilized security officer.

"Now, then. Some quiet." He holstered his weapon and propped his feet up on the counter.

"Stay sharp in the tunnels," Magnus radioed. "They came in this way, so they might try to exfil toward you."

"We copy. They won't know what hit 'em," a raspy voice replied.

The security room was coated in a dim amber glow. Magnus stuck a cigarette in his mouth, ready for a quick break. He clicked his lighter and inhaled the smoke, feeling in complete control of the situation. Ronnie had come through on his end. GPS trackers were in place on the aircraft of his enemy. Now he needed to kill this other team, get the *Portrait of a Young Man* painting, and follow the trail to the rest of the Arma Christi. Taking out their command element was just the start; collecting the whole lot of relics would gain him the world.

Just as he indulged the thought, his satellite phone sent a vibrating buzz through his vest. He flicked open the antenna and pulled the device to his ear.

"Yes?"

"You in place?" Maximillion asked.

"We are, Father. Ronnie came through and is already moving toward extraction."

"Excellent. What's your timeline?"

"I've got them surrounded. I should have it within the next two or three hours. I'll call you once we get airborne."

"Did you get the trackers in place?"

"We did. Ronnie said the surveillance was right on. Their CIC is totally disabled. Time for Grandfather to take care of what's left."

"You've planned well, boy. It's time to call him."

"What's the plan?" Magnus asked.

"Let's just say, we've got an inside man. Someone your grandfather put in place from the beginning."

"Who is it?"

"Not for you to worry about. Not yet, anyway. You'll know when it's time. Stick to the plan."

Magnus hissed and gritted his teeth.

"Aye, Father. I'll call you when I have it."

He pulled the phone away and folded it back into his vest. A long draw on his cigarette stirred his thoughts. It was the first time his father had spoken kindly to him in years, although the elevated mood was due to the Ark being in his custody. Earning some respect from his father, and even his grandfather, might prove useful in the end. All of Magnus' thoughts turned to controlling the ultimate weapon, gaining fortune, and owning the world. He sat back in a cloud of smoke, dreaming of a life without them in it. A life where he was master of all things.

††††††

"Nathan, would you hold my cane for a moment?" Walter asked, handing him the well-crafted, metal and wood stick before he answered. He then tucked in his shirt and tugged at his collar, adjusting himself.

They stood in a more secluded section of the airport. The wind picked up; the C-130 transport was loaded and taxiing for the runway. The roar of jet engines taking to the sky managed to drown out the rotors of the Blackhawks, lifting off for their destination in Maine. Nathan used the deafening sounds to steel himself for the road ahead. Something terrible was on the horizon. Facing it didn't bother him, and running away wasn't an option. However, being ill-equipped and uninformed was a serious obstacle to overcome. Seeing the light at the end of this very long tunnel was what he needed. He was no stranger to enduring pain, but pain without purpose served no decent ends.

The sound soon abated enough to talk.

"How about we cut through the bullshit and you tell me the truth. All of it. Right here, right now."

Walter smiled and grabbed his cane from Nathan's hand.

"I told Archie last year, you'd be the one to take us through to the end."

"Dammit! What end, Walter?"

The old man turned, standing more upright. Energized.

"Walk with me. We have much to discuss."

Nathan stuffed his hands into his trouser pockets, but obliged. He looked back toward the Gulfstream, seeing Rod thanking the Canadian authorities. All of the U.S. military assets were off the ground and on their way back to America. Rod appeared to have everything under control.

"What I'm about to tell you can only be shared with John. And, it can only be revealed when the time is appropriate."

"I'll do as you ask, but can we drop the cryptic speak?"

Walter's eyes crinkled, once more highlighting his age.

"After this conversation," he huffed, "everything will change for you – for all of us. You'll know the details of the final solution. The end of the age of man is upon us. The tribulation draws near."

A ball of tension rolled into Nathan's chest. He could hardly breathe, let alone process the declaration. Walter placed his hand on his upper back, taking away the tension. He couldn't explain how his touch had that effect, but it did; power entered Nathan's body, filling him with hope.

"You know what I'm about to speak of," Walter said. "Accept what I'm going to tell you. Remember it. Believe it. And most of all, have faith in it. For you and John are instrumental in the plan, and the plan is paved with suffering. You've foreseen it."

Nathan's first thought was of his wife – his family. What Walter said sounded so final. The end of all things. All the experiences of Arklight crashed down on him at once. The emergence of the Ark, the Arma Christi, and the golden plate he had witnessed just an hour ago solidified Walter's words. He felt the hand leave his back, and they continued walking forward.

"Tell me about the image you saw," Walter said.

"The imagery was very clear," Nathan said, a lump in his throat. "It reminded me of how Egyptian hieroglyphics are used to tell a story. It's burned into my memory: the first image was of Jesus' crucifixion; a man stood below the cross holding a small chalice with the Roman numeral thirteen above him."

"Did you make an association?"

"I did. Joseph of Arimathea is who came to mind. He was always referred to as Jesus' secret apostle. For some reason the number made sense."

"Did you know that Ancient Templar teachings credited him as the protector of the Holy Grail?"

"I've heard a few theories. Mostly in a few books, or movies I've watched over the years."

Walter chuckled a little at the reference to popular culture.

"It's been argued that life imitates art, and art imitates life; either way, in this case, it does. At least to some degree."

"How so?"

"Joseph was a great follower of Jesus," Walter said, his gaze distant. "I'm not sure how he was led at the time, but Templar legend implies that he made it his purpose to collect certain items from the crucifixion – the same Arma Christi we're chasing after today. It's believed that he was the one who originally forged the Time Key. The Spear of Destiny, the coins, the Titulus Crucis, and the Holy Grail represent the entire Time Key. That much is true."

"I guess if he was around in the period, it's not a far-fetched story."

Walter nodded and grasped his cane about halfway down. His hand wrapped around the bronzed shaft in the middle. He carried it along.

"I like to think Joseph got some instruction along the way. If I had to guess, it's much like the visions some of us have experienced."

"I'm still tracking."

"So, if the Templar legends are right—and I believe they are— Joseph of Arimathea constructed the Time Key. It worked by attaching the Holy Grail to the Spear, while the two folded coins of Solomon fit into the middle of the Spear, down the spine toward the blade."

"Wait. How does a chalice fit onto a spear?"

"That's what many people don't know. It's been a secret of the Knights Templar, since the Arthurian cycle in the Dark Ages."

"Arthurian... as in the King Arthur legend? That's all just a fairy-tale, isn't it?"

"Not exactly. You see, Arthur was a Roman. At the height of the Roman Empire's power, Great Britain was under Roman authority. King Arthur defended the land against Saxon incursions and his influence grew into what we now know as legend."

"What does that have to do with anything?"

"King Arthur was a warrior – a believer. He was the first Templar man tasked with protecting the Holy Grail. Other men, like Constantine the Great and other believers, took other pieces of Arma Christi from Joseph's collection to protect."

"So, now that we're close to possessing all the pieces once again," Nathan said, unfazed by the tale, "I guess finding the Holy Grail will complete the Time Key?"

"Yes. All those stories about the Holy Grail... the many quests and legends that have existed, all throughout time. None of them ever took one simple factor into account, regarding the Grail."

"What's that?"

"Did you ever hear about King Arthur's quest to locate the Holy Grail?"

Nathan stopped walking and turned, realizing they had wandered far away from the plane. He could only recall something about the Grail in a movie he watched once.

"Yeah, I remember something like that, but again – I only know a little."

"According to some of the ancient scrolls of the Templar, Arthur made the whole thing up. To conceal the real Holy Grail."

"What's the one simple fact? The reason no one ever located the Grail?" Nathan asked.

"Joseph of Arimathea had it forged from a chalice into a handle. A handle for the Time Key."

"Why?"

"Anyone's guess," Walter said. "Maybe it was simply to hide it, or maybe he was led to do it. Whatever the reason, the blood of Jesus is what bonds the Spear to the Grail; it's what they both share in common."

"So, the story of Joseph standing below the crucifix collecting Jesus' blood really happened? Obviously, the Bible is clear about the Spear of Destiny."

"Given everything we know, yes, it's very true."

"That's a lot to take in."

"I know," Walter said, as he turned to walk back toward the plane. "Tell me what else you saw on the plate."

"It was very confusing, but I remember several symbols of the Apocalypse: the four horsemen, the seven seals, and destruction. But in the middle, I saw what I can only describe as the Ark, encircled by a ring, and by what you just described – the Time Key."

"Was there anything else?"

"Yes. I was so focused on the images that I almost overlooked it." He concentrated. "On the other side of the Ark I saw a lamb. And a hand holding a sword."

Walter cupped his cane in his right hand and used it once more to guide his path.

"That image, actually the whole image, is what our enemies call the final solution."

†††††

Maximillion sat in a leather-bound seat in the forward cabin of the leased cargo plane. It rumbled down the runway, taking flight from the Halifax-Stanfield Airport. His nerves relaxed once they left the ground. It was no easy task clearing customs, but the right money in the right hands made the difference. He thought they had him when the Blackhawks landed on the other side of the airport, but they didn't have a clue how close they had come.

The plane zoomed upward and Maximillion looked over his shoulder at the large, crated box containing the Ark of the Covenant. He reached into a bag next to him and pulled out a bottle of very expensive wine. There were no wine glasses handy, so his thermos lid would have to do.

It would be a long flight back to Geneva, but for once in his life he felt at peace. He had located the Ark of the Covenant, and the Large Hadron Particle Collider stood ready to operate at full capacity. Once Magnus killed off the final group pursuing them, Maximillion could, at long last, get started on opening the energy portal—the Gateway to Apollyon, as those from the inner circle of The Order of the Black Sun called it.

He poured his drink into the plastic lid. His thoughts wandered to the endless treasures, power, and influence he would carry. The technology now existed to bring an unlimited energy source into the world. Their master race wouldn't need to control anything. The harmony they would create would destroy all those in opposition to their new world order. Peace would be natural because no one would want for anything, save serving the new supreme ruler of Earth.

One government, one people, one thought, not opposed by anything else. Maximillion relished his vision and his father's ideology. Since going off-grid after the second world war, Kieffer's alias—Alfred O'Keefe—had been compromised after Nashville. His command of The Order of the Black Sun was solidified after he had been named as the Führer of the Fourth Reich. The leader of the Nazi-led covert movement had no country, only an ideology and unlimited resources. He grabbed his satellite phone.

"One more call," he breathed, dialing the number. Two rings and the line picked up.

"Max, do you have it?"

"I do, Father. It's magnificent! The artwork on it – it's..."

"Yes, I know," Kieffer said, his elderly voice still gritty and strong. "You realize we still have a long way to go with this plan."

"You know I do."

"Has that son of yours completed his tasks?"

"He told me they have taken out the command element, placed the devices, and are waiting on the Americans to return. He said everything is on track."

"That boy is proving to be more useful than I gave him credit for."

"I told you he would come through for the Order."

"It appears he has."

Maximillion took a drink of his wine.

"Father, is the asset in place? I believe it's time you activate it. They got much closer to finding the Ark than I thought they would. I barely beat them to the airport; I was lucky they didn't lock the place down."

"Right… I think you're correct, Max. It's finally time to finish what the Reich started so many years ago. I only wish the Führer and my dear friend Weber were still alive to see this."

"Weber? That name is familiar."

"Ah, yes. You only saw him a few times when you were a boy. And by a different name at that. Do you remember Mr. Johnson?"

"He was a rather irritable man, if I remember correctly."

"That might be true, but he knew the vision. He gave up his only son to make all of this possible."

"How so?" Maximillion asked.

"After escaping Germany, Weber was given the new identity of Joshua Johnson. You know most of the story already, but I never told you much about him… for good reason."

"I do remember him coming to visit on occasion. I vaguely remember his son. What happened?"

"After the war, Hitler and Himmler set up a small base of operation, deep inside the jungle of Argentina. It was there that we continued working toward the final solution. It was there that we began our search for the Knights Templar journal – the same journal I gave you when you graduated university."

"Yes, Father, I know. It was the key to constructing the Large Hadron Collider."

"What you don't know is that we continued various experiments that Weber oversaw for the Reich. One of these was the ZTP Program."

"Wasn't that Josef Mengele's mind-control program at Auschwitz?" Maximillion asked, adjusting the phone for another taste of wine.

"You always had a great memory, son. Yes, ZTP continued for years in South America, and it was eventually perfected. See, Mengele had discovered at Auschwitz that children around the age of 8 were excellent candidates. Their minds, not fully formed, could be manipulated— molded, even—into the perfect sleeper agents. ZTP used hypnosis, physical stimuli, and mind-altering drugs to develop controllable split personalities. Its extreme effectiveness created agents who didn't even know they had a whole other person living inside of them... until activated, of course."

"That sounds similar to the MK Ultra program used by the American CIA."

"Yes. Like so many other things, they stole the research when they invaded the fatherland. But, without Mengele's personal knowledge, they had limited success. Also, the fact that they couldn't experiment on children kept them from discovering ZTPs true potential."

"So," Maximillion deduced, "Weber used his son for this program?"

"He did. In the late 50's, his son was converted into one of our greatest achievements. We inserted our agent protocol, wiped his mind, and gave him enough background to pass for an all-American boy. It was an elaborate plan. He's still unaware, even today, that he will do whatever I tell him."

"How does it work? I mean, after all these years?"

"Mengele was a genius. He developed a series of activation words that will instantly hypnotize the subject, allowing me to access the sleeper agent. He doesn't have any clue what's happening to him, but he will be under my full control."

Maximillion smiled as he realized the full depth of his family's work. A new world order rising from the ashes of the Third Reich. The Fourth Reich was well on its way toward controlling the entire world. His father always stayed a step ahead.

"The ends justify the means," Maximillion said, just as Kieffer had always taught him, growing up.

"Yes, they do, my son. See you in Geneva. We'll have victory over our enemies soon enough."

Maximillion closed the antenna on the phone with a whole new level of caution regarding his father.

†††††

Rod watched Nathan and Walter walking together in the distance. Helen and Archie were conversing inside the Gulfstream, drinks in hand. He leaned against the wall of the small hangar, not far from the plane. The cool night breeze felt refreshing, especially since it had only been a couple hours since he had been extracted from a dank tunnel beneath a swamp. It was the first real chance he had to collect his thoughts. With the Ark in Maximillion's hands, things had taken a turn for the worse.

His phone rang. He grabbed it out of his pocket. No number showed up on the screen, but he felt compelled to answer it.

An elderly German accent rattled his eardrum.

"Schwartze Sonne – Black Sun."

Rod's body froze in place. A thought flashed through his head. His jaw clenched. The voice continued.

"Weltschmerz – World Pain. Ending. Awaken. Mission. Execute. Activation – Kieffer."

Rod's memory flashed again. He tried to move, but could only hold the phone to his ear. Intense pain shot all over his body. He remembered. He was free even though he knelt to the ground, grunting in agony.

"Klaus Weber," the voice said, "respond to me."

Something took over. Rod faded away; someone else took control.

"Agent, copy. This is Klaus."

Memories of his childhood flooded his brain. Training – intense training. The swastika… he remembered. The lens of Rod's life remained accessible, but Klaus Weber emerged. His mission protocols became clear: undermine Arklight, report to Kieffer, and destroy anyone's ability to interfere with the final solution.

Klaus stood to his feet, once again aware of his surroundings. He saw Nathan and Walter in the distance and furrowed his brow. They closed in on the Gulfstream. No longer was he concerned about Arklight. The Black Sun's mission unfolded in his mind. He knew what needed to happen.

"Klaus," Kieffer said, "are you in a position to receive?"

"Yes."

"What is your current status?"

"Status – nominal. Ready for orders."

"Report."

"I am currently at the Halifax airport, accompanied by the United States Secretary of Defense, Archibald MacManus, Arklight Commander, Nathaniel Grant, CIA operative, Walter "Pappy" Steadman, and his CIA escort, Helen."

"Good. Once you're airborne, seize control, capture the assets, and report in once complete. Do you understand?"

"Yes."

"The Order of the Black Sun awaits your return, Klaus. You're a hero of the Order and the Reich. Sieg Heil."

The phone went dead and Klaus pulled it from his ear. He stared at his hand, his arm, and down to his toes. It had been decades since he felt his own body. He opened his eyes wide, focused on his objective. He dropped the phone back in his pocket.

"Sieg Heil," he muttered, his gaze locked on Nathan and Walter.

✝✝✝✝✝

Nathan looked across the tarmac and saw Rod looking back at him. It had been a long, hard day for everyone. Knowing that Maximillion and Magnus were a step ahead weighed heavily on them all. Walter stopped walking and looked toward the night sky hanging over the eastern horizon.

"Tomorrow will look very different," Walter said. "Remember what I've told you. We're all depending on you."

"I just thought there'd be more time."

Walter turned to face Nathan and handed him his cane once more. He adjusted his jacket.

"The end of this world is only the beginning. Seek the answers you already know to be the truth. That's why you were chosen."

"I still don't know what I'm supposed to do," Nathan said.

"John will know, when the time comes. Just stay true to the mission, live for today. The path will reveal itself."

"I'll do my best," Nathan said, rolling the cane about in his hands.

Walter reached for the cane, taking it back once again.

"Nathan, do you remember the story of Noah?" Walter asked.

The admiral nodded.

"While violence and corruption are not absolute, the time is fast-approaching. We must make a choice. That's what all of this is about. The golden plate you saw depicts that choice for all men. Fight for righteousness, or embrace the sin we all carry. Everlasting life, or judgment and death."

"I know," Nathan sighed. "But how do we accomplish that?"

"Through faith," Walter smiled, bringing his cane up to eye level.

Nathan took a deep breath, accepting that Walter had a plan.

"Okay. I'll work it out," Nathan said.

"Remember one other thing: someone will come to you in your darkest hour – have faith in what they tell you."

Nathan nodded.

"Gentlemen," Rod said, walking up, "Shall we board and get back?"

Walter cut his eyes to Rod and gestured with his left hand.

"After you."

Rod elbowed Nathan.

"It's been a day to remember," he said, walking around to the stairs.

Nathan walked with Walter toward the entrance to the plane.

"Everything is about to change, Nathan. Don't get discouraged. Stay focused. And do not share what I've told you with *anyone* – except John."

"I understand," Nathan said.

Walter eased up the stairs into the Gulfstream and Nathan turned to look toward the horizon. Heaviness invaded his heart. He wanted the feeling of impending doom to loosen its grip, even for a moment. His command phone rang, startling him from the daze.

"Chief, everything alright?"

"Sir, we've taken a hit. A real bad one."

CHAPTER 12: GHOSTS

"Fear and trembling overwhelm me, and I can't stop shaking."
Psalms 55:5

1600-Zulu Time 24May1945 (0100-JST 25May1945 Shuri Castle)

Voices carried into the corridor of the castle's throne room. John entered the chamber, camouflage active. Two Japanese soldiers were talking on the other side of the room. He froze in place and waited as the two men exited into one of the many halls leading out of the building. As soon as they cleared, he motioned for the others to enter. Chappy and Rico split off John's position, with thermal mode toggled on their goggles to detect one another in the room.

"We're taking a chance coming up here," Chappy said.

"I know, but if they don't find the painting down there, it's gotta be up here," John said.

"Shouldn't we give them some time first?" Rico asked.

"There's no time to waste," John said. "We need to recon what's up here anyway."

Chappy huffed and Rico shook his head at John's reasoning for the added danger; they both wanted to find the painting as fast as possible, but deep down, they didn't know if the risk was necessary. Chappy crept past John, covering the door leading into the main courtyard. Rico took the right side of the room, checking the hallway for any sign of movement. He could see the two Japanese soldiers turn a corner and move out of sight.

John closed in on Chappy and grabbed the pull on the main door leading into the courtyard. With his thermal imaging, he could see Chappy turn his head and nod, signaling he was ready for the door to open. John pulled the large wooden door, trying to keep the hinges from making a sound.

Chappy could see a seam of the courtyard along the opening edge, his view growing wider as John pulled. The courtyard was barren, with the exception of three armed guards posted near another building. Chappy stepped through the door and took a position on the exterior of the structure. Rico glided past John, finding a spot parallel to Chappy, on the other side of the courtyard. John followed, careful not to let the door slam behind them.

"That building," John said, "It's the officer's hooch."

"Where's all their troops?" Rico asked.

"Some of these other buildings are being used as barracks," John said, "but the majority of them are camped on the opposite end of the castle."

"You're like a war encyclopedia," Chappy marveled. "I guess we need to take a look around?"

"Stay on me," John said. "Fall back is the cavern."

"Roger that," Rico said.

†††††

The glow of LED flashlights lit the cavern's contents with just enough light to see. Bell pushed a crate off some stacked boxes.

"There's still nothing here that looks like it should hold a painting."

Ian huffed as he searched through a large, straw-lined crate of silver trinkets. Zip stood closer to the corridor leading to the castle. He was monitoring the sensors and, with less intensity, watching Ian and Bell interact.

"We've almost checked everything of consequence," Ian said.

"I know," Bell replied. "If it's still in the castle, we're screwed."

"Why do you say that?" Zip asked.

"Because, there's like, two thousand Japs up there," Bell surmised.

"John and the others are already looking," Zip added. "I gotta believe God has a plan for this trip. He always does."

"Yeah, well," Bell said. "It's easy to forget that sometimes."

Wisp sat next to his captive, within earshot of Bell's commentary. He watched his prisoner's eyes intensify; he understood what was said – Wisp could tell.

"Fujio, you *do* speak English."

Fujio turned his attention back to Wisp.

"You are a traitor to your people."

Wisp turned, looking him in the face.

"If you speak English, then you know why we're here."

"How did you get here? You appeared here like spirits – like ghosts."

Wisp could see the curiosity, even if it was laden in fear. He sat back and realized he had some leverage.

"That's not an easy question to answer... I tell you what, you help me and I'll tell you."

"I'm no traitor," Fujio said.

"I'm not going to ask anything of you that would compromise your integrity, or your honor."

The young Japanese officer adjusted his position on the moist, craggy floor. He held his arms up in the air.

"Free me," Fujio said. "Tell me what you want?"

Wisp didn't hesitate reaching for his combat knife on his load-bearing vest. He grabbed the handle and pulled the cold-steel from his holster, exposing the six-inch serrated tanto blade. Fujio's eyes widened as Wisp stepped in to cut the bindings from his wrists. With a quick slice, Fujio was free and he rubbed the discomfort from his wrists.

"We are here for something specific."

✝✝✝✝✝

On the other side of the cavern, Anne stood watch as Richie, Red, and Jack rummaged through crate and box alike. Refuse lay all over the rock-lined floor, and frustration continued to hasten their search for the painting.

Jack tossed an antique vase aside, shattering it into near powder.

"Hey! How about making a little more noise," Anne said.

"Shut your pie hole, sugar-cakes," Jack replied in earnest.

Anne stepped toward the Marine twice her size. Jack turned and looked down upon her small, yet powerful frame. Red stepped in between the two of them.

"Jack, stand the hell down. She's not some girl. She's an officer. How 'bout you show some respect?"

Anne continued to stare up at Jack, until she realized that the tightness of the space, lack of sleep, and a mission she barely understood were weighing her down. She took a step back, and Jack pulled back his head.

"Anne, what is it? You okay?" Richie asked.

She snapped her head around, looking at Richie.

"I... I don't know," Anne said. "This whole situation is starting to wear me out a little."

Richie turned and nodded at Red, who in turn nudged Jack back to work. The two Marines walked further into the cavern, looking for the painting. Everyone needed to find a few minutes of clarity.

"I've been living this out for years now. Maybe I can help?" Richie suggested.

She turned and sat on one of the boxes nearby. Her hand moved to her mouth, covering it as she rubbed the tightness from her jaw.

"We arrived on a streak of lightning," she said. "I mean, we floated like there was no gravity – no air – no atmosphere. Then just before I couldn't see anything else – there *He* stood."

"Who?" Richie asked.

"You can't possibly understand," Anne said, shaking her head. "I surely don't."

Richie sat back, watching her. Anne couldn't quantify what she saw with rational thought. Even with her superior scientific intellect, it was impossible. Maybe that was why she felt scared – unraveled even.

"When I got shot in Krakow, Poland," Richie said. "My ignorance— my lack of faith—caused me to make mistakes."

"You got shot?" Anne asked, forgetting her plight.

"Yes, But, that's not the point."

"Okay well, this is about me," she snapped. "You won't understand."

"Try me. I'm a little brighter than I look."

"I'm just trying to understand what this all means."

"I get that. Let me help. Lay it on me."

She popped the buckle of her chin strap and removed her helmet. She sat it beside her and pulled the balaclava down, exposing her brown hair.

"I was around, in another capacity, when John and the team went to Bizerte, and later to Nashville," Anne said. "It was weird then, just watching what happened. But now after living it? I don't know what to think."

Richie sat silent and nodded.

"But I don't believe in religion," Anne said. "How could I?"

Richie continued to listen. Anne dealt with her disbelief. It was time to know what she had really gotten herself into. She was lucky enough to see it, but was now too shaken to understand why.

"I think I know what you're talking about," he assured her.

"I have to sound crazy."

"I don't think you're crazy. I just think you're confused by what you can't explain – at least not in terms you can understand."

Anne stared at the floor; her mind busy in thought.

"I remember a story from back home, before I volunteered to fight in this godawful war," Richie said, "Maybe it helps, or maybe it doesn't, but I feel like you should hear it."

Anne stared ahead again, thinking about the face she saw. Instead of fading into her memory, it continued to intensify.

"There was this old rancher I knew, back when I was a boy."

Anne looked at Richie. His teenage face made her want to smile, until she saw the wisdom of a warfighter in his eyes. Richie paused for a moment, realizing as well that he was giving advice to a woman many years his senior.

"Anyway, this guy had hundreds of head of cattle. I remember one day, he lost one of his calves. Instead of worrying about the greater number of cows, he tore off, leaving the herd to search for that one that got away. He spent all day looking for it. Like really on a mission to find this one little calf. Then, just before nightfall, he found that calf – up to its neck in a mud pit."

The uneasy thoughts in Anne's mind faded away as she listened. It was a simple story, yet something about it made her take note.

"So, this old rancher jumped off his horse and into the mud pit to save this calf. The calf was scared, kicking and nagging. Heck, I think the calf even kicked the rancher. No matter how much the calf fought, the rancher grabbed on tighter and tighter, until he finally got a hold of that calf. After one heck of a struggle, he finally pulled the calf out of that muck and eventually led it back to the herd."

"I guess that rancher was pissed?" Anne surmised.

Richie laughed, "Nope. Even though he was dirty and the day had slipped away, he was happy that he saved that calf."

"I don't get it. How's that supposed to help me?"

A brief stillness lingered, until Richie looked at Anne.

"What did you see?"

Anne shook her head and looked at the floor.

"A man with a face brighter than the sun. His hand reached for me, but it was like I left my body or something. I can't explain the feeling."

Richie smiled and patted Anne on the shoulder.

"Sounds like the rancher's reaching out," Richie said.

Anne shook her head, unable to launch an argument to the contrary. For all of her preparation and training, she had no defenses for this end. The one thing she was never able to see, touch, or prove felt like it was the only explanation in the moment that made sense.

"Why? Why try to save me? I'm not a bad person."

"There's an old parable, similar to the story I told you, which says, '"There's more joy in heaven over finding one lost soul than for all of those who haven't strayed away.' For some of us, it's not about being good or bad. It's deeper than that."

"Maybe you're right."

Richie stood up and turned to Anne.

"I kinda like the thought of John getting his good sense from me."

Anne laughed at the statement, reflecting on the similarities the two men shared.

"There seems to be some truth to that," Anne said. "Thanks."

"We're only human and often blinded by ignorance."

"Only you men are ignorant," Anne said, as she slapped Richie on the back.

"Let's get back to finding this painting," Richie said with a smile.

†††††

Three semi-reflective blurs glided across the courtyard of Shuri Castle, like apparitions in the night. The reactive camouflage covered their movements as they passed by several armed sentries on their way to the officers' quarters. Rico posted up next to a brick outcropping by the courtyard wall, while Chappy settled into an outlying, light-streaked corridor. John plowed straight ahead, knowing he was covered from two angles. He keyed up his radio.

"Spear actual, I'm closing in on the main officers' quarters."

Anne's voice came over the radio, reminiscent of missions past.

"Spear six to Actual, we haven't found the painting down here."

John had a feeling he couldn't explain. It guided his movements and sharpened his senses. He clicked his mic twice in response.

Rico watched John close in on the door to the small building.

"Steady, I see at least two heat signatures moving inside."

"Are they looking at the door?"

Rico adjusted his positioning so he could be sure. He leaned to each side, trying to get an idea which way the men were facing.

"Looks like they're oriented facing away."

John reached the door and clicked his mic twice.

"Chap, Rico – I'm going in for a sneak and peek."

Chappy started to leave his spot, fearful that John was about to break a cardinal rule of close quarters combat: always work at least in pairs. John knew from their years together that Chappy would move closer.

"You two, hold what you got," John said. "It's a small space."

John looked back to see Chappy take a knee in the middle of the courtyard.

"It'll be fine. I'm just gonna take a look. Be right back."

Chappy retreated back to his position. John pulled on the lever, and the door opened out toward him. He slipped inside without a sound. Once in, he settled into a corner of the building, his head on a swivel. He switched to night-vision mode and could see shadows on the floor. Two men stood just around the wall in front of him.

He peeled to his left for a better view. An oil lamp illuminated the otherwise dark room, highlighting a Japanese general, another high-ranking officer, and on the wall behind them, the *Portrait of a Young Man*. The general sat on the floor in deep meditation, while the other officer sat at the desk, scribbling with haste.

It would only take John seconds to eliminate the two men and take the painting. He raised his ISR, activating his targeting system. His night-vision picked up the straight infrared laser as it settled on the general's chest. John clicked the weapon to fire, his finger on the trigger. He stopped. He didn't need to kill these men. He let his rifle hang and reached for his TX-9 to tranq the men.

"Spear two – Actual. Six hostiles coming at you. Get small – Rico and I will take 'em out."

"Negative," John whispered in the mic. "Hold."

Chappy worried that John's judgment was still skewed from their last mission; it was no time to get soft, even in the wake of tragedy. He gritted his teeth, hoping John had other motives. Rico sighted in on the six men as they approached the officers' quarters.

The door opened and the six men walked right past John, to the general. The experienced Arklight operator glided through the door before it closed, finding himself back in the courtyard.

"That was freaking close," Chappy said.

"Should've been there."

"So, what's the status?" Rico asked.

"Painting's inside. Now we just need to figure out how to get it out."

"Let's just go in there and take it," Chappy said.

"We don't need to kill them unless it's a last resort."

"The three of us can tranq them," Rico said.

"I think I've got a better idea," John said as he settled next to Chappy.

"Wisp," John radioed, "think you can convince Fujio to help us out?"

†††††

"Copy that," Wisp said.

"Who are you talking to?" Fujio asked.

"My team. We need your help, or your people are going to die."

"Why should I help a traitor?"

Wisp wanted to make some sort of connection with the man, but he could see there was little chance. Fujio was convicted in his imperialistic Shinto beliefs, and his honor was something valued above all else. Wisp knew that he would rather die than betray his beliefs, and that the Japanese state practiced Shinto, brainwashing the populous into ultra-nationalism. He needed a new approach and keyed up his radio.

"Spear actual – Spear three. Who's the general inside the hooch?"

"General Mitsuru Ushijima," John said. "He's the commander of the 32nd Army."

"Copy that."

Wisp didn't like the tactic, but knew it was necessary.

"Fujio, I have a man ready to kill General Ushijima, if you don't do exactly what I ask."

The Japanese officer looked down for a moment and raised his head, rage in his eyes. He sprang from his backside into Wisp with all of the force he could generate. Wisp countered, rolling to his right, using Fujio's own weight against him. Zip heard the commotion, turned, and ran down the rocky steps in time to see Wisp's large frame on top.

With a quick spin, Fujio slipped Wisp's hold and moved to his side, reaching for anything he could use as a weapon. His right hand found a board, swinging it at Wisp's head. The timber glanced off Wisp's helmet and out of Fujio's hand. Zip jumped in, restraining the free arm. Fujio yelled for help, only to be hushed by Bell's hands over his mouth. Wisp clamped down tight as his Fujio struggled under the weight of three men.

"Stop!" Wisp pleaded. "Listen to me if you want the general to live."

The thrashing lessened, be it from exhaustion or rationality. Fujio focused on Wisp. Zip and Bell continued to hold him in place.

"All you need to do is walk into the officers' quarters, get the general out of the room, and we'll be gone. No one has to die. We just want the painting. We aren't here for anything else."

Fujio's gaze transitioned from anger to confusion. His body relaxed and Bell removed his hand.

"You're here for that ugly painting? That's all?"

Wisp looked straight at Fujio; his intent was clear.

"Yes. That's it."

"I don't understand. Why is that painting so important?" Fujio asked.

"In our time, Japan and America are Allies. This war will be over soon, because of a terrible and powerful weapon. The same information used to create that weapon is now threatening the entire world. There's something in that painting that will help us win a war far, far worse than this one."

"You lie," Fujio said. "The Emperor would never ally with the Americans."

"Look at me… I'm not lying. It's the truth. We came here for a bigger purpose. The war we're facing? It knows no race, sex, or ethnicity. It will mean the end of the world if we fail. We fight for mankind – for everyone."

A chill shot down the back of Wisp's neck. Fujio sat back, seeing the truth in Wisp's explanation. He wanted Fujio to believe his story, and knew he needed to press him to comply. He hoped Fujio would do whatever it took to protect his beloved general. One thing was certain, Wisp could sense a certain level of fear and uncertainty coming from his captive.

"Tell me what I must do," Fujio said, his eyes filled with contempt.

†††††

John shifted to an unlit corner just outside the entrance of the officers' building. The six officers that had entered previously remained inside, squabbling to the general. John couldn't understand them, but they all seemed worried. The best he could tell, they must have seen the American fleet closing in on the castle. John knew that he needed to get everyone clear of the area before the *U.S.S. Mississippi* opened up with her 14-inch guns.

"Spear three to Actual," Wisp radioed. "We're in the throne room and ready."

John turned his attention the door and clicked his mic twice.

"Chappy, Rico – hold position. Cover our exfil. Wisp – you and I will enter and handle extracting the painting. Zip, pull back to the throne room. Be ready to cover us. Anne – hold the cavern; we'll be falling back to you and then we're outta here."

A series of clicks registered across the radio system. The plan was simple enough. John scanned the courtyard. Things were as quiet as they could be, considering the bulk of the Japanese 32nd Army surrounded the castle. If Fujio did his part, this would be a piece of cake.

"Go ahead and bring him out," John said.

Wisp straightened Fujio's uniform, stuck the unloaded pistol into his holster, and inserted his sword back into its sheath. The Japanese officer studied him, acknowledging the act, still unsure of how this could be.

"I'll be right behind you – understand?"

"How?" Fujio asked.

Wisp pulled up his balaclava, covering his face, and adjusted his gear, including his ISR rifle. Fujio looked on as Wisp touched a panel of lights on his forearm, vanishing right before his eyes. Shivers raced over his body; terror gripped at his throat.

"Yūrei," he said in disbelief.

"I'm not a ghost, Fujio. It's just technology."

"Aye," Fujio gasped, unable to process what he had witnessed.

The young Japanese officer exited the door of the throne room and walked across the courtyard. John watched him approach, his body stiff, almost robotic. Stepping in behind Wisp, John planned on taking an overwatch position to cover his teammate. Fujio walked with purpose, albeit with a stagger of uncertainty – or maybe fear. Wisp nodded to John as Fujio approached the entry point. John circled in behind, placing his hand on his teammate's shoulder.

Fujio entered, swinging the door open wide. It was enough, allowing Wisp and John to enter simultaneously. Their presence was undetected by all, as Fujio crossed into the main room. General Ushijima stood at a table; officers flanked to both sides. He pointed across the map, discussing the defense of the castle. Once Fujio entered, the general stopped and looked up at the young lieutenant.

The tension of betrayal latched onto Fujio's throat, and he was without words. Almost instantly, sweat beads formed on his forehead. He struggled to get something out – something that frightened him. Wisp placed his hand on Fujio's back. It was as much as a reminder for their deal as it was for encouragement. Wisp gripped his rifle, worried he had made a miscalculation of Fujio's intent. John's thermal vision flared against the oil lamp, distorting his view.

The general left his position at the war table and walked around the other officers. He stopped in front of Fujio, his attention locked on him. Wisp stood behind Fujio, still as a statue, focused on the features of the general's face.

"Y-Yūrei," Fujio uttered. His eyes were polarized with fright.

John couldn't understand what was happening. He held his position, covering Wisp.

General Ushijima stepped back, his stare blank, his jaw falling slack. The flicker of an oil lamp outlined something behind Fujio. He caught a shimmer, the flicker of a shape. Something ghost-like.

He reached for Fujio's sword, pulled it from the sheath, and thrust it into the blurry figure. Wisp tried to parry, but the blade buried itself deep into his lower abdomen, just below his body armor. The Katana blade burned through his core, staggering him into the wall.

He writhed in pain as the sword exited his body. The general pulled it over his head, ready to strike again. Fujio jumped forward, crossing the room in a single bound, escaping the fray. In shock, John ended the general's sword arc with a panicked burst of ISR fire, striking his arm, dropping him to the floor. The other officers scattered, trying to draw their pistols, terrified of the apparitions before them. There was no time; the plan had failed. John emptied the rest of his magazine with precision, dropping everyone else in the room – with the exception Fujio and General Ushijima.

Fujio took two driving steps into the general, forcing their bodies out of the room's window. Glass shattered, sending fragmented pieces to the stone walkway outside in a crash. They hit the ground hard, but both men were on their feet, adrenaline fueling their flight. Fujio grabbed the general, whisking him away in a panic. They ran for cover. The general looked back at the window they had escaped from.

"Yūrei! Yūrei!" Fujio screamed.

"Akuma," said the general, as he watched a shadowy figure appear in the window.

John's camouflage deactivated as he stood there watching the two men run. He had them in his sights. It was too late to stop the alarm. He wanted to pull the trigger, but killing them wouldn't solve the problem. They were compromised. An entire army was about to descend upon them.

He turned toward his downed teammate, dropping his rifle to try and help tend to the injury.

"Wisp, how bad is it?" John asked.

"It's bad," Wisp huffed, wincing in pain.

"Chappy, Rico, get in here! Wisp's down!"

Two blurs entered into the door of the building. Rico had already pulled his medical pouch out and slid across the floor, making contact with Wisp. John deactivated his camouflage so they could see the wound. Chappy cleared the rest of the small structure and settled into an overwatch position in front of the painting.

"What happened?" he called over.

John only shared a look. Rico rolled Wisp on his side. Blood poured from the through and through wound, flowing out of his torso.

"Dammit. It hurts." Wisp said, his respirations labored.

Rico looked at John. He knew it was bad, but they couldn't linger.

"Look buddy, you know the drill… stay calm. This is gonna hurt."

Wisp gritted his teeth and shook his head. There was little he could do to help, other than contain his agony.

"Rico, pack it," John said, squeezing Wisp's hand.

He pulled out all of the hemostatic dressings and Israeli bandages he had. John started tearing open the packages and Rico stuffed them into the wound channel. Wisp's eyes rolled back into his head. A wheeze exited his lungs, and he passed out due to the pain.

"Wrap it tight," John said.

John pulled Wisp's limp body upright, allowing Rico to wrap the wound. The bandage began to turn an oxblood red before it was even secure. They had to keep the pressure on it and avoid causing further damage. An alarm sounded in the distance.

"We gotta move!" Chappy yelled. More armed men than he could count began charging into the castle entrance.

"Chap, grab the painting and haul ass to the cavern," John shouted. "We're right behind you."

Chappy fired a burst from his ISR. Several of the advancing Japanese soldiers fell to the ground, scattering their approach. He grabbed one grenade, thrusting it overhand toward the wedge of confused soldiers. Then a second. Two explosions resonated, and Chappy grabbed the painting off the wall. John and Rico hoisted Wisp off the floor, reactivating his camouflage.

The explosions that rattled the castle were now muffled by the commotion of men descending all around them. Chappy sprinted across the courtyard, clasping the painting as best he could. John and Rico carried Wisp, hot on Chappy's heels. Rounds sparked across the ground around them. The Japanese soldiers fired at a painting that appeared to be floating through thin air. One Japanese soldier focused in on the blur, bringing his rifle stock up to his cheek. His body dropped before he could take aim.

"Hurry up." Zip radioed, as he recovered from his shot. He began taking aim on several more soldiers, covering the extraction.

Chappy entered the throne room, followed by the others.

"How bad's he hit?" Zip asked.

"Through and through – left side abdomen. I think it got a kidney," Rico huffed, out of breath, "John, take him."

John hoisted Wisp over his shoulder, following Chappy into the cavern entrance. Zip continued engaging the mass of soldiers bearing down on their position.

"We can't hold this." Zip said, hoping someone heard him over the sporadic cracks of gunfire.

"Give me 10 seconds," Rico said, arming an explosive charge.

Hundreds of rounds decimated the façade of the throne room. Zip tossed a grenade out the front door as he crawled toward the entrance of the cavern. Rico stuck one charge and then a second on the concrete pillars on front of the corridor. The grenade shook the courtyard.

"Go, Zip. We're out." Rico said, as bullets cut through the wall and into the throne room itself.

Rico followed him into the tunnel system that would lead them back to the cavern. He armed the explosives on his command module as they ran. As soon as they had cleared the area, he pressed the initiate button and fired the shots, shaking the tunnel with a deafening blow. He stumbled from the shockwave, falling flat on his face. A plume of dust and debris covered him, extinguishing almost every bit of light. Zip turned, the taste of dirt entering his mouth with each breath. He couldn't see from all the particulate in the air. Zip felt behind him for any sign of his teammate.

"Rico! You okay?"

"Yeah," Rico coughed, his ears ringing from the pressure, "that's a little closer than I wanted."

Zip's hand found Rico's in the rubble. Rico turned on his helmet light and looked behind him. The entrance to the lower cavern had collapsed, buying them some time.

CHAPTER 13: OUTGUNNED

"So we don't look at the troubles we can see now; rather fix our
gaze on the things that cannot be seen."
2 Corinthians 4:18

1700-Zulu Time 24May1945 (0200-JST 25May1945 Shuri Castle)

"Team. Coming in." Chappy huffed, out of breath as he entered the main cavern. Bell and Ian were close by and turned, seeing the *Portrait of a Young Man* in his grasp. Anne appeared, running up to meet Chappy.

"How's Wisp?" Anne asked.

"He's in bad shape. See if you can help stabilize him. I'll deal with exfil."

Chappy walked past her until he made it to Bell and Ian, now joined by Richie. He sat the painting on the ground, with little concern regarding its priceless nature.

Red and Jack stood a little farther back in the cavern, detached from and unconcerned with the commotion. Jack gnawed off a plug of chew and leaned against a crate. Red stared at the painting, shaking his head at the lengths they had gone through to get it.

John emerged from the corridor with sweat dripping from his nose and Wisp draped over his shoulder. He felt the warmth of the wound against his neck as he continued to press Wisp's body against his own. He hoped the contorted pressure would slow the bleeding.

Anne pushed and kicked parts of crates and boxes out of the way in an effort to make triage space. She saw that Wisp was unconscious and noticed the blood-soaked spot on his side.

"Bring him here," Anne said.

Crouching through the tunnel had exhausted John. He was panting under the weight of his friend's limp body. He walked to Anne and knelt, lowering Wisp to the smooth rock floor of the cavern, with Anne helping guide. There was a lot of blood. Wisp's skin was pale and cold, his respirations shallow.

Zip and Rico emerged from the corridor. A rolling, chalky gray cloud of soot clung to them as they exited. They were coated in dirt, but appeared to be okay.

Ian, Bell, and Richie stood next to Chappy, all shaken and concerned over Wisp's state.

"What happened?" Bell asked.

"I'm not sure," Chappy said. "but it ain't good."

"What do you need us to do?" Richie asked.

"I... don't know."

"Is he going to make it?" Ian asked, watching John and Anne rip off Wisp's gear.

"I hope so," Chappy said, still trying to catch his breath. "We may have bitten off more than we can chew. The whole damn Japanese army came bearing down on us up there."

"We should be able to make it out the way we came in," Richie said.

"That is until the Japs close in on the lower entrance," Bell noted.

"Whatever we do, we need to get him stabilized and get on it," Chappy said, passing the painting to Richie.

"Hold this for a minute," happy said, walking over to his downed teammate.

Zip and Rico traded solemn looks with the Alsos Team as they, too, stepped in beside their downed brother. John and Anne had pulled off Wisp's outer plate-carrier, applying pressure on the wound. Precious life continued to seep through the bandages.

"Chappy, give me another pressure dressing," John said, his gloved hands covered in red. Chappy pulled out the vacuum-sealed bandage and peeled away the wrapper, handing it to John. Their gaze met. No words needed to be said, but the communication was clear. Faces turned sullen; there was little anyone could do.

Two sets of hands pressed on Wisp's wounds, joined by three more sets. John looked up and his chest burned with grief.

"God, don't let this happen," John said, surveying Wisp's face. His wounded teammate's eyes opened, transfixed well beyond his pain, as if looking into the unknown.

"Steady – it's okay. It was my fault, not yours," Wisp said, as his body stumbled into failure. Tears rolled from his cheeks.

A wave of emotion engulfed John and the others.

"We need you," John said, "there's still so much to do."

"My time's over, brother." Consciousness faded, and his senses grew numb. He reached for John's arm and squeezed with what energy he had left in his veins.

"Mission… first. Don't let evil win," he whispered.

John watched his friend's gaze grow still. A final labored rise of Wisp's chest told them all his time had arrived.

"Forgive me…" he murmured. Spear Team surrounded their fallen warrior. Stone silence settled upon the cavern. John sniffed and fought back the tears, trying to focus on what they needed to do next. He raised his head and wiped his cheeks.

"We can't do this right now," John said, standing up and looking around.

Chappy took and deep breath. He swallowed his emotions and looked at John.

"What do you want us to do?"

"Chap, take Rico, Zip, and the Marines. Go and see if we can get out the way they came in."

"Copy that."

"The rest of us will see about extracting the Spear from the painting. Anne?"

Anne's fingers rested over Wisp's eyelids. She choked back her emotions, wrestling to get a hold of herself.

"Anne," Chappy barked, "stow it for later – understand?"

She jumped and turned her attention, staring at him with disdain.

"I heard you the first time," she said as she stood, never taking her attention off Chappy.

"Anne, look at me," John said.

She turned her head, until her eyes followed, meeting John's gaze.

"You've got to hold it together. Mission first – you heard Wisp. Honor *his* wishes."

Her rage was apparent, but she fought back the tears. She shook her head and turned to face Chappy.

"Sorry," Anne said.

"Nothing to be sorry about, little sister. You good to go?" Chappy asked.

"Yeah."

John exchanged a nod with Rico as they walked toward Red and Jack, who had already gathered their gear. Jack exchanged a brief, but solemn, glance of remorse for the loss. He turned and followed the others toward the secret entrance to the cavern.

"War don't change," Jack said, "no matter who you are."

††††††

Anne and John made their way around to Richie, Bell, and Ian. The frame encasing *Portrait of a Young Man* was oversized, considering the painting itself was just over 2-feet tall and just under 2-feet wide. An extravagant, golden, Italian framework surrounded the art piece, twice the height and width. Many experts surmised that the work was the self-portrait of the artist himself, Raphael.

Anne looked at the floor, in the opposite direction of Wisp.

John stood beside Bell. He stared at Wisp's body, wondering what went wrong and why he had to die. Richie grabbed John by the arm.

"I'm sorry Wisp didn't make it," Richie said. "He was a good man."

Anne turned her attention to her downed mentor and patted John on the back.

"This isn't how I thought it would go," Anne said. "Steady?"

John pressed his lips together and closed his eyes tight. Anne could see his torment, and changed the subject as a distraction.

"The frame on this painting looks big enough to hold a small elephant," she said, turning her attention to the task at hand.

Richie rocked the painting forward, inspecting the 500-plus years of patina.

"It looks pretty old," he added.

Ian rubbed the bridge of his nose, shaking off the stiffened daze he had fallen into. He stepped toward John, grabbing him by the shoulder.

"I'm terribly sorry about your man. He's a true hero," Ian said, absorbing the loss covering John's face.

"Yeah. And above that, he was my friend." John tried to breathe deeply. "All that matters now is getting the Arma Christi and driving toward the truth."

"How are we going to get out of here?" Bell asked.

"I sent the others to scout out the exit. We'll figure something out. Let's get a look at the back of this painting."

Richie found a crate close by and flipped the art piece over, exposing the backing. A thin layer of dust on the backing had a few disturbances, most of which were finger impressions from Chappy's hold during his all-out sprint from the castle courtyard.

"The Lance of Long and the Young Man share a destiny," Richie said, cutting his gaze toward Bell in reflection.

"What's that?" John asked.

"It's the phrase that started this whole thing for us," Bell said. "We've been after this for a long time."

John nodded.

"It's the main piece we need to activate the Time Key. I just hope it works. We've got the other pieces already secured at our base."

"What do you think it will do?" Richie asked.

"According to everything we've learned, it should fit together seamlessly; the two folded coins get inlaid into the spear and the other 29 silver coins, along with the Titulus Crucis, somehow interact with it. It's not like there's been any clear instructions from the Templar journal."

"Very true," Ian said.

"We don't have a lot of time," Anne said, looking toward the collapsed corridor.

"Yeah," John said, keying up his mic. "Chap, you copy?"

†††††

"I got you," Chappy said. "Entering the cave now. Jack says the mouth isn't far." He crouched his way through the craggy opening. Wooden ammunition crates lined the walls, and armaments were stacked all around. The damp cave was illuminated by just a few oil lanterns.

"Jack, you and Red hang back for a second," Zip said.

"Hang back my ass," Jack said, gritting his teeth.

"Trust me – it will be easier this way," Chappy said, activating his camouflage. He disappeared right before Jack's eyes.

Zip patted Red on the shoulder and followed suit. Rico trailed the others, looking back to monitor the expressions of disbelief from the two young Marines.

Chappy crept into the center of the hollow, until he reached a point where he could see the jungle beyond. The soft amber glow of the cave faded into the endless abyss of the night sky. If the enemy was present, they weren't moving. He switched his night-vision goggles to thermal enhanced mode. White-hot, glowing figures lit up his display, like fireflies in the night.

"Hold," Chappy radioed, "go thermal. Give me a count."

The other two Arklight operators flanked his right and left. Rico's goggles flared from the numerous human silhouettes to his front. Zip took a moment to assess their situation; the sniper in him knew they were outnumbered at least ten to one.

"Looks like a weapons platoon. Medium sized element," he said. "I count at least two crew-served weapons platforms."

"Are they facing the cave?" Rico asked.

"They are," Chappy said, continuing to count men. "Spear two – Actual. We've drawn a crowd."

"How bad?"

"If it was just us, we could get through – no problem. But with Bell and his crew... not happening."

"I copy," John radioed. "Get a plot on the positions and send it to my command module."

"Copy that," Chappy said, turning his head to find Zip on his right, "Can you get a drone up?"

"Already on it."

Zip pulled a mini-drone out of his gear and found a large wooden box to take cover behind. He sat the drone on the plywood top, activated his control screen, oriented the camera to his heads-up display, and flew the drone out of the cave. The aerial-recon system rose above the Japanese forces gathered outside. Computer-aided thermal targeting was selected, and the drone plotted almost 40 soldiers, all of whom were staring down weapons aimed at the mouth of the cave. Chappy moved to cover and pulled up the information from the drone. He patched it through to John.

"Spear two to Actual. The package is sent. Looks like close to 40. I think they're intending to drive us out from above."

†††††

"Spear Actual, copy." John looked at Anne, who was already reviewing the footage.

"Steady, you seeing this? They got enough ordinance down there to shred anything that pops its head out. Looks like a couple of machine gun nests, supported by a rifle platoon."

"What's going on?" Bell asked.

"They've got us cut-off," John said, scrolling though the footage. "Looks like they're intending to break through up top and force us into an ambush at the cave."

"That's not what I was hoping to hear," Ian said.

Richie continued to focus on the painting. He looked to his right, seeing John and Anne meticulously scrolling through information. Ian and Bell both paced about, worried about escaping the predicament. Richie's hand found its way down to his old faithful companion, his combat knife. Without a second thought, he sliced into the backing of the priceless painting.

"Richie. What the hell are you doing?" Bell asked, breaking contact with Ian and grabbing Richie's arm.

"Skipper, we don't have time to fool around. Let's get this damn spear, and make a run for it."

Bell looked at John, only getting a solemn nod. He relaxed his grip and stepped back, remembering the painting meant little in relation to the Spear of Destiny.

"Go ahead then," Bell said.

Richie turned his focus back to the painting, cutting away the entire backing. John stepped up, grabbing the brittle material. He and Richie pulled until it ripped entirely away from the frame. Anne could see a slight deformity to the woodgrain along the bottom half of the backing.

"See that?" she asked, pointing.

"It looks very similar to the void we found in the backing of the *Storm on the Sea of Galilee*. It's got to be in there," John said, pulling out his combat knife.

Both he and Richie stabbed at the seam of the panel, slicing into the hidden compartment. John's knife soon penetrated the seam, deep enough for him to pry at the cover. Richie stopped his progress as soon as John's knife seated itself. Anne, Ian, and Bell surrounded the painting, anxious to see what they had uncovered. What Wisp had died for.

John's knife tilted away from the cover, and with a *click*, the piece of wood popped away from the frame. He reached down with his free hand and removed the lid. A faint shimmer of metallic bronze reflected off of their faces. John took a deep breath, relieved they had found it. The Lance of Longinus. The spearhead was nothing remarkable; a modified pilum with a double-edged pyramid design, sharpened on one end. The other end was a shank, attached to a wooden staff at some point. A tarnished iron spine had two circular depressions centered along the tang. John worked his hand down into his pocket to retrieve the John Bell Hood coin.

Everyone watched as he held the coin flat in his hand. It looked to be a perfect fit for one of the spots on the spear.

"I think General Hood was right. This is the key," John said, simultaneously realizing that for as much as it had been on his mind, he hadn't the chance to enlighten Bell about their previous mission.

"Wait – General John Bell Hood? As in my great-great grandfather?" Bell asked.

"Yes. I wish there was more time to explain," John said, fitting the coin into the spear.

A shudder vibrated the table. John's hand was locked in place, and he gasped for air. His entire body froze, stiff as stone.

"What's happening?" Richie asked, grabbing John to free him. Richie's body then froze in place, like he was being electrocuted from his contact with John. Anne reached out, but Bell pulled her hand away.

"Don't! I've seen this before," Bell said.

"What's happening?" Anne asked.

"They'll be back," Bell said, looking up toward the ceiling of the cavern. "It's a vision."

Ian stepped in as close as he would dare, trying to search Richie's face, but all he saw was a chilling, blank, emotionless stare.

"A what?" Ian demanded.

"God," Bell said with a faint smile drawing across his face.

Anne pushed Bell's hand away.

"Enough of this," Anne said, drawing back her fist, targeting John's upper arm.

Her strike reached his arm and stopped cold, her knuckles flat against his deltoid. It was only for a split second, but there He was again. Reaching for her. She had never seen anything with as much clarity, but in an instant, her momentum accelerated once more, carrying her forward, striking John. Bell watched the three of them stagger back into motion. Ian's eyes grew wide, and he inhaled sharply, jumping back, at the ready for anything.

"What just happened, chaps?" Ian asked.

John and Richie looked at each other with a determined spirit in their eyes. No words needed to be shared. Anne stumbled away, catching her balance.

"What the bloody-hell was that?" Ian asked again.

"We know what to do," John said.

"That's great, but—" Anne struggled to focus.

"I'll have to fill you in later," John said. "We've got work to do."

Richie nudged Ian, whose stare remained animated with adrenaline.

"Give me the journal," Richie said, his hand extended.

Ian stared back at Richie, still working to comprehend the slowing of time he had witnessed. Richie stood confidently, as if he were possessed by some higher power.

A soon as the journal landed in Richie's hand, he flipped it open to page 112 and started writing.

"Two doors will reveal the Young Man. The Spear is stone, the stone is the path," he whispered.

John overheard the comment and knew this journey was far from complete.

†††††

"Spear two, Spear actual. I'm pretty sure we can carve a path for the Alsos Team. What do you advise?" Chappy asked.

"Actual copy. No need. We have another plan," John replied.

"Roger that. Care to share?"

"You three return to the cavern. Leave Red and Jack in place. The Alsos Team will join them shortly for exfil."

Chappy didn't know what had changed, but John's voice carried a confidence he hadn't heard for some time. It was enough for him.

"Zip, Rico – pull back to the cavern," Chappy said.

Two clicks were heard over the radio. Zip recalled his drone and the three Arklight men retreated into the cave. They were soon out of sight, walking back to where they left Red and Jack.

"Chappy, that you?" Jack whispered.

"Yeah, it's clear."

Jack laid his rifle on a crate and pulled off his helmet, stepping out in the corridor. Red emerged from his piece of cover and took a seat on a metal can.

"So, what's it look like out there?"

"There's a couple machine gun positions and an entire platoon covering the exit," Zip said.

"I guess we're screwed," Jack said, spitting on the ground.

"Not necessarily," Rico said. "Looks like we got another plan. John said for you two to stay put and lay low. We have to head back up. He said the others would meet you back here."

"I ain't waiting around all night," Jack said. "Tell them to do whatever it is and let's get the hell out of here."

"We will, don't worry. Just hang tight, bro." Chappy patted the big Marine on the upper arm.

Rico began following Chappy to the entrance of the tunnels, turning when he sensed a pair of footfalls missing.

"Zip, you coming?"

"Yeah, give me a sec."

Zip walked over to Red and took a knee on the ground.

"It's been a pretty strange day, huh?" Zip asked.

"It's not every day you meet your grandson – who's twice your age."

Zip leaned back trying to not laugh too loud.

"A bit unusual, no doubt. But, I wanted to tell you, it's been a real privilege to see you – like this," Zip said, his eyes narrowing with a smile.

Red nodded and placed his hand on Zip's shoulder.

"What's next?"

"Just be ready. I promise you'll make it. Don't look back once you start running. Understand?" Zip said, remembering the story… or at least, the parts of it his grandfather had elected to tell him back on the reservation. He turned his attention to Jack, who stared toward the entrance to the cave.

"Jack, it's been an honor to meet you. A real honor." Zip extended his hand.

Jack reached out, his meaty paw engulfing Zip's.

"Likewise, old timer," Jack said with a wink.

Zip shook his hand and walked toward the entrance to the tunnel. He turned around before he entered.

"One other thing: you can't tell me we ever met, okay? You know, once I'm born."

"Seeing the man you've become – that's enough for me to know that what you say is right," Red said.

Zip took one more look, smiled, and nodded before fading into the murk.

†††††

Richie handed the journal back to Ian, who stuffed it into its customary pocket inside his jacket.

"What was that all about?"

"It was something vital that needed to be written," Richie answered.

John patted Bell on the back and looked at Richie.

"That's the phrase that brought us here," John said.

"Man, this gets more and more confusing with each passing second."

"Don't worry, Skipper. I know how we're getting out," Richie said.

"How's that?" Ian asked, beating Bell to the question.

Richie looked at John and nodded.

"You'll just have to trust me," Richie said.

Anne stood motionless, still wrestling with what she had seen. John looked at her blank stare, remembering what she had given him earlier. He pulled a tiny black device from his cargo pocket.

"Take this," John said, handing the drone to him.

Richie grabbed the device and looked it over.

"What gives, John?" Bell asked.

"You saw it, right?" John asked. "The *Ghent*. What this is for."

Richie nodded as he held the device in the palm of his hand, inspecting it. It was a black, rectangular box with a flat top, a small red button on the side, and four small metallic balls protruding along the bottom. A diminutive piece of smoked glass covered the base along the underside.

"How does it work?" Richie asked.

"Anne," John said, shaking her shoulder.

"Yeah," she said, her eyes aflutter, turning her focus to John.

"Can you tell them how the drone works?"

"It's an auto laser-imprinting drone."

"A laser what?" Ian asked, raising a brow.

Richie and Bell shared a quizzical look. Anne realized her terminology might be a little advanced.

"Sorry. Okay, all you need to do is lay the surface flat, set the drone on top, press the red button, and let it do the work. It will only take about 20 minutes to encode the entire thing."

"This – this was on the *Adam panel*, moving about. That's what I saw," Richie said.

"What are you talking about?" Bell asked, squinting with confusion.

"I'm a bit lost myself," Ian said.

Richie turned his attention to John. Anne stood back, anxious to hear an explanation. John looked around at everyone before reaching for the Spear of Destiny. He grabbed the pilum and removed the coin, placing it back in his pocket. He flipped over the piece of Arma Christi, examining it for anything remarkable. It had nothing that stood out in its design. However, he could see faint traces of crimson along the blade, lining several crevices along the spine.

"The blood. Look right here," John said, pointing out the flaky splotches.

Everyone craned their necks to see the stains on the bronzed-iron. John looked at Richie and handed the Spear to him.

"You've got to take this out of here."

"I know," Richie said, rolling his small backpack off his shoulders.

"And how do you propose we do that?" Ian asked.

John watched Richie secure the drone and the spear.

"Listen up, you three – Bell, write this down."

Bell rummaged in his breast pocket, finding a small notebook and a pencil. Ian moved closer to John, engaging his well-trained mind to remember the details of the conversation. Richie threw back on his backpack and looked straight into John's eyes.

"It's imperative that all of you make it to the Saint Bavo Cathedral in Ghent, Belgium on April 10th, 1946."

"Why?" Ian asked.

"That's where you three are going to imprint the binary codex into the *Adam Panel*."

"Wait, you said *we* are?" Bell asked.

"But, isn't the binary already on the panel?" Ian asked.

John and Richie looked at each other, unsure how to break the news to the others.

"Skipper, I saw it myself. We have to do this," Richie said.

"That sounds like an incredibly bad idea," Ian said."

"All I can tell you is that it must be done," John said, "and you three have to be the ones to do it. Richie and I both saw it."

"This is hurting my head, but even so, *how* are we supposed to do that?" Bell asked.

"You're going to have to trust me, Skipper," Richie added.

"It's not that we don't trust you, buddy. It's just that I – I mean, we don't understand."

"It does sound a bit tosh," Ian said, looking at Bell for support.

"I get it, I do. But has any of this been normal?" Richie asked.

John stood still, thinking about the journey thus far, himself.

"Point made," Bell replied.

"What's the play, John?" Ian asked.

John looked around the cavern. He could hear the faint voices of the Japanese soldiers carrying through the collapsed corridor. He walked over to the wall – to the exact spot he had touched when they were sent to the past.

"What are you doing?" Richie asked.

"What needs to be done," he said as he turned around. He stepped back to Richie and held out his hand. Richie shook John's hand, then closed in, hugging him.

"I guess it's time?" Richie asked.

"It is," John said. "Take them out through the cave – just like you saw it."

"I'm still trying to see how… the Japs are all over the place."

John pushed Richie to an arm's length and looked at him.

"Bell, what's the salvo cadence of a New Mexico class battleship?"

"Huh?"

"What's the firing cadence of a single battleship, firing on a fixed location like Shuri Castle?"

"A salvo – right. The initial salvo will be a 12-round broadside, with a two-to-three minute reload," Bell said.

"If my watch is still right, the U.S.S. Mississippi is about to start leveling this entire grid," John said, winking at Richie.

"The Japs at the cave entrance will run for cover," Richie said.

"Well played," Ian said. "Let's just hope we don't run into any bad luck."

John smiled and shook Ian's hand.

"You'll be just fine. Just don't waste any time once the first salvo ends. Believe."

"Right," Ian said, patting John on the shoulder.

"Bell, it's been an honor – again," John said, reaching for his friend's hand.

"Sure has, John," Bell replied, with a stare and a quick hand shake.

"Good luck. Make sure you hide that spear well."

"We will," Richie said.

The Alsos Team gathered their gear and made their way to the tunnel. Richie stopped beside Anne.

"You're luckier than most," Richie said.

"What's that?" Anne asked, shaking herself out of a trance.

"You've gotten to actually *see* what others can only have faith in."

Anne nodded with a solemn raise of the corners of her mouth. Her eyes cut over to Wisp's body, lying still on the floor of the cavern. What she had seen tonight was as real as the war they found themselves fighting.

"Thanks, Richie," she said.

Bell stopped by next.

"Sorry, if I was out of line earlier."

Anne looked at Bell and smiled.

"I understand. My advice? Ladies—real ones—like to be respected."

Ian walked up behind Bell, pushing him forward.

"I'm just glad to know that women haven't lost their beauty in the future," Ian said, grabbing her gloved hand ever so gently.

Anne's feelings couldn't stop her face from blushing. Bell followed Richie into the tunnel to the cave. Ian broke contact with Anne, only after kissing the back of her hand. John shook his head, smiling in Ian's wake – a true gentleman, even in the midst of war. He pulled out his combat knife, focusing on the wall of the cavern as the Alsos Team moved out.

CHAPTER 14: WAR

"And you will hear of wars and threats of wars, but don't panic.
Yes, these things must take place, but the end won't follow
immediately."
Mark 13:7

1800-Zulu Time 24May1945 (0300-JST 25May1945 Shuri Castle)

Anne scowled in John's direction, annoyed by the scraping sound of metal to stone, which had removed the last vestiges of her reverie. He stood firm, dragging his combat knife across the rock.

"What are you doing?" She stood to observe more closely.

"Creating the past we need… to get back," John said, his attention still focused on the carving.

"What's that supposed to mean?"

He stepped back to inspect his work. Anne craned her head to the side, observing the exact spear-shaped marker John had touched earlier.

"Wait a minute. You drew what we saw?"

He turned around and faced Anne, and then found the nearest crate to sit on. He unstrapped his helmet and ran his hand through sweaty hair. His solemn poise caught her off guard. She stood, puzzled until she realized he had something else on his mind.

"What's going on?" John asked.

Anne's body felt electrified with chills.

"What?"

"Come on. What's with you?" John asked.

She fidgeted with her hands and took a deep breath. Her ideas, her beliefs, were shaken. Wisp's death was hitting her hard. Her thoughts were so clouded. She exhaled, trying to seem calm.

"I saw something when we came here – and again when I separated you and Richie. I just don't understand what I'm supposed to do. I mean, how do you reconcile what you don't understand?"

213

"It comes down to a choice for most," John said. "Belief, or disbelief."

She nodded. Science and fact had always driven her decisions, not emotion.

"So, you're saying I should choose to believe in what I saw?"

"That's up to you. But, I do want you to realize the gift you've been given."

Tears formed, but she wiped them away, forcing back her emotions. She looked at John.

"I'm not like you," Anne said. "I've never had faith in religion."

John shook his head and laughed.

"Neither have I."

"What?"

"I put my faith in God, not religion," John said, sensing an opportunity to expound. "Religions exist around the world, but they are fundamentally manmade interpretations of Biblical prophecy. Most are fine—some great even—but some are simply twisted to conform to the rationalization of man's flawed will, rather than God's purpose. That's what people fail to understand."

Anne sat down and wiped her eyes. John placed his helmet back on his head and buckled the chinstrap.

"Steady, if I believe what I saw – what's next?"

"That's up to you," John said, smiling without hesitation.

She looked back at him, her head dropped, eyes darting to the ground.

"Let's work on getting out of here first," John said, turning his attention back to the task at hand.

†††††

Chappy, Rico, and Zip entered the cavern, climbing around some crates to spot John sitting alongside Anne. Her eyes were closed and her head was tilted as if she were looking at the ceiling. He realized that she was on the precipice of a choice, much as he was back in Bizerte. He held his arm out to stop Zip and Rico's movement, alerting them to what was happening.

The three men stood motionless. Anne stirred and looked at Chappy.
"What?" Anne asked.

"Nothing," Chappy said. "Just watching y'all sit on your asses, while we risk our lives."

John laughed, standing up and walking down to meet the rest of Spear Team.

"Glad you finally made it back," he said, bumping fists with his team.

"Richie said they have to fight their own way out. What's up with that?" Chappy asked.

"Yeah, we've got our own battle to fight this time," John said, leading them back to the wall where he had carved the symbol. "Come on up."

They followed him to the upper level of the cavern. Wisp still lay at their feet. Anne pulled out her poncho-liner and laid it beside his body.

"Let's get Wisp ready to go," John said, kneeling down.

All of Spear Team helped lift his body onto the poncho liner. John put his hand on Wisp's chest.

"Blessed are the peacemakers, my friend," John said.

Zip nodded and placed his hand on John's.

"Godspeed and calm seas."

"See you in Valhalla my brother," Rico said.

"You're not out of the fight – only resting," Chappy said. He put hand on John's shoulder.

Anne couldn't find the words; she scanned the faces of her teammates.

"You gotta say something," John said. "It's all we might get."

She overcame her grief and choked back the emotion. Her jaw faltered as she choked out the words.

"Thanks for believing in me," she whispered.

Mission focus fell over them all. Only the banging of metal against rock sounded throughout the cavern. The Japanese Army was close to breaking through. John rolled the poncho liner over Wisp's body.

"Secure it and rig some handles. We'll have to carry him to the extraction point."

"Will do," Chappy said.

Zip looked up at John.

"What's the plan, Steady?"

"It's simple." John walked to the carving on the wall, reaching out to touch it. "We head back to our time."

Wind circulated in the stale cavern. John turned around, looking at his team on the ground before him.

"Send us back. I know what must be done," John said, looking up at the ceiling.

A blue static charge arced from the walls and formed a whipping vortex about the cavern. The wind increased, and electrically charged particles surrounded John and the team. Anne looked up into the center of the vortex. She saw the figure. A man's figure, made of pure light. The brilliance blinded her, but the warmth settled into her heart. A blast of lightning struck the ground, thunder shook the cavern, and every feature faded. Arklight disappeared. One final snap of lightning reached out, striking the face of the painting. *Portrait of a Young Man* burned away, erasing itself from existence.

†††††

Richie crawled through the tunnel access and into the cave. His movement drew attention.

"Who's there?" Jack demanded, pointing his rifle at the crag.

"It's just us," Richie said, pulling himself to his feet.

"You damn sure took long enough," Red said.

"Sorry. Had to work out a few details," Bell said, following Richie out of the tunnel. Ian wiggled through last, reaching up to take Bell's hand and climb out.

"What's the plan?" Jack asked.

"That's usually my department," Bell said, checking the magazine of his rifle, "but Richie here says we need to trust him. So – any thoughts to share there, wise-guy?"

He turned toward the sailor, who used to be his subordinate. Where orders and discipline once ruled their relationship, only respect, admiration, and trust remained.

Ian dusted off the knees of his pants and looked at Richie, happy to see him becoming who he was supposed to be.

"Whatever we do, we need to act fast," Richie said. "It's only a couple hours until daylight; it will take us nearly that long to get back to the front lines."

Richie looked around the cave. It had a natural curvature to the right, just before you could see the mouth. He knew there was at least an entire platoon waiting for them. He checked his watch and smiled.

"Jack, you and Red set up over there. Take cover behind those crates. Me, Ian, and Bell will set up here and just to the right of you. When the Japs come running in here, we'll have them in a cross-fire."

"When they what?" Jack asked.

"We don't have much time," Richie said. "Just trust me."

Jack stuck a wad of chew in his mouth and said, "I got sailors telling me how to fight a ground war, some guys and a dame from the future popping in and out like magicians, and we're standing here... about to fight over some stupid-ass painting. I'm about out of damn trust."

"Speaking of – where is the painting?" Red asked.

"It's not important right now. Just do what Richie's asking. We've gotta believe this is all for something bigger," Bell said.

"Easy for you to say," Jack said, grabbing one of the stored Japanese machine guns. "Red, grab a couple extra magazines and follow me. This is freakin' insanity is what this is."

Red took a look at Richie, finding confidence in his stare.

"Jack, just do what he says. We'll be drinking some hooch back at camp before you know it."

The Marines set up a base of fire on the left side of the cave. Richie and Bell picked a covered position to the right, with Ian to their far right. There was little to no cover toward the entrance of the cave. Anything that entered would not have much recourse.

"Listen up: we lay down fire when Ian engages. He has the largest angle, so we'll open up after him, trapping whoever is in the kill-box," Bell instructed.

"I hear you," Jack said, spitting some tobacco to the floor.

"After we knock out the Japs, be ready to make a run for it... in between salvos," Richie said.

The earth shook. Deafening explosions rattled everyone's skulls. Debris fell from the ceiling of the cave. Another rumble of thunder jolted them, then another, until they all realized it was rounds impacting around the castle. A shocking *BOOM* struck just outside the cave, rumbling the Alsos Team's guts.

"That's not regular artillery... those are battleship guns. The Mississippi must have started her run!" Red smiled. "Good call, Richie."

Richie nodded and pulled the stock of his rifle into his shoulder. A commotion of voices could be heard entering and echoing around the cave in chaos. Shadows appeared on the walls as the men ran for cover from the naval gunfire.

"Hold. Let them get closer," Bell said.

Japanese Army regulars appeared, rounding the corner with their rifles at the ready. Their eyes were wide open, scared of what they might find. Another explosion rocked the cave. Several men jumped to the ground, while others ran for the tunnels located behind the Alsos Team.

"Fire!"

Ian opened up on the rear of the group. Jack fired the machine gun, sweeping it side-to-side across the formation. Clouds of ruby mist hung in the air as men collapsed from the barrage of hot metal. Amid the mayhem of the unexpected onslaught, a few random shots were returned from the Japanese soldiers. Jack's machine gun clicked empty, and Red scrambled to load another magazine atop the Type-99 LMG. They soon realized, however, that nothing moved forward of their position. Only a few gurgles of the men's last breaths could be heard.

Jack pulled the charging handle and stared down the sights of the weapon. Bell and Richie hung their heads around the cover they were behind, changing magazines. Ian stood looking over his field of fire, finding no signs of a threat. Heavy impacts from the Allied guns continued to shake the ground. Dirt and pieces of rock rained down from the cave's ceiling.

"Helluva job, fellas!" Jack said.

Richie stood up and walked toward the mouth of the cave.

"What are you doing, Richie?" Bell asked.

"I have to go check our path – it's okay, Skipper."

"I've rarely seen the chap this sure," Ian said.

"Let's go cover him, just in case. Press forward." Bell stood to his feet on the shaky earth; it was like trying to walk during an earthquake.

Jack hung his rifle across his back and tucked the Japanese machine gun under his armpit. The two Marines moved in unison, Red tucking extra magazines in his pockets along the way.

Richie continued to stalk toward the entrance while the other four covered him from all angles. Once he reached the bend inside the cave, he could see the devastation of the naval gunfire. The lush green of the jungle had been ripped apart. He saw the bodies of many Japanese soldiers – the ones who didn't make it inside. Either way, death was all they would have found.

"There's a lull. Should we run for it?" Jack asked.

"Not yet," Richie said, holding up his arm, index finger extended.

"When?" Red asked.

A faint sound carried across the exterior landscape. The atmosphere parted with a sharp buzz and the echo of metallic rain carried across the ground.

"Incoming!" Ian shouted.

Everyone ran back, deeper into the cave, except for Richie. He stood just feet inside the mouth while the others dove into the dirt, trying to become part of the rock wall.

"Richie, get to cover!" Bell yelled.

The jungle quaked and rolled with each powerful explosion. Trees shattered, dirt rained down, and debris scattered in all directions. Richie watched each round close in on the cave's entrance. Everything shook, throwing him off balance. He stumbled to the floor of the cave, still focused on the destruction as it closed in. He counted impacts, even as the vibrations to his gut almost forced him to vomit. Hell was raining down on Shuri Castle, but all he could see was his team's salvation.

The bombardment ceased. Richie counted 12 massive impacts. What he saw in front of him aligned with what he saw inside the cavern with John.

"Let's go! Move!" he shouted.

The other four staggered to their feet, flexing their jaws from the deafening explosions. Their heads pounded and their bodies ached.

"It's about damn time," Jack said, closing in on Richie in the center of the cave.

"I'm not sure we could stand another one of those," Bell said.

"Just follow me, and don't stop!" Richie replied, running into the charred remains of the jungle. A rolling path lay spread before them, filled with craters and smoldering earth. It went on for over one-hundred yards.

Richie took the lead, bounding through the shattered jungle. The rest of his team followed, making it halfway across the craters. A burst of fire opened up on them from the untouched jungle ahead.

"Down!" he yelled, diving in one of the smoldering craters. It was still warm from the explosion and the kinetic impact.

"Hot!" Red yelled, raking shredded foliage under his body.

Rounds impacted all around the crater and flashes popped across the barrier of the jungle.

"What now?" Bell asked, poking his head up to see where the enemy was.

"Wait for it," Richie said, raising his head to look. The next inbound salvo could be heard descending from above.

"Cover!"

"Oh my God!" Jack bellowed.

The ground shook with unrelenting fury. Each powerful rumble sounded like the thunder of the most radiant lightning ever witnessed. Harrowing flashes popped, so bright, the night turned to day. Dynamic shockwaves carried over the Alsos Team. None of them dared raise their heads from the warm soil. Richie counted, even as his guts felt like they would rattle out of his chest.

"Eleven... Twelve!"

The rumble subsided and he raised his head, feeling warm soil roll off his neck. His entire body was buried from the barrage. Anyone in the jungle trying to stop them was surely destroyed or shell-shocked far beyond action.

"Thank God!" Richie said, rising to his feet. "Forward!"

Bell shook the concussion off and looked around, seeing the others stagger to their feet.

"You heard him. Let's go while we can."

"This sucks," Jack said, shaking out the cobwebs, "like worse than Iwo."

"And that's saying something," Red added, trying to muster a jog.

"Hurry up!" Richie yelled, trying to keep the group focused.

"If we make it out of this – no more war for me," Ian said, now keeping pace with Richie.

The five men circumvented as many craters as they could; some they had to run through and climb out of, at last reaching the jungle, clear of Shuri Castle. Richie entered the canopy of foliage, ushering the others into its welcomed concealment. Jack took point, orienting himself by compass on the most direct path to the Marine's front lines.

They soon crested the hill where they had rendezvoused earlier. Jack propped himself against the Sisha statue on the crest. Richie and Red stepped a small way out of the jungle, scanning for any sign of the enemy.

"Relax, fellas. We should be out of harm's reach. I know the safe way back to the front from here," Jack said, inserting another large plug of tobacco in his mouth.

Red walked up to Jack, sticking his fingers in the same tin, extracting a dip for himself. All of them were covered in ashen dirt, debris, and sweat. Ian and Bell both had wet rings showing through their clothes.

"I'd give up the Queen's gold for a jolly good smoke right now," Ian panted, taking a seat on the ground. Bell took a knee beside him.

Richie stepped to the edge of the foliage and pulled out his binoculars. They could all still feel the ground shake with each shell impacting in and around the castle. He watched large chunks explode from the structure while men scrambled for cover.

"I hope John and his team made it out," Bell said.

Richie scanned the castle and then down to the cave from where they escaped the barrage. The once-pristine landscape lay pitted, shattered, and charred. This entire area would be destroyed in a matter of another day.

"They made it out. I'm sure of it."

"How? Why are you so sure all of a sudden?" Bell asked, taking a sip of water from his canteen.

Richie knew he would have to explain what he saw, but he couldn't chance a breach of their secret. The truth would have to wait until the three of them were alone, in a secure place.

"It's just something I know," he said, nodding to Bell.

"Well, I don't know about you," Ian said, running his hand through his wet hair, "but I'm seriously about done with this war. I think we need to go about things a bit differently in the future."

He reached into his breast pocket and pulled out the Knights Templar journal and sat in on his thigh. From his other pocket, he pulled out a flask filled with whiskey.

"I think it's time that we report back to our respective agencies and make the request for something new." He took a draw off his flask, passing it on to Bell, who turned up the small metal container.

"What are you talking about?" he asked, handing the flask over to Richie next.

"I think given our experiences," he said, pausing in thought, "collectively and singularly, we need more leeway to develop the information in a more collaborative way. In other words, we need to form a cooperative alliance to get to the bottom of all of this — you know, once this godforsaken war is over."

Richie took a drink and handed the flask to Red.

"Bell, he's got a point. We need to keep digging. There's so much more we don't know. Plus, we have somewhere to be next year — as a team."

"Do you have any idea what the hell they're talking about?" Jack asked, nudging Red as he guzzled the flask. "And hey, how about you save me a taste?"

"Sorry," Red said, passing the flask to his friend. "Whatever they are talking about, I've seen enough weird stuff for one lifetime."

"Yeah," Jack said, after emptying the remainder of the whiskey. "I'm good."

"Gentlemen, you do realize that you can't speak about what happened here — to anyone, ever," Bell said, standing back on his feet.

"Look, Lieutenant. I'm not saying shit about whatever the hell happened tonight. All I have to show for it, anyway, is a damn headache and crap all over me. At least I can wash that away with a shower, some hooch, and aspirin," Jack said, spitting on the ground.

Bell smiled and tipped his hat to Jack.

"At least you got a sense of humor about it, Marine."

Red stood up and walked next to Richie, surveying toward the castle as it continued to take a pounding.

"I do have one question," he said, cutting his eyes to Richie. "If that was my grandson I met tonight, how am I supposed to deal with that?"

Richie smirked and shook his head.

"We can't let them know."

"What do you mean... them?" Red asked.

"I'm not sure if you caught it, but the leader of that team was my grandson, John."

"Really?"

"Yeah. I had to decide some time ago that I would and will do everything I can to build him into the man I saw tonight, without telling him all that I know, as he grows up. I think it's imperative that we remember the men we saw and shape them toward their future. But, that's just me."

"That sounds like good advice," Red said.

"This war has matured us. Hardened us for what's still to come. How's the saying go? What doesn't kill us..."

"Makes us stronger," Red said, smiling.

Jack hoisted the Type-99 on his shoulder and walked up beside them. Bell and Ian joined the group, and they collectively watched another barrage of naval guns flatten the western wall of the castle. The blasts flashed into the predawn sky as the Eastern horizon signaled a new day.

"If we hump it, we can probably get across the lines before sunrise," Jack said.

✝✝✝✝✝

"Richie," Bell whispered, tapping him on the shoulder. Jack and Red were on point and Richie was in the middle of the small column.

"Yeah?"

"Me and Ian have been talking it over."

"Talking what over?" Richie asked.

"His idea," Bell said. "You know, about continuing to run down Templar info."

"Oh yeah. So, what's the plan?"

"I'm sure we need to keep everything compartmentalized. We both agree," he said, ducking a branch, "that we need to keep working on this as a group – just the three of us."

"Okay, and?"

"If we go to our bosses at the OSS, and he goes to his at MI-6, we think they will bite on the continued joint operation, but we'll have to disguise our real mission. You know, under the cover of continuing the Alsos Missions. He's got a plan for that."

"That's pretty smart, Skipper. Both our governments will be trying to acquire all the atomic intelligence they can muster. Since it's all intertwined, we should be able to pull it off."

"That's what Ian thinks, too."

"Since it involves information on atomic research, we should be able to get a beyond-classified security measure in place."

"Exactly. And I've already thought of the project name."

"Let me guess. Arklight – Project Arklight," Richie said, with a smile.

"I'm pretty sure we can get the right people involved and push the project forward, especially if you and I are in charge."

"What about Ian?"

"We'll share everything – all of it. The Brits deserve to know what we know."

Richie stepped over a small fern and stumbled forward. He caught his balance, catching up to Red and Jack. The foliage had broken open, and the Allied front lay ahead of them. Their night's ordeal was behind them, but war, a hidden war, remained in their future.

CHAPTER 15: CRUSADE

"And many will turn away from me and betray and hate each other."
Matthew 24:10

1830-Zulu Time 24May2020 (2330-EST Over the Atlantic)

Admiral Nathan Grant exited the rear communications deck with a blank stare. The Gulfstream G650 had six plush recliners in the front portion of the aircraft; a well-insulated bulkhead separated the operations section and Nathan's command team. He sat in one of the leather chairs, sinking almost as deeply as his heart. His head fell back against the headrest. He inhaled and tried to expel the choking tension in his chest.

Archie and Rod shared the front row, and Helen sat next to Walter in the second. Hearing his return, they leaned and twisted back to face Nathan, waiting for an update. Only the rush of atmosphere across the fuselage and the hum of the engines resonated. Nathan tried to gather his thoughts. Helen shifted to the very edge of her seat, reaching across the aisle.

"Are you okay?"

He rolled his head forward and looked across the faces of his colleagues, mentors – friends.

"They're all dead," Nathan said, fighting back a tearful rage. "The whole CIC team."

Archie stood up out of his seat at the news.

"What? How?"

Walter gripped his cane, placing his forehead against his hands.

"Have mercy upon their souls," he whispered.

Rod sat back in his seat; his face contorted from the news. Nathan looked at Archie, who sank back in his seat, as well.

"Chief said the attack looked coordinated. Well-planned. Judging by what he was able to recover, probably the work of Magnus."

"What's the chief's status?" Archie asked.

"All he told me was he's fine," Nathan said. "Knowing him, it sounded like he got banged up some, but he's a tough one."

"I still don't understand how they knew we were there," Archie said.

"I hope we can figure that out. A lot of good people died, and now – the whole mission's compromised."

"Maybe not," Walter said, raising his head off his hands.

"No offense, but that gives me very little comfort," Nathan said. "I need an actionable plan, not just hope."

Helen sat back in her chair, electing to stay out of the conversation. Rod closed his eyes repeatedly, rolling his jaw as if he needed to release some pressure in his head. He twitched, turning his chair away from the others. Nathan glanced at Rod, worrying that his emotions were getting the best of him. He focused back on Walter's statement. Archie stood and walked down the aisle, taking the seat beside Nathan.

"Walter, this is no time to hold back," Nathan said. "We don't have much time if we're going to Spear Team."

The old man exchanged a glance with the admiral. His eyes were telling.

For the first time, Nathan understood why Walter operated as he did. He embraced his designed path, and he had a faith far beyond Nathan's own worldly perception. Walter was convicted to a purpose – not of the world he could see, but of the one he couldn't. A chill shot up his spine, and his eyes widened, meeting Walter's. The old man nodded his concurrence. He sat back, trying to understand how Walter could have sensed his epiphany.

"Nathan, we have to assume that Magnus has compromised the mission," Archie chimed in. "If he knew where the CIC was, he probably knows Spear Team's location as well. We need to get the chief some support and launch a counterassault."

"Yessir, I agree." He spun in his chair and knocked on the door to the communications deck, sliding it open.

"Get the chief back on the horn. Tell him—"

A hand grabbed his shoulder, interrupting him. Walter stood behind him and leaned down to his ear.

"Use Expedition Protocol. Tell the chief they need to extract covertly. I have an asset in place."

"What?" he whispered back.

"Trust me. The asset will find them. They have to go dark – now."

Nathan's face grew slack. He took a deep breath.

"Follow the path, Nathan. Our enemies are upon us."

He pulled his head back to get a square look at Walter. The old man's hand patted him on the shoulder, and he returned to his seat with a nod. Nathan entered the communications deck.

Once inside, he glanced back over the forward section of the plane. Helen and Archie were talking among themselves. Rod sat alone in the forward corner of the compartment with the back of his chair hiding his body; something had looked painful in the way his eyes had opened and closed, his brow creased, and his lips curled. Nathan's gaze swung back to Walter, who sat in his chair, hands propped on his cane.

"Go ahead… we'll wait," he said.

†††††

Nathan locked the door to the communications deck and turned to look at his staff of three. He faced the rear of the compartment and looked down the long table to his right, which was stuffed with electronic equipment and computers. The closest to him was Lydia, the senior communications officer.

"Admiral, what can we do?"

"Get the chief back on the horn."

"Will do," she said, turning to dial out.

Beside her sat Lieutenant Frank Mitchell, and beside him, Patricia Smith, the long-time command missions analyst. Frank was the youngest of the crew, brought on only a couple of months ago, but the other two ladies had both worked under the command for some time. Nathan placed his hands on the counter, and he looked over the monitors. At an angle, he could see pictures of the scene at Kadena Air Force Base on Patricia's screen. He walked down the aisle, standing behind her station.

"How bad is it?"

Her eyes brimmed with tears. She had known them all.

"They're all dead. Every one of them."

Nathan placed his hand on her shoulder and squeezed.

"I know it hurts, but we have to hold it together."

She nodded and wiped her cheeks. Frank looked over his right shoulder and up to the admiral.

"We still don't have an ID on who's responsible, sir," Frank said. "We washed all of the images of the tangos through Interpol and the FBI databases. Some of them are on the watchlists for Asian triads, one was German, and two of them are U.S. military veterans. It doesn't make any sense."

Nathan rubbed his chin, already sensing who was responsible.

"It's the work of Magnus O'Keefe. He used a conglomeration of mercs in Nashville; it's the same thing here. The big question I have is: how did he know where to hit us?"

Patricia clicked her keyboard and pulled up footage from the hangar.

"They came straight in, like they knew exactly where to go."

Nathan watched two men peel off from the main assault force, one holding a small case.

"What are those two doing?"

"Not sure," Frank said, "we don't have a camera covering that angle."

A minute passed. The camera caught a single man entering frame, his weapon tilted barrel up. The way he moved was familiar.

"Is that the chief?"

"Yessir. Based on what we know, he killed those other two inside one of the C-17s. That's him moving toward the hangar. He took out a bunch of tangos, sir. But, by the time he got in there – it was already too late."

"I've seen enough," Nathan said, backing away from the work station.

"It's hard to watch," Patricia said, minimizing the feed.

"Admiral, I got the chief back on the line," Lydia announced.

"Thanks." He picked up the red receiver on the console and pulled it to his ear.

"Are you secure?" Nathan asked.

"Yes," said the chief.

"You still in one piece?"

"I've been in worse shape, sir."

"You're a tough old frogman, Chief. What's our status?"

"All of our aircrews are accounted for. I've got both C-17s in the air, headed back with our dead and what's left of the CIC. Thank the SecDef for me. Had he not stepped in, this would be all over the news. I've got a Delta Force Team inbound to extract Spear Team."

"Good. What's their ETA?"

"They're already on the ground in country. Given our last experience, I had them tasked with a training op after we selected our target."

"Good looking out, Chief... I'm sorry about your team."

"Me too, sir. I'm gonna kill that Welsh bastard and the goon who did this when I find them – count on that."

"I'm with you, but I have to ask one more thing."

"What's that, sir?"

"I was told you encountered two of the mercs on one of our C-17s. Is that right?"

"I did."

"Did they have a case, or a box, with them?"

"I didn't see one."

Nathan thought about all of the possibilities. *What was in the box?* He had to find it. Any number of terrible scenarios could result if it went unchecked. He took a deep, mind-cleansing breath and prepared for the road ahead. He knew getting to Spear Team was paramount.

"This might be the last time we talk for a while, so I need you to listen up. You with me?" Nathan asked.

"Roger that, sir."

"Execute exfil plan Charlie – Expedition Protocol. Arklight is compromised. Extract Spear Team and go black."

"Sir?" he paused. "Verification?"

"Alpha, Eight, Four, Delta, Zulu – One," Nathan said.

"Copy that. Good luck, sir."

"Same to you, old friend."

The line went dead. Nathan pulled the receiver away from his ear and lowered it into the cradle. Lydia sat back in her chair, as did the other two communications deck officers.

"We're compromised? How bad?" Lydia asked.

Nathan stood up and ran his hands over his face.

"Complete."

"Patricia, let's contact both C-17 crews. We're going to need them to stop in Guam, off-load, and inspect their cargo. We have to locate that case, or box – whatever it is."

"I'll start the process, sir. Do you want them quarantined?"

The bulkhead next to Patricia vibrated with a sharp *crack*. The wall bulged, springing inward, before retracting back into shape.

"What the hell was that?" Nathan asked, unlocking the door and pulling it open.

Before he could react, a blurred object struck him in the head. The sharp blow came through the doorway, splitting his forehead. A numbing red fogged his vision as he staggered backwards, falling to the deck. He tried to recover, but consciousness faded into fragmented frames of violence. He looked at the blurred figure; the assailant leveled off his weapon, firing it into Nathan's command team. Before he could process what was happening, another heavy blow struck him in the head, knocking him unconscious.

†††††

Rod stood above Nathan's motionless body; his suppressed pistol was warm with the friction of rapid-fire. He felt nothing. Bodies lay slumped over the workstations. People he knew, and had even led, lay dead by his hand. His face grew slack, as if something else stepped in, taking charge of his body.

Looking over his handiwork for any movement, he saw none. He turned to face the forward compartment of the aircraft, ready to seize all control. The SecDef, his head already split open from the fray, sat stunned in his chair. A single shot to the back of Archie's head had taken Walter by surprise, shaking his attention from Helen's body. She had acted valiantly, drawing her weapon to defend against Rod's initial attack in Nathan's absence, but there wasn't enough time. Rod had punched her, knocking her to the floor with an impact that jerked the pistol from her hand. He had shot her first, crippling her on the deck in front of the bulkhead.

With all attention upon him, the old man tried to parry Rod away with his cane, but it proved too feeble a move. Rod kicked the old man from his seat, turning toward Helen as she tried to pushed herself up, wounded but not out. One more kick to the stomach and her body heaped in front of the communications deck. She never recovered. He followed up with a single shot to the back of her head.

All that consumed him was the mission. It ran through his mind like a broken record. Every part of his being was now obsessed with completing his task and avoiding the pain he knew would come if he failed. His movements were robotic, precise, and calculated. He looked down on the floor, grabbing Walter by the collar, dragging him back into his seat.

The old man shook, not from fear, but from the pain of his fall. He glanced at Helen's lifeless body, now sure that his nightmarish visions contained real prophecy. He reached to the floor and grabbed his cane, leaning it on his chair. He rubbed his side and looked at Rod.

"It was never entirely clear," Walter grimaced, "who would betray us."

Rod reached into a compartment just inside the door of the communications deck, pulling out two sets of flex cuffs. He holstered his weapon and stepped into the passenger compartment. He tucked one set under his arm and walked up to Walter.

"Don't make me hurt you again. Give me your arms."

Walter held out his hands, wrists up. Rod placed the plastic bands over his wrists and cinched down the ring, securing Walter's wrists to each other.

He turned and stepped over Helen's body, taking a knee by Nathan, who remained unconscious on the communications deck. He rolled him over and secured his hands behind his back. He grabbed Nathan under his arms, pulling him forward to the passenger compartment, onto the empty seat behind Walter.

"Why, Rod?" Walter asked.

"My name isn't Rod."

Walter sat back in his chair. He watched a man he had known for almost forty-years fade away into something else. There was no doubt that Rod had ceased to exist. He had killed people – some closer to him than his own family. Without warning, he had turned into a monster, something different. Walter watched him drag the bodies of people he called friends toward the communications deck. One by one, he dropped them all on the floor and shut the door.

Without giving it a second thought, he walked to the minibar and washed the gore from his hands. He picked up the receiver to the pilot compartment.

"How long until we get back to Arklight HQ?" he asked.

"If we maintain our current airspeed, 67 minutes."

"Roger that."

"Sir, is everything okay back there? It sounded like someone fell."

"Oh, we're fine. I tripped over my chair," he laughed. "Too much bourbon."

"Understood, sir. We'll be making our approach into Mayport shortly."

"Thanks," he said, as he hung up the receiver.

"So, if you're not Rod. Who are you?" Walter asked, wincing from a broken rib.

The man glared at Walter with contempt. He pulled out a glass, added ice, and poured some bourbon, electing to sit in the chair next to Walter. Nathan was slumped over to one side, handcuffed and unconscious. His breathing was labored, his face covered in blood not all his own. Rod took a drink and looked through the window into the ink-black night sky.

"You know who I am, old man."

He turned back to Walter, and his eyes told the story. They looked different. The change in him was complete. He was no longer Rod; he was convicted by something else. An intense stare burned into Walter. Something from the past sent a chill down his spine.

"Your eyes," Walter said. "They remind me of a man... I once knew. An evil man."

"Evil? You, with all of your wisdom, and all of your experience – yet, you still don't understand that one man's perception of evil is simply another man's quest for righteousness."

"Weber?"

"Yes. I'm his son. Klaus."

"But how?" Walter asked. "You're Roderick Johnson. I've known you for decades. You're a hero, a soldier – my friend. This can't be."

Klaus took another drink and laughed. The commotion stirred Nathan. His head bobbled back and forth. Klaus took what was left of his drink and tossed in Nathan's face, stinging the gash along his forehead. He shook to life and gritted his teeth. His vision was fuzzy, but he recognized Walter sitting in front of him by the hands resting on his cane. His wrists were bound. Nathan looked at Rod, trying to focus on his face.

"Nathan, are you okay?" Walter asked.

"What happened?" Nathan asked, fluttering his eyelids, trying to focus.

"Walter and I were just discussing that fact," Klaus said, standing to walk to the minibar for another drink.

"Rod? Why am I handcuffed?"

"I was about to get to that with old Walter here, just before you woke."

"What?" He worked to sit up and noticed he was seat-belted in place.

Klaus dropped some cubes of ice into his glass and poured himself another round. He focused on Nathan.

"Do you know what it's like to live in Hell? Imagine being trapped inside of your own body for 50 years. Watching through a lens, while some fake persona drives you along. You can't feel, you can't act. Just screaming into an abyss of nothingness. Trying desperately to free yourself from the bonds of that life, only to find out that it's the definition of who you are."

"What the hell are you talking about, Rod?"

Walter sensed his meaning, having heard similar descriptions in the past. He worked on many projects over the years. Certain spin-offs from Project Arklight had developed into other programs.

"MK Ultra – is that how they buried you inside of Rod?"

He laughed, "No—they covered the real me, Klaus Weber, with Rod Johnson, the fake. I hate him – call me Rod again, and I'll show you how much."

"I don't understand," Nathan said.

Walter held his palms up toward Klaus.

"Nathan, Klaus Weber is the son of Colonel Weber, from our Alsos missions. Apparently, MK Ultra was much more effective than I ever knew."

"You arrogant Americans think you know everything. MK Ultra was a stolen, half-hearted attempt to create the ultimate spy – a real Manchurian Candidate. Your country never had the guts to see the program to its full potential."

"What's he talking about?" Nathan asked, his lucidity increasing.

"MK Ultra was a CIA mind-control program we started in 1953, after we seized some research during an Alsos mission. That, coupled with what the Allies discovered at Auschwitz, gave the CIA some strong research to base the program on. I never worked on the program, but after we heard some unsavory information regarding how it was being conducted, it got shut down."

"Okay, but why? Why give up your whole life just to betray us? It sounds insane."

Klaus walked back to his chair and sat. He turned up his drink and crossed his legs.

"Frankly, I was born for this. My father raised me into the Teutonic Knights Order – The Order of the Black Sun. I know the history. The Templar stole away what rightfully belonged to us. Our Führer started World War II in an effort to reclaim our birthright and to initiate the final solution. You may have stopped us then, but it only delayed the inevitable. The destruction of Arklight will ensure our path to true enlightenment."

Nathan looked at Walter, knowing his words carried more meaning than ever before. Everything had changed. Rod was gone and Klaus was the vengeful remnant of the man they all knew and even loved. Everything crashed in on him at once.

"Where's Helen? Archie? Where are they?"

Klaus sat back in his chair; his face filled with satisfaction. Nathan looked behind him on the floor. Gore stained the carpet. He looked on the leather behind Klaus' head – spatters of crimson.

"He killed them," Walter said, his head slumped downward.

A rage filled Nathan's heart, until tears ran down his cheeks.

"Bastard!"

"Easy," Klaus said. "Unless you want me to kill the pilots too."

Nathan gritted his teeth.

"If it makes you feel any better," Klaus said, a German accent forming in his dialect. "Rod never did have the stomach for this sort of thing. I would be yelling out on the inside… for him to shoot you in the face, but he would just keep yammering on – like an idiot. He made me sick. Weak."

"Calm down, Nathan. Save your energy," Walter said.

"So, he can do what, old man?" Klaus laughed. "Die well-rested?"

"That's your plan?" Nathan asked. "Killing us? Then why keep us alive now?"

Klaus sat forward, drawing his pistol. He pointed it at Walter, his finger straight against the slide. Nathan knew he had no intention to shoot either of them.

"You're bluffing," Nathan said after a pause. "You need us both alive."

"You're a smart guy." Klaus pulled his weapon back and placed it in his holster. "We do still have to get past all that biometric security."

"Security? What are you after?" Nathan asked.

"You know, I may have been trapped inside my own body, but I wasn't blind. What do you think I'm after?"

Nathan's mind reeled thinking about how close Rod had been to the program. Too close. He had designed most of the protocols, and he even built Arklight's headquarters. The man knew everything.

"The Arma Christi," Nathan said.

A buzz resonated in the cabin. The receiver to the pilot's cockpit flashed. Klaus walked to the device and picked it up.

"Yes?" Klaus answered.

"We've got a plane off our port side. U.S. markings. They radioed us and said they're a priority flight. They said you would verify."

"Roger that, son," Klaus said, his voice shifting. "They're a new Arklight security component. Have them follow us in. They have priority clearance to the Arklight hangar."

"Will do, sir. I guess you'll alert the admiral?"

"He's right here. He'll be thrilled." He hung up the phone.

"What are you up to?" Nathan growled.

"Let's just say – we have a plan." A satisfied grin spread Klaus' mouth.

"Look, no one else needs to die. We'll give you what we have, but don't do this," Nathan said, his stare pleading.

"Even with everything we have, you still won't have all of it," Walter added. "How are you going to activate the Time Key without all of the pieces?"

"That's not my concern. However, I'm fairly certain that Kieffer will enjoy seeing you both," Klaus said, grabbing Walter's chin, "one more time."

"Alfred Kieffer," Walter said. "So, he's still the man behind the curtain, is he?"

"He's our Führer now. His family will rule this world before it's over, and I will stand beside them with pride. Once the final solution is activated, the world will be ours, and the Fourth Reich will rule in peace."

Klaus sat back in his chair, no longer interested in conversation.

"Walter, does this all go back to Bizerte?" Nathan asked.

"Not exactly. This – this battle goes back to the beginning," Walter said.

"What are you talking about?" Nathan asked.

"The greatest battle man has ever faced. Our toughest challenge."

"What's that?"

"Our own nature. The choices we make," Walter said.

"Maybe I don't understand. Are you talking about our mistakes?" Nathan asked.

"It's deeper than that," Walter said. "One line burns as the light and the other is an abyss of gloom. One is life and the other is death. The Templar and the Teutonic Knights. Arklight and the Black Sun. Where there is darkness, there will always be a light to engulf it."

Nathan took in his words. He was no stranger to the ways in which good can oppose evil.

"Shut up, old man," Klaus said, sitting forward, tired of the comparison. "There's never been a choice. There're only the falsehoods of the Templar. Our Führer knows all about your lies. You created religion, the notion of Christ, the Bible, only to bring order upon men. Not for any other reason. You took relics that have scientific qualities and hid them from the world, stalling our development. You're not some hero; you're the villain – a vile lie to the masses."

"You're insane," Nathan said, looking at Klaus.

"No," Klaus said. "We're the only ones who see the world clearly. That's why we're destined to rule, disproving all of your lies."

"And how do you think you'll accomplish that?"

"The final solution will wipe you all out – religious zealots, along with anyone else who opposes our master race. Your time will close, nearly as abruptly as it started with your Jesus Christ. The lies will end once the Führer shows the world what you've been hiding from them. They will make him a king. A righteous master of the world."

Nathan looked at Walter, his concern evident. The final solution sounded much like mass genocide. Even with his knowledge of the Arma Christi and the Knights Templar journal, he had no clue how The Order of the Black Sun would accomplish their plan. He had to figure a way out of this terrible situation. Too much was at stake.

CHAPTER 16: SHADOW

"And for those who lived in the land where death casts its shadow,
a light has shined."
Matthew 4:16

1830-Zulu Time 24May2020 (0330-JST 25May2020 Shuri Castle)

A cigarette hung from Magnus' lips as he scanned the camera monitors from his perch inside the security office. He adjusted the thermal goggles on his head as an extra precaution.

"Tunnel team. Radio check."

"Clear and in place."

"Copy. Make sure your thermals are ready to go. It might be the only way we see them coming."

"We copy."

He pulled the cigarette from his lips and exhaled a cloud of smoke. He laid the radio across his lap and pulled out his sat-phone, dialing up Ronnie.

"Hey," Ronnie answered, "you headed this way yet?"

"No. Still waiting. What's your status?"

"I'm here. No tails. We're all set."

"Good. Did you get the diversion set?"

"Primed and ready. Was Ayana helpful?"

"You can say that. She's free now," Magnus smirked, burning through the last drag of his cigarette.

"Whatever, let's just get this over with, and you pay me what I'm due."

"You'll get everything that's coming to you, mate. The payday of a lifetime – I promise. Just focus on what's ahead, and be ready to go when I call you."

"Okay."

Magnus cleared the phone and pressed the call button for Maximillion. He scanned the monitors as it rang.

"Before you say anything," Maximillion answered, "we are in the final phase now – the asset is active."

"When were you going to tell me?"

"I just did, you ungrateful sod!"

Magnus sat forward in his chair, sighed, and rubbed the bridge of his nose. There was never a chance to win with his father.

"Yes, Father. Who's the asset?"

"Your grandfather and I have decided to hold that information for security purposes at present – until you return to Geneva. We will give you the details there, in person."

"Then why tell me anything, now? You knew I'd want to know."

"You've always been short-sighted, Magnus. Sometimes I find it hard to believe that you're *my* son. Stop acting like a selfish imbecile, get the job done, and don't be an idiot."

Magnus clenched his jaw. All he could think of was getting his hands around his father's throat; choking the life out of him was the one thought that kept him focused.

"Yes, Father."

"Now listen, the asset has seized control of the primary command element. We have a team in place to neutralize their base and extract the Arma Christi."

"How?"

"Like I said – stop being so short-sighted. Our asset has been in place since the beginning. This goes far deeper than you're capable of comprehending."

Magnus lit up another cigarette, growing tired of being treated like some pawn. He thought maybe his father would give him some respect now, but the man was only riding a high from getting his hands on what he wanted. He took the smoke into his lungs, exhaling away the rage.

"What do you want me to do?"

"The asset confirmed that they went to retrieve the Spear of Destiny, as we thought. But they have another piece of the Time Key with them. A coin – carried by John Steadman, their team leader."

"A coin? What kind of coin?"

"It's one of the folded coins we've been looking for. According to the asset, it's an American civil war coin, marked General John Bell Hood. We have to retrieve it as well."

"I'll get it off of his dead body."

"Whatever it takes, Magnus. We need both relics."

"I understand. Anything else?"

"One more thing. Today marks a new beginning for The Order. No more running. Our enemies will be no more. Don't fail our family, Magnus. We will establish the Fourth Reich and fulfill our Führer's grand vision – the final solution."

"Aye, Father."

The line went dead. He was sick of being left out of the loop. He had done everything asked of him over the years, but his father still treated him like a child. Whatever the ultimate weapon was, it was going to belong to Magnus and no one else. The Order of the Black Sun would be his to control, along with whatever power that entailed. He sat back in his chair smoking his cigarette. It was all just a matter of time.

✝✝✝✝✝

The electric-blue radiance flashed; static-filled light reflected against the rock, and a final arc surged throughout the cavern. In the terminal strobe, five silhouettes were standing. One other profile lay horizontal, suspended by the others.

"I can't see," Anne said.

"It gets a little less-blinding each time. Just let it settle," Zip consoled.

"Set Wisp down for a minute," John said, lowering the makeshift body bag to the ground. He stood back up and reached for his radio, flipping the switch back to digital. He keyed up the transmitter.

"Spear actual to Command – you copy?"

There was no response, only static.

"We're still deep underground," Chappy said.

"Let's get up to the throne room, then. We should be able to exfil from there."

"Sounds good to me," Rico said. "I've had enough time in caves for the rest of my life."

"Me too, buddy. Anne, you take point. We'll get Wisp," John said, crouching down to help lift.

"Roger that." She stepped toward the tunnel, flipped down her night-vision goggles, and activated her camouflage. John and the others followed her up the path, making for the throne room above.

"What's the extraction plan?" Chappy asked.

"Depends," John said.

"Since when do you fly by the seat of your pants?" Rico asked.

John looked down to his hand gripping the body-bag.

"Since Nashville. We have to stay fluid."

"No doubt," Chappy said. "I don't want to get shot again if I can help it."

"That hard head of yours saved us all," Rico said, forcing a smile.

"I'm topside," Anne said.

"Spear actual, Command – anyone copy?" Only static registered.

"Steady, I got multiple contacts; looking at the playback now," Zip said, addressing his command module.

"You were right. Magnus is here – isn't he?" Chappy asked.

"I got about a dozen contacts I can see," Zip said. "There may be more. Looks like he's got everything covered."

"What about the lower exit from the cavern?" Rico asked.

"It might be clear. Can't tell," Zip said.

"Set Wisp down," John said. "I need a minute."

The team lowered Wisp's body to the ground. Anne moved side-to-side, checking for any movement inside the throne room. John took a knee beside his fallen friend, closed his eyes, and grew silent. Chappy looked at John and soon realized what he was doing. Without a second thought, he placed his hand on John's shoulder. Zip and Rico looked back then at each other.

"Looks all clear," Anne said.

When she didn't get an acknowledgement, she turned, seeing them all still and silent.

"What in the hell are you doing? We have to figure a way out of this mess."

She scowled, turning her attention back toward the throne room.

"This is bullshit," she whispered, edging forward to exit the corridor.

A hand grabbed her ankle.

"Freeze," John whispered.

She locked her body in position. It was then that she saw the faint glimmer of a laser tripwire in front of her.

"See it?"

She nodded and retracted her body back toward the others. She turned toward John, lifting her night-vision goggles.

"So, what's next?" Anne asked.

"I need you to trust me. Have patience," John said.

"Okay," she said, making herself small against the wall as Rico crawled up to the boobytrap. Her eyes were wide with concern. This behavior seemed odd, even for this bunch.

Rico pulled out a fogging device and sprayed a burst toward the laser. Only one line was visible, but it was placed in an advantageous position.

"It's a direct-feed system best I can tell." He pulled out a micro-burst electro-magnetic disruptor. "This should disable the system, but it won't take them long to realize it."

"Okay, once he gets the laser disabled, let's secure this structure and strongpoint the entrance. I'm going out to meet Magnus."

"What? That's freakin' suicide," Anne said.

"No. It's something more," John said.

She took a deep breath, prepared to further oppose John's position, but Chappy's hand landed on her shoulder.

"It's what must be done," John said.

"But… I mean, why?"

"I just have to."

"This is completely insane," Anne said, looking at Chappy. "Magnus will kill him."

"Listen to me. You've seen some things tonight that you can't explain, right?" John asked.

She nodded.

"Okay, then. Practice exercising a little faith in me now. It will all work out how it should." He looked down at Wisp's body. "Death here—for this cause—isn't death."

"What's that supposed to mean?" Anne asked.

"Steady, laser disabled; moving," Rico said, pushing his way forward.

John pushed past Anne's shoulder. The team moved out of the narrow corridor and into the throne room. Rico covered to the right and Anne to the left. John pushed into the middle of the room. Chappy and Zip dragged Wisp's body out onto the floor. They both stood, Chappy tapping Rico and Zip tapping Anne. Each pair of operators cleared to their respective sides of the room. John held cover on the main door leading into the courtyard of Shuri Castle.

Chappy flanked to Rico's left, covering the rear hallway. A shoulder appeared, sitting in a chair. It didn't stir. Chappy leaned in, placing two silenced rounds in the man's chest. He slumped, never awakening, no longer able to draw breath. Rico entered the hall and an infrared light flashed on the floor. A fist emerged from the area of the faint green light, pinky extended, thumb up. It was Anne and Zip. Rico flashed his own laser, letting them know the area was clear.

Anne stepped into the hall and Zip followed, turning around to verify Rico's position. She edged up to a closed door – the only one in the hallway. She rested her hand on the knob and searched Zip's face; he nodded, and she turned the handle. The door opened, startling the three men in the room, who had been watching a security feed. A succession of rapid-fire rounds impacted the trio, collapsing them to the floor in a heap.

"Clear?" Anne asked, scanning her side of the room.

"Clear," Zip answered. He closed distance on the small handheld tablet, still clutched in one of the men's hands.

Zip picked it up and could see several cameras affixed to the exits of the throne room, including the corridor they had just breached.

"Spear five... Actual."

"Go," John's voice crackled over the radio.

"All clear on our side. Got intel on the exits and the enemy coms."

"Roger that. Collect it. Let's take a look," he said as he searched the door seal in the main room.

"Spear two, Actual – all clear on our side. One exterior door."

"Copy. Rico, rig up something in case we have company. Let's harden this location – time's not on our side."

A series of clicks sounded over the radio. John sat his rucksack on the floor and pulled out a silenced drill. He picked a spot in the middle of the door and placed the tip up to the wood. Once he actuated the drill, spirals of wood shavings fell from the hole as the bit sank into the solid surface. John felt the bit give, void of any other resistance. He then removed it from the hole, careful to avoid any noise. He placed the drill back into his rucksack and pulled out a fiberoptic camera, sliding the fisheye lens into the freshly bored hole. He lifted his night-vision goggles from his face and put his eye up to the base of the camera. The courtyard was moonless, quiet, and undisturbed, aside from Spear Team's initial entry. John could see a silhouette perched atop the security building. A sniper no doubt, set up in an obvious hide.

He heard his team's footfalls approach behind him.

"What's it look like?" Chappy asked.

"Well," John said, cycling through the scopes visual capabilities, "if we didn't know they were here, we'd be done. I just found our distraction, though. Maybe this works out."

"Let's hope," Chappy said.

John shook his head and took a deep breath.

"I ain't scared," Chappy said. "I just want to take out this asshole."

"He'll get what's coming to him," John said.

Zip and Anne walked closer. Rico moved to the corridor of the chamber and set a new boobytrap of his own. John broke his concentration away from the camera's eyepiece and looked at Chappy with fierce determination.

"Remember this, all of you: the bad things that happen are beyond our control. Stay focused," John said, his head dropped to Wisp's body. "But in the end, we're gonna get it done."

John patted Chappy on the arm, smiled, and looked back into the camera.

"What're we do'in?" Zip asked.

Rico had finished rigging explosives on all of the doors, except the main one where the team was posted. John continued scanning the courtyard, and Rico joined them.

"All set, Steady."

"Good," John said, trying to anticipate where Magnus would be. "Rico, rig a wall charge to my right. Zip, when I open the door, it'll set off their sensor. You should have a good look at the sniper. He's posted 12 o'clock high. Take him out."

Rico nodded and turned to the wall. He inspected the material and began building a wall shot. Zip dropped the magazine from his ISR platform, extracted the round, and separated the upper receiver from the lower. He lowered his rucksack to retrieve a 6.5 millimeter upper and replaced it on his rifle. He nestled the 300 Blackout ISR back into the rucksack and changed his ammunition over to the specialty 6.5 Grendel magazines. He powered up the enhanced thermal scope, granting himself precision ability in all lighting conditions.

"What do you want me and Anne to do?" Chappy asked.

"Be ready to haul ass with Wisp. Rico and Zip will cover."

"Where?"

John broke contact with the camera and handed the eyepiece to Chappy. Their gaze fixated on one another just long enough for Chappy to see that John had a plan. Maybe not a good plan, but whatever it was, John believed in it.

Chappy pressed his eye up to the camera. He could see that they were outnumbered and surrounded. He pulled the camera out of the hole and turned to John.

"Okay. Whatever, man. This is a level of crazy beyond me, but… I'm with you, brother."

"Well, I don't like it," Anne said, slumping, as she sighed away the tension.

John looked at her and put his hand on top of her helmet, just behind where her night-vision goggles sat. She curled her lips and took another deep breath.

"Look at me," John said.

She turned her head, tilting her eyes up to John's.

"Believe whatever you will, but you have to admit – this is beyond what you thought you knew. It's okay to make peace with that."

"This blind faith you keep acting on – it sounds crazy," Anne said.

"Come on, now," John said. "You're too smart *not* to see what's happening here. I saw the real you down in the that cavern. Don't second guess what we're doing here."

"If this is real," Anne huffed. "Then, how do I? I mean how can I possibly be enough?"

John realized she was wrestling with her past.

"I want you to be okay," John said. "I can't force you to let go or to move forward. You just gotta choose."

"But it's not that simple," Anne said.

"Why? Because you don't feel worthy? Or because you think this is all some dream?"

She dropped her gaze to the floor and sagged her shoulders.

"I've done things... killed – some worse. My mind crawls with those thoughts. Terrible thoughts sometimes," Anne said.

"You think I'm any different?" John asked. He looked at Chappy.

"Anne, you just described my every day, hour, and minute," Chappy said.

Anne picked her head up and looked around. Zip and Rico both paused their tasks, exchanging glances with Anne.

"How can you be messed up?" Anne asked, looking at John. "You're the only person I know that has it all together."

"I'm no better than anyone else," John said. "I'm probably worse off than most. But, you gotta have hope. All of this—including this war we're in—it's purely about fighting a lie, and people are going to have to make a choice. For everyone on Earth, that choice is coming. It's coming like a freight train, bearing down on us all, equally. Your choice is what matters."

Anne wiped her nose with the back of her hand and nodded. Time was weighing on John's mind, but he believed that her peace of mind was essential, and just as important as the mission. She shared a final glance with John, turned, and walked over to Wisp's body. She tugged on the body bag, moving him closer to Rico's extraction point.

"It's up to you," Chappy said, walking over to help.

"Okay, let's get ready," John said.

††††††

"Sir, one of the sensors is down," a voice carried over the radio.

"They're here, mates – get ready," Magnus growled, standing up from the monitor station, extinguishing his smoke.

"Cavern team, check in."

"All good here."

"Throne room?" he listened. "Throne room – answer."

He walked out of the security building and glanced up at the sniper posted above. He checked his right and left flank personnel.

"Stay alert!" he barked.

Men shifted to life around the perimeter of the courtyard. A few metallic clicks and pops resonated throughout the stone-clad buildings. Magnus found a spot of cover and checked the camera feeds on his tablet. The entrance to the cavern was blacked out.

"Cavern team, hold position. If they come that way, you know what to do."

"Copy."

Magnus shifted his view on the tablet, realizing all of his communications could be compromised.

"All teams, go dark. Switch to alternate channel two. Repeat – switch to channel two. Coms compromised."

He switched his radio over to the secured channel and entered the security code, allowing him access.

"Smart. But now I got you," he said under his breath.

A few seconds passed. He fished out his satellite phone, hitting the speed dial.

"Is it done?" Maximillion asked.

"About to be. I think we have contact, finally."

"Good. Just make sure you get the Arma Christi intact. Our asset is about to take out their base. You want to know what they call themselves?"

Magnus scanned the front door to the throne room. He press-checked his pistol.

"Bloody pains in the ass," Magnus said.

Maximillion paused.

"No; they call themselves Arklight. It's a squadron of six operators."

"That's good to know."

"Make sure none of them escape – understand?"

"Aye, Father."

"Good. Call me when it's done. And Magnus, don't waste any time getting back to Geneva. We still have much to do."

††††††

"It's just like we thought, John. They have the cavern covered," Zip said, trying to figure out which channel Magnus was now using.

"Forget it. That's an encrypted system. It's useless without the channel and the code," Rico said.

"Alright, then, it's time," John said, looking ahead at Zip. "You ready?"

Zip nodded and sank into a kneeling, shooting position, deep inside the room.

"Rico, charges armed and ready?"

"All set."

"Anne, you good?"

"Faith and trust," she muttered under her breath.

"Anne?"

"Good to go," she said.

John took a deep breath and stood beside Chappy; whose hand was ready to open the door.

"Promise me this, Chappy," he whispered. "Whatever happens, *you* get the team off the X."

Chappy looked at John, his face slack with sudden uncertainty. John grabbed his shoulder and squeezed.

"You hear me, brother?"

Chappy couldn't muster the words, but managed a woeful nod.

"Standby. Three, Two…"

The door opened and a flash illuminated the upper portion of the security office, exposing the sniper. A deafening discharge exploded from the end of Zip's rifle, splattering a mist in the air where the sniper had been positioned. John stepped into the doorway.

"Magnus! Let's talk," he yelled. "Me and you – before things get ugly."

"You bloody smart bastard!" Magnus responded, emerging from his cover by the security office. "How'd you guess I was here, mate?"

"Let's just say, someone let me know."

"Okay, I'll consider your parlay. Meet me in the middle of the courtyard."

"John, don't do it," Chappy whispered from behind the door. "We can't cover you."

"Stay the course," John said.

"Dammit," Chappy said, easing the door shut. "Game on."

John slung his rifle and let his hands relax by his side, knowing that he was surrounded. He walked into death's valley, praying to himself that God would save his team. He scanned the perimeter, feeling numerous enemies locked on him over the barrels of their weapons.

Magnus emerged through the shadows, blotches of gradient light catching his face. His rigid features accentuated the contempt in his narrow eyes. He gripped his pistol tight, bouncing it on his thigh as he walked. John showed his empty hands. Magnus holstered his pistol. He looked willing to talk. John stopped a little more than arms-length away.

"John Steadman," Magnus said, "I'm surprised you're willing to talk, after what I did to your men."

"Magnus O'Keefe – or should I call you Magnus Kieffer?" John asked, trying to counter knowledge, fighting his emotions.

"Aye, so you know about my family, then?"

"I know enough."

Magnus pulled out a pack of cigarettes, tapped the container, and offered one to John.

"No, thanks."

Magnus shrugged and pulled one out, pressing it between his lips. He placed the pack in his pocket, extracted a lighter, lit his smoke, and inhaled. A plume of smoke lingered in John's face.

"I think we were in Iraq around the same time," Magnus said. "Prior to 2006."

"Maybe so," John acknowledged. "What do you want?"

"You know I've got you surrounded, outnumbered, and outplayed, right?"

"Maybe." John said, scanning the courtyard. "But, have you thought about every possible counter? Every angle, every contingency?"

The Welshman inhaled another stream of smoke from his cigarette. John looked around, aware that no plan is ever one-hundred percent.

"Let's cut through the bullshit, mate," Magnus said. "You've got something I want – a spear. Let me have it, and I'll let you and your team leave."

John smiled, realizing the Spear of Destiny was still safe. If Magnus wanted it now, then there was no way they had discovered it to date.

"It seems that you might have a problem then, *mate*," John said.

"What's that now?" Magnus asked, his eyes narrowing.

"We don't have the Spear you're looking for. It's not here."

"What? I know you have it. Give it to me before I take it," his hand crept closer to his pistol.

"Don't let your emotions ruin a profitable exchange, Magnus." John held his right arm up in front of his chest, making a fist.

"What's in your hand?" Magnus asked, planting his hand on his pistol and backing away one step.

"Something I can offer you in trade."

"What do you mean?"

"Let me and my team out of here, and I'll give you a big piece of the Time Key."

"Which piece?"

John opened his hand.

"The folded bronze coin over gold. The John Bell coin – the piece that activates the Time Key."

Magnus edged closer, making sure it was the original. John could see that Magnus knew what he was looking at.

"Where's the Spear? The Spear of Destiny is supposed to be here."

John couldn't afford to waste a single moment. He raised the explosive in his left hand, planting the coin into the soft, clay-like plastic block. His thumb flicked the actuator, priming the device.

Magnus drew his pistol, realizing he had been distracted.

"Wait! I don't have the trigger. It's with my team. Shoot me, and they'll blow you to hell."

John didn't think any of the Arma Christi could be destroyed, but he was hoping Magnus didn't know any better. John looked down the barrel of the pistol and dropped the explosive device on the ground. It landed between them, settling at their feet, exposing the radio-controlled trigger. He focused past the pistol and into the enraged stare of Magnus.

"Listen, I'll leave that here. When we're clear, it's yours."

"What, so you can blow me apart?"

"As much as I would be okay with that, no. A deal's a deal. You get this piece for our freedom. No tricks."

Magnus sneered; fire evident in his soul. He searched his mind for other options. No matter what, this Arklight team wouldn't be leaving alive, anyway.

"Let's say I agree to this – deal. Why would I take your word about the Spear? There's proof in the journal that it's here."

John couldn't afford to turn toward deception at any point; only the truth would convince. He lowered his hands, stepping in front of his archenemy. The barrel of Magnus' gun, pressed against John's torso, stopped him from getting any closer.

"The Spear was taken out of here in 1945," John said. "We've seen it… it exists, but it couldn't pass through time – not like the folded coin."

"What do you mean?"

"The coin travelled forward in time. It's the only piece of Arma Christi—"

"Capable of altering time… the 30 folded secrets are the mystery. A key to the temple hidden in 30, activated by the one, controls the ultimate weapon – power for the one."

John's brow furrowed, remembering the cryptic phrase buried somewhere within the journal; Magnus was focused on the power for the one. It was his drive, his motivation. John knew that Magnus wanted it all for himself.

CHAPTER 17: EVADE

"My heart is troubled and restless. Days of suffering torment me."
Job 30:27

1900-Zulu Time 24May2020 (0400-JST 25May2020 Shuri Castle)

Magnus withdrew the pistol from John's abdomen, holstering it with a click. John's hope of getting his team out lay at his feet. His actions gleaned the importance of the coin, a clear crux of the negotiation.

"Bloody damn journal," Magnus said, shaking his head, "So, where's the Spear in our time – now?"

"I don't know," John said without the slightest twitch of deceit.

"Okay, how's this trade gonna go?" Magnus asked.

John knew Magnus couldn't be trusted. Any slip on Spear Team's part would end badly. He felt prepared to deal with the ruthless psychopath. John took a step back.

"The device can be remotely detonated," John said, pointing to the sky, "There's a drone up there, watching it. Anybody goes near it, it detonates. You move, it detonates. You get the picture, right?"

"Aye, so what guarantee do I have? Why not just shoot it out – right here and right now?"

"Because you want that coin. You *need* that coin. We're going to walk out of here, and once we're far enough away, the device will disarm. The red light will turn green. The coin will be yours."

"I'm afraid that's not gonna work for me, mate."

"Look, I know you'll be trying to think of a way to take us out the whole time. I can see it in your face now. You want the coin? You want to live? We do this my way."

"Smart bastard," Magnus hissed, grabbing his radio. "Nobody fires. I repeat: weapons hold, copy?"

"Copy."

John keyed up his radio.

"Spear Actual – we have terms. Hold."

Two clicks registered.

Magnus stared at John with loathing, placing a hand on his hip.

"I'll be killing you next time we meet."

John felt empowered in the moment. He balled up his fists to maintain control of himself. He wanted nothing more than an opportunity alone with the salty Welshman. He gritted his teeth and stared straight through Magnus.

"Until then..."

The two men stared each other down as John backed away toward the entrance to the throne room. Magnus reached in his pocket, pulled out his pack of cigarettes, and lit up another smoke. He stood firm over the small explosive device at his feet and looked into the pitch-black sky. John knew Magnus would try to find a way to kill them before they could escape. The door creaked open behind him.

"Well?" Chappy asked.

"Pray for a miracle, Chap," he said, stepping inside of the building, "and leave the door open."

John side-stepped out of the doorway, clearing himself from view. Zip still knelt, deep in the throne room, his sights affixed on Magnus' chest. Rico checked the link on the explosive device. Every connection showed green. The mini-drone was hovering out of sight, but well within range of the explosives. John looked over the faces of his team.

"How long before we lose coverage on the drone?"

"It's hard to say," Rico said, "Maintaining this link will zap the battery pretty quick. Maybe 10 minutes – tops."

"How are we getting out of here, Steady?" Anne asked.

"I'm happy we got this far. What's the plan?" Chappy asked.

"I'm to the point we just have to believe this is for something. We'll get out of this. I know it."

"That's not telling us much," Anne said, sighing.

John rubbed the bridge of his nose, tired of the scrutiny.

"Anne, I'm doing the best I can," John said. "Just trust me. Let's get ready to move."

"You heard him," Chappy said, "Let's get the hell out of here."

"I'm down," Rico said, throwing his rucksack over his shoulder.

"He'll get us out, Anne. I know it," Zip said.

"I'm just ready to get off the x," she muttered, still struggling with the harsh realities she'd experienced on the mission. Her entire system of beliefs had been shattered, and as a result, she still fought to debunk what she had witnessed. Her mind fought itself, arguing every aspect of fact, lashing out at anyone and everyone who challenged her own thoughts. *Focus, Anne. Mission first; deal with your own damn drama later.*

†††††

Magnus exhaled another thick smoke stream, looking into the inky void beyond the door of the throne room. He could feel the pressure on him, knowing any sudden move would find him splattered against the stones of the courtyard.

A voice clamored over the radio in Magnus' ear.

"What do you want us to do?"

"I'm trying to think, ya wank. Shut your damn mouth for a second."

The eerie stillness was broken by Magnus scratching his head, seeking another option to get out of his current predicament. With a bomb at his feet, the matter seemed settled. It was then that he heard the buzz of the drone, hovering above him to his front; the blades were almost silent, but his well-trained ears managed to pick up on the soft, bee-like hum. He strained his eyes, searching for the source. There it was – hovering some thirty feet away, darting back and forth, making for a hard target. He smirked. The key to his escape, and the completion of his mission, hung in the air, a pistol shot away.

The ground began to vibrate under his feet. Confusion disrupted his thoughts for a moment before he was able to make sense of the distinct, familiar sound and feel. Everything was about to get chancy.

"Incoming!" Magnus yelled, scrambling away from the coin-laden explosives, "Helo, inbound!"

†††††

"John. Prepare to exfil." The Chief's voice crackled over the radio. "Boomer, that you?"

"Sorry to leave you hanging, boss."

"Get us out of here, and I'll let it slide," Chappy said, his eyes growing wide with hope. A smile emerged on his face.

"Can you get to the North gate?" asked the chief.

John knew it was the only spot wide enough to set down a helicopter.

"We'll find a way," he radioed.

The building vibrated as the Blackhawk settled into a low orbit. Two shots of small arms fire popped from outside, until they were targeted under the growl of a minigun. Hot brass rained down on Shuri Castle. Spear Team had to move.

"Breach that wall," John said, grabbing Anne and Chappy by their sleeves.

"Get clear." Rico yelled, priming the charge.

Zip grabbed his rifle, disappointed that the distraction had allowed Magnus to escape his sights. He closed in on the team.

"I took my eye off of him for a second, and he was gone."

"We'll get our chance," John replied.

Chappy reached down, scooping up Wisp's body and laying him over his shoulder. John tried to help with the weight, but Chappy patted his shoulder.

"I got him," Chappy said, "just cover my ass."

John nodded and turned, squeezing Rico's shoulder. Another burst from the minigun fired from above.

"Fire in the hole." Rico said, clicking the actuator.

BOOM.

He looked up as the dust and debris cleared the breach.

"Door's open! Get some!" Rico said.

Smoke rolled in through the hole in the wall, and rotor wash blasted the courtyard. The deafening buzz of a minigun chewed up bits of the ground and walls. The rotor blades chopped at the air, pounding in John's chest as he followed Rico through the breach.

Rico cut right, covering the walkway toward the back of the building. John took the left, catching one of Magnus' goons trying to get a shot off at the orbiting Blackhawk. He flicked the safety down and pressed the trigger of his ISR, ending the shooter's opportunity.

"Clear. Press toward the North gate." John said, launching weapons forward from the corner of the building into the courtyard.

Anne exited next, followed by Zip and then Chappy. She ran across the opening as John fired on another man who was hiding from the barrage of deadly fire from above. She made it to cover and poked her head around the stone. The first round passed so close to her head; she felt the sonic snap. The second round ricocheted off the side of her helmet. She tucked in, pulling her hand to her temple, feeling for a gash. Anne pulled her hand down, sure she was okay, but angry she had gotten shot. At least she had the gunman's position pegged.

"Frag out!" Anne yelled, as the spoon flipped off the grenade.

She heaved the ball frag over her head toward the threat and shouldered her ISR. The determination in her voice motivated Zip as he watched her operate like a lion among sheep. Anne attacked the corner, firing short automatic bursts as she cleared the flank.

"Clear," Anne called over the weapons fire.

"Copy that," John said, his gaze fixed on the explosive-rigged coin resting in the courtyard.

Zip stopped next to John, pulling his weapon into his shoulder. He scanned the roofline across the courtyard, finding a target. The two rounds discharged so fast from his sniper rifle that they sounded like one. He located another threat, blasting another round at the movement from afar. A second Blackhawk sank below the outer wall of Shuri Castle, just beyond the North gate.

"Cover me," John said, assessing his chances for retrieving the coin.

"Wait," Zip said, engaging another shadowy figure across the courtyard. "I'm going with you!"

John felt a squeeze on his shoulder and looked back. Rico had his weapon up, running toward the North gate, ready to set up the bound to safety. He paused, turning to engage threats, lowering his rifle to clear the path to the helo. Chappy followed, struggling under the dead weight that was burdening his every step toward escape. Another snap of an incoming round collapsed Chappy as it cut through his leg. He fell to the ground, spilling Wisp's body in front of him.

Time slowed. John could see the faces of his team all laser-focused on the fight. A sudden lump of fear gripped his throat.

"No!" he howled, scrambling toward Chappy, "Cover me!"

Zip radioed, "Helo 1, get some fire across from us. Marking with red smoke."

He threw the mini-cannister smoke grenade across the courtyard. It expulsed thick red smoke and the gunner of the Blackhawk opened up on the area. He shifted his focus to the coin, aware of its importance to John. He scanned the area for an opportunity.

John slid on the ground and snatched Chappy up by the back of his vest as he pushed himself back onto his feet. The right leg of his combat pants grew wet with blood. Chappy reached down, assessing the damage.

"Chap, you good to move?"

"Yeah, I'm good." he said, grabbing his thigh.

"Go. I got Wisp."

John scooped up his friend's body with near superhuman strength. Adrenaline was coursing through all the reaches of his body.

"Zip! Anne! Extract!" John yelled, ensuring he had their attention. He could scarcely be heard over the noise of war.

Anne made eye contact and backed in his direction. She fired well-aimed bursts in two different directions.

Zip tilted his weapon up, looking at John. Instead of moving to the helicopter, he saw a chance and ran toward the coin. A crystal clear, orange tint reflected from his eyes as dawn fell over the castle.

Anne made it to John and paused to see what his focus was on. John took a step toward the castle. Horror filled her mind.

"No!" she yelled.

"Zip, it's not worth it – fall back!" John radioed.

They could merely watch. Zip shouldered his rifle, firing shot after shot as he closed on the coin. He reached to his vest with his off-hand, yanking a grenade from its pouch. With the precision of a thousand repetitions, he sank his thumb in the pull pin, flicked it, freeing the spoon, and underhand tossed the grenade forward. All the while, his weapon stayed up, in the fight.

"Spear actual, get some cover on Zip! He's still in the courtyard!"

"Coming around," said the Blackhawk pilot.

Anne stepped forward, leaning to run in Zip's direction, only to be stopped by John's hand.

"Get to the helo."

"But we can—"

"There's nothing we can do. Go!"

She tried to pull away.

††††††

The growl of the minigun and the deafening *thump* of chopper blades forced Magnus to retreat into the relative safety of the security office. The windows were shot out along the façade, but he was well inside the stone-walled building—deep enough that the helicopter's gun was at too high of an angle to be effective. His ear buzzed with voices trying to fight back against the barrage of gunfire. His plan was falling apart.

"Get some fire on that chopper crew," he said, realizing his words couldn't be heard.

Magnus pulled the radio from his ear and stood up, regarding the weapons cache they had brought in with them. He picked up an RPK rifle and looked through the shattered windows. Light glared in his eyes, but he could see a silhouette charging through red smoke, into the center of the courtyard. Stone and concrete fragments showered around Magnus. Rounds were striking around him as he took aim down the sights of the rifle.

The figure threw something in his direction; he caught the outline of the spoon flipping off a ball grenade. He had a few seconds to deal with that, but for the man – he just needed one. The soldier was running toward the coin and was in the open.

"Not on your life," he snarled as his finger depressed the trigger. He jumped away from the grenade's trajectory, firing a long burst of RPK fire forward the soldier. Rounds ripped through flesh, dropping him to the ground. The grenade came into the security area, exploding just one room away from himself. He dropped the RPK rifle and picked up a rocket-propelled grenade launcher.

"You aren't getting away – not now, not ever."

He had one shot.

††††††

John watched in horror as Zip's body collapsed to the ground. A cloud of crimson mist drifted over him. He never moved. Anne jumped, ready to run into the fray.

"No!" she screamed.

John knew he had lost another friend and brother. He jerked her in his direction, forcing her to the Blackhawk.

"He's gone! Go!"

Anne struggled with John, who worked to press her back through the North gate. He lifted her off the ground and turned her toward the helicopter.

"We can't leave him!" Bullets chewed up the path in between them and the castle.

"We have to go, now!"

John couldn't even feel the weight of Wisp on his shoulder anymore. The Blackhawk was a few feet away. The chief met John, helping to balance Wisp's body.

"Where's Zip?" asked the chief.

John's jaw clenched—not from sadness, but from rage. He shook his head.

Anne jumped into the helicopter; only death remained within the walls of Shuri Castle. John and the chief got Wisp inside. Once onboard, they grabbed a bench adjacent to the side door. The Blackhawk lifted off, turning toward the Northwest and the open waters of the bay. Bullets *tinged* off the fuselage as they gained altitude. John could see blue lights from the approaching police cars, several streets below. He turned, looking over his team – what was left. All he could see was Anne. Her intense stare cut through him. Anger burned within her at the loss of another teammate.

Rico slid the side door shut, hoping to increase their ascent speed from the target.

No sooner did the chief put on his headset.

"RPG!"

The Blackhawk jolted violently. Sparks and smoke sputtered from the top bulkhead. A series of shudders ripped through the aircraft. Alarms sounded from the cockpit. Both side doors locked from the force of the explosion.

"We're going down!"

Chappy grabbed the bulkhead.

The chopper shimmied and shuttered into a spin. The RPG took out the tail, or at least part of it. John reached for the door handle and tried to slide it open, but it wouldn't budge. They were going down in the bay.

"Chap, get your door open!" John yelled, still struggling to open his side.

"I can't get mine open!" Chappy added.

The compartment filled with smoke as the pilots fought for control. The turbulent spin generated G-force, pinning the team down inside.

Rico moved to help Chappy, and they tugged with all their combined might until the door opened – only a few inches. It was at least enough to clear some of the smoke and the overwhelming scent of burning wires.

John and the chief strained to push back, trying to kick open their door, but the force overwhelmed their attempt, sliding them against it, instead. Anne reached for the fire extinguisher, but the effort was futile.

"We ditching?" John asked the pilot.

"Yeah, it's going to be wet."

"Blow the doors!"

"Roger, everybody clear!" the pilot yelled.

John looked back and saw everyone trying their best to clear away from the doors. He tucked into the middle of the chopper. Nothing happened. Alarms continued to sound. One turbine quit, slowing the rate of the spin.

"The system's fried – get those doors open however you can. I'll try to hover and get y'all clear."

John patted the pilot's shoulder and returned to the rear.

"Emergency ditch. Get those doors open."

Spear Team worked to get the rear doors open. Chappy used his rifle as a prybar, snapping off his buffer-tube in the process. John tugged with all his strength on the emergency handle of his door. Nothing budged.

"I can't hold it!" the pilot yelled, "We're going down!"

The Blackhawk's second engine seized, and the pilot tried to auto-rotate into the water below. The entire aircraft began spinning, slamming nose first against the water of the bay. Everyone rolled to the right, on top of Chappy and Rico. Water poured in through every crease. The

ARKLIGHT: Task Force Crusader

aircraft began to fill with seawater as it shuttered into complete silence. The blades sheared off as they smashed into the water.

"Everybody okay?" John asked. It was all he could muster.

The Blackhawk rolled another ninety degrees. It was upside down, water entering from every crack. The team emerged for a breath, one-by-one. Chief, Anne, Chappy…

"Where's Rico?"

John submerged and saw him. He was underwater, looking at the side doors of the helicopter. John grabbed him by the vest and pulled him up, unaware that his actions had purpose.

"Rico! You breathing?"

"Yeah, let me get back to it before we all die."

"What?" Chappy asked.

"I've got a breach charge left. I'm gonna blow the door."

"What about the overpressure?" Anne asked.

"I got worked out," he said, smiling before taking a breath and submerging once more.

"Chief, how are the pilots?" John asked, unsure of Rico's plan.

"Checking."

"Strip off your kits," John said, flipping his helmet off.

Soon, the chief popped his head out of the water and shook it at John.

"They aren't moving."

"Can we get out through the cockpit?" John asked.

"No. I couldn't squeeze through – the nose is collapsed into the compartment."

"What the hell's Rico doing?" Anne gasped.

The water level rose, forcing her to take a deep breath. Everyone was submerged in turquoise saltwater. Light faded. John looked into Anne's eyes, realizing, himself, what Rico was doing. His back was turned as he worked on the door charge.

Rico's arms moved with quick determination; his hands sure. He placed the primer into the breaching charge. He closed his eyes, praying it would be enough to set his team free. He turned his head and smiled into John's anguished face. He winked, hoping his sacrifice would save his team. Rico pulled his body into the charge, using his own mass to force

261

the explosive blast into the door, away from his teammates. He initiated the explosion. His body absorbed the shock.

The blast-wave enveloped him, producing red bubbles. The door peeled away from the fuselage, and Rico's body floated toward John. Blood wept from the numerous fragmentation wounds. His face was distorted from the overpressure—shredded, even—unrecognizable. John grabbed him and followed the other remaining Arklight members out of the sinking coffin.

He broke the surface of the saltwater bay, taking a deep breath, coughing from near shock. The four remaining SEALs used every bit of their training to escape. Chappy did his best to hold Wisp's body on the surface, and John kept his arm wrapped around Rico, tugging him through the water as he tread. The chief could see cherry red gore encircling them all with every kick of the leg or stroke of the arm made.

"Chappy, you got to let him go. You're going to bleed out with that leg if you don't relax."

"Can you get a tourniquet on it?" Chappy grimaced.

Anne looked around, trying to get her bearings. She checked her command module.

"Steady, Oki is that way," she said, pointing above the water line.

John swam closer to her, his breathing labored, trying to keep both himself and Rico afloat.

"Check for vitals," John said, still treading water.

Anne pulled off her gloves, taking a long, sullen look at Rico's battered face. His eyes were open and affixed. She ran her hand over them, closing his blank gaze.

"He's gone," she said, trembling.

"Rico sacrificed himself to save us," John said, on the verge of breakdown. "Why? Why's it got to be this way? Tell me!"

He pulled Rico close.

"Brother, this is so far less than you deserve."

Anne watched John release Rico. His body sank in the salty sea. She put her head under and watched him float downward. Anne came up for a breath and found John looking at her.

"Remember him for who he was," John said.

She nodded. John swam to Chappy.

"Chap, let him go," John said, pulling out a tourniquet, "You have to. We've gotta save you."

"He's dead," said the chief. "You're alive. It sucks – I know."

"Once we put this on, that leg won't work so good – you know how this goes."

The chief pried Wisp from Chappy's grasp.

"Anne, grabbed onto Chappy, inflated her safety vest, and started floating. Chap – relax," John coaxed.

He pulled the tourniquet over Chappy's leg, above the wound, and drove it all the way up his leg. A quick adjustment to the strap and John started twisting the lever, cutting off the bleed.

The chief was a few feet away from the others. Wisp had already started to sink.

"Until Valhalla, brother," the chief said. "I'll see you again."

Chappy cut in, undeterred, "But, not until we find and kill that bastard. Not until then."

Chief watched Wisp sink, gathering his strength to swim. It wasn't time to mourn. They had to keep fighting. He saw John tending to Chappy. There had to be reason they were all alive and had lost so many.

✝✝✝✝✝

Magnus emerged from the house containing the secret entrance to Shuri Castle. He paused to take in the fresh, salty air of the morning, along with the sirens in the background. He stepped into a waiting car and got on his phone.

"Ronnie, we still set?" Magnus asked.

"I was starting to get a little worried," Ronnie said. "How'd it go?"

Magnus looked down to his palm. The John Bell Hood coin rested in the flat of his hand, free of explosives. He admired the markings, but he was aware of what hid beneath the surface. The coin's clever disguise only added to his intrigue. Although he didn't have the Spear of Destiny, this piece was far more precious in his mind.

"It didn't go to plan," Magnus said, "but I got something we needed."

"What about the Americans?" Ronnie asked.

"They tried to escape, but I shot their asses down. I saw the helicopter crash into the ocean."

"Any survivors?"

"After that crash? No chance," Magnus said with a smirk. "I even killed one of them trying to get a piece of the Time Key back. I gunned the desperate bastard down."

"I'll be here waiting on you with the engines running."

"Okay, mate. Be there in a few."

Magnus ended the call and dialed Maximillion's number. He picked up on the first ring.

"Is it done?" Maximillion asked.

"Yes, with one exception."

"What's that?"

"They didn't have the Spear," Magnus said.

"What? It was there!"

"Before you get upset, it was there – but in 1945."

"What's that supposed to mean?"

"Another team took it out of the castle, in that time."

Maximillion paused.

"The Alsos Team," he said, remembering their importance.

"Who's that?" Magnus asked.

"Your grandfather is very familiar. I'll have to let him know."

"While you're at it," Magnus smirked, "tell him I secured one of the folded coins from the Americans – before I killed them."

"What? How?" Maximillion asked, his voice

"It's a long story, but it's real."

"The Time Key is crucial to activating the ultimate weapon, but without the Spear of Destiny, we are no closer to its initiation. I'll let your grandfather know. At least he'll be pleased you got the coin."

"There's more. The Americans, this Arklight unit, is wiped out, but I do have a clue of where the Spear might be."

"A clue?"

"Yes... the American in charge told me the Spear couldn't pass through time. Not like the folded coin I hold. It had to have left here in 1945—he said as much."

"Right," Maximillion said. "The Alsos Team would have had it if that's true. I'll start looking through the journal for any clues to where they hid it. That's a good start, son."

Magnus didn't acknowledge. His father's compliments fell far too short these days. All he wanted was to figure out what his father and grandfather were hiding from him.

"We'll be extracting soon," Magnus said. "I'll call you once we get in the air."

"Aye. Make sure that coin gets back to Geneva."

"I will."

††††††

"You still with us?" John asked, side-stroking toward dryland.

Chappy replied with a thumbs up.

The chief had hold of his upper body, pulling him along like a lifeguard would a drowning victim. Chappy just relaxed and focused on floating. His leg throbbed more from the tourniquet than the bullet wound.

Anne stared at John, fuming, nostrils flaring.

"What?" John asked.

"We could've helped Zip. You just let him die."

"Is that how you see it?"

"I tried to go. You didn't let me."

"Because then you'd be dead too," John said, blowing out to catch his breath.

"We had to try. You didn't," Anne said.

"I told him not to go out there. Once he was gone," John turned his gaze toward Okinawa, "I knew we wouldn't get him back."

"You should've tried harder."

"Maybe. Then what? What about the mission? What about the rest of you? I had to make a split-second decision. Die with Zip, or get the rest of us out," John said.

She cut her glare away.

The chief overheard the conversation, identifying Anne's inexperience and willingness to sacrifice herself. Perhaps she felt guilty for living; three of her teammates were dead, and there was little she could have done to stop it.

"Anne, listen to me," he panted, pulling Chappy along. "Zip made the decision. It doesn't make it hurt any less, but John's right. Get over it – and quick. We got bigger problems."

John rolled on his back and looked at the chief.

"Bigger problems than this?" John asked.

"I'm afraid so, sir. Magnus' mercs knocked out our entire command unit at Kadena. I haven't been able to contact the admiral, General Johnson, or the SecDef. Not to mention that the Japanese Police are probably not going to be very cooperative if they catch us. So, yeah… we got problems."

John tugged on Anne's leg.

"Be mad at me later, but get your head right for now. Understand?"

She looked back at him, at least able to recognize the stakes at present, and nodded. Her head dipped below the surface of the water for a few moments. She came back up.

"There's a boat. Sounds like it's getting closer," she said, prompting them all to scan the waterline.

"I see it," John said, "looks like a civilian boat. No government markings."

As it approached, the sound of the engine throttled down. The boat came to a stop between Spear Team and the early morning sun. The silhouette of a man with a wide-brimmed hat stepped in front of John, looking down at him. An elderly face with sunglasses blocked the light. John squinted, trying to make him out.

"Something told me you frogmen would be here," the old man said.

"Who – wait… Bell?" John asked, recognizing the voice.

"Throw them a line," he said to one of the crew. "Sorry I'm late. Got held up in the marina."

"But how?" John asked.

"Let's get you onboard first. We need to get out of here before the authorities arrive."

†††††

Anne and the chief worked on Chappy's leg. A full medical kit lay at their feet, and they had already started an IV. He looked like he would be fine. Feeling a slight sense of relief, John turned his attention to the aft deck of the boat. Bell sat next to the stern; he motioned for John to join him.

John exited the cabin and sat down. The man was nearly 100 years old, but moved well, even on a boat.

"I thought you were dead."

"I feel like it somedays," Bell said, with a grim smile on his face. "Truth is – Kieffer, Alfred O'Keefe, sent a kill squad after me many years ago. I let him think they got me. Only your grandfather knew I was alive."

"You going to tell me how you got out here?"

"You already know the answer to that question. He sent me, because it's time," Bell said.

"Time for what?" John asked.

Bell's leathery face crinkled in the sun, his sunglasses reflecting the rays.

"It's time for the end of an age. A new beginning awaits."

"Now?"

Bell laughed and craned his head toward the horizon.

"It's not that simple, John. Darkness has closed in around us. The apostasy is nearly complete. Now, we have to take the fight to them and begin the next evolution."

"You mean, Magnus?" John asked.

"Not just him, but the entire Order of the Black Sun. They have everything they need to open the Ark. Well, except for this," he said, pulling out the Spear of Destiny from the large, inner pocket of his jacket.

"You still have it? Thank God."

"Even so, we have much to do," Bell added. "Much to prepare for."

"If you can get us out of Okinawa, that would be a good start."

"It's already been handled. This is something we've been preparing for since the beginning."

"Beginning? Since Bizerte?"

Bell smiled and said, "I wish there was a simple answer to that, my friend, but all your questions will be answered in due time."

"I'm lost," John said, his face sullen.

"No. Not at all. You've only just found yourself."

The boat powered ahead over clear waters. John didn't know what Bell meant by it all, but there had to be more – much more.

CHAPTER 18: ENDGAME

"Why do the wicked prosper, growing old and powerful?"
Job 21:7

1300-Zulu Time 26May2020 (1800-EST Arklight, HQ)

The enormous lift descended into the Arklight base, groaning as it lowered into the hollow below. Nathan and Walter were relocated to Nathan's office, where four armed guards stood over them. They sat bound and helpless, unable to stop Klaus and his mercenaries. The two C-17s that sat on the lift had just returned from Okinawa; the crews had no clue Arklight was under siege. All the two men could do was watch as their enemies moved in, taking the air crews captive.

Klaus stood behind Nathan's desk, overlooking a clump of Arklight personnel seated on the floor of the vast, underground hangar. They were surrounded by several Black Sun soldiers, supplemented by mercenaries, all with weapons at the ready.

"They move – beat them," he said, turning to walk out of the room.

"Rod? Why?" Nathan asked, turning to look at what used to be his friend.

Klaus stopped, and his face twitched. He turned on his heel, walking up to Nathan.

"I told you, Rod's gone. It was just a cover."

"I don't believe that."

"Right," Klaus said, drawing his hand back and following through with a knuckled jab to Nathan's face. The viciousness of the strike rolled Nathan out of his chair, onto a knee.

He touched his tongue to his lip, tasting the metallic bitterness. He gathered himself, pushing his body back into the chair.

"I still don't believe it," he said, eyes cutting into Klaus.

"We'll get back to more of that soon enough, then."

"What are you going to do?" Walter asked.

Klaus backed away from the two men and smirked.

"That's up to the Führer. He'll be with you shortly," Klaus said, crossing the threshold of the room.

"Führer? You mean that old asshole, Kieffer?" Nathan asked.

Klaus spun back around and faced Nathan.

"No!" he snapped. "The Führer of the Fourth Reich. The chancellor of The Order of the Black Sun. Our one true leader, and the harbinger of the Final Solution. His eminence, Alfred Kieffer. If you disrespect him again, I'll cut out your tongue."

The door slammed shut. Nathan turned and looked at Walter.

"What, no cryptic words of wisdom?" he asked, still pressing his tongue to the cut on his lower lip.

Walter looked down and gritted his teeth.

"Not unless you have something to numb the pain in my arms," Walter said, flexing his hands.

Nathan sat up and stretched his achy back. He looked at the guard next to him.

"Look, I understand me, but can you let the old man loose for a few? He's not a threat. I assure you."

The guard pulled back his rifle, preparing to butt-stroke Nathan. The door to the office opened, exposing the silhouette of a man, bent by almost one-hundred years of life. He held two canes, one in each crooked, gnarled hand. His head hung low, until he craned it, looking ahead. The old man wore all black, his gray hair thinning over the freckled crown of his skull. Two beady blue eyes stared a hole through Walter.

"Kieffer? That you?" Walter asked.

The old man used both canes, closing the distance, answering his question—a nod without words.

"Why are our guests still handcuffed? Klaus, cut them free and bring some – refreshments."

Klaus nodded to the guards closest to their captives. They pulled out some cutters and removed the zip-tie style handcuffs. He motioned to one to the guards outside the office.

"You heard the Führer. Refreshments – now!"

The man moved out with purpose.

Walter pulled his hands in front of him and kneaded his wrists. Nathan pulled his arms toward his chest; the sting of tense muscles burned as he stretched his shoulders. Kieffer stopped, passing Walter his cane before walking around Nathan's desk to overlook his men on the floor.

"I couldn't help but admire your cane," Kieffer said.

"It's just what I use to get around these days," Walter said, thankful to feel it back in his possession.

"The craftsmanship is quite detailed."

Walter ran his hand over the metal, feeling for any inconsistences. It felt intact. Kieffer was fishing.

"After what you did to us back in Canterbury, I needed a decent walking-stick to get around."

Kieffer turned and sat in Nathan's desk chair. He placed both elbows on the desk and his brow creased.

"If you would have simply died back in Poland, I wouldn't have had to resort to such tactics."

Kieffer and Walter stared at each other with daggers in their eyes. Nathan knew there was a bitter, deep-seeded history between the two men.

"What happened in Canterbury?" Nathan asked, breaking an awkward silence.

Kieffer sat back and took a deep breath, reminiscing.

"Admiral. To answer your question, we're discussing who's the rightful owner of the Knights Templar journal."

"What happened?" Nathan asked.

"Kieffer, get to the point. What do you want?" Walter asked.

"Ahhh," he said, leaning back in the chair, "what I have always wanted. What is rightfully mine."

"The journal?" Nathan asked. "But, you already have it."

Kieffer looked from Nathan to Walter. His expression narrowed.

"No, Nathan. He wants the Arma Christi," Walter surmised.

"You were always a smart one."

The door to the office opened, and one of Kieffer's men walked in, holding a tray. He had water bottles and an assortment of junk food from the Arklight breakroom.

271

"I know you must be thirsty. Please have something. You're going to need your strength."

Nathan grabbed a bottle of water, ripped off the cap, and emptied it in a matter of seconds. He dropped the empty bottle on the floor and reached for a second, wiping his chin with his sleeve.

"Well, you're not getting it, no matter what."

"You are mistaken, Admiral," Kieffer said, motioning to Klaus. "We already have it. You just need to finalize the transaction."

Klaus walked over to the bookshelf and pressed the hidden switch, opening the door into the briefing room.

"Please, gentlemen. With my compliments, let's negotiate," Kieffer said, holding his hand toward the door.

Nathan stood to his feet and helped Walter up. The two men, weak from captivity, walked into the briefing room. Klaus made his way over to the safe, while Kieffer hobbled in, clutching his canes for support. The old Führer held his hand up to one of the mercenaries.

"Stay here at the door. We'll try to do this like... gentlemen."

The mercenary stopped, watching Nathan's every move.

"Okay, so you know about the safe. It'll still take you days to cut through it. By that time, our protocols will have kicked in and the entire military will be breathing down your neck. Don't believe me? Ask him," he said, nodding his head toward Klaus.

Klaus stood firm. Kieffer sat at one of the chairs at the table.

"You're going to give us the passcode," he said.

"Hell no I'm not!"

"Do you know why Klaus here pushed for you to be the commanding officer of Arklight?"

Nathan turned away from his voice.

"Why is that?"

"Because of your compassion," Kieffer said. "But I think after everything you've witnessed so far, you know it won't bother me at all to kill every single Arklight person on that hangar floor. I already know you're going to give me what I want. I've foreseen it."

Nathan dropped his head, knowing Kieffer was going to make this impossible.

"Show them the video from Okinawa."

Klaus pulled out his cell phone and opened a video box. Walter looked away, wincing as if someone punched him in the gut.

"Nathan, remember what I told you," he said, "The time draws near – feel your way."

"Shut up!" Kieffer yelled, breaking Walter's thought. "Show him!"

Klaus rotated the phone around as the video started to play. Nathan watched the shootout with Spear Team and Magnus' men. He saw John... they were carrying someone. The helicopter lifted; a rocket fired, striking the Blackhawk. The camera zoomed, catching the military bird nosedive toward the bay. Nathan's fists tightened, he had yet to take a breath.

"See? Your quest is over. Don't let this old fool next to you get the rest of your people killed."

Nathan ran a hand through his already disheveled hair. He stared at the floor.

"The passcodes – now!"

He grabbed a chair and sat down. He stared at Kieffer. He had never wanted to kill someone out of pure anger in his life, but now he did.

Kieffer stared back at Nathan, shifting his gaze to Klaus. The Führer held up two fingers and nodded. Klaus pulled his radio toward his mouth.

"Kill two."

Two shots echoed from the hangar. The muffled screams and yells vibrated into the conference room. Nathan's eyes filled with furious tears. He exploded out of his seat and charged Kieffer, only to be struck in the head with the rifle of an armed mercenary. He collapsed to the floor, his head bleeding, thoughts clouded.

"Shall we kill two more?" Klaus asked Kieffer.

"No... please."

"Override code – 4562045Q1R," Walter said.

"What was that?" Kieffer asked.

"It's my administrative override code. It will open the safe."

"Walter, why?" Nathan asked.

"It's over, Nathan. No one else needs to die today. Especially you."

Klaus walked to the access keypad of the safe and entered the code. The door clicked, opening to expose the Arma Christi and the other artifacts Arklight had collected over the years. Klaus entered the vault, his gaze transfixed on the treasures just inside.

"It was all we had," Nathan mumbled. His head sank to the floor.

"What was that, Admiral?" Kieffer asked.

Nathan raised his head. Red dripped from his scalp as he stared a hole through the German Führer.

"Remember what I told you," Walter whispered to Nathan. "Have faith."

Klaus exited the vault with a small stack of items in hand, including the plastic, divided box containing 29 silver coins and the one folded coin. On top sat the near forearm-length petrified wood of the Titulus Crucis.

Kieffer stood and met Klaus in the middle of the briefing room. He extracted the journal from his pocket, holding it tight, as if it would disappear if he didn't. His crooked, bony hands caressed the leather cover and his right index finger found the Templar lion talisman in the middle. He traced over the branded symbol, a devilish smirk growing across his face.

"The last time I had to retrieve this journal, I failed to realize something. I failed to realize that you knew far too much to kill. You know, it's been nearly 56 years since that day."

"You tried to kill me then and failed," Walter said from his chair, his hands gripping his cane. "Now you're just making an excuse for your failures – like it's some epiphany."

Kieffer's eyes narrowed.

"Maybe you're hard to kill, or maybe you're just lucky. Either way, I'll be taking both of you with us. I will enjoy extracting every ounce of information out of you. Only then will I allow you to die."

Nathan sat back in his chair, loosening his collar.

"Do your worst," Nathan said.

Klaus sat the Arma Christi on the conference table. In one motion, he backhanded Nathan, stunning him. His hand traveled around as he drew a fist, punching Nathan in the nose, splitting the bridge open.

"Silence! You will not speak to the Führer like that – ever."

Nathan's hand cupped his nose. Blood ran down his face as he checked for a broken bone. He moved to the edge of his seat, ready to attack. Walter's hand landed on his shoulder, urging restraint.

"There's nothing for us to share that you don't already know," Walter said.

"I'll be the judge of that," Kieffer said, admiring the Titulus Crucis.

Nathan and Walter both sat, looking over the Arma Christi. Klaus stood next to Nathan; his gaze trained on the admiral. Kieffer now picked up the Crucis, studying the wooden title of the cross.

"The Order of the Black Sun looked everywhere for these relics. Who knew that time itself hid them from me – from destiny. They are quite unremarkable in person, but I can feel their power."

"Yes, His power does flow through them," Walter said.

"His power," Kieffer laughed. "The power of this being you call God? That's the limitation of you Christians – you fail to consider truth. You fail to understand science, evolution, and supremacy. When assembled, the energy that will flow through this device is easily quantified. It's a conductor of sorts… opening an ancient energy stored within the Ark itself."

"Or, it's purely the power of God," Walter said, his head raised in defiance.

"Silence!" Kieffer yelled, slamming his hand on the conference table

"Silence my ass!" Nathan said, shifting as Klaus stepped closer. "You still don't have all of the pieces. It won't work."

Kieffer produced an insidious smile and he sat back in his chair, arching his hands, drawing them under his chin. Klaus drew his hand back, ready to strike Nathan in the head.

"Yes," Kieffer said, motioning for Klaus to refrain, "maybe I don't have the final piece – yet. But, it will find its way to me soon enough. I have seen that day."

"You mean, pieces. Even if you've acquired the John Bell Hood coin, the way I see it is you still need the Spear of Destiny and the Grail. Neither of them are in your possession," Walter said.

Kieffer took a deep breath and smiled, excited to tell Walter the truth.

"The Holy Grail. Ah, yes – the other piece of the puzzle." He relished the moment. "It's already mine."

Walter tightened his grip on his cane. Despite hearing the terrible news, a sense of confidence eased his mind. He distorted his face to show surprise, anxiety, even fear—an old spy-game tactic; something Ian had taught him years ago: he acted.

Kieffer smirked when Walter stared ahead, his face frozen in shock.

"How?" Nathan asked.

"You remember Hildebrand Gurlitt, don't you, Walter? The man you abandoned to die in Poland? Funny thing was that he had located the Grail back in 1934, a year after Himmler visited Halifax. The stone Himmler found—"

"You mean stole," Nathan said, Klaus' hand now gripping the back of his neck.

"The stone revealed a clue," Kieffer continued. "Eventually, he discovered that the Holy Grail had been hidden within the *Just Judges Panel* of the *Ghent Altarpiece*. Hitler sent operatives to Belgium, where they stole the painting. Hildebrand swore to guard the relic, hiding it away, even after the end of World War II. Only a few high-ranking Nazis knew the significance of what the *Just Judges* contained."

"Choltitz. He knew – didn't he?" Walter asked.

"A very sound deduction. He was smart enough to figure it out, so yes. That's when I first overheard the story, myself, that night in Paris."

"How did you get it from Gurlitt?" Nathan asked.

"Let's just say that he met an untimely demise, after defying us."

Walter lowered his gaze and rested his forehead on the top of his cane. He strengthened his resolve, knowing the truth.

"You killed him for it?" Nathan asked, careful to guard his knowledge. "His accident – that was you?"

Kieffer smiled, his ice-blue eyes almost sparkling with delight.

"So, you see, Walter. We've had the Grail this entire time. Now that we have all of the other pieces firmly in our possession, the Spear will come to me soon enough – no matter what you tell me."

Walter's head dropped.

"Your team took the Spear out of Shuri Castle," Kieffer said. "You know where it is."

"True, we did take it. However, John Bell was the one who hid it from the world. I'm afraid the Spear's whereabouts died with him."

Kieffer stood up and turned, motioning to the security detail at the door to Nathan's office.

"Let me show you something," Kieffer said, turning to walk toward the elevator.

The security detail walked in, focusing on Walter and Nathan. Klaus pushed Nathan toward the lift.

"Walk," Klaus said. No emotion existed. He was a machine.

The security detail grabbed the two men and walked them into the elevator, pushing them into the back corners. They were made to face away from Kieffer and Klaus, their bodies forced into the corners of the lift as they descended to the exterior team entrance on the hangar's floor. Nathan ran scenario after scenario in his head, trying to formulate an escape plan. The security was too tight; there were too many factors, and there was no clear way out. Everywhere he looked there were armed mercenaries, and even a few soldiers, wearing the symbol of the SS. All of their attention focused on him, knowing he was a real threat.

"Where are you taking us?" Nathan asked, attempting to build on any intelligence that might help.

"Shut up," a guard said.

The doors to the elevator opened. A hand grabbed Nathan by the shoulder, turning him around to face the interior of the massive, granite-walled cavern. He could see his entire command, packed into a section on the floor. Some sat, while others propped on a knee. Their faces were all sullen, and Nathan couldn't bring himself to look at them. The situation was too dire. All of them stared at him. Narrow hope existed, but he had no answers.

"That's far enough," Kieffer said, signaling his mercenaries to stop Nathan and Walter short of the others.

The faces in front of Nathan looked shaken, still in shock from what was happening. An entire base of military personnel went about their daily routine on Mayport's Naval Air Station while Arklight was under siege in the depths below. Nathan scanned over his people, settling on the tearful face of one of his intelligence team. Her cheeks were stained with streaks of mascara, her eyes swollen from loss. Beside her laid the lifeless body of someone from her group.

"What's it going to take?" Kieffer asked, placing his hand on Walter's shoulder. Walter dipped away from Kieffer, disgusted he'd even touched him.

"Like I said before, I can't tell you what I don't know. Bell had the Spear. He's dead. You know this, because your people had him killed."

"Lies!" Kieffer yelled, stepping beside Nathan. "Are you going to let him keep lying, Admiral? You know he isn't telling me everything. I can see it in your face."

Nathan had slipped away, his mind blank. He continued to stare ahead, losing his focus in fear. The short, dark hair of the female in front of him reminded him of Anne. Kieffer turned to see what Nathan was looking at, smirking with evil intent when he caught her gaze.

"Fine! Klaus, grab that one."

Nathan snapped out of his trance when Klaus grabbed her by the hair. He dragged her away from the group as her eyes darted around the cavern. Her scream echoed in the subterranean hangar. The rest of the prisoners were powerless to help.

"No!" He held his right arm out toward the female. Everyone called her Sam, but he had always chosen to call her Samantha. She reminded him of his own daughter.

Klaus and one of the other mercenaries forced her to her knees. They grabbed her head and forced her to look at Nathan.

"I haven't done anything!" Sam screamed, a barrel resting against the back of her head.

"Shut your mouth!" Klaus commanded, jerking her around.

"This is senseless!" Nathan yelled, looking at Kieffer, who wandered back to Walter.

"Is it? I'm afraid that Walter here is the only one that can answer that question, Admiral."

"What's he talking about? Walter!"

Walter had settled into his own thoughts, weighing the terrible costs of this war. The plan was initiated; people were going to die. The mission given to him could not bow to the needs of a flesh-driven, broken world. His position was clear, full of burden.

"She can live or die! It's up to you."

"Dammit, what the hell is he talking about, Walter? Tell him something."

Walter thought, knowing he still held an ace up his sleeve. It had to be played, but only later. For now, he would do what he could. Somehow Kieffer knew the truth, or some of it.

"Okay! I'm not lying about the facts. I don't know where the Spear is," Walter said, Klaus still pressing his pistol against Sam's head.

"Wait!" Nathan exclaimed.

Walter turned a stony gaze to Kieffer, who stared back, awaiting the confirmation. They were face to face.

"How did you know?"

"You're not the only ones who can intercept intelligence," Kieffer said. "Now tell me, or the girl dies."

Walter took a deep breath. He glanced over, seeing the terror in Sam's eyes. A calming touch landed on Walter's shoulder, but he looked and could see nothing. He still felt it – a touch assuring him it was okay to part with the truth. The vision he had seen was true. Walter stood relieved of the burden and was freed.

"He's alive. John Bell's alive and well," Walter said, hanging his head down.

"Where is he?"

"I don't know," Walter said. "I haven't spoken to him in weeks."

Kieffer grabbed Walter's chin forcing his head up, staring at him. Walter pulled his head back.

"The problem is… you've lied so much, I can't tell if you still are or not. Kill her!"

"No!"

An instant later, a single shot discharged, human bits splattering on Klaus as Sam's body fell limp to the floor.

Nathan erupted toward Kieffer, only to be electrically stunned, by one of the mercenaries behind him. The rapid-fire, distinct sparking of fifty-thousand volts surged into Nathan, dropping him to the ground, as if he were having a seizure. Seconds went by as the mercenary held the trigger down, zapping what energy Nathan had left. Two more men closed on Nathan, applying a fresh set of flex-cuffs. The clicking soon ceased. He just laid on the floor, his mind scrambled, trying to catch his breath.

"Where is John Bell?" Kieffer asked, looking in Walter's eyes once more.

"I don't know."

Kieffer patted Walter's shoulder and walked toward his plane, which his men were ferrying onto the lift, replacing the two C-17s that had arrived earlier from Okinawa.

"Klaus, secure them on our plane. Put the rest of their people inside the cage. It's time we leave."

"Yes, my Führer."

†††††

Nathan felt movement and regained a painful consciousness. He was strapped to a seat in a sizeable commercial aircraft. The hum of the engine whined. It was a jet – a cargo plane. They were still on the ground, taxiing. Nathan looked to his right, seeing Walter beside him in the window seat. They were surrounded by soldiers and mercenaries, who settled into their seats in the cabin.

"I'm glad you're awake, Admiral," Kieffer said.

Nathan turned his battered head, looking behind him. There he sat, an impish look on his face.

"Where are you taking us?"

"You ask too many questions," Klaus said from across the aisle.

Nathan looked over, realizing Rod was no longer himself. Maybe he was never really there.

The engines throttled up and the plane rolled faster down the Mayport NAS main runway. Nathan looked out the window at the gigantic hangar – the one that served as the entrance to Arklight's base. Nothing appeared out of place on the surface, but below, he knew his people struggled to escape.

Kieffer watched Nathan as he stared. He pulled out a cellular phone and looked at the speed dial button on the keypad. The jet lifted off the tarmac and soared into the sky above the Atlantic.

"It's not fair, really – leaving all that tech behind."

Nathan turned his attention back around to him. Klaus sat back unconcerned, since Nathan's hands and feet were bound.

"You know something, you're a real asshole – even for a Nazi," Nathan said, twisting back in his seat to look straight ahead.

"I know you don't understand us. I'm not going to try and explain it. You are ignorant to the importance of our cause. One day history will show what heroes we truly are."

"I guess not much has changed. That's the same bullshit rhetoric Hitler used to convince an entire nation they were a special race, somehow more deserving than every other."

Kieffer laughed and ran his finger over one of the buttons on the phone.

"Maybe we aren't special. But then how do you explain all of this, happening like it has?"

"I can't..." he looked down towards his feet.

"You know why?"

Nathan sighed, recovering his gaze to the back of the chair in front of him.

"Destiny, Nathan. I have seen it. The end of this terrible, bitter, divided world draws near. The beginning of a new world order is soon to begin, with me ruling at the center of it."

"You're crazy."

Kieffer picked up the receiver next to him and pulled it to his ear.

"Pilot, are we at the safe distance?"

Nathan heard the question, struggling to understand what it meant.

"Turn the plane for our guests."

"Turn for what?"

Walter looked out the window as the plane turned left. Mayport NAS came into view, many miles away in the distance. Kieffer pushed the speed dial button on the phone.

"Look at what used to be your home. Behold."

A brilliant flash of light erupted from Arklight's massive hangar on the far side of the base. All of them looked away from the illuminated sky. The light faded, exposing a towering mushroom cloud climbing into the air. The aircraft shuddered from the shockwave. Nathan's eyes blurred from exposure, but he continued to bear witness to the devastation of the base. Everyone they had left behind was lost. Everything, gone in an instant.

"You see, there is no hope," Kieffer said. "Only my destiny remains."

Walter's hand covered his mouth, knowing what caused the blast. The pocket nuke they let getaway in Germany made itself known to the world. All this time, all these years, the Nazis had planned this day to the most finite detail.

Nathan sat back in his chair, unable to breathe. His heart ached from intense sorrow and his mind could no longer absorb the reality of what was happening. All seemed lost.

"Nathan, I'm sorry," Walter said.

"This is a nightmare."

"No," Kieffer cut in, "this is the gateway to a new world. You will see soon enough. Once we arrive in Geneva, my plan will be in action."

"I… we don't have a chance, Walter. We have nothing left – no one," Nathan said, his grief quivering his lower lip.

Kieffer sat back in his seat, enjoying the intense pain he had caused.

Walter's hands remained free and he rest them both atop his cane.

"It's always darkest before the light," Walter said, looking at Nathan.

"Well, it's pretty damn dark, Walter." He looked at the old man like he was his only friend left in the world. He might as well be. Everyone else was dead.

Walter ran his right hand down the handle of his cane to the ornamental, metal piece in the middle. Hidden from view, his right index finger tapped the piece.

"Faith and belief," he said, his eyes unleashing a truth.

Nathan realized what Walter was telling him, and he tried not to give himself away.

"How?" Nathan asked.

"We're in the endgame now," Walter whispered.

Nathan sat back, maintaining a defeated posture. Klaus was asleep, snoring in the seat next to him. He looked around the cabin, watching all of Kieffer's men celebrating Arklight's destruction. There was no way to quantify the loss. Nathan's thoughts turned to his wife. It was then he remembered what Walter said in Halifax: he and John were the keys – John had to be alive.

"Faith and belief," Nathan whispered. "God help us."

CHAPTER 19: PARADOX

"The wicked frustrate the plans of the oppressed, but the Lord will
protect his people."
Psalms 14:6

2200-ZuluTime 10April1946 (2300-CET Ghent, Belgium)

The shop keeper's bell chimed as Ian walked into the pub down the
street from Saint Bavo's Cathedral. He stopped, lit up a cigarette, and
scanned the room beneath the flickering light of the pub lanterns, looking
for someone familiar. The war was over for the world, but not for the
Alsos Team. Much still needed to be done. They needed answers. He
spotted Richie and began weaving his way across the room.

The smoky bar was filled with the joy of young men and women
trying to get on with their lives. Laughter was the one thing Richie had
almost forgotten existed in the world. After Okinawa, the team returned
home, but life as they remembered it was lost. Nothing felt the same.
Every time Richie closed his eyes, all he could see was the chaos of battle
and the death that had accompanied it. With every meal, he could almost
taste it. Even though he had come home, gotten married, and learned to
smile on the outside, a bitter and brutal history haunted his every thought.
A devious enemy still lurked about.

"Good to see you, old man," Ian said. His upbeat tone shook Richie
from his cold, lonely thoughts.

"How've you been?" Richie asked. "It's been too long."

"Frankly, I'm glad to be back in the field. MI-6 had me writing cover
reports about our little adventures for months. I came up with a
wonderful cover, calling us the 30AU Commando Unit. Evidently, they
thought well enough of it to put us back on task, under the guise of T-
Force."

"T-Force? What's that?"

"It's a joint special operations branch... they never told you?"

"OSS doesn't tell us anything. We've been at this so long, I think they've forgotten about us—but at least the funding's still there."

"We'll have to shore some things up once we get back. I've gotten an entire report ready for you to lay out for your President. Otto Hahn and the minds at Farm Hall have come up with some interesting ways to help jumpstart Project Arklight. I think even Bell will be pleased. We've codenamed the project 'Thunderball.'"

"You Brits come up with some eloquent ways to cover your tracks, that's for sure."

Ian laughed before taking a long drag of his cigarette.

"That's not the half of it. I've been given the cover of foreign manager to the Kemsley paper group. MI-6 upgraded my operative status to double-secret. I can go anywhere at any time."

"OSS put me and Bell back to work. Nothing fancy, just continuing doing what we do. I'm glad we still get to work together, though – I've missed you, buddy."

Ian took another pull of his smoke and patted Richie on the shoulder.

"Speaking of missing, where is Bell?"

"He's down the street, watching the target."

"Excellent. I can't wait to see his sour face. How's he been?"

"He's been Bell… just a little more relaxed."

"Bell, relaxed? That has got to be a sight."

"Let me clarify: as relaxed as Bell can be," Richie countered, feeling a familiar comfort return. The team was back together, and he knew what needed to be done.

"I can already see the wheels turning. What's the play?"

He slid closer to Ian, careful to re-check their surroundings.

"We've been watching the cathedral for over a week. They should close up for the day any minute now. When they do, the main floor is locked up tight; however, we found a door that Bell thinks we can enter. He made an approach last night and it looked feasible. Once we get in, we'll need to actually get to the *Altarpiece*."

Ian cut his eyes toward two military policemen as they entered the pub.

"At least the occupational forces are friendly," he said, craning his neck to see what the MPs were staring at. "It appears that our neighborhood protectors are more interested in the ladies than patrolling."

"Yeah, we've noticed. Good news for us. You ready to take this to task?"

He stubbed out his cigarette and stood.

"Lead the way."

Richie stood up and grabbed his backpack, careful to scan the pub once more upon exit. The two MPs were hitting on a couple local girls, which guaranteed they would be indisposed for a while. He stopped on the curb of the Lumburgstraat and took a deep, mind-clearing breath. Ian stopped beside him.

"Saint Bavo's... what a beautiful church," he said, glancing across the street to his left.

Richie nodded and pulled his black watch cap down low on his head.

"This is where it all started for us, if you think about it."

They began to walk parallel the cathedral, careful not to look too closely.

Ian smiled, "I didn't really think of it like that. The *Ghent Altarpiece* did start us down this path."

"I think that was just a small piece of the puzzle."

"You figured out why we had to be here on this exact date," Ian said, his gaze locked on Richie's face for a reaction. "If... if that's not it, then what's your meaning?"

Richie had grown his spy-craft over the months. Not even a lie-detector could read him. His face revealed nothing to Ian, until he chose to allow it with a smirk.

"You've gotten good. Now, spill it!"

"There's Bell," Richie said, happy to make him wait a little while longer.

Ian nodded like a proud sibling, and they crossed the street. Bell was standing in front of the cathedral, his hands tucked into his trouser pockets. He turned his head, sensing his friends approach.

"Hey, buddy," Bell said, his hand out for Ian's.

"How've you been, old man?" he said, grabbing both hand and elbow for the greeting.

"Better than I deserve. You?"

"Back where I belong and ready for another adventure."

Richie enjoyed seeing the team back together, but time was short; of late, his visions had a bad effect on his mood.

"Glad we're back, but we gotta get to it."

"Right," Bell said. "Follow me."

Bell walked along the front of the cathedral, turning the corner at the lesser-traveled Kapittalstraat. Ian followed close behind, while Richie took time to scout; no one was watching. Bell jumped the gate, followed by Ian. Richie closed in last, still vigilant of their surroundings. The cover of night made them hard to see. He leapt over, following his team down the stairs to a below-ground entrance.

"Anyone see us?"

"We're good, Skipper."

A lock-picking set was already in Bell's hands, and he got to work. Ian rubbed the soot from a small glass panel in the center of the door and tried to see what was inside. The main contrast was between grayish shapes and accents of black lines.

"Almost got it," Bell whispered, wiggling the lockpick set, "and... voilà!"

The door pushed open, rusty hinges creaking.

Ian entered the dingy basement area, careful not to bump into the stacks of wooden boxes littering the floor.

"I see a little bit of light," he said as he crept across the room. Bell looked back, watching Richie pull the door shut behind them.

"It's a hallway that looks to go up to the cathedral," Ian said. "Hold tight while I check ahead."

He crept down the hall to a set of ascending stairs. As he closed the distance, he began to hear the click of heels striking the marble floor above. Careful to conceal his presence, he climbed the steps. His head rose from the stairwell, and he worked to keep his focus trained on the source of the sound, despite the grand opulence of the cathedral's architecture. Giant stone columns extended toward the high ceiling, and statues stood all around, like guardians from long ago. He found the source of the footfalls: one of the priests, walking along the front of the altar. The priest moved away from Ian and exited through a door on the opposite side with a *clunk* that echoed inside the great hall.

"Is it clear?" Bell asked from below.

The beauty of Saint Bavo's made Ian forget they had a mission to complete. He crouched low enough to see Bell's face and motioned them ahead.

Bell moved in behind Ian, and Richie walked in front of them both. His mind took stock of the *Ghent Altarpiece*, freed from the clutches of the Nazis. It hung, once again, over the pulpit—as it had before the war; the most-stolen artwork in history had been returned to the care of its rightful protectors.

"We need to pull down the *Adam Panel*," Richie said.

"Are you going to finally tell us what you saw?" Bell asked. "You know, what all of this is about."

Richie looked at his friends.

"All I know is that I saw us, right here, in this place – and we all had our hands on the *Altarpiece*."

"And?" Ian questioned.

Richie took a deep breath and twisted his head. His eyes darted to the floor.

"What is it, buddy?" Bell asked.

"We all see... Him."

"I don't think I understand," Ian said.

Richie sighed and looked at Ian, then Bell.

"Something incredible happens. Something I can't describe. I only know that we need to do this—we have to do this—right now."

"I've never doubted you, and I'm not gonna start tonight," Bell said. "Let's get to it."

Ian smiled, noticing a ladder propped against the wall behind Richie. He stepped across the floor to retrieve it. Bell shifted his gaze to the *Ghent Altarpiece*.

"God, huh? You think *He's* gonna want to look at us, after all we've done?" Bell asked.

Richie hung his head, ashamed of what he had become because of the war. The emptiness he felt affected every aspect of his life. Nothing felt the same after they escaped the hell of Shuri Castle. Not even his wife could get to him – the real him. The man he had been before the war seemed lost.

"We gotta try, Skipper. Our only hope lies in what we do tonight. That's all I'm certain of."

"But I don't get it," Bell said. "This *Adam Panel* is a recreation of the real one, the one buried in Bizerte. Arklight hid it in that hovel, and we made sure it was hidden the next day. This is a fake."

"Yes, I know; that's what's been so strange to me – there's literally no connection to the Arma Christi in this piece… but think about what does connect."

"The date? That's all I can think of."

"John said we had to be here tonight, specifically," Richie said.

"It's the anniversary of the original theft—the one in 1934. But wasn't that theft involving the *Just Judges* and the *Saint John the Baptist Panels*? Why are we concerned about the *Adam Panel*?"

"It's just something I saw. I can't explain it. I just need to get it down, so we can all put hands on it and see what happens."

Bell nodded and patted his friend on the shoulder.

"What the hell. Maybe God will give us a break tonight. Or better yet, tell us what all this is really all about," he said, a smirk emerging on his face.

"Skipper, we're in a church. How about watching your mouth for once?"

"Sorry."

Ian passed by the two of them with the ladder on his shoulder.

"If you two are done, could I bother you for a hand?"

Bell turned and Richie followed him to the base of the *Ghent Altarpiece*. The *Adam Panel* hung in the top left corner, suspended by cables secured to the ceiling.

"How do you propose we get it down?" Ian asked, propping the ladder on the floor.

"The cables are hooked into another frame piece and the painting, itself—frame and all—is held in place with a couple of wooden dowels."

"How do you know that?" Bell asked.

"That's how it was secured before the Nazis stole it. Since it's in the same carriage, I'm making an educated guess. Now, hold the ladder. I'll have to use the top step to reach it."

Bell and Ian grabbed the ladder from either side. Richie scaled the steps until he was forced to balance on the apex. He struggled to hold his position as he reached up to the *Adam Panel*. A jolt of déjà vu surged into his thoughts; this was familiar. A warmth flushed his skin.

His hand touched the canvas, and blue, static-charged particles danced around his fingers. A gust of wind blew out the prayer candles in front of the altar, throwing him off balance. He swayed, working to steady himself, hands on the frame of the *Adam Panel*. He located the two wooden dowels holding the panel in place within the superstructure.

A shiver shot up his spine as he removed both supports and tilted the *Adam Panel* out of the external frame. He took great care in lowering the priceless work of art into the waiting hands of Bell. Ian did his best to throw more of his weight onto the base of the ladder, better supporting Richie's balancing act. Bell lowered the painting to the floor while Richie climbed down from the ladder.

The three men soon found themselves staring at the painting. Richie still couldn't figure out why this panel recreation burdened his every thought. He pulled out a magnifying lens and a flashlight from his small backpack. The light clicked on and he studied the panel, trying to find the binary code – or anything with meaning.

"Just what I thought. Nothing," Richie said, his voice echoing within the cathedral.

"Keep it down," Ian whispered. "What are you looking for?"

"There's no binary coding on this piece. So, it's a fake – for sure."

"I could've told you that," Bell said. "Uh, matter of fact I did."

"I guess I just figured some miracle may have happened. I'm still wondering what the significance of this piece is," he said, still inspecting the panel.

Bell gripped the art piece, and Richie ran his hand along the outer portion of the framework. Ian watched over Richie's shoulder, curious, observing what he was doing. A gust of wind circulated around the three men, and the same blue-arc of static tickled Richie's fingertips.

"Ian, touch the painting," he said.

A vortex formed around them. Electric light flashed from above, as the air was violently pulled upward. Ian struggled to look up into the small portal of brilliant energy. He squinted; he couldn't see anything but light.

The cyclone pulled him off his feet, and he grabbed the painting's frame to avoid falling – but instead, he floated in the air, suspended in a powerful vacuum of luminescent, blue lightning. He locked his gaze on Richie and then Bell, both of whom also clung to the painting as if their lives depended on it.

"What's happening?" Bell asked.

"I wish I knew," Ian said.

Richie held on tight, mind churning until he remembered something his grandson said, back in Bizerte.

"May we walk on a righteous path today," Richie said.

"Oh my God!" Bell said, staring up with eyes wide like dinner plates.

A flash of light blinded them. Everything stopped. No sound, no wind – nothing. Richie's own thoughts were interrupted by a peace he had never felt before. It was as if time itself stopped. The intensity of the light was so bright, he covered his face. Another arc of lightning snapped, and all three men found themselves kneeling on a hard, cold floor, blind, and in shock.

"Richie? I can't see a damn thing," Bell said.

"Yeah, I'm here."

"What was that?" Ian asked, covered in chills.

Bell reached out, finding Richie's shoulder and pulling himself to his feet, before helping up his teammates. All three men struggled to open their eyes, seeing the blurs of gradient blacks.

"Did either of you see what I saw?" Bell asked, trying to gather his senses.

"It… it was like the finger of God pushed down on us," Ian said. "Like we stood still for a time. I felt such peace, but it was only for a second. What was that?"

Richie staggered about, still trying to adjust his focus, until he realized they were in the dark. It hadn't been very bright in the cathedral before, but now it was pitch black. Ian pulled out his lighter and rotated the ignitor. A spark turned into a soft flicker of yellow light. Richie plucked one of the altar candlesticks from its base nearby and held it toward the flame. He lit one candle after another, until a glow radiated off the columns in the cathedral.

"Richie? If we were holding onto the painting down here on the floor, why is it hanging above us now?" Ian asked.

Bell continued to blink himself into a functioning state. He tilted his head up and saw a figure staring back at them. A lean man with wire-rim glasses and a thick mustache stood just feet away, frozen in place. Fearing his team's compromise, he launched himself at the catatonic man, taking him to the ground. The man's glasses flew off his nose, and Bell covered his mouth with his left hand, his right drawn back into a fist. The man's stare broke from the trance, and he started to panic.

Ian and Richie scampered into the fray. Ian secured the man's flailing feet, and Richie grabbed one of his arms.

"Shhh," Richie said, placing his free hand's index finger to his mouth, hopeful to avoid any further noise.

The man shifted fear-filled eyes to Richie's face. Richie reached beyond the man's head and retrieved his glasses for him. By the condition of the man's suit, he was well-to-do, and educated.

"Do you speak English?"

The man nodded.

"We aren't here to hurt you. We need your help. Can you help us?"

The man's attention darted back and forth; Bell relaxed his grip, and the man nodded once more.

"What if he yells?"

Richie reached under his jacket, until his hand met a familiar friend. He pulled out his knife and held it where the man could see it.

"You understand, if you try to call for help, we cannot allow that. We don't want to hurt you, so don't make us, okay?"

The man's gaze was focused on the long blade of the combat knife. He shifted his focus back to Richie and nodded in one distinct movement of understanding. Bell and Ian released the man, but hovered over him, ready in case he changed his mind. Richie leaned back, finding the sheath for his knife.

"Who are you?" Ian asked.

The man shifted his gaze to Ian.

"You're British and American?"

"Yes," Bell said. "Now, *who* are you?"

"I'm Arsène Goedertier. I am a trustee of the church. How… did that happen – how you got here?"

"What are you saying?" Ian asked.

The man's eyes darted back and forth between the three strange men.

"What's your name again?" Ian asked.

"Arsène Goedertier. I'm a stockbroker, here in town and I… I volunteer here at the church. I help with their finances."

"Could you tell us what today's date is?" Ian asked, sensing something was amiss.

Bell and Richie felt he was on to something.

"The… the 10th of April."

"What year?" Ian asked.

"Why would you want to know that? It's 1934. Everyone knows that."

"What the hell? We're in the past?" Bell asked.

"This is it – this is what I saw," Richie said, standing to look at the *Ghent Altarpiece*.

"I won't even get into what I saw," Bell said. "There's no doubt in my mind now – God exists. Did either of you see? The face?"

"Face of what? I was blinded by what felt like a dozen suns at once," Ian said.

"The face of God," Bell said, chills breaking out on his arms. "Richie? Did you?"

"Skipper, it was Him, no doubt. But it was for a very distinct reason. We need a ladder—we don't have much time."

"I'll find one," Ian said, turning to search.

Arsène pulled himself up to his feet, dusted off his suit, and straightened his glasses. Richie looked him in the eye.

"What are you doing here?"

"I could equally ask; how did you get here?" Arsène replied.

Richie turned his attention to the *Ghent Altarpiece* hanging above.

"I think you know that much, but the thing you'll want to know is… why we're here."

"I just saw you appear in front of me. Like magic."

"Well, it ain't that simple," Bell said.

"We're on a mission from God. We need your help," Richie continued, hoping to enlist the man's help.

"You're angels?" Arsène asked, his voice cracking.

"Well—" Bell started.

"Yes, Arsène, something like that," Richie said. "We're here to protect something. Something hidden inside one of these panels."

"What is it?"

"What do you know about the Knights Templar and the Arma Christi?" Richie asked.

"Not much. Well, maybe a little. I know what the Knights Templar is, at least." Arsène said.

Ian walked up, with a ladder riding over his shoulder once more.

"Does Arsène know anything?" he asked, reconstructing the ladder below the *Adam Panel.*

"Nope," Richie said, climbing to the top.

"That's strange." He secured the ladder from below.

"What are you two talking about? We've somehow gone back 12 years. I'm so confused," Bell said.

Richie wiggled the *Adam Panel* out of framework and passed it down to Bell.

"Bell – tonight, remember? Arsène here is the prime suspect."

"Me?"

"Yes," Richie said, having made his way back to the floor. "But, I think the actual suspects are on their way here now, which is why we have to hurry."

Richie opened his backpack and pulled out a small case containing the device John had given him back at Shuri Castle.

"Bell, set the panel flat on the floor."

"What's the plan?" Bell asked.

"I'll deal with this. You and Ian grab the *Just Judges Panel* and the *Saint John the Baptist Panel* and bring them down here."

"Which ones?"

"It's the one on the far left below where this one was," he said, pointing at the *Ghent Altarpiece.* "*Saint John* is attached to the back. We need to separate them."

"Got it. Ian, hold the ladder."

"Why are you taking down these panels? They're priceless. You're going to damage them," Arsène said.

Richie motioned for the man to come over to him.

"Come here. I need to explain something to you that you're not gonna like."

"You are really not how I imagined an angel would be," he muttered. "What am I not going to like?"

Richie pulled the drone out of the case and flicked on the power switch, just as John had shown him. He set the small device on top of the *Adam Panel* canvas. He pulled his hand back and the drone began scanning the painting.

"What is that?" Arsène asked.

"It's something we don't need to disturb. I don't even know how it works, myself, but it's going to hide a code within the lines of this painting," Richie said.

"Code?"

"Yeah, but that's not got anything to do with you."

"I'm lost in all of this," Arsène said, rubbing his head.

"I need you to listen to me very closely."

"Okay."

They watched a red light start to flicker from below the drone.

"Men are on their way here, tonight. They're going to steal the *Just Judges Panel* of the *Altarpiece*... and we need to let it happen."

"What. No. We can't," Arsène said, his stance shifting back.

"Arsène, the fate of the world depends upon it. Man's part in the end of times is right before us. What we do right now is all that matters."

"I... I can't. I don't understand."

"That's why it's called faith; put your trust in God."

"Trust not in the ways of men," Arsène continued, "or of earthly riches."

"That's right – it's just a painting. What it holds is what we have to protect. Arsène, you're a believer, right? I need you to believe in what I'm saying," Richie said.

The man's face was dazed with confusion.

"Take a minute to let it sink in."

Ian and Bell had lowered both paintings to the floor. Ian separated them from one another. Richie patted Arsène on the shoulder and walked over to get a better look.

"Why did we need to get both?"

"I want us to check and make sure the *Saint John Panel* isn't hiding anything."

Bell leaned the panel forward to better expose the thick, wooden exterior frame. Richie pulled out his flashlight and scanned for any secret compartments. He circled the entire piece, finding nothing out of place.

"Arsène, will you hold this panel for us? So it doesn't get damaged."

The man nodded and took the *Saint John Panel* from Bell. Ian held the *Just Judges Panel*, rotating it to let Richie and Bell inspect.

"What are you looking for?" Arsène asked.

"Yeah, Richie. What *are* you looking for... exactly?" Bell asked.

"Something General Choltitz said back in Paris has been bothering me. He said that Gurlitt had pieces of the *Ghent* hidden away."

"Go on," Ian said, leaning the panel further back to expose the frame.

"If Hitler had stolen the entire *Altarpiece*, why would Gurlitt have just pieces of it hidden away? Why wouldn't they be intact?"

"I'm still not following you, buddy," Bell said.

"There was an entry in the journal from 1434 that referenced a 500-year prophecy called the *Just Judgment*," Richie said, feeling along the seam of the frame. "It said that the handle of Arimathea would reveal itself to the Templar protectorate after 500 years. It went on to say that it would remain in the hands of the protectorate until the last day."

"So, what's that mean?" Ian asked.

Richie stopped and smiled.

"Flip the panel over and lay it with the back facing up."

"I'm still not following."

"Yes, yes... go on," Arsène said, interested in the story.

"Well, it's 1934, so it's been 500 years. Joseph of Arimathea was the original protector of the Grail. This is the *Just Judges Panel*, which was created 500 years ago. We all know that Gurlitt, Himmler, and Hitler had been pursuing the Arma Christi as far back as—"

"The early 1930's," Ian finished. "Brilliant Richie... absolutely brilliant."

"So, you think the Grail is hidden in this piece?" Bell asked.

"There's a strong possibility. Everything points to it."

Richie pulled out his knife and dug it into a well-constructed, almost invisible seam along the backing of the *Just Judges Panel*. He pried at the wood until a fitted piece of block released, revealing a secret compartment. He shined his flashlight into the void and discovered a cloth-wrapped, cylindrical object.

"That's a little skinny to be the Holy Grail... isn't it?" Bell asked.

"It is," Richie said, pulling the object out, "unless the Grail was modified into the handle for the Time Key, like the journal suggests."

The cylindrical piece had the heaviness of bronze, and Richie could feel the detail along the crevices. Even wrapped, the craftsmanship on the footlong piece felt distinct—handmade. He unwrapped the petrified cloth, revealing an ornamental bronze handle, adorned with several sparkling red rubies. One end was hollow, and the other was capped with a cross. Richie and the others inspected the piece, finding what appeared to be traces of dried blood along the hollow end's decorative edge.

"Wow. This has to be it. Now that I'm holding it... it feels right."

"What feels right?"

"Our exit. Bell, there's a small chalice on the altar. Get it for me."

Bell shrugged his shoulders, confident that Richie knew what he was doing. He looked over to see the drone had stopped darting across the painting. Their mission was complete.

"Ian, hang the *Adam Panel* back up and I'll hand you this one next," Richie said. He looked to Arsène. "I need you to take the *Saint John Panel* and go over there by the stairs."

"But why?"

"There's no time – just go. I'll explain later. Bad men are about to be here. Hurry," he urged.

Arsène picked up the panel and carried it to the stairs where the Alsos Team had entered the cathedral in their time. Bell returned with the small ceremonial chalice, handing it to Richie.

"This will have to do," he said, wrapping the antique cup with the stiffened cloth. He stuffed it inside the void, replaced the block, and pushed it into place, concealing the compartment. Richie inspected it one last time. The fit was perfect and looked untouched.

"Quick, hand it back to Ian," Richie said, as he stuffed the Grail into his backpack.

Ian was careful to set each of the paintings back in their cradles just right. He scampered down as the front door of the cathedral creaked. He folded the ladder and leaned it against a pillar on his way to the others.

"Hurry, out the way we came," Richie said, as they all ran toward the stairs. Richie grabbed Arsène, and all four men escaped down the stairwell, into the lower storage room. Ian took point and cracked the exterior door. It was dead quiet, with plenty of shadows to conceal their escape.

"Looks clear."

"Let's get across the street," Bell said, pointing, "That cheese shop will do as a good place to lay low."

"Okay, let's go."

Richie grabbed Arsène by his jacket and the four men exited the cathedral, walking with haste. Ian and Bell scanned the area, thankful it was late and no one appeared to be in the streets. Once they cleared the street, Ian pulled out his lock-picking set. The men entered a small alley beside the cheese shop, and Ian got to work on the locked door. Within a few seconds, all four men and the *Saint John Panel* entered the closed business. They were all out of breath. Ian peered through the front glass, hoping they went unnoticed.

"Why did you have to take this part of the *Altarpiece?*" Arsène asked.

Richie found an empty chair and sat down.

"Because I wanted to save it from the Nazis. They would have destroyed it. Plus, you couldn't possibly have given it back to the cathedral if they had it."

"Nazis?" Arsène asked.

"Those men I told you about are in there right now. They're stealing the *Just Judges Panel*, because the Nazis believe it holds a piece of Arma Christi."

"The Holy Grail you took... you took it to save it from the Nazis?"

"Yes."

"What are we gonna do with it?" Bell asked.

Ian walked beside Richie and placed his hand on his shoulder.

"We are the protectorate of the Grail."

Richie looked up at Ian and then to Bell.

"We all need to learn everything we can about the Knights Templar, so we can understand all that's at stake."

"What am I supposed to do? I'll surely be arrested. You said it yourself, I am the prime suspect," Arsène said, his voice cracking.

"Richie, I have to admit, it's kind of a raw deal for our friend here," Bell said.

"Arsène, I wish I had the time to explain everything. You're a smart man – a good man. No one can know we were ever here. Everything good in this world depends on you keeping this a secret. Do whatever you have to, but it needs to look like you stole both panels," Richie said.

"I'll spend the rest of my life in prison if they catch me."

"No; you won't. There's a plan for you. You may not understand it, but you will be rewarded for how you handle this."

"I pray you are right. I've never done anything, or have seen anything, like what's happened tonight."

"I know," Richie said. He pulled off his backpack and flipped open the top.

"If you're angels…"

"We're no angels, Arsène. Just men," Bell said.

"Then how did you just appear?"

"We may be but broken men," Ian said, "but we have been touched to do something righteous."

Richie stood up and pulled the backpack strap over his shoulder. He held the Grail in his right hand and looked at his teammates.

"It's time we get back," Richie said.

"Back where?" Arsène asked.

"To where we belong," Bell said, walking toward his team.

Ian nodded and grabbed the Grail.

"Fair winds, Arsène," he said.

Bell reached last, grabbing the Grail. Blue, static, electric energy jumped around them, and a gust of wind billowed about as Arsène looked on in amazement. A flash of light shocked his senses. He turned away. When he looked back, the three strange men were gone without a trace.

CHAPTER 20: ABSOLUTION

"They are at death's door; the angels of death wait for them."
Job 33:22

1500-ZuluTime 04June2020 (2000-EST Virginia Beach, VA)

Lord, why... why must good men suffer and die? John thought. So many had died, so many had suffered, and his mind was tormented with doubt. Since they had encountered Magnus, not much had gone according to plan, and now three of his teammates were dead, their bodies left behind amidst the chaos. *Jesus be with them... I feel so lost. Help me.*

"John, we're here," Chappy said, shaking him from his daze, as the jet came to rest in the hangar.

The voice brought a sliver of hope to help buoy him; how Chappy held it together, he might never know.

"How's everyone holding up?" John asked.

"Bell ain't changed," Chappy said, "even though he's pushing a hundred. Chief and Anne slept through the landing, but I just got 'em up."

"What about you?"

"My leg's sore, but the chief did a good job stitching me up."

"I'm not talking about your leg."

"It ain't the time. I've got to believe there's more fighting to do. No time to grieve. We've got to finish this thing."

John marveled at Chappy's steadfast resolve. He wished that sorrow hadn't already grabbed hold of his own soul over the past few days. If he let the anger in, he feared he would lose control. Maybe that's what needed to happen, but without focused purpose, it would be futile—at least, that's what he kept coming back to.

"You're right. We need to finish this."

"Let's do it." Chappy grabbed his shoulder.

Bell hobbled up to John, looking at the embattled leader.

"We've got much to discuss," he said, his voice stronger than most men half his age. "Time to get yourselves together. There's no turning back from what must be done." He continued on his way.

Chappy looked at Bell, then back to John.

"He's been tight-lipped since he fished us out of the water. It's time for some answers."

"I know. It's my fault. My head's not been in the game," John said, watching Bell exit the private jet's front stairs.

"We can't pull this off without you, boss. Get it together."

"I will," John nodded as he stood to exit.

"Steady, Bell said we're going to a black-site somewhere south of here," said the chief, passing by on his way to deboard.

"Yeah, it sounds like we'll have a chance to figure out what's next," Anne said from behind John's seat.

John followed them out, ready to hear what Bell had to say. He exited the plane to find that they were inside of a closed hangar. Two SUVs sat idle, just beyond the tip of the wing.

"John, you're with me. Have the rest of your team get into the trail vehicle."

"I get it. Whatever he's got to say… it's for your ears only. We'll be right behind you," Chappy said.

Two men in suits stood around the hangar. John assumed they represented Bell's personal security detail – likely CIA contractors, with limited, compartmentalized knowledge. The chief, Anne, and Chappy walked to the second vehicle.

"Stay safe," John breathed, stepping around to the backseat door opposite the one Bell had entered. The driver and Bell's bodyguards made sure they were all ready to move out.

"John, I imagine your head is swimming with questions, and I guess it's time you get some answers."

The anger started to boil over. Just one question plagued John's thoughts.

"Why wasn't it me?" he asked, tears welling.

"The answer you seek will not be found here. It's a complicated matter."

The SUV rolled forward and Bell closed the partition, separating them from the front of the vehicle. John waited until the compartment was sealed.

"Did they die needlessly for this cause? I know you know something… tell me at least why," he pleaded.

"It wasn't needless. They died for a reason – they died for you… for the team, so you could survive to fight another day. Their love for you was why they died. You will see them again, just like I'll see Doc and Sam. There is no greater love than to lay down one's life for one's friends."

John remembered that morning in Bizerte, back when the tables were turned.

"But, why them? Why not me?"

"Your story isn't finished. God is far from done with you. You have to realize that," Bell said, grabbing John's arm. "You'll find your way through this. You just need to put your faith back into motion."

"It is—I mean, I am… I just don't understand why it's gotta be *this* way. I can see their faces looking at me. Like I failed them. And I did."

"What? You failed them? John, you know it doesn't work that way. Those are the lies we believe when we stop believing in our path – our calling. If you believe you failed them, then you are lost."

"That's all I can feel: loss," John said, his face covered by his palms.

"You need to regain your perspective. You need to understand that your men didn't fail. They didn't fail to protect you. The failure here – is you're blind."

"Blind?"

"Yes. You're blind to their love. Their sacrifice. Their lives had meaning, and their deaths had purpose."

"What purpose does death serve?"

Bell patted him on the back and looked out the window as the city passed by.

"It only serves a purpose if you let it. Our dying here, on this earth, is only death if we refuse to believe. Zip, Wisp, and Rico's sacrifices are among those of the martyred. Their sacrifices were great, but they aren't dead. They live on – you know this."

John pulled his head up and wiped his face. His sorrow and inner torment found some comfort in Bell's words. He sat back and looked out the window.

"I understand. It's just not easy to accept they're gone."

"If anyone knows that feeling, it's me. Back in Bizerte, I felt the same way... after losing Sam and Doc. You'll never forget. The pain never leaves. You just have to get through it – even if it doesn't seem to make sense."

†††††

"I hope the old man can get through to John," Chappy said from the driver's seat, looking ahead to the lead SUV. "I've never seen him like this before."

"We just lost our friends," Anne said. "I think he's entitled to feel like shit."

Chappy sat back in his seat and gritted his teeth. The chief leaned forward from the back and said, "Anne, careful..."

"All of this is just too much to take," she continued. "We could've done something different – made better decisions."

"We did the best with what we had to work with," Chappy said, glancing out the driver's side window. "How you feel right now, that's just the anger building, telling you it's someone's fault. Somebody's got to get the blame, right?"

Her face was flushed, rage hidden just under the surface.

"Yes, dammit. It's someone's fault. Someone screwed up."

The chief reached over the passenger seat and gave her shoulder a gentle squeeze.

"Anne, you're right. Someone is to blame, but it's not John. We've been infiltrated. Someone with executive-level clearance set us up. There's only a handful of people who could have done it. Think about it: our base was nuked. The SecDef, General Johnson, Walter Steadman, and Admiral Grant have all disappeared. One of them – that's who's to blame. One of them is the traitor."

"How else could all of these terrible things have happened?" Chappy asked.

"Why would any of them sabotage the mission?"

"Who knows. But I promise that's what we're going to find out. Them and Bell are the only ones who knew all of the details. Our staging locations, entry points, times... they knew it all."

"He's right," said the chief, "we have to figure out who the rat is, then cut off its head."

"Who had the motive?" Chappy asked.

"Given what I've seen, Walter, Bell, and the admiral are far too invested to be our traitor," Chief said.

"Yeah, but I don't think we can rule anyone out at this point."

"We don't need to trust anyone – even John Bell," Anne said.

"Let's see what he tells John. That should give us some insight into his intentions moving forward. I'd think if he's our traitor, we'd be dead by now. But, that's just a hunch."

"I'd trust your gut over just about anything," said the chief.

"Thanks, but it's been off a little lately... I'm not sure I know what to believe anymore."

"So, best case scenario," Anne said, "Bell doesn't have us killed, isn't the traitor, and Magnus thinks we're dead for starters. How in the hell are we going to find him? We don't have any resources. Our base is gone, and even though the government covered up the attack, the world remains on the brink of war. Oh, and we can't call for help. That sum it up?"

"Yeah, pretty much," Chappy said, looking ahead.

"We'll handle it one step at a time. Just like we always do. John will find a way. He has to."

"How did Magnus get his hands on a suitcase nuke?" Chappy asked.

"Bell told me during the flight back that the bomb was a low-yield device," Anne replied, "but I was only aware that the Russians possessed those types of weapons. Bell said it wasn't the Russians; he said the uranium came from Germany – back in 1945. He said Hitler and Himmler escaped with the nuke, establishing the Fourth Reich and The Order of the Black Sun, which explains a lot. If he's telling us the truth, this goes all the way back to World War II, like we thought. The history of the world will be rewritten over this."

"Why didn't you share that earlier?" Chief asked.

"Honestly, I thought the old man was suffering from dementia. It didn't make any sense at first."

"Whatever the case, our government thinks we got nuked by the Russians, or China. Hell, take your pick. We've got to get to the bottom of this, before something else happens," Chappy said.

"I swear, the old man seemed to be talking out of his head, but he said something else, too. Maybe you guys will know what he meant... he said that Kieffer is behind everything. Something about Geneva being ground-zero."

"Alfred Kieffer – Magnus O'Keefe's grandfather," Chappy grumbled.

"I remember hearing that name back in Okinawa."

"That's right. He's also the father of Maximillion O'Keefe. The chief scientist over the large hadron collider project in—"

"Geneva," she remembered from the briefing.

"I guess we know where to go looking," said the chief.

"Hunting's more like it," Anne said.

Chappy's gaze remained forward, trained on John's SUV.

†††††

"It's time I know the truth. All of it. What's going on, Bell? First Nashville and now this. I thought we were doing God's work?"

The urban scenery had transitioned into blurs of green beyond the passenger compartment. Bell nodded and reached into the lining of his jacket, pulling out the Spear of Destiny. He sat it on the console dividing the rear seat.

"Do you think we would have this," Bell said, pointing at the dull, pitted bronze spear head, "if God wasn't with us?"

"I don't know anymore. My men – my friends – they're dead. There's no reason they needed to die. I... I can't – I mean, I don't understand why."

Bell pulled both of his hands back to his lap and cupped one over the other, rubbing his knuckles.

"Do you remember that morning back in Bizerte? After Doc and Sam got killed?"

"Yeah, I do."

"Of everything I've ever experienced, that moment sat with me – more than any other."

"Because of losing them… I know, but this is different."

"How's it any different?"

John took a deep breath, knowing he was on the edge of losing his composure.

"It just is."

"Maybe in the sense you're thinking, but I want to offer another perspective."

"Dammit, Bell. I can't take another trip down that rabbit hole. I just want the truth."

"The truth. You think it's that simple – even now."

"What?" John said, eyes welling as he faced Bell. "Why can't it be that simple? I just want the freaking truth."

"Truth is, we're all going to die. How's that?" Bell asked, his tone clear, yet abrasive.

"What's that supposed to mean? Of course, we're all going to die, everyone dies."

"Do they?"

John cocked his head and took another deep breath to try and clear his mind.

"Okay – get to your point."

"When Sam and Doc died, it hurt. It sat with me, initially, like a raw nerve, constantly jolted into a painful burn at every turn. After a while, it healed, leaving a scar. A constant reminder. You know why?"

"Because they died? Because they can't be replaced?"

"No. Their deaths changed how I viewed everything. That change motivated me. It drove me – even Richie. We wouldn't have chased this," he said, patting the Spear. "We wouldn't have had that power within our soul to live on."

"What are you saying? They were meant to die?"

"Not at all, but clearly the opposite. Their lives meant something— maybe everything. Can't you see that?"

"I don't know anything anymore. I thought when we first started this... maybe I understood. But now, I can't see past all of the loss. Hell, I can't see past my own grief."

"Exactly. Your sorrow has taken away your ability to lead – to see the big picture here. You must realize that Rico, Wisp, and Zip's sacrifices are not your fault... even though they happened under your watch. Their lives meant something to you – to all of us. Their passing, while tragic, is yet another reason for you to be right here, right now."

"Magnus. He's gonna pay for what he's done."

"The road ahead won't be easy, but you're the only one that can pull this off. Everything depends on you, John."

"Why me?"

"Why not? God made you special, as he did with all of us. But you... You're who He chose for this purpose."

"If He chose me, then why am I failing?"

"That's just the lie talking. You aren't failing. You've only just begun."

"What's that supposed to mean? We've been at this for years now. We're losing."

"You're thinking in human terms. You need to change your focus. This world is just a temporary stop. You need to shift your perspective, and things will start to make sense."

John reached into his pocket and pulled out the tiny Bible he always carried with him. He gripped it and looked out of the window, taking a moment to remember why he had faith. The stakes had grown exponentially since Bizerte. The battle's very meaning had multiplied beyond his understanding, transcending all of humanity, if Bell's theory was to believed. The Time Key, the Ark of the Covenant, and the Large Hadron Collider all worked together to open something—this he knew.

"Tell me what this all leads to, Bell. I need to know," he said, turning his attention to the old man.

"All I know is that you, and you alone, are the key. You will face Magnus again. I'll be there when you do – remember that. Every believer's soul will be looking at you: the catalyst of their salvation. This is what I've foreseen, but beyond that, I don't have any answers."

"Was it a vision?"

"Yes. I've seen you repeatedly over the years, facing down Magnus."

"What do you mean by 'you are the key'?"

"I've seen you holding the Time Key, but I can't see anything else. I'm not going to lie to you, John. You… you're bleeding – broken in my visions. It's a nightmare I've lived with for years now. The next thing I see is you. Alone."

"That's not going to happen."

"Maybe not. But you have to get to the Time Key and assemble it."

"And how do you suggest I do that? We're thousands of miles away – fugitives from our own government. We have no resources, and there's a good possibility our own command staff has betrayed us."

"Rod. Yes, I know."

A molten heat rolled into John's chest.

"You knew?! And did nothing?"

"No, it wasn't like that. The vision hit me when I got in the boat to find you, after your helicopter was shot down. I wasn't even sure of what I saw, until we were flying back to the States."

"That's strangely convenient. What else are you hiding from me?"

"You've had the visions yourself. You know how they work. Sometimes they make sense and sometimes they don't."

John exhaled and rubbed the bridge of his nose.

"So, what do you suggest?"

"We're almost to the black-site. Once we get there, I'll brief everyone. I just need you to keep an open mind, clear your head, and remember that our focus can no longer be limited to this world."

John sighed and flipped open his Bible, anxious to find some words to help guide him. He looked over to see Bell staring out of the window. The old man was right about one thing – he wanted to find Magnus so bad it was burning a hole through his heart. There was one singular thought running in the back of his head. He would find him, and when he did, there would be no escape.

†††††

The two SUVs had driven down a long, winding, dirt road, deep in the country, close to a town called Moyock. The trees lining the road soon gave way to an open field with a butler-style building sitting prominently in the middle. Armed security was scattered all around. The two vehicles came to a stop at the front doors.

Bell stepped out of his side of the vehicle, moving for the front door. The evening air was crisp—cool, even—with a hint of salt still lingering in the breeze. John walked around the back of the SUV and met Chappy, Anne, and the chief in the graveled parking lot.

"Well?" Chappy asked.

"You guys are going to need to sit down for this one," John said. His gaze met each of theirs, landing on Anne's. "I really hope you can come to grips with what's happening."

"What the hell are you saying, Steady? It gets worse than it already is?" Anne asked.

The chief stared at John, placing his hand on Anne's shoulder, squeezing hard enough to get her attention.

"It's about that time, isn't it?"

"Yeah," John said, meeting his eyes with a truth so bold, it was going to be hard to put into words.

"So, what are you talking about – the final solution?" Chappy asked.

"My God," Anne said, shaking her head, "it can't be true. It can't be. How?"

"Because the science of man has finally evolved enough to open the door," John said. "In all of our existence, since the beginning of the world, there's always been a time for something. We've had our time – our time to live on this earth. But that time-cycle is coming to a close. Failure's not an option."

Anne stepped back, remembering her conversation with Richie, back in Okinawa. Remembering what John had her make. The drone and the *Adam Panel* code.

"Wait a minute. That drone you had me make – does it have anything to do with what's happening? You caused this?"

"The world we live in nears the end of days," John said. "I didn't cause anything; I simply saw what needed to happen."

Anne stepped toward John, her rage on the verge of ripping through him. Chappy and the chief grabbed her by the arms.

"You killed them," she said, looking straight through John.

"That's what you think? Anne, if it were up to me, it would've been me instead! You've got to know that – I wish it were me!"

Anne pulled away from Chappy and Chief's collective grip.

"Let me go!"

"You're angry and just looking for a fight, Anne," said the chief. "John's right. You've got to realize that this is all happening because it must. We've got a choice to make. We can believe, or we can choose to not believe. But I'm telling you, and you've got to know, this is the truth. Think about everything that's happened. Search your own mind. If you just let go and believe, you'll see."

She turned away from John and the others. Her heart ached so badly that she grabbed her stomach, kneeling to the ground, in an attempt to hold in the pain.

"You know me," Chappy said. "I used to not believe all of this stuff. But, I gotta say, you can't explain any of this away. Everything we've done has gone according to a plan. A grand plan we can't begin to understand."

"Plan?" Anne asked, sliding her gaze up to the dark wood line across the open field.

Chappy walked up to her, settling beside her.

"Yeah. There's a plan. Think about it. The visions, traveling through time, and who we've encountered – not to mention the *when*. You know there's no way any of that happened without some higher-power aligning it."

Anne shrugged her shoulders and looked to her right. Chief walked up on her other side and crossed his thick forearms.

"I know you're struggling with their deaths, but understand that it was their time. Their sacrifices have brought us to this point and you can't deny – it's providing motivation."

"And while terrible," John said, stepping up beside Chappy, "all of the victories, even the defeats, the losses, and the setbacks have brought us to this point. We're almost to the end now. What lies ahead might be unknown to us, but we were all built to weather this storm."

"He's right, Anne. Every plan we've carried out, every person we've encountered, and everyone we've lost – they brought us to where we are."

"I miss them so much," Chappy said, "but I've found peace – even in the face of their dying."

"How?"

"I know they're not dead," he replied. "They're living on. I've seen it."

"What are you saying?" Anne asked. "You've seen it?"

"Yeah, I have. I can't stop thinking about it."

John looked over at his friend, also surprised.

"What did you see?" John asked.

"That last trip back, I just let go, choosing to believe that I could see through the light. You know," Chappy said, looking toward the night sky, forming a circle through his hands. "It's not a finger that touches us, when we travel through time. It's a place – a pure place. It was only for a second, but I was awestruck. I mean it was so real."

Chappy dropped his arms and his face relaxed into a blissful neutral stare.

"Like a city of pure light?" Anne asked.

"Yeah, but the peace I felt… I never wanted to leave. Everything stopped – I mean everything. For that brief moment, all I felt was joy. And not some fleeting, emotional, sensory feeling; it was complete, utter joy."

Anne's entire body broke out in chills. What she had seen was real, and no figment of her imagination. She, too, had stared into the distance, accepting that she wasn't alone. It wasn't her imagination.

"I don't need to see it," said the chief, "Hearing it. That's enough."

"I wish I had seen it, myself," John said.

"You weren't ready," Chappy said, turning to look down upon Anne. Her eyebrows flared, remembering. She snapped her head around at Chappy. The words just came to her.

"No. No, you weren't."

"What's that supposed to mean?" John asked.

The chief even stepped back and asked, "What are you saying?"

Chappy looked at Anne, knowing. They both saw it: a flash of something to come. Almost as if they both looked on, powerless to stop it – like they were out of their own bodies.

"It's nothing, John. You're just going to have to trust us," Chappy said, patting Anne on the arm.

"I think I get it," Anne said. "I'm sorry."

"No harm done, Anne. But what's going on with you two?"

"It's like you've both seen a ghost," Chief said.

"No, I think we're good," Anne said, looking at Chappy with a smirk. "I just wanted to say it. I think, for the first time, I really understand."

"Good," John said. "We all have to be on board for what's to come. I'm glad you see that, Anne. We need you."

"I'm ready," she said, her mind cleared for the journey to come.

†††††

John entered the building, followed by Chappy, Chief, and Anne. The security team showed them to a safe room where they found Bell sitting at a conference table. The design appeared to be an earlier configuration of the chief's briefing room. The team entered, and the door was secured behind them. The lights dimmed to blue, before switching back to white.

"Take a seat," Bell said.

The four remaining members of Arklight all sat across from Bell. They took their seats as the middle of the desk lowered, sliding into a space below. A metal frame extended upwards from the gap, flickering to life. The holographic monitor allowed for Bell to see through the frame and speak to the team.

"Alright, Bell. We're all here. Time to tell us what the plan is," John said.

"And no bullshit," Anne added.

Bell smirked, pulling up a map of Europe. He moved its focus over Switzerland.

"Here's where you'll need to go," he zoomed the map in, "just outside of Geneva."

"Is this where Magnus is?" John asked.

"All of them are going to be there, when the time comes."

"Dammit, Bell, don't start with the cryptic speak – not now," Chappy said.

Bell took a deep breath and realized he couldn't hide the truth from them any longer. He closed his eyes and exhaled, seeing that the time for unfettered truth had arrived.

"The truth is not going to be easy to hear."

"We're all grown-ups," said the chief. "Spill it."

"And besides, I think you know we're ready," Anne said, placing her elbows on the tabletop.

"There's a time for everything, Bell. I think you know how we feel," John said.

"Okay." He turned off the screen. "No more holding back, but I think you all know where this is headed."

"Yeah, we're pretty sure," Chappy said, leaning forward. "But, we're ready."

"Even if the truth means suffering – and dying?"

"I think we all know that none of us are walking away from this one," John said.

"We're all in, no matter what that means. Magnus has to be stopped," Chief agreed.

"All of them. This Order of the Black Sun, whatever the final solution is… we can't let them get their hands on the weapon," Chappy said.

"You mean the ultimate weapon?" Bell asked.

"Yeah, and what is it, really? I know you know. I can see it in your eyes."

Bell stood, placing his hands on the table.

"Yes, I know what it is. And you've all learned a great deal about how the Knights Templar protected the Arma Christi relics – of which the ultimate weapon is formed. The Titulus Crucis, the 30 pieces of silver paid to Judas, the Spear of Destiny, the John Bell Hood coin, the Holy Grail, and the Ark of the Covenant represent the key and the lock. The Large Hadron Particle Collider—built in Geneva—represents the door, or the portal. Collectively, with a coordinated effort, they form the ultimate weapon."

"The Time Key opens the Ark, but how does it work?" Anne asked.

"More specifically, how does the collider work with it?" asked the chief.

"What we call science is simply our growth into understanding our Maker… but we will never be able to replicate, or even touch, what He can. You're all very intelligent, in this world, and that makes some of this even harder to understand. None of the power of this weapon is of this earth. It is truly other worldly – God's greatest gift to mankind."

"Jesus?" John asked. "Jesus is the weapon?"

"As in Jesus Christ," Anne said as she sat back, "so, we're talking about Biblical prophecy?"

John looked at Anne, nodding.

Bell sat forward and balled up his hands in front of his face.

"Yes, and the tribulation. It's why we cannot fail. The legend says, if evil opens the breach first, it will trigger the Apocalypse, trapping everyone, even believers, here on earth. Seven years of unimaginable suffering before the next breach forms, starting the Battle of Armageddon. However, if we get to it first, a beacon of righteousness will open the breach, bringing forth the rapture for all of God's people, sparing them from the terrible suffering and persecution of the tribulation. The Bible tells the story, but the order in which it occurs is up to us – mankind. See, it goes back to choice. Adam and Eve made a choice, which cursed the Earth. Now, we need to make a choice. We have to do this part ourselves, as a people."

"So, we're all going to die – like no matter what happens?" Chappy asked. "That's heavy, man."

"Yeah, but it's been written. Now the only thing that matters is… how we choose to live in the time we have left," John said.

An ominous cloud settled over Anne.

"We die, or we die?"

"We've all gotta die," John said, "The thing you've got to understand is that if we live for what's right, our passing is simply a new beginning. Remember that glimpse you and Chappy talked about? That's the life that's before you – not darkness."

"I'm still trying to get my head around all of this," Anne said.

"It's the truth," Bell interjected, "and it's already set into motion. Like it or not, you four are all that stand in the way of pure evil."

"What about you?" John asked.

"My part in all of this is nearly done."

"How? We still have pieces of Arma Christi to find," Chappy said.

"No. All of the pieces," Bell said, setting the Spear of Destiny on the table, "except for this one, are together in one place."

"But, how? The Ark and the Holy Grail are still out there," John said.

"No. They're not, old friend. Kieffer has them all. Soon he'll have this piece as well."

"The hell he will. Over my dead body," Chappy said.

Bell turned his chair, stood, and walked around the table. John and the others tracked his movements.

"I need you to hear me out, because I have something very specific – actually, me and Richie, have one more role to play – before we leave."

"Leave? You can't leave, we need you."

Bell laughed and stopped at the head of the table.

"No, John. Everything you need to complete this mission sits either beside you, or will come to you, when the time is right. But only when the time is right."

"Okay, how does this play out?" Anne asked.

"I'm going to take the Spear of Destiny to Kieffer. They're already spinning up the Hadron Collider for an August 14th collision attempt. When all of the pieces are in place and the collider fires, the door will be opened. They already have Nathan and Richie—both are being held captive on their farm, just outside of Geneva, which just so happens to be in the exact center of the collider ring."

"The place you were about to show us on the map?" asked Chief.

"Yes. That's where you'll have to go. That's where they'll have me, in the evening of that day – as well as the others."

"I don't understand. Why take them the piece? Why take any chance they could accidently figure out the weapon?"

"I've foreseen what must happen. The Spear and I must be surrendered over to Kieffer, freely. Richie and I must face him together."

"Can't we use the element of surprise? We sneak in with you and take them all out before they even know we're there? Plus, Bell… I'm not sure my grandfather and the admiral can hold out that long; the collision attempt is over two months away. We've got to move on this."

"I gotta say, I'm liking John's plan better than what you're suggesting," Chappy said.

"I don't expect anyone to understand why it has to be this way, but I know that Kieffer won't be able to activate the weapon without one important factor. Well, actually – two."

"What are they?" John asked.

"You have to remember, all of this is happening for a purpose."

"Okay, but what factors are you talking about?" Chappy asked.

Bell gripped his cane and leaned on it, struggling to share.

"So, you're basically telling us to have faith? Just surrender? We need to plan this out. We need to move," Anne said.

"Sometimes surrendering is the only way to win, you see. Am I afraid of what they'll do to me? Yes. But, I must do this or all will be lost. I can't explain it beyond that. You're just going to have to trust me," Bell said, his stare locked on John.

The room grew quiet. John crossed his arms and took a deep breath. He exhaled and focused, hoping to see something. All he could feel was the intense ache of his heart. The plan made no sense, but the conviction Bell showed moved him, stirring his memories of being on the other side, leading. He just couldn't get past one thought: Jesus surrendered to the Romans and suffered, paying for the sins of all mankind. Maybe Bell was right, and following the example of Christ was the only way. Dozens of scriptures flooded John's thoughts, supporting Bell's theory.

"So, what course of action should we take?" John asked.

"You four need to regroup and heal up," Bell said. "Start training here. Once you're ready, I'll go to Geneva, you'll follow, and we finish this. Together."

"What about my grandfather – and Nathan?"

"They're both fighters. They still have purpose."

"You can't be considering this... John?" asked the chief.

"It's a bad deal. I know that. But we have to consider what's at stake. We can't let emotion drive us. Not now."

"I'm with you, brother," Chappy said, "the old guys haven't been wrong yet."

John nodded at Chappy and looked around the group, landing on Bell's face.

"Okay. We'll do it your way, then. Now, tell us about why Kieffer won't be able to start the weapon?"

"Have you ever looked closely at your grandfather's cane?"

CHAPTER 21: TIME

"Terrors surround the wicked and trouble them at every step."
Job 18:11

2000-ZuluTime 09Nov1956 (2100-CET Dusseldorf, Germany)

The rumble of the inline six cylinder engine hummed along the two-lane stretch of road, just down the street from Hildebrand Gurlitt's home. He drove alone in the night, following a check on his priceless collection of art. After WWII, he had successfully managed to forge documents and outwit the Allies' questions about the mysteriously acquired collection, which housed some of the most important works of art in the world. Some were hidden away, while others hung in the numerous houses he owned all around the city. He had all but forgotten about the war, enjoying a life of comfort and luxury. The horrible secrets of his fortune were buried along with the Nazi Third Reich.

He pulled his car in front of the brick townhome and stepped out into the mist of a cold rain. Popping up the collar on his coat, he scampered up the steps to his front door. Keys jingled as he looked for the correct one. He entered the foyer, closing the door behind him. The house was dark; no one else was home – not even the maid. His family had left for the weekend, leaving him alone to obsess over his one true love: the art.

The sixty-one-year-old war profiteer shrugged off his jacket and hung it on the coat tree before stepping into his parlor. He flicked on a switch as he walked across the room toward his desk.

"Doctor Gurlitt," a voice sounded from behind him, "I'm so pleased you are home."

Gurlitt's heart grew cold in an instant. He turned to face the intruder.

"Colonel Weber? Is that you?"

Weber stood up from the chair in the corner of the room. His woolen suit and tie made it even more difficult to recognize him; the last time Gurlitt saw him was in Krakow, Poland, after the Allies had barely escaped Hans Frank's villa.

"Yes. It's me, old friend," Weber said, his face twitched.

"W-what brings you back to the fatherland?"

"I've come to collect something. Something that you know is important to the Führer."

"Hitler? He lives?"

Weber smiled with devilish intent as he walked closer.

"What I meant to say was – it *was* important to the Führer. Now it's important to our entire cause."

A creak of the hardwood floors in the next room caught Gurlitt's attention. A shadowy figure emerged into the light of the parlor.

"Kieffer? You're alive as well. Such – good news."

"Hello, Hildebrand," Kieffer said. "I think you know why we're here. Where's the Grail?"

"Grail? What Grail?"

"The one you told the Führer and Himmler about," said Kieffer.

"I said no such thing. If I had found the Holy Grail, I would be sitting atop a fortune."

"Who said anything about Holy?" Weber asked.

"I...," Gurlitt choked, "I simply assumed that is the Grail he was referring too."

Kieffer stepped beside Gurlitt and proceeded to pour himself a glass of cognac.

"Hildebrand, do you remember the night we got you out of Paris – just before the fall? The night you almost got caught by the Allies?" Weber asked, walking toward Gurlitt and waving his hand in gesture for the art dealer to sit down. After all, it was his home—even if overrun with unwelcomed visitors long presumed dead.

"Yes. I was very thankful – I am very thankful to both of you."

"So, you realize that we know everything," Kieffer said, pouring a second glass. "We know about your meeting with Hitler, Himmler, and General Choltitz... the general told us everything before Paris fell."

"I'm afraid that I don't know what it is you're insinuating."

"Enough!" Weber snapped, slamming his fist on an end table. Gurlitt jumped, turning his head to Weber.

"Any idea where your family is?" Kieffer asked.

"Why would you ask such a thing?" Gurlitt asked, refocusing on Kieffer.

"They're away at your wife's sister's again this weekend," Weber added.

"How?" Gurlitt asked, rubbing his throat.

"They'll be dead in the next hour if you don't tell us where the Grail is," Weber said, his face contorted, revealing his intent.

Gurlitt's eyes flared with a fear, and his stomach soured at the choice. "You can't!"

"We can and we will," Kieffer said.

Gurlitt's will folded and he slouched back into the couch.

Kieffer took a drink of the expensive brandy and focused on Weber. The two men exchanged a knowing glance.

"Please. You don't understand. You have to listen to me. The Grail... it's not what I thought it was."

"Liar!" Weber shouted.

"So, you do have it?" Kieffer asked.

Gurlitt nodded and said, "What Hitler wanted with it – it's the guaranteed destruction of the world as we know it. I've seen it. You cannot go through with the final solution. It is death."

"What nonsense are you rambling about?" Weber asked.

"I've been studying something called the *tunc clavem*. Have you ever heard of it?"

"No, but why should we believe anything you say?" Kieffer asked.

"I may have lied about having the Grail, but I lied because I've spent years chasing these answers. Hitler's final solution will bring terrible suffering and death to the world."

"Of course. An apocalypse will come to the enemies of the Reich – that has always been the promise. Once we find the ultimate weapon, we can use it to eliminate those who do not share our beliefs."

"Is that what they teach you... in the SS?" Gurlitt asked, rubbing his hands together.

"It is the truth of the world. Who are you to challenge it?" Weber spat.

"The truth, in this regard, is something no person can be sure of. The truth is, we are all doomed if you fail to listen to me."

"Say what you must, but know this," Kieffer said, "you will take us to the Grail tonight – or your family dies."

Gurlitt's face fell flat, his jaw slack.

"I understand."

"What's the *tunc clavem?*" Weber asked.

"It took me years to finally understand what it was. The Arma Christi—the weapons of Christ—are directly linked to the *tunc clavem*. What I discovered is that the term, translated from the Latin, means 'Time Key.' This key uses certain pieces to activate the ultimate weapon you speak of."

"So, you found some Latin term. I learned as much from Doctor Clarke, before he was killed in Casablanca," Kieffer said.

"And we know from the Knights Templar journal that the Arma Christi are part of the ultimate weapon," Weber added.

"No. They are not part of the weapon. They simply form the key. The ultimate weapon is something else entirely."

"Go on…" Kieffer said, finding a chair across the parlor to sit in.

"I came across an ancient Hebrew scroll on one of my trips to Israel. The scroll referenced the *sermita in armis*: the path to the weapons."

"Yes, the Knights Templar journal," Weber said, sitting down, himself.

"At the base of the scroll were several lines of text that made no sense. Not even the greatest scholars have been able to make anything of it. The discernable content of the message was the reference to the Knights Templar journal. Many believe the message to be a cipher that can only be decoded using the journal."

"You're just wasting our time," Weber said. "I should have your family killed and make you watch."

"No! I promise – I'll cooperate. Just leave my family alone – promise me," he pleaded, looking at Kieffer.

"They won't be harmed, but you need to get to your point. Weber is not as patient as he once was."

"I think the scroll contains the whereabouts of the ultimate weapon," Gurlitt said, hoping to pique their interest and buy more time.

"Interesting. Elaborate," Weber said, his eyes burning a hole in Gurlitt.

"You are aware of the discovery around Wadi Qumran? The Dead Sea scrolls?"

"Yes. I've heard about that. What's it got to do with the weapon?" Kieffer asked.

"Everything. One of the scrolls mentioned the *tunc clavem*. It said, *'he who unlocks the weapon must be filled with light, for death cannot touch him.'* And it went on to say, *'Armageddon awaits the false god and those who seek out that path.'* Much of it was destroyed, but it was enough… enough to tell me that seeking out the ultimate weapon is a bad idea."

"Doctor Gurlitt, you're a man of great intellect. You helped start the Führer on his quest for the Arma Christi. Surely you understand that these scrolls are just another one of our enemies' tactics to thwart our success. You have to see that."

"I don't know what to think anymore. I'll give you the Grail and the copy of the scroll I had made. Just don't kill me, or my family. And please look at what it says, before you go any further."

"I'll look at it. But know there is much at stake."

"Where do you have it hidden?" Weber asked.

"In a house I bought after the war. It's not far. I'll take you there."

"Yes, we'll ride with you," he said, pulling open his jacket to expose the handle of his Luger. "No games, Doctor."

"I understand. I just want to be done with this." He cast a glance to the floor at his feet.

Kieffer looked at Weber and stood up.

"I'll have our man follow us. He's parked across the street."

"Excellent. That will give you and I more time with the doctor. Time for us to get… reacquainted."

"I will give you what you ask for, I swear. All I ask in return is that you look into the information I've come across. Please, look into it before it's too late. If you assemble the Time Key and I'm right – the world could crumble."

"And if you're wrong?" Kieffer asked.

"Then it would make Hitler right. The final solution could occur as he foresaw it."

"And that," Weber said, "that is why your concerns are inconsequential. The Führer shared his vision with Kieffer and I. He even foresaw you, being an obstacle to our endeavors."

"When? When did he tell you of this vision?"

Weber and Kieffer exchanged a glance. Weber turned, walking into the foyer. Gurlitt turned to Kieffer, his expression lifted.

"He's alive. Isn't he?" Gurlitt asked.

Kieffer nodded.

"What did he tell you about his visions?"

"He told us that after his death, another Führer would rise. A man who would see the final solution through to the end. A true leader. One whose heir would rule the entire world."

"Yes… yes, that is what he told to me – so many years ago. But, did he share what else he saw?"

"The flash? He described it as a blinding light. Almost like pure energy, consuming all of our enemies on one singular moment."

"That is how it was described to me. But, what if that singular moment represents something else? What if that moment of consumption isn't death to our enemies? What if it's the beginning of the end of times?"

Kieffer stepped back and laughed.

"Oh, Doctor, he told me you would say exactly that. There is no God – no second coming. There is only power, and we will obtain it. You were with us once; you should come back to your senses."

"You have to listen to me, Kieffer. You have to look into the truth like I have done. There are powers at work we don't understand."

"The only power at work is your imagination," he said, turning toward the foyer. "Get your coat, Doctor. I wouldn't want you to catch a chill."

The three men stepped through the front door as the rain continued to pour. Gurlitt grabbed the handrail, feeling his feet slide about on the concrete. Patches of frost had built on the metal atop his car. The drive across town would be tricky in the wintery mix, but he needed all the time he could create—to develop an escape plan.

Gurlitt's white knuckles almost glowed on the steering wheel. The rain had turned to snow, and the roads were covered in patches of ice. Weber sat in the passenger seat, his pistol trained on Gurlitt's gut. Kieffer sat in the back, making sure to look behind them at every turn, ensuring they didn't lose their ride out of Germany. The car trailing behind followed at a distance, keeping them in sight.

"How much further is it, Doctor?" Weber asked, prodding him with the barrel of his Luger.

"We're here." He pulled the car to a snow-dusted curb and shut the motor off. A four-story brick and concrete building was on their right. Weber looked up; no lights were on inside.

"This better not be a trick," he said, pulling his pistol into the concealment of his jacket.

"It's no trick."

Kieffer looked over his shoulder, watching the trail vehicle pull to the curb a block behind them and turn its headlights off. All three men soon found themselves standing on the sidewalk in front of a plain, yet highly secure door. Kieffer counted no less than four different locks.

"This is the old Reisholz district?" Weber asked, looking around the area.

"Very good guess," Gurlitt said.

"It's not nearly the industrial area I remembered it to be."

"Ah yes," Gurlitt replied, juggling a massive ring of keys, "the old refinery was bombed during the war. This whole area was leveled. Since the end of the war, they've rebuilt into more of a residential area. I've managed to acquire a couple of small buildings."

He opened the door and reached inside, flipping on a light. A narrow stairway led up to the second floor. The faint smell of fresh paint lingered in the air.

"If you would be so kind, please lock the door behind you," he said, not looking back as he lumbered upstairs.

Weber followed Gurlitt, crowding his space. Kieffer turned to close the door. The hinges creaked under the weight of the steel hatch. Once closed, he noticed a wheel mounted on the back of the door—an obvious crank to bar the door from the inside. He recognized that such extreme measures were taken in order to guard something of great importance.

Kieffer secured the door and ascended the stairs with little effort, catching up to Weber as he stepped onto the hardwood floor of the second level. Streaks of light glistened on the floor from the stairwell; a flip of a switch later, and the whole floor lit up. The colors in the room were almost staggering. All of the windows had been painted over and covered with plywood. The room was painted white, with paintings hanging on every surface. It was Gurlitt's own private art gallery – beautiful and elegant.

"Is that Lieberman's *Two Riders*?" Kieffer asked.

"Beautiful, isn't it?"

"Where's the *Just Judges*?" Weber asked.

"It's the one covered in the middle of the room," Gurlitt said, pointing to the covered easel. "Please be careful – it's very old. However, if it's the Grail you want, that's in the safe."

"What safe?" Kieffer asked.

Gurlitt walked across the room to a bookcase, where two smaller paintings were displayed on the shelves.

"May I?" he asked, showing his hands to Weber, who nodded.

He reached beside the painting on top, feeling for a spot on the wood. There was an audible click, and he pulled open the bookshelf, exposing a hidden wall safe.

"I'm impressed the lengths to which you've gone to protect your collection," Kieffer said.

"I was always cautious, but after that incident in Krakow – I became obsessed with security."

"Open the safe, Doctor," Weber insisted.

Gurlitt knelt to the floor and turned the dial once before stopping.

"What will happen to me?" he asked, looking at Kieffer.

"Just open the safe," Weber said, his voice rattling with impatience.

"No. Not until you promise me my family won't be harmed."

"No harm will come to your family, Doctor. And if you give us what we've come for, no harm will come to you," Kieffer said.

Weber cut his gaze to Kieffer and huffed.

"Now, hurry up and open the safe. You act like we're your enemies. Remember, we're the ones who pulled you out of the trouble in Paris and Krakow," Weber said.

"Fair enough." He rolled the dial.

Weber stood straight and gave the doctor some space to work. He reached into his jacket, gripping his pistol. Kieffer nodded his approval of the Führer's kill order—just not before they had their hands on the Grail.

Gurlitt continued spinning the combination on the safe. The hair was standing tall on the back of his neck. He knew they would kill him. Weber's face never could conceal a lie.

"Weber would you be so kind and hand me that key. The one on the table, over there," Gurlitt said, pointing across the room.

Weber saw the key he asked about and walked to the table, his eyes still affixed on Gurlitt. Kieffer stooped down, behind the doctor, as he turned the knob. Weber reached for the key and waved it.

"This key?" he asked as he held it up.

Gurlitt and Kieffer both turned to see Weber standing across the room, grasping the single key at eye level. It was all he needed. He reached to the wall, flicking a rope off a hook. A small sandbag, used to counterbalance one of the paintings, crashed down on Weber's head, collapsing him to the floor. Gurlitt threw open the safe door, reached into it, and out came the Grail. He smashed it into Kieffer's face, knocking him to the floor.

The savvy, degenerate art dealer worked his way to the exit, while he could. With the Grail in hand, he scampered down the stairs with all the speed he could muster.

Kieffer's face was bleeding from the cheek and nose. His head throbbed like it was in a vice. He heard Gurlitt's shoes clicking down the stairs and felt for his pistol. He staggered to his feet, trying to give pursuit.

Weber's neck and head cracked under the weight of the sandbag, but the weight was not significant enough to render him unconscious. He sprang up on his feet, gun in hand.

"Where'd he go?" Weber asked, rubbing the back of his neck.

"Downstairs! Hurry!" Kieffer yelled, leaving smears of his own blood on the handrail as he used it to steady himself.

He made it to the door only to hear Gurlitt's car breaking traction on the slick road; they would have to chase him down. He exited the building, waving to get the attention of their driver.

Headlights came on, and the car accelerated forward. Weber exited the building, still gripping the back of his neck and grimacing in pain.

"I'm going to kill him slowly now," he said through gritted teeth.

"Not if I get to him first," Kieffer said, turning to show Weber his marred face. He wiped away more of the blood, which was threatening to obscure his vision. The car slid up to the curb. Weber jumped in the front and Kieffer entered the back.

"Chase him down!" Weber yelled at their driver. The young man pressed the accelerator, careful to maintain as much traction as possible. His hands gripped the wheel, steering with sure-handed precision.

"Faster, Kurt!"

"Sir, it's ice. I'll catch him, but not if I kill us first. Calm down!"

He built upon his speed as they watched Gurlitt slide all over the road in his car. Kurt had experience on ice, and Gurlitt was panicked out of his mind. They were closing in on him, even as speeds increased.

"You're catching him! Good," Weber said, as he slapped the dashboard.

"Do whatever it takes to stop him," Kieffer said from the backseat.

"Yessir," Kurt said.

The icy roads grew more treacherous as they accelerated, moving behind the reckless driving of Gurlitt. Weber looked for a clean shot, wanting to bring the chase to a close.

"No, Weber! We have to wreck his vehicle; the shots will bring too much attention to us," Kieffer said, his stare flaring with bloodlust.

The engine of the car revved as their driver fought for constant control on the slick pavement. Kurt saw an opportunity approach in the distance. A short bridge lay ahead, with steel grates instead of pavement—sure traction.

Gurlitt's car jetted back and forth on the slippery road, while Kurt held their car steady, just off his tail. They bumped Gurlitt's car, their headlights disappearing in his rearview. Even in the intense cold, Weber was sweating profusely, ready for a kill.

The cars hit the bridge, almost leaving the ground as they sped along. Gurlitt darted his car to the left, trying to cut-off his pursuers. Kurt jerked the wheel right, accelerating ahead and aligning their front bumper with Gurlitt's rear passenger quarter-panel. Just before leaving the sure grip of the bridge for frosty pavement once more, he slammed the front part of their car into the right-rear of Gurlitt's.

Gurlitt spun out of control, momentum increasing as he hit fresh ice, and he crashed into a brick wall at incredible speed. The collision collapsed his entire driver's side.

"Good work, Kurt!" Weber yelled, looking back at Gurlitt's crushed vehicle.

Kurt pumped the brakes, bringing their car to a halt. He put it in reverse and backed up to the smoldering wreck. Weber and Kieffer opened their doors, stepping out of the car.

Weber bent down, inspecting the outline of Gurlitt. He wasn't moving. His face was crushed.

"Out of the way," Kieffer said, pushing past. He tried to pry open the passenger side door, but it wouldn't budge. He saw the Holy Grail, still clutched in Gurlitt's hand. He brushed the glass out of the way and climbed through the window, cramming his upper body into the bent and broken space. He grabbed the Grail as Gurlitt's grip tightened around the chalice's base. In a fit of rage, Kieffer punched Gurlitt in the face until he released the Grail, blood streaming from his mouth.

"It's mine! Now die!" he said, snatching it and pulling himself out of the passenger side window. He held the Grail up to Weber and smirked. "Now you can finish him. But, hurry. We need to leave before anyone sees us."

"My pleasure," Weber said.

He pulled himself into the passenger window, staring at Gurlitt's broken body.

"I wish I had more time," Weber said, his ice-blue eyes sparkling with excitement.

Gurlitt coughed, and a line of ruby red spit spewed from his mouth. His face had already swollen from the trauma.

"You will only guarantee your death," he mumbled through his bloody teeth.

"Then I'll see you in Hell," Weber said, his hands closing around Gurlitt's throat. He clamped down, exerting all the rage he had on tap. He crushed Gurlitt's damaged windpipe with his hands, feeling the distinct snap of cartilage giving way. Gurlitt convulsed, fighting for air. Weber placed his hand over the man's nose and mouth, smothering all life from his body.

"Is it done?" Kieffer asked, from the backseat of their car.

"Yes," Weber said as he watched Gurlitt's face transfix.

He climbed out of Gurlitt's car and looked around. The streets were clear, but a few lights were flicking on along the block. He jumped back inside their own car, and Kurt pulled away from the wreckage.

"Finally, we have the Grail," Kieffer said, rubbing his hands along the bronzed edges.

Weber turned in his seat and looked at the prized piece of the Arma Christi. The Holy Grail was in the possession of the Führer.

"It's a very nice chalice. Hard to believe it's almost two thousand years old. Looks remarkable for its age," Kieffer said.

"Now that we have it, what are we supposed to do with it?"

"We take it back to Argentina and then find the Knights Templar journal. Himmler said the journal is the key to finding the Arma Christi needed to construct the Time Key."

"His dream for The Order of the Black Sun seems to be coming to light," Webber said.

"So long as we stay in the shadows, we will be victorious. Everything Hitler has told us has come to pass, and he has left nothing to chance."

"All, but one thing."

"What's that?" Kieffer asked.

"Who his successor will be. He has yet to name one, and he grows sicker by the day."

"He will name one, in his own time."

"Kieffer, I think it will be you. At least, you're who I will support," Weber said, turning to face forward. Kieffer looked back at the Grail, still stroking it as they drove along. The thought of becoming Führer of the Fourth Reich and leader of the Black Sun filled his mind with possibilities. With Weber at his side, he would be unstoppable.

Bell lowered his binoculars. Gurlitt's car smoldered in the distance as the other car pulled away.

"How did you know they'd kill him tonight?" Bell asked.

Richie stepped away from the window and looked around the room of their CIA safehouse.

"It came to me in a dream, Skipper."

"Weird. Accurate, but weird."

"At least they're killing each other," Richie said.

"Ian will want to know about this."

"I told him we'd be here tonight. He's been pretty busy, so I told him we would meet him in London."

Bell lowered the blinds and stepped into the middle of the room.

"Now our trip to Ghent makes sense. The Nazis think they have the real Holy Grail."

"The one thing we need to remember is, even if the tables turn, we have possession of the real Grail," Richie said, pouring a glass of bourbon.

"The Spear of Destiny and the journal, as well."

"I talked to Ian about that. He believes that each of us should hide away our pieces, even from one another," Richie said.

"In case one of us gets compromised?"

"Exactly."

CHAPTER 22: RESOLUTION

"Lord, do not let evil people have their way. Do not let their evil
schemes succeed, or they will become proud."
Psalms 140:8

1900-ZuluTime 14August2020 (2100-CET Geneva, Switzerland)

Walter sat alone in a small, dank cell, praying for the end. His body
shivered, despite the heat of summer. He felt himself slipping away
under the harsh conditions of Kieffer's grasp. The historic battle he had
waged for all his existence, the war, the Arma Christi, the final solution,
life itself, and even death, still hung in the balance. The time was near.
The time of grace was coming to a close; his focus was all that remained
intact. The end of days approached, but there was still much left to do.

"John, don't lose faith. The hope of all rests with you," he whispered.

"Walter?" Nathan said, his parched voice struggling, "That you?"

"Nathan – it's good to hear your voice."

"You too."

"You sound like hell," Nathan said, wiping the dried crust from his
lip. The grime on his face was more gore than dirt.

"Lord, my God, I've cried for You to help. You've kept me from
falling into the pit of despair," Walter prayed, crawling to the edge of his
cell. The bars didn't allow him to see where Nathan was being held.

"I'm not sure God can hear us in this place." Nathan pulled himself
to his feet. The cold from the bars was the only soothing comfort he could
afford the swollen-knot on his forehead.

"He hears us. Have faith." He grabbed the bars of his cell, pulling
himself close and straining to see Nathan across the room.

"What's it been? A couple weeks?" Nathan asked.

"I've lost track, but it's been awhile since they put us together." He
was relieved he wasn't dreaming. The pain he felt was sobering.

"Can you get to your feet?"

"No. My body is shutting down," Walter said, rolling on his side to get a better look at his friend.

"I'm barely hanging on, myself."

"You're right, my friend. The time is fast-approaching."

"Time... it's a funny thing."

"Yes, it is," Walter sighed, "I need you to listen to me carefully. Make sure John gets... you know – to what I showed you. He'll know what to do."

"How about you give it to him yourself. You can't take the easy way out, old timer. There's no dying today."

"It's not my choice to make," Walter said, "you have to understand that."

"What? But—how do I go on?"

"You'll know. Just don't lose faith. Remember, get to John... You must not fail."

"What's going to happen?" Nathan asked.

"When the time is right, He will show you."

"Dammit, Walter. Even in captivity I can't get a straight answer?"

Walter managed a labored smile.

"Unfortunately, the answers are not mine to give."

A buzzer rang out. The squeak of hinges swinging startled Nathan, who retreated toward the back wall of his cell, unable to control the reflex. Sweat dripped off of his face.

Magnus entered the basement-level prison with Ronnie and one of his hired goons.

"Grab the old man," Magnus said.

Ronnie walked to the cell and threw open the door. Walter couldn't muster the energy to move. He felt them grab his upper arms. After a cry of pain, he lost consciousness. They carried his near-lifeless body to the stairs and out of the makeshift dungeon.

With each footstep, Nathan flinched. Then it grew quiet once more, except for one click of presence in the room. The creak of a shoe and a nail-curling scrape chilled Nathan's blood. The grinding of a heel to the hard-concrete floor tortured his mind.

"Admiral Grant," Magnus said, turning to look into the cell, "I can't wait until our next meeting. I know you're very anxious about it."

Nathan pulled his legs under him and tried to cover his ears. The sound of Magnus' voice carried into his bones. Every syllable struck raw nerves. Nathan began to shake uncontrollably, and his stomach rolled.

"Nothing to say?" Magnus asked, spitting into the cell. "I better hear the words... make them for me."

Nathan panted and convulsed in the corner of his cell. His heart started beating out of his chest from severe terror. No control, pain would follow.

"Leave me be," Nathan said.

"Now, that's not what I wanted to hear, mate."

Nathan hyperventilated, knowing his resistance would be punished. Magnus pulled the hose from the wall and turned it on, spraying Nathan until he was soaked through.

"I'm comfortable, being uncomfortable," he mumbled to himself as he forced back the bile in his throat.

"What was that?"

"You're gonna die!" Nathan yelled.

Ronnie and the other hired gun returned and stood behind Magnus. The mercenary smiled, enjoying Nathan's suffering. Ronnie's face grew long, tired of the constant exposure to suffering and pain. He was supposed to have been free of this life by now, enjoying the spoils of war, but Magnus had a firm hold on his lapdog.

"While I'm gone," Magnus said, turning to walk out of the room, "string him up. I think he could use a little shock therapy for today's activity. We'll teach the wretch some manners."

"The only easy day was yesterday," Nathan muttered, trying to get a hold of himself.

†††††

The late day sunlight shone into the large plate-glass windows of the Swiss estate. Nestled between the mountains and surrounded by lush pastures, the main home sat prominently on the beautiful plot of land. Horses roamed the surrounding acreage of the farm. The home marked the exact above-ground center of the Large Hadron Particle Collider. The massive underground ring ran at capacity, its magnets guiding specially charged particles of matter on a collision course. The experiments strived to separate the God-particle, holding it open to expose the dimensional portal. The estate sat in the same location where Kieffer had first showed his son, Maximillion, the marked stone of Abaddon, or as the Order knew him – Apollyon the traveler.

The natural exquisiteness of the area stood in stark contrast to the ominous presence of the O'Keefe home. Maximillion bought the land after his father had introduced him to the Order's doctrine. There was no room for deviation. Everything he had studied, the struggle for understanding, now lay in the concrete and metal ring encompassing his home. Whomever occupied the center of the ring would know a power unlike no other. The ability to rule the world, to bring complete peace, and to wipe out all resistance made Maximillion's chest swell. His father's vision of the future danced in his thoughts.

"Father, I had the old man taken to your study," Magnus said, as he approached.

Maximillion stared out of the living room window, taking in the colors of the mountains in the distance. The sky against the marbled shades of blue granite mesmerized him.

"Good. Your grandfather will be there shortly."

"I'm going to go back down to the basement. The other one, he's still got some fight left in him."

"Wait a moment, son. Come stand here with me. Take it all in."

Magnus walked across the hand-hewn hardwood floor and stood beside Maximillion. He put his hands in his pockets, his upper arms resting on the twin pistols hanging in their holsters.

"I've seen this a thousand times."

"I know, but after today, everything will be different for us. No more hiding out and no more running. We will take control of every government on Earth, once they see the power we possess."

"You've been saying that for years. I still don't know what it is you're talking about. How about you tell me how you intend on accomplishing that? I've been running all over the world – taking all the risks. Tell me why."

"You're not capable of understanding most of it."

Magnus looked away and gritted his teeth.

"I'm not a bloody idiot. You sit on your high-horse looking down at me – your only son. I'm more than capable…"

"Shut up, boy," Kieffer said as he entered the room, walking toward them. "You're no more capable than an insolent child."

Magnus curled his lips and turned around. The fire in his eyes matched the thought in his mind. He pressed the two pistols into his side, ready to be the last man standing.

"Father," Maximillion said, "how are you feeling today, my Führer?"

"Fine. Did you bring Walter into the study, as I asked?" Kieffer said, staring down the contempt Magnus couldn't hide.

"Yes, my Führer," Magnus replied, fighting to keep is emotions in check.

"Very well." He turned to leave. "Explain to the boy… if you like. His mind is not like ours. He won't see like we see."

Kieffer exited the room with two suited guards following him out.

"Why does he treat me like rubbish?"

"It's just his way. You don't exactly give him the respect he deserves."

"How am I supposed to take his abuse and not fight back?"

"You have to submit to him, boy. He'll show you a different side of himself, only after you dedicate to his purpose."

"Have I not risked everything for his cause already? I've taken out all of his enemies. Isn't that enough?"

"You forget – you failed him on more than one occasion. You didn't recover the Spear. You didn't recover the Crucis. You barely recovered the folded coin. All he sees are the failures. He treated me much the same way when I was young. He even beat me at times, but it made me realize the importance of what we're doing."

Magnus thought back to the beatings he took at the hands of his own father. The long nights he would spend chained under the house, thinking about his missteps. It seems the monster he knew growing up still had demons of his own.

"Listen to me," Maximillion said. "I went to the best schools, studying physics, and I founded the research on the Large Hadron Particle Collider. Using the journal your grandfather had, we constructed one of the modern marvels of our time. The collider is the key to solving everything from time-travel to galactic-travel, and we will even be opening portals for interdimensional contact. Don't you see the power that we will have?"

"I get it. The technology, itself, I may not understand, but how does what you are talking about help the Order with the final solution? How does it give us control of the entire Earth? The governments, more specifically."

"Technology – science, that's real power, son. The Order has long held to the original teachings of the Teutonic Knights of old. The original Grand Master, Sir Heinrich, was the first of our line."

"Yes, I remember the teachings."

"What wasn't shared was Sir Heinrich's original encounter with a traveler on his way back from Rome. Some called him Apollyon, or Abaddon, but he had many names."

"Abaddon? Who is he? And why didn't you share that with me?"

"Because, it is information reserved for the highest levels of our order. Only myself, your grandfather, and now you, will know the truth."

"Tell me."

"Sir Heinrich was an ancestor along Himmler's family line."

"Heinrich Himmler?"

"Yes. Your grandfather and Klaus' father, Colonel Weber, smuggled Hitler and Himmler out of Germany in 1945. They staged both of their deaths, using body doubles and papers, so that the Allies wouldn't pursue. I won't go into the details, but our existence is proof the plan worked. Hitler and Himmler never gave up on their pursuit of the ultimate weapon. Your grandfather and Weber were indoctrinated into The Order of the Black Sun to continue the quest. For years, Hitler and Himmler continued to live on in secret, working from a compound in Argentina."

"Grandfather actually knew Hitler?"

"They became very close. That's how he was named Führer of the Fourth Reich and Grand Master of the Order."

"What's the story on Himmler's ancestor?"

"Oh yes, Sir Heinrich," Maximillion said, pulling a scroll from his jacket pocket. "This scroll has been the most closely guarded secret of the Order. It contains Sir Heinrich's account of his encounter with Abaddon."

Maximillion handed him the scroll. He untied the ribbon, holding the scroll in one hand.

"Be careful. The parchment is almost a thousand years old—and don't touch the writing on the paper."

"Aye."

"You see Abaddon wasn't some devilish angel from Hell. He wasn't the destroyer of the world. He wasn't a destroyer at all. It was all fabricated as a further means of control over the people of the Earth. Abaddon was a traveler of sorts, and when Sir Heinrich encountered him, he showed him the truth about our world – about all things."

Magnus couldn't read the parchment. The writing was in Latin.

"I guess I'll have to take your word for it. I can't read the bloody thing."

"You hold on to it. Take it for transcription, yourself. You'll only see that I'm telling you an absolute truth, boy."

"You said traveler – there was more?"

"Yes… a traveler from another dimensional plane, another world."

Magnus cut his eyes to his father.

"An alien?"

"In a way, but Sir Heinrich described him as no different than any other human."

"Go on," he said, rolling the scroll into the leather case.

"Abaddon asked Sir Heinrich to help him escape. You see, he was being hunted down, and would be killed for telling anyone the truth. Abaddon asked Heinrich to embark upon a quest. A quest to obtain the power of the Black Sun. Limitless, clean power that would reshape our world."

"So, am I to assume the quest encompasses all of the pieces of Arma Christi we chased down, and the Ark?"

"Yes. These artifacts hold certain cosmic properties, still-unidentified elements, that will cause a chain reaction, once they are coupled together. They are otherworldly—proof that other life exists. Proof of resources beyond measure."

"How did they get here?"

"Likely the same way Abaddon came, and left. There's a theory called the Einstein-Rosen bridge. You may know it more commonly referred to as a wormhole."

"I'm familiar."

"Imagine folding time and space on itself – into a direct line, capable of opening a portal to another world."

"The particle collider."

"That's only part of the truth. You see, Abaddon told Sir Heinrich all about the technology, the artifacts, and what they represented. Heinrich wrote it all down on his scroll, later sharing it with the murderous, lying Templar Knights. Sir Heinrich could hardly believe what he was told, so Abaddon placed his hand on Heinrich's head and gave him the vision—a vision that has been passed down from generation to generation. A vision that was twisted by the Knights Templar and ripped from the grasp of the Teutonic Knights."

"The journal."

"Yes. The Knights Templar saw Abaddon as a devil. The archaic thinking of the time created this lie, which has been spread throughout religion, even in the Bible itself."

"It's a tale that's rather hard to believe," Magnus said.

"In the final line of Heinrich's scroll, he said a flash of light, like blue lightning, consumed Abaddon in an instant. He disappeared, likely back to his world – taken by those who pursued him. I tell you, that's the proof. It's the source. I've been researching it my entire life, and now we finally have the technology to complete Heinrich's quest."

"A bridge to another dimension… So, if Abaddon is to be believed, unlimited power would be ours for the taking."

"Yes. The power of the sun and beyond would be ours. No one would be able to stop us, and we could finally bring peace to our world with the truth. No more starvation, no more suffering, and no more lies created to simply control us. We would be the masters of our own fate."

"Masters of a new world order," Magnus smirked. "Now I understand what Hitler was really chasing – what Grandfather's grand-vision truly is. With power like you're describing, we could easily defeat anyone who stood in our way. I—I mean, we, could rule everything. Peace at last, through conquest."

"Yes, my son. Hitler saw this as well. Once we open the portal, you and I will be unstoppable."

"You and I?" he asked, raising an eyebrow.

Maximillion scanned the room, pulling himself closer to his son. It was a very unfamiliar feeling for Magnus – his father embracing him, pulling him into his arms.

"It's your grandfather's ideals that fail him. They are the same fascist ideologies that ended the Third Reich. Ancient thinking… small-minded concepts of race, sex, religion, and human culture, restricted to a single plane of relativity. Imagine the most vast, far-reaching reality you can think of. We will rule the world through our understanding of science, reaching into the beyond – imagine the untapped resources of the universe, itself."

"What are you proposing?" Magnus asked.

"When the time is right," Maximillion said, turning his mouth to the ear of his son. "You must kill him."

Magnus' eyes narrowed. His father's conviction concerning this otherworldly reality was convincing; the planning and the calculating had taken a lifetime of commitment—something they both shared in common. A forced succession. The betrayal of his own father. Magnus understood. He felt the exact same way.

✝✝✝✝✝

Walter could barely sit up in the chair. His strength faded. Two men in suits stood behind him, watchful of his every move. One of the guards took a half step back, offended by the wretched smell of the old man in his keep. Walter coughed, wincing in agony with every labored breath. The very same pain forced his head back, revealing before him the Ark of the Covenant. Suddenly, all his discomforts vanished, replaced by a laser-focused energy he hadn't felt in some time. His heart felt a release, aligning his dreams with the hope of visions long past.

"Lord. You are my strength," Walter said, his spine finding support once more. "Death has no grip on me. I can do all things through You."

"You and your God," Kieffer said, circling into his view. "You believers are only lying to yourselves. Hiding from our greatest moments of triumph – it's sickening."

"Kieffer, we're all the result of a lie. Mankind exists on the reality of our own sins. Our brokenness."

"What you call sin, I call the truth. Your faith? That's simply the prison for progress—a place your predecessors chose to hide the real truth. We're not alone in this universe, and once I open the portal, nothing will be able to stop me. This world will become so much more."

Kieffer stepped past the Ark, continuing to a window on Walter's left. He stopped, taking in the scenery, basking in his success.

"This is my crowning achievement. You will soon see the power that your kind has feared for over two thousand years. Your secrets will be shattered, and your God? He will be exposed."

Walter focused his energy, staring into the center of the Ark's top. Two golden angels sat on opposing ends. They faced downward, into the center of the Ark. Their wings were outstretched and covered their heads, almost touching one another. They sat prominently, like protectors of the contents—guardians of the light within.

"You're only bringing death to yourself and those like you."

"The words of a feeble excuse for a man. Look at yourself, Richard Walter Steadman. You're the one who will be experiencing death. Not me. The time of my rise is near, and your time is at its end."

Walter coughed and laughed. More energy returned to him with every passing second.

"Your plan will fail."

Kieffer turned and walked over to Walter, looking down at his long-time nemesis. A smile broke through his wrinkles, and the burning slap of his hand smacked across Walter's face.

"You will die." Kieffer said.

The strike was vicious, opening up Walter's lower lip. Redness from the blow had already settled upon his cheek.

"The Hadron Collider is spinning at capacity, ready to open the portal. As you can see, the Ark—your precious covenant—sits before you."

The doors of the study opened behind Walter, permitting Maximillion and Magnus. They each carried relics of Arma Christi. Walter watched Maximillion's hands, relieved to see the false Grail he had slipped into the *Just Judges Panel*. He scanned the room, looking for his cane. The men sat all of the pieces of Arma Christi on the desk. Walter craned his neck and his eyes grew wide. Kieffer smiled, his surprise having the desired effect.

"You thought we didn't have the Spear of Destiny," he taunted. "You thought we wouldn't complete the Time Key, but your own partner betrayed you."

"Klaus, bring him in!" Maximillion shouted.

The doors opened and John Bell used his cane to walk toward Walter. Klaus followed behind, watching Bell take each labored step. Kieffer walked around the Ark, joining his son and grandson next to their prizes.

Bell arrived, standing beside Walter once more, placing his hand on the shoulder of his lifelong friend. In that instant, they both remembered their promise: a promise made before God.

"Richie, you smell awful," Bell said, taking the chair next to him.

Klaus stood behind the two elderly men with his blank stare to nowhere, shaped by years of torture and mind-altering drugs.

"I've been better, Skipper."

Bell squeezed Walter's arm and sat back in his chair. He took a moment to take in the ornate study. It's high, coffered ceiling and handcrafted antiques gave the room warmth; however, it wasn't enough to melt the bitter chill residing in hearts of the enemies before him. He tapped Walter's foot with his own and looked into the center of the Ark.

Kieffer broke his concentration on the pieces of Arma Christi and looked into Bell's eyes.

"Max, assemble the key," he said, almost unable to contain his anticipation.

"Yes, Father. Magnus, set the Crucis flat on the desk and hand me the Spear."

Magnus picked up the Spear from the container and handed it to Maximillion. He reached back into the plastic box, retrieving the petrified piece of wood. Both sides were flat and smooth. The ends were jagged and cracked. He set the Titulus Crucis on the desk and turned his attention to Maximillion, who handled the Spear with care. It had a broad head, made from bronze, with a single spine running up the centerline. Two open circles lined the center of the Spear, with the spine splitting them into halves.

"Remarkable craftsmanship for its day," Maximillion said, speaking more to himself than anyone else. "Hand me the journal."

Maximillion sat the Spear on the table and flipped the journal open. He looked for a specific entry.

"Hand me the two folded coins," he said, stretching out his left hand. Magnus picked up each one and placed them in his father's palm.

"Now, take the 29 pieces of silver and line them up on the Crucis," he said, sliding the book to where Magnus could see it, "like this."

Magnus took and placed each coin on top of the Titulus Crucis in two rows of ten. He then staggered the remaining nine coins on the center of the two rows, one coin at a time. As he laid the final coin into place, a static charge stood his hair on end. The estate's power failed, and Magnus stepped back. A blue haze of energy illuminated the room, pulsing from the Titulus Crucis. The coins had liquified into a mirror-like, shallow pool, floating atop the ancient wooden title. The lights flickered back to life, but the glow remained.

"Amazing," Maximillion said, pushing Magnus to the side.

"I knew it would work," Kieffer said, stepping up to the Spear of Destiny. "Now assemble the Time Key."

Maximillion swallowed and looked back into the journal's pages. Sweat beads formed on his lip. He sighed, reluctant to follow the next step.

"Do it. Do it, now!" Kieffer insisted.

Magnus moved to the side and stared into the liquid silver. His gaze stayed locked in place.

"Yes, Father," Maximillion said, extending his left hand to touch the liquid metal.

"It won't burn you," Kieffer said. "Do not be afraid."

Maximillion almost touched the metallic surface before pulling his hand away.

"I always knew you were weak."

Magnus stepped forward, pushing Maximillion aside. Without hesitation, he touched the liquid with four fingers, sinking his hand into the wood.

"It's cold. I can go further."

Kieffer looked on and rubbed his hands together.

"Yes. This is it."

Magnus closed his thumb and pushed his entire hand into the liquid. It looked as though his hand had passed through the wood and into the desk. Soon, it was up to his wrist. Maximillion moved back up, mesmerized by the spectacle.

"It's freezing, but not like water. It's as if nothing is touching me."

"Max, what does the journal say?" Kieffer demanded.

"Ummm," he shifted his focus to the open pages. "I don't see anything in the journal. All it says is, 'the path to the weapon ends at the cross.'"

Kieffer stepped closer, overlooking the verse. Magnus rolled his arm around inside the silver pool. His mouth widened; he felt something.

Bell tapped Walter's foot, getting his attention. Walter's trance on the Crucis broke. He turned his head toward Bell. While Kieffer and the others were distracted, Bell looked past Walter, motioning to the bookshelf behind Magnus. Walter's head turned, following his friend's lead, finding it on the shelf: his cane was still intact. The Holy Grail was still hidden. Kieffer was none the wiser.

"It's about time," Bell murmured.

"Thank God," Walter said.

Klaus grabbed them both.

"Shut up."

Both men sat back in peace, confident that their lives had served a divine purpose. Bell reached across, grabbing Walter's hand. The two old sailors shook their heads.

Magnus jerked violently, slamming his free hand on the desk. His body drew up, locking in place. His eyes opened wide and blackness filled them, like ink dumped into water.

"Argggh!" he wailed. His jaw clenched shut. "I… I see it. It will be."

"What do you see?" Kieffer asked.

"Th-the end… beginning…"

"What does that mean?" Maximillion asked, grabbing Magnus by the arm.

A violent jolt shuttered through Magnus' body, and his hand shot out of the silver liquid. The coins reanimated and the liquid was gone.

"Magnus?" Kieffer asked.

"You okay, boy?" Maximillion asked, shaking his son.

Magnus stepped away, flexing his eyes and rubbing the hand he pulled out if the Crucis.

"Tell me what you saw," Kieffer said.

"It wasn't so much what I saw, but what I felt. The power was immense, and beyond anything I've ever experienced. I saw the Ark open. It's time to try."

Magnus reached in front of Maximillion and pulled the Spear of Destiny in front of him. He grabbed both of the folded metal coins, taking a moment to admire the markings on the John Bell Hood coin. He inserted them into the open circles of the Spear. The lights flickered and the Ark of the Covenant began to glow. A soft, golden haze covered the large chest, and a beacon of light appeared between the two guardian angels perched on the lid. Kieffer walked to the side of the Ark, admiring the glow.

"The power of the universe will soon be in our hands."

Magnus reached for the chalice, the false Grail, and held it next to the Spear. Something was wrong.

"I don't see how this attaches."

The speck of light between the angels grew into a softball size orb of energy, swirling its way open.

"This is it," Kieffer said.

A massive surge of blue light pulsed from the Ark, blinding everyone in the room. The estate's power failed once more, darkening the room. Another electric arc of light, followed by a blast of air, drove Kieffer into the bookcase behind him. Maximillion and Magnus covered their faces with their forearms. Klaus looked away. Magnus opened his eyes and saw only empty chairs remaining where Bell and Walter had been.

"Where'd they go?" he asked, dumbfounded.

"What are you talking about?" Kieffer asked, trying to see for himself.

"Them," he said, pointing to the empty chairs in front of Klaus.

"What happened?" Maximillion said.

"Why is the Ark not glowing?" Kieffer asked.

"Klaus, find them," Magnus said, still trying to shake off the effects.

All of the men glanced about, disoriented. Klaus stumbled to the entrance, turning on his flashlight. The door closed behind him as he left to search for the prisoners.

"How did they disappear?" Maximillion asked.

"I… I don't have a clue," Magnus said.

"That's the promise. It's already starting to happen. The power we'll have," Kieffer said.

"What are you saying, Father?" Maximillion asked.

"Abaddon promised Sir Heinrich that once we obtained the Time Key, we would control the power. Our enemies would be crushed. Don't you see?"

"But, the portal isn't open yet."

"They didn't run away," Kieffer said. "We control the key. There's no other explanation."

"I can't assemble the Time Key is what I'm trying to tell you," Magnus said, switching on his flashlight. "It doesn't fit together."

"It must!" Kieffer said. "Max, get in that journal and find out how to assemble it, now!"

CHAPTER 23: REMNANTS

"A remnant will return; yes, the remnant of Jacob will return to the Mighty God."
Isaiah 10:21

1900-ZuluTime 14August2020 (2100-CET Geneva, Switzerland)

John and the chief were settled in the tree line. Their camouflage blended with their elevated position in the Alpine setting. The O'Keefe house sat in the middle of an open plain, surrounded by mountains. Every approach was exposed, across fields and green pastures. The grass was kept low, and the cameras at the front gate provided an additional layer of security. Roving guards kept to a tight schedule, making an infiltration difficult, even in the dark. John peered through his binoculars, awaiting Bell's signal.

"He's been in there for a while now," he said, continuing to scan the grounds for a possible way in.

"Yeah," said the chief. "He said he'd handle it. I guess we have to trust that."

"I don't see a good way to infiltrate. When we get the signal, we've got to go – and fast."

"Yep. To hell with it, John. I think all we can do is hit it direct. We don't have many options. We're gonna get bloody on this one."

"I know, but we've got to stop them at all costs."

There were no technological advantages. All of their equipment and resources had gone up in flames with the base. Even though they were able to get some equipment into the country, it wasn't much; a few weapons, ballistic plate carriers, and a basic communications package was all they could smuggle through customs. Thanks to Bell's planning, each of them operated under an assumed identity. The remnants of Arklight had become ghosts, operating with one sole purpose: stop the Order and the final solution.

"It's time for a little payback," Chief said.

"Absolutely."

John grabbed a handheld two-way radio from his backpack.

"Chappy, you copy?"

Some static crackled.

"Go ahead."

"What's your status?"

"We're about to pick up the rental. Any requests?"

"Yeah, try to get something with four-wheel drive and enough room for all of us. I've got an idea."

"Copy that. We'll be at the jump-off point in thirty."

John clicked the radio talk button twice.

"What's this idea of yours?"

John took a second look through his binoculars. The chief pulled his up, trying to look in the same area as John.

"See the main road down below?"

"Yeah."

"Look back to the curve, down to the left... see the access road? It looks like it parallels their land. I'm thinking we go dark and ride that trail until we get down to the pasture. We turn there, and make a beeline to the house. We hit the residence, drop Chappy and Anne outside, and the two of us take the inside. We'll have no time to waste. Bell said he would take care of the power and cameras, but I don't know how much of a window that will grant us. It's risky, but I think the four of us can make it work. If we surprise them, we can create enough confusion to buy time, at least."

"How are we getting out?"

John pulled the binoculars away and paused. The chief dropped his and looked back at John.

"I'm not sure we are. All I can think about is stopping Magnus. The rest of them – they'll get what they deserve for what they've done."

"We'll figure it out. Hell, we'll probably be dead anyway," said the chief, his teeth emerging into a smile under his mustache.

"At least we'll go out fighting," John said, returning a smile.

He balled up his fist and bumped it against John's.

†††††

"Anne, let's go," Chappy said. "You got the extra mags?"

The two of them gathered small technical gear into their backpacks. Chappy had two suitcases, which were packed with four operator kits, weapons, and grenades. The hotel they were staying at was on the outskirts of Geneva, selected for its proximity to the O'Keefe estate.

It was time to leave, pick up a rental from across the street, and get to the rally point.

"I've got everything," she said, throwing two backpacks over her shoulder.

Chappy stood at the door as she passed through, making her way to the stairs.

"What did John say?"

"He wants a four-wheel drive. Said he had an idea."

"After looking over the place yesterday, I hope it's good. Their property isn't exactly easy to get to."

"No resources, no backup, no decent tech. We're just gonna have to fight this one out toe-to-toe. No shortcuts," he said, following her down the stairs to the lobby. The weight of the suitcases was a strain to carry, but he managed.

"I'm ready for an old-fashioned fight. These evil bastards need to die," she said, turning on the platform to another set of stairs.

Chappy grunted as they hit the lobby floor. Anne made for the front door and he followed, trying to not draw attention to his departure. The clerk at the front desk had been waiting to see him. A package had arrived. Like the others, Chappy had checked-in using an alias provided by Bell's CIA team in Moyock.

"Herr Duncan," the clerk said. "Herr Duncan!"

Chappy slowed, and then stopped, reminding himself that was his name—at least currently. He turned and carried his bags to the front desk. With every step toward the clerk, he grew more concerned that this was a trap. *How could anyone know?* Maybe it was a message from Bell's people. Maybe it was a trap. There was no time to waste. He looked around the lobby for any sign they were compromised.

"Yes?" he answered, watching for duress on the clerk's face.

"Herr Duncan, this came for you a few minutes ago," the clerk said. He slid an ornamental wooden lockbox on the counter. It was handmade, by the looks of it, and the initials carved into the top read *E.C.*

"Thank you. Who delivered it?"

"An Englishman. He said he was with the Colnaghi Foundation – in London, I believe. Left his card," the clerk said, placing it atop the wooden box.

"Colnaghi," Chappy whispered to himself, trying to remember where he heard the reference. He looked at the initials and ran his thumb over the letters. It hit him.

"It can't be. Emaline?" he asked aloud.

"Sir?" the clerk asked craning his neck.

"Chap—I mean, Duncan!" Anne's voice rang from behind him, "We're gonna be late."

"Yeah," Chappy said, grabbing the card, stuffing it into his pocket. He tucked the book-sized box under his arm and picked up the bags. He shuffled out of the hotel, following Anne's hasty steps to the car rental shop next door.

"What was that about? Oh, and by the way, they've got a four-wheel drive available."

"Good," Chappy said, his head swimming with questions, his heart aching to open the box. *How?*

He dropped the bags he carried and pulled the box from under his arm. He held it now, unsure of what it meant. It couldn't be her... the one woman he had ever loved – even if it was short-lived. She died more than a hundred years ago. He still struggled with the fact that he had only known her for those few hours in 1864, but it felt like a lifetime.

"Chap, you okay?"

"Just go in and rent something we can use. I... I need a minute," he said, staring at the box, his chest burning.

"What's in the box?"

"Anne, seriously – I need a freaking minute."

"Whatever," she huffed, walking inside the storefront.

Chappy sat on one of the bags, setting the box in his lap. He stared at the initials, hopeful, yet terrified. It couldn't be. He flipped up the latch, opened the hasp, and folded the top open. Anticipation and reluctance comingled in his mind. Sealing wax stamped with the letters *E.C.* held the top flap of a letter in place. He grabbed the parchment, remembering the demure features of her face, feeling the coarseness of the yellowed paper.

"It can't be," he breathed again, hopeful.

With one finger, he popped loose the wax seal, pulling out a handwritten note.

> *'Billy,*
>
> *I've prayed what seems a lifetime that this letter finds you. During our visit to London, Sarah and I both had visions that were so real we couldn't ignore them. Part of our deal with Colnaghi and Wertheiner was to insert this box into a trust. For a very generous price, it was left with instructions that it be delivered to Thomas Duncan, in Geneva, Switzerland, on August 14th, 2020. I didn't need to understand it in my time, but maybe you can in yours.*
>
> *Everything was shown to us on the eve of delivering the painting as John wished. If this letter has found you, then you should know it was by the hand of God. He is how all things are done. Count this as one of the many miracles of my life. Please take my words to heart as you set out on your mission. This will not end how you might envision.*
>
> *Sarah and I have seen your day come to pass, both in our dreams, and in visions. We've seen the battle you are about to embark upon. Please take these few words and use them wisely. Commit your actions to the Lord, and your plans will succeed. Don't allow vengeance and wrath into your plan, instead fortify yourself as a Weapon of Christ. A sacrifice must be made and it must be made with the right spirit. John is the key and you are the protector. Remember, sometimes winning means surrendering.*
>
> *For the short time you were with me, from the time our lips met, and until the day that I no longer draw breath, you are all I ever wanted. Your embrace, you next to me, is the only time I've ever felt whole in this life. Know that I believe in you, and I'll be waiting for you. Now go face the devil, remember my words, and know that I am with you — even now.*
>
> *All of my love,*
> *Emaline'*

Chappy read the letter twice, wiping tears hanging from his nose, running his fingers over Emaline's name, remembering her like it was yesterday. For him, it had been a short time since that fateful night. *If Emaline wrote this letter on the eve of their donation of* The Storm on the Sea of Galilee, *that would put its penning sometime in 1870.*

"Unreal," he muttered, tucking the letter into his pocket.

Anne exited the storefront and jingled the keys in her hand. She was too far away to see Chappy's tears.

"You done, or what?"

"Yeah," he said, drying his cheeks, "just go get our ride, smartass."

Anne presented a one-finger salute and jogged over to the midsize, four-wheel drive SUV. She unlocked it and jumped inside. Chappy wasn't far behind, opening the rear passenger door and lugging the suitcases into the backseat before hopping into the front.

"You ready?"

"I am, now," he said, a smile breaking on his face.

"What's that supposed to mean?"

"Let's just say I got some encouragement from someone very special to me."

"The box?"

"You wouldn't believe me if I told you."

"Try me."

Anne pulled the SUV off the lot, maneuvering toward the rendezvous location John had set earlier. Chappy pulled the letter out of his pocket and showed Anne, pointing at the name of Emaline.

"Are you serious? How?"

"I don't know. She said that she and Sarah saw this day. That they knew what we were about to go do. It was her—that I know—and everything she wrote in the letter was important. She cautioned me about my mindset."

"But, how? How did they know back then where you would be? Who you would be?"

Chappy laughed and opened the letter once more.

"Only God knows the answer to that. I can't even begin to get my head around it."

Anne felt her senses heighted with each moment of acceptance that there was more to life, much more. Chappy had received supernatural guidance from a woman he barely knew—a woman he fell in love with in 1864. She glanced the letter as she drove. There was no rational explanation for it.

"I'm sorry," she said, staring at the road ahead.

"Sorry? What for?"

"For giving you guys so much crap. I think I understand… there's more than just what we see."

"It's cool, Anne. It took me seeing it for myself to start believing."

"Yeah, but this – what we're about to do. What happens to me?"

Chappy's brow wrinkled as he tried to understand her question. It sounded a bit selfish, but he hoped she was getting at something he could identify with.

"I mean," Anne said, "that didn't come out right."

"You mean what happens in the end?"

"Yes. If I die. If I've never believed? What happens then?"

The SUV exited the town, and they entered the lush hills of the country.

"Well, take it from a very imperfect me. I was much like you when we went into Bizerte – you remember."

Anne smiled, reflecting on the man Chappy used to be and admiring the man he had become.

"John got me started that very night, right after I changed my mind. Honestly, it's the best thing I've ever done."

"What did he do?"

"Nothing. It was what I did. I asked to see the truth."

"That's it?" Anne asked.

"It was a start, but I found that it gets deeper and more complex with each passing conversation."

"You talk to God? I thought you were supposed to pray to Him. Worship Him, even."

Chappy laughed.

"That's the thing. After you start talking, pretty soon, everything starts speaking to you – in a different way. It changes your heart."

Anne couldn't deny that she carried a heaviness in her chest she couldn't describe—like she was weighted down by invisible chains, bound to an immovable object. She wanted freedom. She wanted to fill the void she had always felt.

"I think I get it," she said, turning off the main highway onto a secondary road. "Can I ask you something else?"

"Sure."

"How do you feel about Emaline? You've never really said much about it."

"What did Zip—" the loss tugged at his throat, stealing his voice. "What did the guys tell you?"

Anne hadn't been able to accept they were gone either. She glanced at Chappy, who stared straight ahead. They both missed their teammates and friends.

"Zip told me you… uh, made out with her, and Rico said you *loved* her. I won't even mention what Wisp said." She cracked a smile.

Chappy smirked, trying to remember the sound of their voices.

"Yeah, they didn't cut me much slack. I can say this, I've never met a woman that impacted me like her. I could just say anything and it was okay. I thought I had been through a lot, until talking to her. She was a real, genuine person. She made me feel whole. I respected her in a way that's hard to describe."

"Did you fall in love with her?"

"I guess I did – as much as time would allow. She moved me and her loyalty was unshakable. This letter proves that."

"So, do you believe what she said in that letter your holding?"

"I do."

"Then listen to her. Women don't throw words around lightly, especially when they love someone."

"Yeah. I just wish she had been more specific."

"Have Walter or Bell *ever* been specific – about anything?"

"I guess you've got a point."

Anne slowed, looking for the logging road John picked out for their rally point. Chappy pointed it out.

"There."

"Roger that," Anne said. "Did the three of them make it, you think?"

"To heaven?" Chappy asked, knowing who she meant.

"Yeah."

Chappy turned and looked at her as she drove along. Just as it had happened to him, it was happening to her. Time was short, dissipating in the very air, like a fine mist.

"There is no greater love than to lay down one's life for one's friends. Each one of them showed us how much they loved us."

"Is that enough?" Anne asked.

"Not always, but, for them? Yes. They all lived with honor and the right heart. So, I'm sure they all made it. You will too."

"Pray for me?" she asked, gripping the wheel tight.

"Already did, little sister. Already did."

†††††

"Did you see that?" asked the chief.

"What?" John asked, swinging his binoculars in the direction of the chief's view of the house.

"The power just went out, but came back on. I thought he said it would stay out?"

John could see a large set of plate-glass windows toward the rear corner of the main house. The power twitched once more, but this time John saw a blue spark reflect against the glass.

"We're getting close. He'll make it happen."

"He better, or we're all screwed."

John cracked a faint smile and pulled the binoculars back from his face.

"You know something?"

"What?"

"We're going to do this. I know it."

"I hope you're right, John. Otherwise, we all die and Magnus wins."

"I won't let that happen."

Chief started scanning the grounds once again, plotting the team's path into battle. John picked up the radio.

"Chappy, status?"

"Roger. Five by five on the copy. We're standing by at point x-ray."

"Copy that. Get everything ready to go and find a way to get the doors off that rental."

"What?! Did you say take the doors off?"

"Yeah. We've got to shed some weight."

"And how do you expect to get our deposit back?"

"They can bill us after we get out of prison, since we're about to break any number of international laws."

"Good point, boss," Chappy said with a chuckle. "You want it, you got it."

John sat the radio down and picked up his binoculars. Scanning the perimeter, he counted about a dozen security personnel he could see in the open. There was no telling how many guards lingered inside—not to mention the fact that the O'Keefe's, Kieffer, and Klaus all had to be in there. At least the house was large enough for them to split up and confuse the enemy force. John's gaze followed a drainage ditch along the left side of the home. It dropped off toward the back. It was deep enough to provide cover, and it ran toward the rear – a sound infiltration point for a couple of assaulters.

The blue sky faded as the sun fell behind the mountain. It would be only minutes before nightfall covered them. John looked up, sure that the plan would not fail, so long as God stayed close. He let go of worry, letting it all fall away.

A flash beaconed through the windows on the rear corner of the house. Brilliant light flickered, contrasting with the clear evening sky. The lights inside the house turned off, and all of the lights on the property failed. He scanned the area again, seeing only a few flashlights beaming.

A powerful feeling surged within him; his body shook, and he dropped his binoculars. It was as if a veil of understanding had been laid over him. An overload of noise in his head forced his eyes closed. His hands cupped his forehead, and he gritted his teeth.

"Everything's changed," John whispered.

"What?" asked the chief.

"It's happening."

"What are you saying?" asked the chief, placing his hand on John's shoulder.

"Purpose. Right here, right now."

"John, what in the hell are you babbling about?"

"Don't you see it? We're the watchkeepers," John said.

"Okay? You aren't making sense."

John starred ahead in deep thought.

"I don't know what's gotten into you," said the chief, "but your freaking me out."

"Don't worry. I'm still me," John gasped, shaking his head. "Let's just call it a little injected wisdom."

"Huh? Did you see something?"

"I did," John said. "I saw my grandfather and Bell. It was like they were young again. Strong."

†††††

Chappy had the suitcases laid open on the side of the dirt trail. He was adjusting his ballistic plate carrier and pulling the one-point sling for his rifle over his head. His hands reached into the case and pulled out a helmet. He prepped it and placed it on his head, tightening down the worm-drive screw and chin strap.

"Lord, make us swift, make us light, and make us deadly," he said to himself. "May our actions serve Your will and Your purpose."

"You praying?" Anne asked as she press-checked the chamber of her assault rifle.

The bushes shook, and a twig cracked behind her.

"Cannon," she snapped.

"Fodder," Chief's voice answered, providing the stand-down code.

"Team, coming out," John said, exiting the tree line.

Chappy adjusted his belt-fed M-249 light machine gun and turned to hear what John and the chief had learned.

"What's our status?" John asked.

"We're a go," he said. "You ready?"

"I was born that way, brother."

"I know you were."

The chief stood by John and Anne closed in, forming a loose circle. John looked at the remaining faces of his team—his family. He knew the sacrifice each of them stood ready to make. It was the one of the things that made Arklight great, and so long as their bodies held breath, it would be their legacy. John choked back his fear, knowing what was about to take place. The certainty of his conviction, the pain of his emotion, and the oblation of his life carried in his tone.

"You've all fought for something greater than yourselves. You've all felt the loss, the pain, and the suffering that sacrifice can bring. This, tonight, is something I must do. Your lives are yours – no one else's. If you decide to go..."

"No need to say anything else," Chappy said, grabbing his team leader by the shoulder. "We're all with you. We all know that this is a one-way trip. None of us would have it any other way."

"For all of those we've lost. May we see them on the other side," John said, wrapping his arms around them all. They enjoyed a moment of calm, before the storm.

"So, what's the plan?" Anne asked, wiping a tear from her eye.

"I've seen something unexpected," John said.

"You saying that reminded me," Chappy said, handing Emaline's letter to John. "Look at what I received today."

He opened the letter and pulled out a small red light to read the contents. His body tightened and chills shot all over as he read her words.

"You're part of the Arma Christi, John. *You* are the key to it."

"Like predestiny?" Anne asked.

"Maybe," Chappy said, nodding.

"So, no matter what we do, the end will be what it already is?" asked the chief.

"No, not necessarily," Chappy said, "I think what Emaline was saying needs to be in our hearts – before we walk into this."

"Like how?" Anne asked.

John thought about it and said, "Clear all thoughts of wrath and vengeance from your minds. Commit yourselves to God's will and purpose. Let Him guide us. We can't chase after what *we* want."

"After what they've done, we're to ignore that?" the chief balked.

"No," Chappy said. "We just don't need to be driven by it. It will lead to our own undoing. Think of it like this: we need to balance our scales, not be influenced by the past. Clear that from your mind and let's go into this with one collective thought: serve our purpose, whatever that may be."

"It'll be hard, but I get it – I think," Anne said, adjusting her kit.

"Okay. This is far bigger than me… or what I want. I'll try," Chief added.

John grabbed Chappy and gave him a hug. He pulled himself back and placed his hands on the strong shoulders of his friend.

"I've never been more proud to be your friend, Chap."

"I'll be with you until the end," he said, punching John's shoulder. "Now get your shit on, and let's do this."

John stood back and watched the others make their final preparations for the assault. He looked toward the heavens and took in the ultra-clear, starlit sky.

"Lord," he whispered, tears threatening to brim over his eyelids. "I wish this didn't fall to me, but since it has – give me the strength to carry out Your will."

CHAPTER 24: DECEIT

"If you repay good with evil, evil will never leave your house."
Proverbs 17:13

2000-ZuluTime 11August1964 (2100-CET Canterbury, England)

The dimpled white ball rolled along the green's short-piled grass and into the cup with a *ting*. Ian stood tall, propping on his putter. Almost twenty years had passed since the war, and his success was now cemented in history. The Englishman enjoyed the life he had always dreamt of.

"That's the round," Ian said, a smile on his face.

Bell and Richie both pulled a single American dollar out of their pockets and walked over to him.

"I still say you're sandbagging," Bell said, handing over his dollar.

"I'm appalled you would insinuate such a thing," Ian replied, trying to hide the smirk.

"Good game, Ian. I should've known you'd find a way to pull it out."

He took both dollars and stuffed them in the front pocket of his trousers. One of the caddies saw an opportunity, digging into a small backpack he had carried the entire eighteen holes. Ian stepped back, reacting to the motion. The young man produced a book, gripping a pen over the cover.

"Mr. Fleming, would you please sign this for me? It's for me mum. She loves your writing."

He recovered himself and walked up to the caddy.

"I tell you what, lad. My friends and I are about to step into the clubhouse for lunch. How about you tend to our clubs and I'll sign your book afterwards."

"Yessir. Be glad to, sir. Thank you."

The young man gathered all three bags up from the two younger boys. Ian turned toward his old friends.

"Shall we?" he asked, extending his arm toward the clubhouse.

"I think we shall," Bell said, giving his best British accent.

The three men walked off of the golf course and entered the rear of the clubhouse. Ian wasted no time finding a cigarette and puffing it to life as they walked into the hallway. Several guests stopped him along the way, shaking his hand, congratulating him on his success. He was a bit of a celebrity and loving every moment of it.

Bell and Richie had found they enjoyed life in the anonymity of the Central Intelligence Agency, but they made every effort to see Ian as often as they could. Besides which, he did still hold the Knights Templar journal and sit on the advisory committee for MI-6. He stayed in the know and always made time for his war buddies. The journal, the existence of Arklight, and their deductions about The Order of the Black Sun still remained a closely guarded secret between them. They discussed theories often, and today was no different.

They entered the restaurant area and Ian held three fingers up to the hostess. She walked over smiling at him, obviously a fan of his work.

"You know," Bell said, leaning toward Richie. "Nothing's really changed if you think about it—he still has women blushing."

"Yep. And you… keep driving them away," Richie said, laughing to himself.

"I can't help it if broads don't understand me."

"You win some…"

"And you lose some, yeah, yeah."

Ian turned and stood by his table inside the clubhouse.

"Is this sufficient?"

"Why yes, it is," Bell said, pulling out a chair.

"Thanks," Richie said, finding his seat as well.

Ian pulled an ashtray in front of him as a waitress stepped up to the table, trying not to stare.

"What may I get you gentlemen?" she asked, her Scottish accent thickened by nerves.

"I'll take a Martini, darling – shaken not stirred," Ian said, without hesitation. "Oh, and try not to let my glass go dry, would you?"

"I'll take a stout," Bell said, "and bring me some fries."

"I beg your pardon?" the waitress asked.

"He means chips, dear," Ian said, clearing up Bell's lack of couth.

"I'll take a double of Jameson," Richie said.

The waitress scribbled a few notes on her pad. She looked at Ian once more before prancing away, like she had just met the Queen of England.

"I know you two are judging me. I can feel it. What's wrong with indulging in the fruits of my labors? I spent the entire first part of this year cooped up in Goldeneye, writing. I'm just enjoying myself... a little. These are my fans after all."

"No judgment here, buddy," said Bell, unable to contain his smile.

Richie laughed. His whole face glowed.

"This is what I enjoy most," Ian said, extinguishing his cigarette. "Seeing you two laugh again. I wish she would hurry up with our drinks. This deserves a toast."

"Yeah it does," Bell said.

"Time helps to heal all wounds," Richie added.

"Absolutely," Ian said, looking over his shoulder for the waitress.

"I'm watching for her, Ian. Hey, Richie, you forgot to tell him about the news."

"News you say?"

"Yes, I'm pretty excited for him—my son was accepted to Annapolis – the Naval Academy."

"That's outstanding! How's that boy of yours doing by the way?" he asked, pulling out another cigarette.

"He's doing well. Wants me to stop calling him Junior... you know, he says he's grown up now."

"Indeed, he has. The Academy will surely finish what you started. Speaking of which, Caspar turns twelve tomorrow. He started asking me about women this year. I feel as though I'll have my hands full with this one."

Bell laughed and said, "Consider it karma my friend."

"I should say so, old chap," he laughed in return.

"Richie, tell him the... *other* news," Bell said as the waitress returned.

"Gentlemen, here are your drinks." She sat each on the table, one after the other. "Need anything else?"

"My fries... I mean chips."

"They'll be right out," she said, pausing to look at Ian once more.

"Thank you, Miss," he said.

"O'Bannon, Charity O'Bannon."

"Charity, thank you. We'll order lunch in just a few."

"Oh, yes," she said as she turned to walk away.

"What is it with you?" Bell asked. "Is it the cologne? I don't get it."

"They say it's pheromones, but I like to think it's my charm."

"You're killing me," Bell said, picking up his beer for a taste.

"Are you two done?" Richie asked.

"Certainly not," Ian said, taking a drink of his martini. "I do so enjoy your company."

"Anyway, the other thing," Richie said, scanning the restaurant in both directions. "We've made some progress with… the project."

"Really? What have you discovered?"

"Do you remember our conversation from last year? The one about Prince Henry Sinclair?"

"Certainly. That was quite the stimulating discussion."

"Well, you know Richie and I have been involved with the Freemasons since the end of the war."

Ian nodded and sat forward, cigarette in hand.

"I've recruited a friend. A guy by the name of Jackson Oliver. He's an up-and-coming real estate investor and has some decent resources. His family has been involved with the Masons for generations," Richie said, taking a swig of bourbon. "His father's a 33rd level Templar Mason and he's able to view the Templar scrolls."

"Interesting."

"It's better than that," Bell added.

"Anyway, Jackson's father attended a ceremony. It was called the Sinclair ceremony," Richie said.

"Wait," Ian said, feeling his pocket empty. "Damn, I left the journal in my room, but I seem to recall a passage I read."

"Yes, that's right—can you remember what it said? I think it had something to do with the Ark."

"We need to head back to the hotel. I think you're right."

"Finally, something makes sense," Bell said. "I'm feeling like tonight will be a good night, fellas."

†††††

The Royal Saint George Golf Club bustled with activity on a muggy summer day. A black sedan pulled into the valet carousel in front of the clubhouse. The rear suicide door swung open. Kieffer stepped out of the back of the car wearing a white linen suit and a matching fedora. Weber slid out behind him, his suit in all black. They nodded at the valets, their driver pulled off, and they entered the club. Short beards covered their faces, age concealed their appearance, and an era of peace camouflaged evil intent.

"It's a beautiful day... don't you think?" Kieffer asked.

"Yes, my Führ—" Weber said, catching himself, since they were in public.

"Remember, my friend," Kieffer said, placing his hand on Weber's shoulder. "You are Joshua Johnson and I am Alfred O'Keefe. We're just a couple of business associates out for lunch."

"It's so hard to not call you by your true title," Weber said, his mind filled with loyalty and conviction.

"I know, but let us play the hand we've been dealt."

They entered the lobby of the golf club and approached the front desk where a young man in his twenties awaited.

"Gentlemen, may I have your membership numbers?"

"I'm afraid we're only guests here," Kieffer said, his accent now graced with a touch of Welsh. "We were told that we would be allowed to tour the facilities today. You know, prior to joining."

Weber stood behind Kieffer, his beady, ice-blue eyes darting around the room.

"Um, I'm sorry, sir – I wasn't made aware of your arrival. Let me call my manager."

"There's no need to inconvenience anyone, lad," Kieffer said. "We'll just show ourselves around. Be back in a jiffy."

"But..."

Kieffer turned and Weber paused, making unsettling eye contact with the desk clerk. The young man froze, not to utter another word. Weber's face twitched before he turned to follow his Führer.

Hitler had passed away of natural causes. Himmler, on the other hand, mad with dementia, had gotten in the way of Kieffer's progress. Weber was glad to snuff him out of the picture. Both men had taken on new lives and families, all while continuing their pursuit of the ultimate weapon. The Fourth Reich and The Order of the Black Sun stood at the forefront of everything they touched.

Colonel Weber lived under the assumed identity of Joshua Johnson, an American businessman. He had found a suitable mate in Argentina and she bore him a son, Klaus. She was wiped from existence in order to maintain the necessary secrecy. Raised by subjects loyal to the Reich, Weber's son was turned over to Josef Mengele and his mind-altering experiments. The process was nearly complete, and Klaus would be abandoned in the United States, to be raised without any ties to the Reich. Klaus' assumed name and personality, Roderick Johnson, would wipe away all traces of what lay beneath the surface.

Alfred Kieffer had assumed the last name O'Keefe for his travels. His son, Maximillion, was born and raised in Wales. Of course, Kieffer's wife had been selected by Hitler, himself. For members of the Order in line for Führer, maintaining the bloodline was of monumental importance. Maximillion was exposed to higher learning, an aristocratic lifestyle, and all of the resources available to train his mind for success. Often times, Maximillion was disciplined for disobedience; however, intellectual achievements were expected, and punishment followed when the strenuous goals set forth were not met.

The long-term plan was in full swing. In the short term, they had gotten word that the famed Ian Fleming was in Canterbury. It only took a phone call from one of their many informants to find out where he was.

"There he is," Weber said, as they passed the vestibule of the restaurant.

"No – there *they* are. The entire Alsos Team. Fortune shines upon us, my friend."

"You're right, of course… John Bell and Walter Steadman, the CIA men – they must be conspiring about the journal. Why Himmler made us wait so long to come get it, I'll never know."

The two men found their way towards the bar in the opposite room. The busy atmosphere masked their movements and allowed them a partially obstructed view of their intended targets. Men and women passed by, and the wait staff was bustling. Kieffer adjusted a bar stool and took a seat where he could watch the three Alsos men.

"What should we do?" Weber asked as he sat beside his leader.

"We wait. We wait until they leave," Kieffer said.

"What if we lose them?"

"Not this time. I already know where he's staying. He always books the same suite, in the same hotel. I think he feels safe – thinking that his war is over."

"So, we'll take them out at the hotel?" Weber asked.

"Yes, later. We need to have patience. We need to cover our tracks."

"Of course. What do you propose?"

"The MK toxin we developed should do the trick," Kieffer said.

"We'll have to get close."

"The three of them have already started drinking. The alcohol will do most of the work for us."

"I'll make sure it's ready," Weber said with a twitch of his cheek.

†††††

Ian missed the keyhole on two attempts before finding the mark. The door to his penthouse suite opened, and he staggered inside, looking for his family.

"Ann? Caspar? Ann darling, are you here?" Ian asked, checking the room. He looked back at the door and waved in Bell and Richie.

"Come on then," he said, checking the other side of the suite. "She must still be out. She'll be back later, I'm sure. I know she'll be delighted to see you both."

"We don't want to impose," Richie said, stepping inside the well-decorated room.

"You got any booze in here?" Bell asked, finding the first chair he saw.

"Of course. Martini?" Ian asked.

"How about a real drink. Got any bourbon, or scotch?"

"Right away, old boy."

He picked up the receiver and concentrated on the numbers.

"If it's not too much trouble," he said into the receiver, "could you have someone send up your best bottle of scotch? Yes, put it on my tab."

He set the receiver down and began to mix a martini together, just as he liked it.

"What's it like to be famous?" Richie asked, admiring the view from the balcony window.

"It's quite demanding and no one respects your privacy," Ian said, a smile drawing across his face. "But, I wouldn't trade it for the world. All of the adventures we have lived gives me so much to write about. I'm content allowing the world to think I rode a desk during the war. It's likely the greatest success MI-6 has had to date is – maintaining my cover."

"You Brits have always been good at that. I'm just glad the CIA has learned a few tricks, herself. Hell, me and Richie don't officially exist anymore. How they did that, I don't know."

Richie laughed and poured himself a shot of Ian's vodka.

"Half the guys we recruited for Project Arklight call me Pappy, since I'm the oldest guy in the room," he said, still laughing. "Bell escaped that title – since he chose to do the fieldwork."

"I did edge you out in seniority and brains," Bell said, a smirk forming across his face.

Richie smiled and lifted his glass toward Bell.

"This one's for you, Hells Bells," Ian toasted. "May your brain not fill with the crap of a thousand goats."

"I'm flattered."

"I've missed you two," Ian said. "You'll both have to come visit me at my home in Jamaica. It's perfectly charming."

"Absolutely," Richie said.

"Sorry to disrupt our good time, but I figure we better take a look at the journal before we get more drunk than we already are."

Ian smiled and picked up his martini.

"Yes, let me get it."

He walked over to the credenza and opened the middle section, inside of which sat a safe. He started working the dial and within moments, he unlatched the lock. He turned, holding the ancient journal in hand, timeworn leather cover displaying the branded Templar lion symbol.

Richie stepped toward Ian.

"May I?"

"Of course," he said, more concerned with his martini. The coarse leather of the journal was cool in Richie's hand. He opened the book, looking for a passage on a specific page. The journal's contents were cryptic at best. He knew there was a key to the coding, but until they could locate it, many secrets would remain a mystery.

"See here," he said, his finger on a passage, *"The Ring and the Stone at 90 are the path. Bring back the Birch – E.o.O."*

"What the hell is that supposed to mean?" Bell asked.

"Obviously this ring and stone are interconnected. The way the birch is described sounds like they are condoning some sort of corporal punishment. Of course, the tree comes to mind as well. What does *E.o.O.* stand for?" Ian asked.

"Could be anything. The middle letter is lower case, bookended by capital letters. That's a bit odd."

"You mentioned Prince Henry Sinclair at lunch," Ian said, turning toward Richie.

"Yes."

"Do you want to know what his Lordship's title was?"

"Don't hold back now," Bell said.

"He was titled the Baron of Roslin and – the First Earl of Orkney. E.o.O. would be the initials, I believe."

"So, maybe the Templar Masons have Prince Henry Sinclair's ring? That might be tied to this other entry," Richie said, flipping the pages.

A knock at the door interrupted his search. He tucked the journal into the small of his back, at the beltline.

"Relax, old man. It's just a bottle of scotch," Ian said as he walked toward the door.

Richie followed behind Ian, finding a seat next to Bell.

"If what you found holds true," Bell said, "we'll need to get more involved with the Masons."

"I'm glad we joined after the war. It's going to take us years to reach the 33rd level," Richie said.

"Yeah…"

Ian turned the knob and opened the door. Before he could react, a dart impacted him in the chest. He reached for it in shock. A second hit him, and his legs gave way, collapsing him to the floor. Kieffer and Weber pushed their way through the door, their pistols leading the charge. Richie and Bell jumped to their feet, but they were too late, and unarmed.

"Sit," Kieffer insisted, waving his pistol in the air. "I said, sit down! Keep your hands where I can see them."

Weber grabbed Ian's seizing arm and dragged him into the room, shutting the door in his wake. Once inside, he knelt down and fired a third dart into Ian's chest.

"There's no escape this time, Mr. Fleming."

Ian's eyes were wide open; his body tensed and released with each seizure. He couldn't speak. He clutched at his chest, his mouth in a froth.

Richie and Bell sat, powerless to act, with Kieffer's pistol pointed at them. Weber patted Ian down, finding nothing of use, and pulled the three darts from his chest.

"John Bell and Walter Steadman. We meet again – dare I say for the last time. Check them for the journal."

Richie stared at Kieffer's face. White-hot rage surged within.

"What did you do to him?"

"It's a simple toxin we developed from shellfish. I'm afraid it's too late for Mr. Fleming. He's received a fatal dose. Soon his body will fail, and he'll have a massive heart attack. The toxic is most undetectable and the darts leave no marks."

Weber stood Richie up and noticed the bulge in the small of his back. He lifted the jacket and pulled out the Knights Templar journal, showing it to Kieffer.

"Excellent. Bring it to me. Cover them."

With his weapon trained on Bell and Richie, Weber back-peddled to his Führer, his smile filled with bloodlust. He handed it over. Kieffer stuffed the long slide of his pistol into the front of his pants and took his time, admiring the outside of the journal. He opened it and thumbed through the pages.

"The way I see it is, we're taking back what belongs to us. Mr. Fleming here killed Doctor Clarke. In turn, he—and by proxy, you—get to die for your crimes against the Reich."

Richie and Bell turned, their eyes meeting, formulating an escape plan without words. Bell stepped toward Kieffer, and Richie toward Weber. A stinging pain surged through Richie's body—his mid-section was on fire. He looked down and saw two darts in his chest. His breath was taken away by the powerful toxin. He fell to his knees, watching Bell meet the same fate. An uncontrollable twitch shot through his arms, and everything went numb.

"Weber, grab the laundry cart in the hallway. We'll leave that one, but these two are CIA. They need to disappear."

Richie was now flat on the floor, shaking as each surge of toxin pumped into his heart. There was nothing he could do but stare ahead. His gaze found Bell's. He strained to see Ian, who lay in a twitch on the floor. Kieffer knelt down, placing his face in front of Richie's.

"Save your strength for the drive to the coast. I wouldn't want you to expire before we drown you."

Black spots coursed through Richie's vision. He labored to draw breath. His body grew frigid, his mind blank. Everything faded away. The frigid embrace of his failing heart pulled him into unconsciousness.

†††††

"Walter... Walter Richard Steadman, awaken," rang a voice as strong and majestic as he had ever heard.

The blackness exploded away in an instant, and gleaming light, brighter than the sun, replaced the emptiness. Richie looked at his hands. The beam of light felt warm. He could move once again. He felt his chest, confused. *Where am I and how?* He felt his throat. The grip of death no longer restrained him.

"Hello? Is anyone here?"

"No, Walter. It is only you," the voice said, so deep it rattled every inch of his mind.

"Am I dead? Is this heaven?"

"You are neither dead, nor are you in heaven. Not until I am done with your purpose on Earth may you rest. I have prepared a place for you – for you are of the line descended from the tribe of Judah. You are the heir of David's throne."

"God?"

"I am known by many names; I am the one true God."

Richie fell to his knees and placed his hands together in the center of his chest. It was as if he were weightless, free of the bonds that held him down.

"I am unworthy, Lord."

"It is your humility that binds you to your ancestors. The time nears for the seven seals to be broken. Your line will be responsible for opening the door. Know that I am with you."

"The journal, Lord. But how?"

"Have faith. I will provide you the path."

A blinding flash shook Richie's body. He jerked his arms and legs and began to flail about, treading a watery resistance. He opened his eyes, adrift in the waters of the ocean. He surged his head above the water line, in shock from the sudden change. In the blink of an eye, he went from standing in the presence of God to fighting to stay afloat in the harsh, salty surf of the open ocean. He coughed, regurgitating water from his lungs.

He saw an arm break the surface of the water in front of him.

"Bell!" he shouted, grabbing the arm and pulling it toward him.

He tugged, flipping Bell on his back and pounding a fist on his chest. Bell sprung back to life in an instant, gasping for breath. Disoriented, he flipped around, reaching out for Richie in a panic.

"You're alive," he said, coughing.

"Barely. Can you swim?"

"Yeah," Bell said, his well-practiced skills kicking in. "I can see the shoreline. It's not far."

They stayed close to each other, just like they did during their training days as Navy Raiders. With each side stroke, they grew stronger, more confident they would make it to shore, until they did. Bell found his footing first, pulling Richie in. The two of them made their way to the sandy beach and collapsed.

"How are we still alive?" Bell asked.

Richie sat up and looked toward the night sky.

"God. He saved us – for a reason."

"You too? I thought I was imagining it."

"We have a very important purpose to serve out," Richie said. "We have to see this through."

"I've got a lot of work to do. A lot of fixing. Not only for Him, but within myself. We've got to get that journal back, find the Arma Christi, and open the doorway. We can't let Kieffer and Weber succeed in their plan... I saw a brief glimpse – what'll happen if they do."

"We've got a mountain to climb, that's for sure."

Bell covered his face with both hands, obscuring fresh streaks of hot tears.

"What about Ian—you think he made it?"

"Not in manner we might like," Richie said, placing his hand on Bell's back. "But he made it."

"He told me who you are."

"That I'm of the line of King David?"

"No, that you are the protector, and I'm to be – whatever that means."

Bell wiped his face and took a deep breath. He shifted his focus toward the horizon.

"Richie, let's get out of here. We need to shift Arklight into high-gear. These Nazis aren't getting away with this."

"Let's be sure to honor His will. He will guide us – in His own time, and way. That I'm sure of."

"Yeah, I know. We've both got a long way to go, my friend."

CHAPTER 25: KEY

"And the last enemy to be destroyed is death."
Corinthians 15:26

2100-ZuluTime 14August2020 (2300-CET Geneva, Switzerland)

Branches scraped along the paintwork of the SUV, some slapping inside the passenger compartment where doors once covered. John steered the stripped vehicle down a steep embankment on the edge of the O'Keefe property. Chappy sat in the front passenger seat, grasping the handle on the pillar.

"Cut it back your way," he said, looking at the ground below.

"Got it. Hang on." He gassed the accelerator on a short hill, pressing to the overgrown access road.

The truck jutted back and forth, slamming everyone's guts toward the floor.

"Dammit," said the chief. "I didn't think it would be this rough."

"Just a state of mind," Chappy said, a smile emerging through the camouflage face paint.

"Until today, I've never gotten car sick," Anne said, rubbing the back of her neck. "I think my spine might need to be fixed after the ride down that hill."

"It did get a little dicey there for a minute," John said as the vehicle leveled off on the narrow dirt trail. "Now we just need to find that ditch I saw."

"What you thinking?" Chappy said, tugging a branch off the hood.

"I thought it looked deep enough to conceal our approach – did you, Chief?"

"I think so. We just need to find the damn thing."

"John, see that clearing up ahead?" Chappy asked.

"I see it. If I figured right, the ditch should be to the right of this access road. Let's park here. It should be plenty close."

"Anne, let's go ahead and rig it," Chappy said as he jumped out of the passenger seat.

John grabbed his rifle and stepped out, turning to look at the chief.

"What do you think our chances are?"

"We got this. The good guys are due a win."

John nodded and press-checked his rifle before slinging it over his shoulder.

Chappy pulled out a fragmentation grenade, locking a makeshift piece of metal over the spoon. The strip was attached to a small actuator, rigged to release by a radio-controlled switch on Chappy's gear. The house was a quarter of a mile away. Having a diversion in place was critical to their success.

He checked the release device over and looked at Anne.

"Pull the pin, and let's hope we don't blow ourselves up."

"You're full of winners today," she said, extracting the pin.

The device held together, and he placed it on top of a full gas can on the backseat.

"Should make a really nice fireball."

"Nothing like a good IED," she said, checking her kit and making sure she had everything.

"Let's go," John said. "I got point."

He walked to the edge of the wood line and oriented himself to the property line. Without night-vision they were at a disadvantage, but if the ditch was deep enough, it wouldn't matter. They could be on the house before anyone realized it.

The pastures were outlined with a series of electrified enclosures. The hot wire ran along the top, keeping the horses off the fencing. The team would need to traverse the first pasture in order to reach the ditch. John stopped and listened for any sign of movement in the area. Their prior surveillance revealed that most of the security personnel stayed closer to the structures; he could recall two patrols of the property all day, and since night had fallen, the likelihood of running into a patrol seemed improbable.

He looked over his shoulder and motioned for Chappy to come up.

"What's up?" Chappy whispered.

"I'm going under the fence to scout the ditch. Hold here."

"Roger that."

In an instant, John slid under the fence and was up, jogging across the open field. Chappy watched him slow and jump down into what he hoped was the ditch they needed to find. Chappy scanned the area, seeing nothing move but a couple of horses in an adjacent enclosure. John's head emerged from the pit. His hand indicated it was all clear. Chappy looked back and motioned to Anne and Chief.

"Yeah?" Anne asked.

"You two haul ass to John. He found the way in."

Anne tilted her rifle barrel up and looked at the chief.

"Don't slow me down, old-timer," she said, scrambling to her feet.

Chief narrowed his eyes, beating her to the fence, sliding under in one well-trained move.

"I'll show you old," he said grabbing her by the vest and pulling her up. "Make sure you keep up."

They both sprinted across the field with Chappy covering their movement. Once they disappeared from sight, he made his way to them, jumping in the long, narrow drainage ditch.

John looked straight at the O'Keefe house, working the next problem.

"See that security crew?" Chief pointed toward the back of the house, "The one on the left?"

"Yeah."

"They're a new group. Means they should be there for a while…"

"Without a rover to check on them," John said. "Good spot, Boomer."

He faced the surviving trace of Spear Team.

"We're moving, stealth to contact from this point on. Once we take out the security group on the Northwest corner, me and Boomer will take the back. Chap, you and Anne be ready to set off the diversion. Chaos theory – good luck."

Chappy's hand grabbed John's forearm.

"You too, brother. Until the end."

"I don't mean to break up your love-in," Anne said, "but, we got business ahead. Let's get to it."

The chief smiled and patted Anne on the back.

"She's like the daughter I never had... plus, she's right. Hooyah!"

"For Arklight," John said, assuming a determined stance as he faced back towards their foe. He checked his kit once more and looked back at Chief, who nodded he was a go. The team moved down the trench toward the main house.

Two sentries were posted on the corner. The men leaned against their vehicle, complacent from the long hours, cigarette smoke billowing off their hands. John and Chappy crept to the edge of the ditch, crawling prone on their stomachs. The suppressed barrels of their weapons penetrated the edge of the grass, protruding enough for a clear shot.

A slight breeze masked their movement. Their intended targets stood still; assault rifles draped across the front of their torsos. John tapped Chappy's elbow.

"In three, two..."

"Hold," Chappy said, headlights reflecting off the men in their field of view.

"What?" asked John.

"Who's this?"

A black sedan stopped before the two guards. The headlights flipped off, and a familiar face emerged from the vehicle. John zoomed in a far as he could with the hybrid CQC three-power optic.

"General Johnson. It was hard enough believing Bell's story, but seeing it – that's worse."

"Traitor," Chappy said, looking behind him.

"Look at how he moves now. What a mind-job."

"He's not Rod anymore, John. He's Klaus now. We've got to put him down."

"I know," he said, breaking his focus from down range. He rolled to the side and made eye contact with the chief and grabbed Anne, pointing to their rear. She nodded and turned her focus one-hundred and eighty degrees.

"What's up?" whispered Chief as he settled in beside John.

John bounced his eyes to the target area and found his cheek weld once more. The chief's eye found his optic; he focused on the three men talking in the distance.

"Traitor. Let it be me."

"You've got the call, Chief," John said, emotion tugging at his throat, clawing to get out.

Chief zoomed in, settling his platform. Knocking Klaus' lights out wasn't enough for what he had done. The betrayal of trust was far beyond anything he could have ever imagined. It was total—complete.

Crosshairs settled over Klaus's chest. The chief's thumb clicked the safety, and his finger dropped to the trigger.

"In… Three, Two, One."

A simultaneous metallic blast of subsonic air exited their rifles. The two sentries went down, and small clouds of pink haze drifted in the space their heads had once occupied.

Klaus staggered backward clutching his chest, his face in shock. Chief jumped from his position, slid under the fence, and ran across the gravel lot. John and Chappy scrambled up after him, hoping Anne had the presence of mind to cover them.

By the time Chief arrived over Klaus, his knife was in hand. The shell of the man they had all followed, admired, and had even loved, lay on the ground, gasping his final breaths. The suit jacket he wore was soaked through with his blood. The chief grabbed him by the face, looking him in the eye, his knife at his throat.

"I hope you rot, whoever you really are."

Klaus gasped for air, the trance-like blur in his stare fading with each pulse of his heart.

John and Chappy settled up beside Chief.

"Just end it," Chappy said, "this can't be about revenge."

"He's right, Boomer."

"It's not. It's about mercy. Hide those bodies. I got this."

John could see something very different happening inside the chief. He nodded at Chappy, and they moved to clean up their mess.

"Rod, I know you're in there – somewhere."

Klaus started to tense, gasping to breath. His gaze focused on the chief's.

"Rod?"

"N-Nathan," Klaus struggled to say a reflection of Rod in his eyes. "He's in the basement."

Chief's eyes stung with tears and a burn infected his chest from the pain it caused him. He could see what remained of Rod, if only for a brief moment. He locked his gaze on his old commander.

"Why?" he asked.

"Because," Klaus said, grabbing the chief's knife hand, "Y-you have to…"

Klaus pulled the knife toward his chest. The old SEAL knew what had to be done.

"Forgive me," Klaus said.

In one quick move, the chief covered Klaus' mouth and dropped all of his weight down on him behind the serrated steel. Klaus' body fell limp and Chief wept as life ran out of the man he had once known and followed.

John paused, watching the chief pull himself up from what he had to do. Chappy moved the body of the man he had killed into the front seat of the security vehicle. The chief grabbed Klaus' body and John helped, sitting his corpse inside the sedan he drove up in. Anne walked up, covering them all.

"Is that?" she asked.

"Yeah," John said.

"He was Rod… at the very end. He told me Nathan's in the basement."

"He's alive?" Chappy asked, easing the door shut to the vehicle.

"Sounded that way."

"Let's go bust out the admiral. Chap, you and Anne move on the perimeter sentries. We'll hit the house," John said.

"Roger that," Chappy said, grabbing Anne. "Let's go."

†††††

Wet sponges of electrified agony racked against Nathan's bare, extended rib cage. His hands were bound above his head, and his feet couldn't touch the ground. He thrashed about with an intensity that had ripped the flesh and nails from his toes. Ronnie looked away; it was more than he could bear to watch. Death surrounded him in Magnus' presence. He had learned what a man was capable of doing to another man. A lesson he thought the war had taught him was trumped by the extreme cruelty of what Magnus could conjure.

"Tell me why the Ark won't open," Magnus hissed against the flicker of lanterns. "Tell me why it's not working!"

Nathan's shoulders burned with pain, ready to come out of the socket.

"D-don't know," he said, his right eye swollen shut from the constant abuse. Life was fading from him. He welcomed it.

The thick rubber gloves on Magnus' hands arched the jumper cables. He closed in for another round, his face filled with hate.

"I don't know!" Nathan screamed, hoping to pass out at the least, die at best.

BOOM.

The exterior door to the basement imploded into the room, knocking Ronnie and Magnus off their feet. John entered, seeing Ronnie reach for his pistol, his eyes widening with shock.

"No!" Ronnie shouted.

John wasted no words, plugging a burst of fire into the Merc's torso. Ronnie fell limp and John turned his attention to Magnus, who was on his hands and knees trying to recover. The chief raised his rifle, ready to end his days.

"No! He's mine, Chief," John said, closing in on Magnus. "Hands! Show me your hands… now!"

Magnus turned his head, seeing it was John. He didn't change his position.

"So, we meet ag—"

John ended his sentence with a round straight through his left arm.

"Arrgghhh! Okay - okay!"

The shot forced Magnus on his back. Both hands were in the air, where John could see them. He closed in further, stepping on Magnus' good arm. The warmth of his suppressor sat under Magnus' chin. He found both of the pistols Magnus carried, tossing them across the makeshift dungeon. John backed off for a moment, remembering they had made some noise getting in.

"Chappy, you copy? Go!" he said, over the radio.

"Go?" Chappy asked.

"Blow the diversion! Go active!"

"On it!"

A moment later, an explosion was heard in the distance. Automatic machine gun fire rattled the front of the estate in bursts. John motioned to the chief.

"Cut the admiral down."

"You got that shitbird covered?" asked the chief.

"I got him," John said, his finger trained on the trigger of his assault rifle, the barrel pointed at Magnus' chest.

Chief stepped up to a near lifeless Nathan.

"Admiral? You still with us?"

All Nathan could muster was a disconnected stare. He reached up with his knife and sliced through the rope that suspended the admiral off the ground. With his other arm, he caught most of Nathan's weight, softening his collapse to the floor. John threw a set of flex-cuffs to Magnus.

"Put those on, before I decide to end you right here." He adjusted his barrel toward Magnus' other arm.

"Bloody hell, okay." He slid the hoops over his wrists and used his teeth to pull the bonds tight. He held them up in the air, so John could see they were on properly.

"Don't freaking move. Got it?"

"Aye."

John backed up to Nathan, never letting Magnus out of his sight.

"Chief, cover the doors."

"Roger."

"Admiral... you okay?" John asked, his hand wiping the stain from Nathan's face.

"That you, John?"

"Yeah, boss. Can you move?"

Nathan's body shuttered. Shock had already set in. His organs had begun to shut down days ago. The admiral could feel life seeping out of his body with every drop of blood that hit the floor. He struggled to hold open the one eye he could still see out of. His hand reached for John's.

"I've got one thing – left, to tell you."

John moved closer, shifting his focus to Nathan's words.

"The handle to the Time Key. It's in your grandfather's cane. He said you'd know... what to do," he said as he lost consciousness.

"Sir? Admiral!" John yelled, feeling for a pulse.

He was breathing, but it was labored. John couldn't hold back his emotions any longer. He collapsed on top of Nathan, or what remained of him. A tight ball of fury burned in his chest, rage filled his core, and his fists shook in anger.

Magnus coiled himself up like a snake in the corner.

"Shame, really," he said. "We were just getting to know each other."

John turned his head, focus locked on the enemy of his lifetime.

"Shut your damn mouth, or I'll—"

"You'll what?" Magnus asked, his face filling with delight. "Come and beat me? I'm not afraid of you. I thought I killed you already. Guess I should've done a better job."

John was back on his feet, cornering Magnus at a clip. The chief knew it was a trap, bait to draw him in, but John could handle anything – even a devil like Magnus.

"Steady, don't let him bait you!" he yelled. More bursts of rifle fire pounded the front of the O'Keefe house.

"I don't care anymore," John said, throwing his rifle to the floor.

Magnus started laughing.

"Yes, come on then. You and me. Take these cuffs off. I'll still take you with my good arm, mate."

John knelt beside Magnus; his teeth gritted together.

"No chance," John said, as he punched Magnus in the gut. "Shut your mouth or I'll kill you – right here – right now."

Magnus seized about on the floor, trying to draw air into his lungs. Seconds passed before he could inhale again. He struggled to breathe and regain his composure.

"Where's the Ark?" John asked, holding Magnus' collar.

Another burst of fire erupted from the front of the house. John didn't know what was happening, but hoped he could leverage the noise to his advantage.

"Don't you hear that?" he asked. "It's the sound of my men moving in. It's the sound of you losing. Tell me where the Ark is – now!"

The chief jerked to one side of the door he was guarding, firing one burst and then a second.

"John, we've got no time. We've got to move!"

He looked back over his shoulder, and Magnus coughed out a few words.

"I'll show you where it is."

"No tricks," John said. "I won't hesitate to put you down."

Magnus nodded. A plan formed in his head.

††††††

"Anne, cover left!" Chappy yelled, jumping to the ground.

He let loose a burst of fire from his M-249, and then another, cutting down two more mercenaries. Anne rolled to the ground, flipping around to their flank and catching another marauder in the chest.

"Moving!" she yelled, making her way to the front of the main house.

Chappy came up to a knee, checking his round count. The box was almost empty. He covered Anne as she closed on the front doors. When she reached the wall, he charged forward across the circular drive. Halfway across, he felt the burn, even before he heard the shot. His right leg spasmed with a familiar pain, tumbling him to the ground. He rolled, hearing the shot come from his right. A silhouette flashed in his sights. He squeezed the trigger, bursting the last of his rounds in the shooter's direction.

Anne peeked the corner, seeing the sentry hit the ground.

"You're clear. Come on."

Chappy reached down to his thigh, and his hand felt warmth gushing from the wound. He rolled to his feet and limped to Anne, collapsing on the ground beside her. His bloodstained hand found the tourniquet on his vest.

"I'll get it." she said, realizing the bullet hit an artery.

"No, dammit. Cover us."

He winced, getting the device in place.

"High or die," he winced.

He cinched down the nylon, and twisted the bar, gritting his teeth together with every rotation. He locked it in, vomiting a bit in the process.

"It's pretty bad, Anne," he said, out of breath. "I think it nicked my femoral."

She checked the front of the house and quick-peeked the inside foyer before kneeling down, pulling Chappy's pressure dressings out of his kit.

"I can do it," Chappy said, his voice labored from blood loss. "Just cover us."

"Shut up. Move your freaking hand!"

Chappy pulled his hand away from the wound. It was still weeping. She let go of her rifle and reached for the tourniquet.

"I've got to give it another twist."

"Just do it," he said, his face pale.

Anne unhitched the bar and twisted it as hard as she could, getting another half turn.

"Ahhhh! Dammit!"

She packed the wound and applied a pressure dressing. Chappy shook the cobwebs out of his head. Despite the pain, he drew his pistol.

"You have to go," he said, reaching into his left cargo pocket. "Here's the door charge—get in there. John's depending on you!"

"I can't leave you."

"You have to," he said, forcing the looped det-cord into her hand.

"Okay, I'll be back... Cover me from here?"

"I got you. Nothing's getting through this door," he said, struggling to his feet. "You'll move faster if I stay here. I'm fine. Just *GO!*"

Anne inserted the primer and looped the charge over the knob. She grabbed Chappy, helping him out of the blast range of the breaching device. She put her thumb on the charger as an energy field developed only a few feet away.

Within moments, an orb of light surrounded the O'Keefe estate. All became still, and the house was cut off from the rest of the world. Pure light fell like a dome around the main residence, but the inside remained dark, consistent with the time of day. The curtain of energy maintained time on the interior, but accelerated it on the exterior. The sun rose and tracked across the sky, from morning, to the middle of the day, and into sunset. The orb was a transparent white with blue arcs of energy swirling through it. The main house of the estate was engulfed by darkness now.

With each sunrise and sunset, the pace increased. Time outside of the energy field moved ever-faster.

"What's this?" Anne asked, her expression wide in awe.

"I wish I knew," Chappy answered, almost forgetting the pain in his leg from sheer amazement.

She stepped forward and reached out her hand, unsure what would happen. Her fingers made contact; the energy field was solid, like a wall, and warm to the touch.

"The Hadron Collider... that has to be it. It's created an energy field around us. Around this house."

"This is it! It's what I saw," Chappy said, a deranged smile emerging on his face. "Anne, no matter what happens, you've got to get in there."

"What did you see?"

"Time is moving forward." Chappy said, pointing toward the outside of the orb. "Look!"

Anne turned her head and looked. The world was moving like a movie on fast-forward. Day became night and night became day. Horses roamed the pastures so fast they became blurs. The clouds jutted through the sky, only to be swallowed by twilight.

"Oh my God," Anne said.

"Yeah. You've got to go – I'll be right behind you."

She took one more look. The days started moving so quickly, the exterior of the orb began to strobe. She turned away from the energy field, placing her thumb on the actuator of the door charge.

"God, forgive me."

"Seeing *is* believing," Chappy said, tucking his head for the breach. *Click. Click.*

"It's a dud," she said, checking the actuator.

"Figures," he said, reaching for the knob. He stumbled, grabbing the door, and it opened. "What do you know?"

She saw the door swing and grabbed Chappy's arm.

"I'm not leaving you out here. It's non-negotiable."

"Okay, okay," he said, gritting back the pain.

CHAPTER 26: LOVE

"I looked up and saw a white horse standing there. Its rider carried
a bow, and a crown was placed on his head."
Revelations 6:2

Time unknown – Date unknown (Geneva, Switzerland)

John pushed Magnus into Maximillion's study. The room was clear—no
one else was present. The Ark of the Covenant sat in front of the desk.
An oscillating, white beacon of light caught John's eye. It hung in the air
between the two angels that sat atop of the golden chest. The chief walked
into the room, clearing the corners, looking for a place to secure Magnus.
He walked toward the large windows, which forced him to squint.

"What's going on out there?"

"Not sure," John said, pushing Magnus toward one of the two chairs
in front of the Ark.

"That's some crazy flashing. Like nothing I've ever seen."

"You know what this is?" John asked, poking Magnus with the barrel
of his rifle.

"The Hadron Collider is producing an energy field," Magnus
growled. "We're sitting right in the middle of the ring."

John turned around, hearing footsteps in the hall. He took an angle
on the doorway.

"Cannon."

The footsteps stopped. John tensed up, ready to engage.

"Fodder," Anne's voice answered back.

The chief crossed to the doorway, relieved they had made the
rendezvous. John held on to Magnus, weapon at the ready. Anne's hand
grabbed the frame of the doorway, and her head emerged.

"You want to give me a hand?" she asked.

John stepped forward, seeing she had Chappy's arm over her
shoulder.

"What happened?"

"He got hit. It's pretty bad," she said, looking at John.

The chief dropped his guard and stepped over to help.

BOOM.

A shot rang out from John's left. Anne collapsed to the ground, Chappy landing on top of her. Blood coated the side of John's face. He staggered. Two rounds hit his chest, knocking him to the ground. As he fell, everything slowed.

The chief went down shooting, hitting his knees hard, his barrel breathing fire into the ceiling. John's eyes made contact with the chief's, just before a final round collapsed his body to the floor. John pushed himself up, grasping at his rifle, looking for the threat. The back of his head met the buttstock of a rifle before he could react. He fought to catch his breath, his head swimming in a fog.

"John Steadman," Kieffer said, stepping through a hidden panel in the wall, his rifle still smoking.

John couldn't muster words.

"Max, cut that waste of life you call your son loose," he said, turning his attention back to John. "And you. Roll over, so I can see you. Do it slowly."

Maximillion covered the chief, loosing rounds into his lifeless body. He moved to Magnus; whose confidence grew.

"He's dead, Father. Now, cut me loose and let's finish this."

A swipe of Maximillion's knife cut the cuffs from Magnus' wrists. He stood up, walked over to John, and grabbed his rifle off the floor. With a sinister smirk, he pointed it at the Anne, releasing a burst of fire, finishing her off with John's own weapon.

John wanted to act, but all he could do was look on with shock. His mind shuddered at the loss. He was all alone, surrounded by evil.

"Magnus! What are you doing?" Maximillion insisted.

"Making sure they're dead. Like I should've done in Okinawa."

He knelt down to John, his face blank.

"Now you're alone. All mine." He punched John in the side, below his plate carrier.

"Magnus! Stop!" Kieffer said. "I need him first."

"No, Grandfather. I know why the weapon won't activate. I heard the admiral tell him the secret," he sneered.

"Alright then, what's the secret?" Kieffer asked, his trigger finger tapping the wood on the lower receiver.

Magnus tilted his head and stood. John ran one hand under his plate carrier, the other down to the pistol on his side. A shot snapped by John's head, rupturing his eardrum. He flinched, feeling his right arm throb. He looked down. His forearm splattered on the floor.

"Just returning the favor."

John winced from the pain, grabbing his arm. He could tell something was broken, even though the wound didn't bleed much.

Magnus turned and closed ground on Kieffer.

"Just tell *you* the secret – like that?"

"I am your Führer! It is my destiny to open the ultimate weapon. You will hold a place… on my council."

Maximillion stepped to the side. He didn't want to get anywhere between them. His focus was on the Ark. His lifelong dream of unlimited power was becoming reality.

"You're a tired old man," Magnus said, focusing on Kieffer like a snake to prey. "You would be nowhere without me!"

John sat back, gripping his forearm, trying to formulate a plan. There was no way out of the fray. Surrounded by devils and greed, he clenched his teeth and prayed to God for help.

"You disrespectful, Imp!" Kieffer snapped, pulling his rifle up.

Magnus fired first, and then again, dropping Kieffer to the floor. He walked across the room and looked down on his grandfather as he drew his last breath. He stepped on the old man's face, turning to stare down his own father, taking what was his.

John blinked his eyes in disbelief. It wasn't exactly the help he asked for, but he figured evil begets evil.

"Father? And where do you stand?"

"Son," Maximillion said, laying down his rifle, "I'll do whatever is necessary to make you the Führer. I just want access to the power that's been promised."

Magnus laughed, waving the rifle around.

"I know you'd slit my throat if you had half a chance."

"No, no, I'm the one who told you to kill him. Remember?"

"Only so you could control the weapon. Only so you could control me."

John couldn't believe the showdown happening right in front of him. The O'Keefe's were so consumed by their own lust for power, they were killing each other. Movement caught John's eye outside the doorway to the study. A swollen, beaten face emerged from the shadows. Nathan crawled up, just on the other side of the wall. He held one of Magnus' pistols. How he had managed to crawl up the stairs was a miracle in and of itself. The answer to John's prayer.

"Magnus, listen to me... You and I can rule this world – as father and son! I'm for you. You have to believe me. Why else would I have told you everything about our lineage – our destiny?"

"Okay, Father," Magnus said, deciding his expertise was still valuable. "Step away from the desk. Move over there. Give me some space."

Maximillion held his hands out and away from his body. He circled the opposite side of the desk, moving toward John.

"See, son? Easy. Tell me what I can do."

"How about you shut it," Magnus replied, looking over the Arma Christi on the desk. "Where's the cane we took from that old bastard, Steadman?"

"It's on the bookshelf, behind you," Maximillion said.

Magnus turned around, taking several glances over his shoulder, untrusting of his own father. John looked at Nathan and nodded. The pistol slid across the floor and John grabbed it with his left hand, kicking Maximillion's legs out from under him. Magnus heard the ruckus and pivoted, leveling off his rifle toward John. Shot after shot he fired, trailing John as he dove behind a couch. Bullets tore through the upholstered leather as he crashed on the floor.

Maximillion scampered out of the study, meeting Nathan's diminished, but still effective right upper-cut. The shot to the jaw staggered him, causing him to fall on the floor. Nathan ducked as bullets penetrated the wall, scattering debris all over the room. He crawled to where Maximillion fell, feeling for his leg.

John took a chance, stopping his forward progress and turning in the opposite direction. It paid off, as Magnus' rounds continued to carry across the room. A rapid burst to the right, and he stood, leveling off his own pistol at Magnus. The first round hit him, knocking him back into the bookshelf. John closed in, firing as Magnus darted to the side. A trail of hot lead followed him until the pistol locked back empty. John threw it as Magnus jumped up from behind the desk.

"Too bad for you—I've got my vest on," he grinned.

The holes in Magnus' shirt contrasted over the black of his bullet-proof vest. Bits of copper were stuck in his trauma plate.

"Come on!" John said, rounding the corner of the desk.

Magnus checked John's movement with a straight-leg kick to the gut. It gave him some confidence, and he ran his fingers across the open bolt of his rifle.

"It's empty. It's just you and me."

†††††

Nathan shuffled back to his feet. He swung his entire body, trying to take in enough of the room to find Maximillion. His one good eye strained in the dark. He could hear John and Magnus going at it in the next room. He heard a rub and turned again. A blinding blow numbed the side of his face, spinning him to the floor.

"Die!" Maximillion shouted, raising a heavy bookend in the air and aiming for Nathan's head.

The admiral rolled into Maximillion's knee, latching on to it before pulling him forward. He fell with a *thud* and Nathan crawled up his back, grabbing him around the neck. He tried choking him out with every bit of energy he could muster.

Maximillion reached behind his own head, finding Nathan's face, clawing at the badly swollen eye. He dug his thumb into the golf ball-sized knot as spittle blasted from his lips. Nathan tried to hang on, but the pain was too intense. He disengaged, punching his adversary in the back of the head before rolling away.

Dazed by the strikes, Maximillion staggered to his feet, falling into the wall, shaken. His hand found one of the bows he kept mounted—a

386

display for the animals he had hunted and killed over the years. In a feverish panic, he ran his other hand along the wall for the quiver full of arrows that was hanging alongside his prized bow. Just as his fingers wrapped around the leather strap, Nathan grabbed him, throwing him toward the front door. Arrows scattered across the floor, but several remained in the quiver through the tumble.

Maximillion regained his balance, grabbing an arrow and splitting it between his fingers. He drew back the pull string. Nathan charged as he loosed the arrow. It struck him in the chest, but the dump of adrenaline carried him straight into Maximillion. He tackled his foe straight out of the front door, into the flashing energy field around the house. Maximillion carried into and through the wall of energy, his motion slowing as he fell. Nathan pushed himself up to his knees, bewildered at the altered time. Maximillion's body was almost inanimate; his slow fall appeared to take hours. His head, then his face, faded through the field of light.

"I guess," Nathan said, trying to catch his breath, "you're going somewhere else."

He looked down at the arrow and stabilized his wound, wrapping his hand around the shaft. Pain set into his core, but he stood, staggering his way back toward John's struggle in the study.

†††††

"It'll be my pleasure to end you," Magnus sneered, tossing his rifle to the floor. He reached down, snapping a sharp folder-knife from his pocket. His hand wrapped around the grip, the silver point toward John.

"Make your move," John said, unclipping a fixed blade from the sheath on his plate carrier. His tanto was pointed down, his thumb over the heel of the knife. The close quarters behind the desk didn't offer an advantage. John stepped toward the middle of the room and Magnus mirrored his movements. They stared at each other as the desk and the Ark, with its centralized ball of energy surging, passed between them. John scanned the room, stepping over the chief's body. He fought back the rage – it would make him vulnerable. He took stock of where Anne, Chappy, and Kieffer lay across the room.

They charged one another, locking in single combat. Magnus blocked John's thrust, sliding under his arm, slicing across his ribcage in a single move. The sting of the gash forced John to close down on his left side. He turned to face Magnus, only to feel the piercing agony of steel in his abdomen. He grabbed Magnus by the head, slamming his own forehead into the Welshman's nose and driving him back. He tried to fight through the pain, but Magnus' blade had struck deep. Wet warmth spread down his body.

Magnus closed in; he had never lost in close combat. A wicked smirk crept across his face, and his eyes narrowed as he found an angle of attack. Both of them were wounded in their dominant arms, wielding knives by their weak hands. Magnus, however, was no stranger to fighting with both hands. His advantage was clear.

"What are you waiting for?" he asked, breathing heavily, moving in front of where Anne and Chappy lay.

John stopped and stood upright as he bled, dropping his defensive position.

"I tell you what. I surrender," he said, relaxing his grip.

Magnus paused his movement, caught off guard.

"Surrender? Are you bloody mad?"

"Can we talk terms? It can be all yours."

The Welshman stood upright, relaxing his position. John held his arms out, shoulder height, his palms up. Everything Magnus wanted flooded his thoughts. *Power. Absolute power could be mine. On my terms.*

"So, what are you talking about, mate?"

John flipped his knife to the hardwood floor. The blade stuck in the wood. He held his hands up, palms toward Magnus.

"You're going to get everything. All you desire."

John dropped to his knees, bowed his head, and opened his arms.

"I give *You* my life," he said.

Magnus saw his opening and charged at John, defenseless and alone. With a murderous gleam in his eyes, he flew across the room, the tip of his pointed blade leading, with his body behind it. He took one final step, thrusting himself toward John, blade aimed straight for the jugular.

The orb of light above the Ark pulsed, as if it had gone supernova. Lightning sparked around each angel perched on top, firing two rays of jagged energy between Magnus's charge and John's surrender. Magnus' blade stopped against a wall of impenetrable radiance, breaking the blade of his knife. His face met a massive fist wrapped around the golden hilt of a sword, and it staggered him backwards across the room.

Two angels stood before John, cloaked in golden armor, wielding both sword and shield. Much larger than any human, each stood almost ten feet tall. Their cloaks and sheathing illuminated the entire room as if it were the middle of the day. Brilliant white wings shielded John; the angels stood firm as his protectors.

Magnus landed on Anne's body, rolling to the floor in shock. He pushed himself to his feet, squinting at the massive protectors. Intense light covered their faces. Magnus held his broken blade, shaking it in a fit of shock.

"This can't be! The weapon is mine!"

The angels dropped their wings, pointing their swords at Magnus. Glorified, younger versions of Walter and Bell stood before him, strong and invincible. Sworn angelic protectors of the Ark, soldiers of the Archangel Michael, and the loyal keepers of the light.

"Magnus," Bell said, "Your fate is sealed. Unto you, he will come."

"We shall see you again, on field at Armageddon. Go now. Reap what you have sown," Walter said.

"Bloody, hell! Make me!" Magnus yelled, his vile spit carrying in the air.

"That task," Bell said, lowering his sword, "is reserved for another."

Magnus stepped to the side and took a long look at the Ark. He looked back at the angels. Anne's body rolled over. Something moved along the floor behind him.

"Bring it on!" he yelled at the angels.

Magnus felt a powerful jab burn the back of his leg. Then another. He tried to kick free, turning at the source of the pain. Chappy sliced across the back of his leg, collapsing him to the floor. Wounded, but not dead, Chappy grabbed Magnus' knife hand, beating the blade free of his grasp. The Welshman clawed at the floor, pulling himself into the next room. Chappy clung to his ankle, matching Magnus' panicked, blood-trailed scurry along the floor.

Shock gripped the Welshman. His progress stopped as his head curled against a pair of legs and mangled feet. Nathan stood above; his eyes made contact with Magnus'. Chappy saw the admiral.

"Let me finish him," Chappy said, as he crawled atop Magnus, overpowering his ability to fight.

"No," Nathan coughed. "He must go through the field of light."

Nathan looked at the front door. Chappy pressed Magnus to the floor. Maximillion's body still hung in a state of falling through the energy wall. Magnus saw his father and what was happening to him.

"No!" he screamed, trying to fight off Chappy's steel grip.

"Asshole," Chappy said, as he continued to bleed upon his enemy.

He let go of Magnus' arm and punched him in the jaw with everything he could muster. Magnus fell unconscious. Chappy grabbed the Welshman by his belt, staggering to his feet and dragging him to the front door. Nathan stumbled along, doing what he could to help.

"I got this, Admiral," he said through bloodstained teeth. He tossed Magnus into the field next to his father, and they both hung in place, unable to be in the now, or the future that continued to flash by outside.

He turned, working to catch Nathan before he could fall to the ground. The two mortally wounded SEALs crawled and dragged their way to back Maximillion's study.

"John!" Chappy shouted. "You still with us?"

John had collapsed to the floor, holding his abdomen. Blood pooled beneath him. Chappy and Nathan labored to pull themselves on the floor beside him.

"John?" Nathan asked.

"It's pretty bad," John said, his breath labored.

"Roll over so I can see, brother," Chappy said, pulling some hemostatic bandages out of his vest.

"Where's Magnus?"

"Asshole got what he deserved, buddy." He pulled up John's shirt.

"He'll get more—what's coming to him," Nathan said, coughing blood into his hand.

Chappy packed the wound and tied on a pressure dressing. John grimaced.

"Damn, that hurts," John said, trying to sit up.

"Hey man, I gotta ask. What's with the two angels? And, where are they?"

"I don't know. I never opened my eyes. When I did, they were gone."

"Angels?" Nathan asked.

"It was John Bell and my grandfather... somehow they knew. They came back and protected me. I could see them, even with my eyes closed, massive beings of pure light. It was amazing."

"I'm not feeling so good, John," Chappy said, laying down on the floor. "You've got to get this done. It's time."

"Yeah," Nathan said, leaning against a bullet-torn chair. "Your grandfather said that the metal piece in his cane is the real Holy Grail. He said that you alone can activate the ultimate weapon."

"Hang in there," John said as he struggled to get to his feet. His wounds continued to bleed. Once to the desk, he found his grandfather's cane on the bookshelf. The Spear of Destiny still lay on top of the desk, the coins inset along its spine. John grabbed the cane and unscrewed the wooden poles from each end.

"Chappy? Nathan?"

Nathan didn't move and Chappy lifted a hand.

"Stay with me," John said.

Strength drained from John's own body with each passing second. He spun the Spear tip away from him so he could attach the Holy Grail handle. With the handle in his left hand, he moved it to toward the Spear. Visible electrical static, in all colors of the rainbow, popped and cracked between the two pieces of Arma Christi. The Spear drew itself to the handle, arcing in John's hand, creating a brilliant gold glow. The entire room illuminated. John tried to raise it high enough for the others to see.

"Chap! Admiral! Look," he said, but his friends were no longer conscious. John dropped to a knee; his body weak.

"Lord, I don't have the strength. I'm all alone. Please help me... do what must be done." He closed his woeful, tired eyes.

The top of the Ark sparked once again, and the orb of light pulsated. On electrified streams of lightning, Walter and Bell appeared to him.

"John – look at me," Walter said, placing warm, soothing hand on John's arm.

"It's okay. We won't leave you," Bell said, pulling John to his feet.

"How? How can this be?"

"We are descended from the tribe of Judah," his grandfather said. "You are the heir to the throne of David, John. Only you can open the doorway. It is the door He must pass through in order to fetch his bride. Today, He comes to claim His prize."

"The church," John said.

"You see," Bell said, lifting John off the ground and carrying him to the Ark, "the 24 elders identified you as the link to the Lion of the tribe of Judah. You won the victory, so the lamb of God may open the scroll, breaking the seven seals. All you need do is open the doorway – the doorway to eternal life."

"The rapture?"

"Yes, John. That is the ultimate weapon. Jesus will prepare us for the battle to come, and for you, our Lord has already prepared a place – a place of honor," Walter said.

"What about my team, the admiral, the chief?"

"They, too, have sacrificed. They have proven quite worthy, but none are as worthy as you," Bell said.

"John, activate the doorway. In this, we must leave you – but you will never be alone."

Bell and Walter positioned John in front of the Ark of the Covenant. A channel appeared at the seam, where the top and bottom met. It was glowing of pure energy. John's wounds no longer mattered. The time had come. As fast as his protectors had materialized, they disappeared back into the two angels of the Ark. He looked at his friends. Their earthly bodies were dead, but he knew in an instant he would see them alive once again. They would all rise into the sky, leaving for a short time.

All of man's feats and accomplishments mattered no more. God's people were to be raptured away, while the ones left behind would feel the true horror of judgment. John took a deep breath, pointed the spear at the keyhole and inserted it.

Everything stopped. Time, sound, pain, and suffering all froze in place. John moved his hand; the wound remained, yet it no longer hurt. He stepped back as the top of the Ark transfigured into a rectangular doorway of pure light. All other times, the brightness had blinded him, but now he could see.

"John?" Anne asked, her hand on his shoulder. He flinched and turned, seeing a translucent apparition in a robe of white. He looked through her—her body was still on the floor.

"Anne, you should see yourself," he said, taking in the golden tones of her features.

"I have," she said. Joy was in her presence, "Thank you."

She lifted into the air and was gone in an instant. John looked across the room. The chief's soul stood over his body. His golden presence offered a salute as he drifted away.

"Thank you."

He couldn't believe what he was seeing. They were being raptured right before his very eyes. He smiled, allowing himself to focus on life.

"It's beautiful, Lord."

A hand landed on John's shoulder, startling him.

"Yeah, it's pretty cool," Chappy said, his spirit hovering beside his friend.

"Chap... I'm sorry I couldn't take Magnus on my own."

"It was my task to complete. I can't wait for you to see what I can see, brother. Everything has been God's will. This you know. There's a place made for each of us. I'll see you soon," he said, before his soul disappeared into the light of the doorway.

John's heart filled with the hope of eternal life. He looked back once more, finding Kieffer's body motionless. The last Führer of the Reich was dead. John watched him sink through the floor, knowing that his deeds had earned him a place in Hell.

"John?"

He turned back to the Ark. A hand was extended through the light.

"It's time."

He reached out and took the hand. The light flashed once more as millions of people vanished from the Earth at once. The energy field collapsed, beginning a time of tribulation.

EPILOGUE

"Their king is the angel from the bottomless pit; his name in the Hebrew is Abaddon, and in the Greek, Apollyon – the Destroyer."
Revelation 9:11

The energy field pulsed, flashed, and closed. Maximillion was thrown to the pavement outside of his home. His bow, the quiver, and arrows lay scattered along the driveway beside him. He landed on his back; air knocked from his lungs. Disoriented, he struggled to breathe. Both of his hands felt his body, checking for breaks or tears. He rolled on his side, glad to be alive and unharmed, with the exception of throbbing bumps and bruises.

He sat up, dusting himself off, wiping his face. A snap of thunder startled him. Magnus appeared in front of the house, in midair, tossed over his head into the pasture behind him. His son landed, with only large strands of bladed grass to break his fall.

Magnus could move again, but his ears were ringing from the fall. The sting of the knife wounds burned his leg and the gunshot to his arm was still oozing. He checked himself over, realizing that he would live.

Taking in the state of things, he sat up, rubbing his neck. The house looked weathered, run down, and in a state of disrepair. Trees stood several feet tall, where manicured grass once occupied. The grounds of the estate looked as if years had passed. Every plant was unkempt and wild. He put a hand down in the grass. It brushed against something hard and jagged. Magnus looked down and saw his hand on the skull of a dead horse. He jerked and shuffled onto his knees, before standing, confused. He stood on his lacerated, torn leg.

"Magnus? You okay, boy?" Maximillion said, standing up in the driveway rubbing his jaw.

"This is your fault! I'm going back in there to take what's mine!"
Maximillion looked at the house with a fearful gaze.

"I'm not going back in there," he clamored, stepping away from the front door.

"Fine, then!" Magnus said, limping across the driveway.

The Welshman had no gun, so he stepped over to his father; the bow and arrow would do. He reached down, collecting them up. He drew an arrow back on the line, limping through the front door, clearing the parlor. He turned the corner into the study to discover long-decayed remains on the floor. His grandfather's body was gone—only ash remained.

Bone and tattered clothing lay scattered where the dead had fallen. The Ark sat in the middle of the room, the Time Key inserted into the side. He stopped, realizing the top was missing. Whatever happened, it became clear that years had passed in an instant. The angels were gone. Nothing stirred. He walked across the floor of the room. The wood creaked beneath his feet. He arrived at the golden box and looked inside, hopeful something of power remained for him.

"Empty," he scowled. "Dammit!"

Light-headed from the stress and blood loss, he turned around, making his way back outside, his anger building over the loss.

"What did you find?"

"Not a damn thing. Death and decay are all that's left. This is not what I saw. This is not what—"

A heavy, ominous voice rang out from inside the house.

"What you deserve?"

Maximillion and Magnus both turned. Out of the front door stepped a man. He was no ordinary man. Whatever he was, he fought to conceal something under copper-toned, near-perfect skin. His eyes glowed red, bubbling the paint on the walls from where he had passed. A dark power surged through him. Magnus was drawn in, affixed on the presence. Maximillion stepped back, afraid of the man.

"Magnus," the man said, ashen smoke rolling from his tongue, "you have fought valiantly, just as Sir Heinrick once did. The victory you sought stands before you. I am here to offer you power beyond your wildest dreams."

"It worked? Who are you?"

"I go by many names. Abaddon, Apollyon the traveler, Shiva the destroyer – some even call me a god. But I want you to call me, is brother."

The devil of a man, the encounter, froze Maximillion inside his own trembling skin. This was not what he imagined, nor the power he foresaw.

"No... how can this be? It was power and scientific breakthrough that I wanted. Not this."

"Silence!" Abaddon shouted, pointing at Maximillion.

Magnus could feel the power radiating from this beast of a man. Raw, unrelenting, and fierce power surged through him. He stepped closer.

"You want me to call you brother?"

"Yes. I want to share limitless power with you," Abaddon said. "Together we can rule the world – bring about the final solution."

Magnus relished the feeling. The sting of his wounds fell away, the closer Abaddon stepped. He could feel himself gaining confidence, power, and strength from the mere presence of the man.

"Magnus! We've been lied to! This isn't what Sir Heinrick promised. Apocalypse is what he offers – not power," Maximillion said, retreating further down the driveway, desperate to escape the sinister being they had unleashed.

"Kill him!" Abaddon growled. "Kill him and we can become one. I need a sacrifice. I need an offering – something to bridge our worlds."

A glimmer of red sparked in Magnus' eyes. Without hesitation, he raised the bow at his father and drew back the arrow.

"No! Magnus!" He raised his hands, back-peddling.

"Shut up," he said, releasing an arrow that struck his father in the chest. Abaddon smiled, bringing his hands into his core, breathing in the bloodlust of the kill. Maximillion collapsed to his knees, a stare affixed on his son, before falling flat on his face.

Abaddon walked toward Magnus, picking up his pace, before vanishing into a cloud of fiery, black smoke. Magnus watched, until the smoke ran into his mouth and nose, forcing him on his toes in a most unnatural state. His entire body balanced in the tips of his shoes, leaning him into the burning, soot-filled cloud. The seizure continued until every bit of Abaddon had transferred into Magnus' body. A flash of embers sparked. Magnus fell to the ground unconscious, full of the fallen one.

†††††

Chappy's hand plunged into the crystal-clear water of a river. The scope and vastness of it all filled him with complete joy. Worry didn't exist. The pain washed away—love remained. The judgment seat behind him. Eternity remained an adventure of service, growth, and wisdom. He lay on his stomach in a field of beauty with colors he had never seen. Creatures of all kinds rode the sky, singing aloud. All of his thoughts brought him comfort. He could see his life; the only lingering thoughts were of what blessings were left unclaimed. The wonder of the future lay ahead in a millennial kingdom yet to come. He stared into the water, seeing the bottom, mesmerized by the intense depth of all things.

"Billy?"

Chappy pushed himself up and turned around. The voice staggered him, but the figure that appeared, even more so. Her body, while human-like, shined with a glowing purpose. Her face was even more virtuous than his memories could have ever produced.

"Emaline?"

"I told you I'd be waiting for you."

"How?"

"Because," Emaline said, her smile radiant, "you have a place prepared for you. I get to be with you on your walk."

"This is amazing."

"Wait until you see what He has in store for you."

"Where did you—"

More people appeared. Chappy could see their faces: Wisp, Anne, Nathan, and the chief appeared around him. Others appeared, almost instantly in the distance, ready to welcome him home. Communication was immediate with them—no words needed to be spoken. He felt everyone around him, looking to Emaline.

"What's happening?"

"Our Lord has lifted all His children," she said.

"Where's John?"

"He's been given a special place. He has received every crown and serves with the Archangel Michael. Jesus Christ and the Saints prepare for Armageddon and the new kingdom."

Chappy perceived a majestic blue mountain with clouds blended across the peak. There, the armies of heaven trained. John's glorified body stood much taller than he imagined. A shield of gold draped across his back, a sword of light in his hand. He stood flanked by Walter and John Bell. Jesus looked over them all, filling them with the power of God.

"How will I serve?" Chappy asked, seeing John in the distance, ready to do battle with the devil.

"Our spiritual gifts are very different from our earthly ones. Those like John are highly-trained in spiritual combat. They've earned a special place. For us, our place is one where we still have much to learn, but we also have much to give. We are all God's children. I get to lead you to *our* special place."

"I'm so at peace. I'm so happy to see you."

"And, I you. This kingdom will take its place on Earth soon. There, you and I will have all the time we need. Until then, we have much to discuss – much to learn."

Chappy took her hand and she guided him to an eternal future. Everyone drifted on their own path, an interweaving of consciousness and light. A life beyond measure carried Chappy forward with Emaline alongside. The tribulation had begun, but God's people, the church, rested until their glorious return to Earth on the battlefield of Armageddon.

†††††

A hot, sticky piece of meat raked along Magnus' face, jerking him back to life. He rolled on his back, only to be assaulted by the smell of bad breath and the slime of saliva. He opened his eyes and there stood a white horse, licking his face in the pasture. Magnus pushed the steed away and staggered to his feet. He looked around, seeing his father face-down on the driveway. Sick of his cowardice, Magnus was happy to see him dead.

The horse stood beside him, fat from grazing—much healthier than some of the equestrian skeletons littering the property. He shook his head, trying to regain his composure. The pain from his arm was gone and his leg didn't burn from gashes any longer. He felt his body. The wounds were healed. He felt strong and energetic. He reached down and grabbed the bow. He stared toward the mountains, where many plumes of smoke rose into the air beyond the O'Keefe property. He wondered how much time had passed and why the world seemed to be on fire.

A wicked voice spoke to him – from within his own mind.

"It's time, brother," Abaddon said.

"You're inside me?"

"Yes. I need a host, until we prepare this world for the coming of our master."

"A host? So, you meant that we were literally doing this together."

"Of course we are," he hissed, his voice pounding like a drum. "There's no time to waste. Get on that horse and take me to Geneva. We have much to do. Riches to gain. Kingdoms to conquer."

"How does this work?"

"Just do as I command, and you will become the most powerful *man* in the world. I will lead you, fulfilling your every desire. Together, you and I will rule the Earth."

"Who is your master?"

"What is mine is now yours," Abaddon said, every word infecting Magnus' mind, tormenting his brain with each syllable.

"Why are you pounding my bloody head?"

"It will stop when your pitiful questions cease. Now, take me into town as I have commanded."

"You said we were brothers – that we would rule together. Why are you plaguing my mind, stabbing at my thoughts?"

"I will torment every inch of your body if you continue to question me, imp!"

Magnus felt his head in a panic. He wanted it out. Pain shuttered throughout his body, ripping at his core. It was as if his heart was being pulled out of his mouth. He dropped to a knee, wrestling to break free.

"Alright!" he yelled, tears streaming down his cheeks. "I'll do what you ask. Just don't do that again."

"That was only a taste of what I can do. Never question me again, boy!"

Magnus stood enslaved, afraid, and sullen. The voice shook his core, reminding him of all his past abuse – both given and received. Fear, anger, and mania found a foothold in his mind, burning his throat with each terrifying moment from which there was no escape. He walked to the horse, grabbed its mane, and climbed on, bareback. There they sat on the white horse, bow in hand—a rider, and the demon within. The first seal had been opened.

†††††

The sword of light was as a feather in his hand, and his brilliant wings extended what seemed like forever. John stood, overlooking so many souls moving into a place prepared for them. Chappy and Emaline walked along the water's edge, joined together for a journey of immense growth. His vision narrowed to the field beyond. He smiled, seeing Doc and Sam, their faces full of splendor and life. Anne and Chief stood together, acknowledging their thanks. Wisp smiled, saluting into the walk made for him.

"John," Walter said, "those are the souls – proof of your good deeds. That is why you were awarded so many crowns. That is why you are among the warriors of heaven."

"But I am so unworthy of this honor."

"And that," a voice said, "is why you are worthy."

John saw Bell standing beside him.

"Why are they all down there? Why aren't they here with us?"

"We all serve a purpose – even here," Walter said. "It's not that we are any more, or less, special than they are. We just serve in our own way, based on our unique gifts."

"We'll all unite soon enough. But for now, we must focus on the things to come."

"What's ahead?" John asked.

"The most decisive battle of all time," Walter said, looking up to the peak of the mountain.

"We must make our final preparations," Bell said.

Another golden-clad, winged warrior-angel appeared. John's eyes grew wide, his heart warmed recognizing the voice.

"We've still got to teach you how to ride a horse properly," Zip said.

"I was wondering where you were," John smiled.

"I'll be beside you in the battle to come, my friend," Zip said, smiling in return.

"What about me?" Rico said, appearing beside Zip, and placing his hand on John's shoulder. "Good to see you, too," he winked.

John was happy, seeing his friends – his family. Time moved at a different pace, collective consciousness flowed, and the tree of knowledge flooded his mind with wisdom. He now knew why.

"There is no greater love than to lay down one's life for one's friends," John said, pure joy igniting his sword with limitless energy.

Appearing behind Zip and Rico were other Saints, ready to fight the devil's army. Ian Fleming, Sarah Estell, and John Bell Hood stood among them, their swords glowing, sparkling with pure light. John felt peace, knowing the time was near. Life ever-lasting would be filled with faith, hope, and love.

ABOUT THE AUTHOR

J.M. Myrick is a former U.S. Marine and a decorated law enforcement professional. He has served in SWAT special operations at all levels, assisted in high-profile cases with the United States Marshals Service Gulf Coast Regional Fugitive Task Force, and is a Medal of Valor recipient. He currently resides in Birmingham, Alabama, with his family.

Thank you for reading Arklight: Task Force Crusader. I hope you enjoyed this series! Please leave me a review on Amazon and/or Goodreads. Writing this series was a great opportunity to grow closer to God.

THE ARKLIGHT TRILOGY
ARKLIGHT: Operation Nightfall
ARKLIGHT: Force Interdiction
ARKLIGHT: Task Force Crusader